C. SURVEY: Buyer, at Buyer's expense, within time allowed to deliver evidence of title and to examine same, may have the Real Property surveyed and certified by a registered Florida surveyor, pr[...] employed to conduct said survey takes the time to return your phone calls, let alone complete said surve[...] survey, which ended up being done on the lot adjacent to the Real Property the B[...] itself, discloses encroachments on the Real Property or that improvements loc[...] ments or lands owned by your second cousin, Harold, or violate any restrictions, c[...] regulations, the same shall constitute yet another among a long string of title de[...]

D. TERMITES: Buyer, at Buyer's expense, within the time allowe[...] perty inspected by a Florida Certified Pest Control Operator to determine if there [...] e damage from termite infestation in the Real Property. If both are found, which is gcnerally [...] company doing the inspection just happens to be the same company offering the $1,875 tenting service, Buyer shall have 4 days from date of written notice thereof within which to have cost of treatment, along with any and all damage inspected and estimated by a licensed builder or general contractor who is so backlogged with work that he can't even think about looking at your unimportant job until sometime after the holidays four years from now. Seller shall pay valid costs of treatment and repair of all damages up to the amount provided in Paragraph XIII-V Section "D." If estimated costs exceed that amount, and you can bet your sweet ass that they will, Buyer shall have the option of canceling this Contract within 5 days after receipt of repair estimate by telling the Seller that he can take his termite-infested house and shove it. Termites shall be deemed to include all wood-destroying organisms required to be reported under the Florida Pest Control Act, as amended and updated daily by bureaucrats who never see the light of day.

Way Under Contract

E. INGRESS AND EGRESS: Seller warrants that an Ingress is a small white heron, having yellow legs and black feet while an Egress is a much larger bird, with long white plumes and a bright yellow beak. Or is it the other way around?

F. LEASES: Seller shall, not less than 15 days before closing, furnish to Buyer copies of all written leases and estoppel letters (whatever the hell they are), from each tenant specifying the nature and duration of the tenant's occupancy, rental rates, advanced rent and security deposits, provided the Seller hasn't already spent most of their security deposit in an effort to rid the property of the termites identified in item "D" above. If Seller is unable to obtain such letter, or decides not to bother to provide same, within that time period in the form of a Seller's affidavit, then Buyer may thereafter contact tenants to confirm such information, provided tenants, who haven't paid the rent in months, who never answer their phone or sign for their certified mail that carries their eviction notice can be contacted. The Sellers shall, in any event, assign all leases to the Buyer and wish him or her luck in trying to squeeze blood out of a turnip in their efforts to get any rent out of their deadbeat tenants. That being the reason they decided to sell the joint in the first place.

G. LIENS: Seller shall furnish to Buyer at time of closing an affidavit attesting to the absence, unless otherwise provided for herein, of any financing statement, claims of lien or potential lienors known to Seller and further attesting that there have been no improvements or repairs to the Real Property for 90 days immediately preceding date of closing. This of course is exclusive of the new roof the Seller has just had installed for $6,563; the entire sum of which he still owes the roofers; or the plumbing repair of $3,245; the electrician he still owes $2,197, and the $9,532 he owes to any number of contractors, subcontractors suppliers and materialmen. All of whom he has been avoiding paying until after closing when he plans to move back to New Jersey leaving the entire angry mob of unpaid contractors to have at the Buyer with any number of death threats and mechanic's liens until they finally get paid.

H. PLACE OF CLOSING: Closing shall be held in the county wherein the Real Property is located, at the office of the attorney or other closing agent designated by the Seller, provided the Buyer and Seller have been kept informed of where the closing is and do not panic the day of same, wandering around said county aimlessly looking for a deed.

I. TIME: In computing time periods of less than six (6) days, Saturdays, Sundays and state or national legal holidays shall be excluded. But in actual practice almost any possible excuse, however unbelievable, to delay the closing generally by the Buyer but sometimes by the Seller will do. These excuses include but are not limited to fluctuations in the stock market, health problems, inability to get a loan, random disappearance of Buyer or a terminal case of Seller's remorse wherein the Seller refuses to sign anything. **Time is of the essence in this contract. Right.**

J. DOCUMENTS FOR CLOSING: Seller shall furnish deed, bill of sale, construction lien and affidavit, assignments of liens, tenant and mortgage estoppel letters (whatever those are) and corrective instruments, which from the sound of it have something to do with eyeglasses. Buyer shall furnish closing statement, mortgage, provided they were able, at the eleventh hour, to even get said mortgage, mortgage note, security agreement and undoctored-up financial statements.

K. EXPENSES: Documentary stamps on the deed and recording of corrective instruments shall be paid, albeit very reluctantly, by the Seller. Documentary stamps and intangible tax on the purchase money mortgage and any mortgage assumed, and recording thereof shall be, albeit equally reluctantly, paid by the Buyer. Of course this doesn't preclude either party from whining excessively about these closing costs, and ultimately, getting their real estate agent to pay for same, thereby effectively reducing their commission to equal the hourly wage slightly below that of an average convenience store employee. Without benefits.

L. PRORATIONS, CREDITS: Taxes, assessments, rent, interest, insurance and other expenses of the Property shall be prorated through the day before closing. Buyer shall have the option of taking over existing policies of insurance, provided the Seller has bothered to insure the property, if assumable, in which event premiums shall be prorated. Cash at closing shall be increased or decreased as may be required, which it generally is because the new girl at the title company closing the transaction has not had any training and the arithmetic on the HUD statement appears to be a random set of computer-generated numbers that have little or nothing to do with the price of the home or its closing costs. If closing occurs at a date when the current year's millage is not fixed and no other information is available, tax Property shall be prorated through the day before closing. Buyer shall have the option of taking over existing policies of insurance, provided the Seller has bothered to insure the property, if assumable, in which event premiums shall be prorated. Cash at closing shall be increased or decreased as may be required, which it generally is because the new girl at the title company closing the transaction has not had any training and the arithmetic on the HUD statement appears to be a random set of computer-generated numbers that have little or nothing to do with the price of the home or its closing costs. If closing occurs at a date when the current year's millage is not fixed and no other information is available, taxes shall be prorated on last year's tax, which was quite a chunk of change by the way. A tax proration based on an estimate shall be prorated on last year's tax, which was quite a chunk of change by the way. A tax proration based on an estimate

Way Under Contract

a *Florida* story
by Charles Sobczak

Read below what critics, readers & realtors have to say and why they enjoyed *Way Under Contract*.

Way Under Contract is told with tongue in cheek and offers a light, comical look at a serious business. His descriptions of characters most of us have come across, and not only in real estate, are amusing. Watch them manipulate, scheme, connive and lie their way to the top of their business only to be taken down by the only force large enough to level the playing field.
- Harold Hunt, *Cape Coral Daily Breeze*, Cape Coral, FL

Way Under Contract: a Florida Story is a novel about money-hungry real estate agents and land-hungry developers; but more than that, it is a call to the environmentally minded to do something already!
- Samantha Puckett, *St Petersburg Times*, St. Petersburg, FL

Excellent book. I was totally into **Way Under Contract**. *I couldn't put the book down, and when I did, I couldn't stop thinking about it.*
- Mike Gadaleta, FL

I just finished **Way Under Contract**. *All I can say is how disappointed I was that it ended...I wanted the story to continue... bravo...*
- Kelly Cathey, IL

I thoroughly enjoyed it, and I think it should be a "requirement read" for all Florida prospective licensees. There were times I had to put the book down because I was laughing so hard.
- Alison Thibos, FL

I am also a realtor in Arkansas. I laughed so hard on the returning flight to Little Rock that I think they were suspicions as to my competence. The inside front cover "contract" was a real piece of art. Great Book!
- Lynne Haubenreich, Realtor, Little Rock, AR

Over my 40+ plus years I have seen them come & go and I think this should become required for all going into the (real estate) business and for the old timers like me as well. Thanks for the most enjoyable reading. Every agent should read it. They would all profit from it.
- Jim Hermes, Realtor, MN

This is a second edition printing: January 2003
Printed in the United States

Published by: Indigo Press LLC
2560 Sanibel Boulevard
Sanibel, FL 33957

Visit us on the web at **www.indigopress.net**

Library of Congress Control Number: 00-134215

ISBN 0-9676199-4-7

Cover photo by Charles McCullough
Cover layout and design by Charles Sobczak & Bob Radigan

Acknowledgments

First and foremost, I would like to thank the thousands of people who have purchased and enjoyed my first novel, *Six Mornings on Sanibel*. Your many kind words, e-mails, letters, reviews and phone calls have helped inspire me to continue with this journey, this journey of the heart.

But there are some individuals who give far more than these few words of thanks could ever give to them in return. I appreciate their reads, their comments and their critiques of the early drafts of this manuscript and acknowledge the time and effort each of them has put forth.

I would like to thank Scott Martell, editor of the *Islander* and *The Island Reporter*, for his honest remarks during the weekly meetings of the DP Society. Likewise I have treasured the comments of John and Nancy Jones, Harry Kotses, Kandee Grossman and Jennifer Rando, all of whom have tried to keep me honest. I could not have completed this book without the dutiful copy editing of Phoebe Antonio, Sharon Heston, Norm Zeigler for his help with the back cover copy and especially Libby Grimm. I pray for Libby's swift recovery.

I would like to thank Charles McCullough, whose pensive photograph graces the cover of this book. His sublime patience was noted while I rifled through 50 years of photographs looking for the one shot that said, "Yes, this is it." His work can be found at the Tower Gallery, 751 Tarpon Bay Road, Sanibel Island, Florida, and an outstanding body of work it is.

Of course I would be completely lost without the contribution of my friend and artist, Bob Radigan, who once again has designed a beautiful cover for this Florida story.

I also wish to thank my two boys, Logan and Blake, and my lovely wife, Molly, for their unending support during the years it took to put this tale on paper. I must make special note of my hard working assistant, Marilyn Gary, who covered for me on many a hectic morning while I carved away at this novel.

But most importantly, I need to thank all the people who work, believe in and contribute to the Sanibel-Captiva Conservation Foundation (SCCF). They have shown me that there is still great integrity and conviction, and the world is a far better place for it.

I would like to single out Erick Lindblad, for his time and guidance on the true meaning of conservation, and Dr. Willard W. Payne, for his contributions and input into the *Epilogue*. I deeply appreciate the help of Dee Fulk and Beverly Ball in better understanding the lives of Florida's loggerhead turtles. We share our beautiful beaches with these ancient creatures, and I hope we can continue to do so forever.

And finally, my thanks to everyone who cares about this lovely planet Earth: its flora, its fauna and its humanity. We can make a difference. We shall.

Charles Sobczak
September 2000

Part I
Acquisition

570-9898
The Main Switchboard

It was a cacophony of phone lines: some ringing, some being answered, some being dialed and some being put on hold. On hold forever. Customers and clients listening impatiently to a Muzak rendition of a Bob Marley song, interrupted every 25 seconds by a tape-loop promo about the wonders of living at Shoreside.

It was a man's voice on the tape loop. A voice as smooth as the best chocolate malt ever made, as sincere as Mt. Rushmore on the Fourth of July and as reassuring as one of Norman Rockwell's illustrated doctors. It was a voice you wanted to believe in.

"Shoreside Island IS the only place to live in Florida," said the deep, melodic voice inside the telephone to the person on hold. "Shoreside Island IS the right choice. Be sure to contact one of our real estate professionals about the many fine ownership opportunities we have available here at Shoreside Realty. Townhouses, condominiums, estate homes, or just a simple island getaway; Shoreside Realty is here to make your dreams come true. Please continue to hold. One of our associates will be right with you."

Bob Marley was glad he was dead.

Betsy Owens picked line four up and answered it politely, "Thank you for calling Shoreside Realty, could you please hold?"

Before the caller could say a thing, she was sent directly to Muzak. A battery of muted trumpets was playing through the chorus, "Don't worry about a thing, 'cause every little thing, gunna be all right."

Within a few more bars, the tape loop came back on. But the man's voice didn't do a thing for the woman making this particular call. It didn't sound sincere or reassuring at all. To her, it sounded like that computer voice in the film *2001*. It sounded like Hal's voice: calculated and condescending.

The woman on the other end was calling because the house she and her husband had recently purchased through Shoreside Realty was leaking like a colander in a monsoon and she wanted to get in touch with the agent who had sold her the property. Something needed to be done about the roof and it needed to be done ASAP.

Betsy picked line four back up. "This is Betsy, can I help you?"

"Yes you can," said Mrs. Jensen. "I need to speak to Linda Hinkle."

"What is this regarding?" Betsy asked. She normally would have patched a client right through, but she could tell by the tone in Mrs. Jensen's voice that this was going to be good and she wanted all the gory details. Betsy had recognized Mrs. Jensen's voice immediately. Mrs. Jensen had called a dozen times over the past two weeks. Her accent was pure Tennessean, probably from somewhere near Knoxville, one of Betsy's favorites.

"Our roof is still leaking. That roof repairman Linda sent over last week didn't do a thing except track roof tar all over our brand-new, white Berber carpet. I need to speak with Linda immediately."

Another line lit up. Betsy went into automatic.

"Linda will be right with you, please hold."

Linda, Mrs. Jensen's real estate agent, wasn't in. Betsy didn't know that. Linda never let Betsy know if she was in or out. Only one agent at Shoreside Realty let Betsy know if he was in or not and that was Sam Goodlet. Linda Hinkle was showing property to someone who still believed in the sound of the man's voice in the tape loop. They had called last Thursday looking for island property. They were cash buyers.

When Mrs. Jensen heard the man's voice repeating his automated message for the fourth time, she hung up. She was frustrated.

"One Love" was being methodically destroyed by 101 Strings just as the receiver clicked down. Somewhere high above the island, Bob Marley asked an angel if she knew where he might be able to score some good reefer. The angel said that she'd ask around.

The phone kept ringing. Betsy had seen line four go dead. She knew Mrs. Jensen would call again later. They always did.

It was the calamity of real estate that kept Betsy Owens working the phones. She had been offered a dozen other jobs over the past five years, but she had turned them all down. Being there, on the cutting edge of Shoreside Realty, kept her intrigued and amused in a way that no other job could have.

It was like being in a movie that was part human interest, part melodrama, part tragedy and comedy combined. The people on Shoreside were constantly buying, selling, renting, dreaming, divorcing, complaining, suing, or sending gift baskets in a chin-deep confusion of gratitude and angst. It was the most entertaining job in the world, thought Betsy. She loved every spectacular minute of it.

Betsy Owens was 26 years old. She was pretty. Not beautiful, but pretty. She had a face that belonged to a crowd. A face that drew absolutely no attention to itself. Ordinary looking was the only way to describe her. Not homely. Not beautiful. Just ordinary looking, like most of us.

She had plain brown hair that hung just past her shoulders. She was 30

pounds heavier than she should have been. Full figured was the p
putting it. She had brown eyes, a pleasant smile and wore a *i*
makeup.

Betsy didn't need to look beautiful. Hardly anyone ever saw her. The
switchboard at Shoreside Realty was in the back of the building. Only the 27 real
estate agents and Doris Smothers ever came to see her. The agents came to
double check their messages, and Doris to cover for Betsy during her lunch
break.

Betsy's job was to answer the phones, and the phones rang constantly at
Shoreside Realty. Two more lines had just lit up. The callers were both put on
hold. Everyone was put on hold. Even God.

If the agents weren't in, and if Betsy actually knew that the agents weren't
in, then her instructions were to page the agents. She had an alpha-numeric
pager system to accomplish that. A satellite-based digital system. State of the
art.

In between the next four incoming phone calls, Betsy paged Linda Hinkle
with the following message. *Mrs. Jensen called again. Her roof still leaks. Call
her ASAP.*

Betsy laughed to herself as she typed in the message. She knew that after
Linda closed on a sale the chances of a buyer getting a return phone call from
Linda plummeted further than a sports car off the cliffs of Malibu. Mrs. Jensen
would keep calling and sooner or later Linda would be in. Sooner or later
somebody would fix that leak.

Either that or Mrs. Jensen and her invalid husband from Knoxville would get
so frustrated that they would decide to sell the "goddamned leaky house."

That's what the people who owned it before the Jensens ended up doing.
They couldn't find that insidious leak either.

I think it was Dr. and Mrs. West, thought Betsy to herself as she double
clicked the "SEND MESSAGE" icon on her computer screen. Or was it Mr. and
Mrs. Carleton?

It didn't matter. When Mrs. Jensen finally got to the point of wanting to list
the house, Linda would promptly return her call. It was a good listing. The next
buyers could find the leak.

Line four lit up again. The caller was asking for Adam Bartlett.

"Extension 17," mumbled Betsy to herself while pressing one of the 33
buttons on her console. Extension 17, she thought. Forty-one percent of the
incoming calls went to the agent and his real estate machine on the other end of
extension 17. One of Adam's three personal assistants had done the arithmetic
to verify that. It was in all of Adam's four-color brochures.

Adam Bartlett, Shoreside Realty's superstar.

570-9898 Ext. 17
Adam Bartlett's Desk

"Adam Bartlett's office, may I ask who's calling?" Chris had picked the transferred call up on the very first ring. She was good.

"This is Harris. Is Bartlett in?"

"I'm afraid not, Mr. Harris. Adam's out on a listing presentation. I can page him and have him get back to you if you would like, or would you rather go into his voice mail?"

"I hate that goddamned voice mail. I mean voice jail," answered the decisive attorney.

Chris Taylor didn't flinch at Harris' choice of language. Years ago she had discovered that doctors and lawyers, over the privacy of a phone line, can swear with the best of them. Mr. Charles Harris, the attorney for TLD, Inc., was as good as a drunken longshoreman when it came to profanities. He could swear a blue streak if he had reason to. Adam did his best never to give him that reason.

"I understand, Mr. Harris. Do you have a number where he could reach you?"

"Yeah. Have him call me at my office at 574-8783. Tell him Boyle's getting cold feet again and we had better do something to calm him down. Maybe Adam can call him or better yet, go have a drink with Boyle tonight. Maybe we could all meet at the Yacht Club, for christsake. Just tell him to call me."

"Fine, I'll page him in just a minute, Mr. Harris," replied Chris.

"Goodbye now."

"Goodbye."

Chris hung up and turned to her computer. She wouldn't use the alphanumeric pager on this call. Harris meant big business. She'd use Adam's private pager.

❂

Fresh leather. Adam Bartlett was waiting for the light to turn green. For the briefest of moments, he wasn't in a hurry. Instead, he was preoccupied with inhaling that rich, smoky aroma of fresh leather. Intoxicated by it, slowly sifting the interior air of his brand-new BMW through his nose in some post-modern, luxury car mantra. He just stood there at idle, savoring every waft of that delicious smell, like an upholstery junkie.

It was the smell of his new car, the scent of fresh leather, that Adam so enjoyed. For five years running, Adam had traded in his BMW *750 iL* annually to the day. After a year of driving around the island, he knew that the leather smell faded. His well-tuned olfactory senses noticed the slow decline of the aroma from the day he drove his new pearl-white four-door out of the dealer's lot. Adam tried to be reasonable about it. The dealership put up with his twelve-month leases, but Adam knew that anything less than twelve months would prove all but impossible to negotiate. Even for Bartlett.

At $1,900 a month, Adam felt he had paid for this aroma of fresh leather. His CPA had insisted that leasing was still cheaper than buying in the long run and 100 percent tax deductible. Ninety-five thousand dollars for a car, thought Adam to himself as he sucked in another dose of fumes, that's a hell of a lot of money for a set of wheels. Leasing didn't tie up all of his capital. Adam's CPA was right. He always was.

Adam had picked this particular lease up a month ago. It was a good car, Adam thought to himself. It was holding on to its leather smell better than most.

He flipped down the visor and the light on the mirror instantly came on. He took a brief look at the face in the mirror and Adam liked what he saw. Although a few wrinkles were gathering on the edge of his bright blue eyes, his hairline was holding up well and his teeth were a showcase for Crest. He smiled. Adam had a great smile.

Charisma, that was his strong suit. Good looks, sharp clothes and big plans. It was inevitable that Adam Bartlett would find himself selling Florida real estate. He had taken it up on a lark ten years ago, after getting tired of waiting tables, and he had been laughing all the way to the bank ever since.

Adam had the touch. He could sell refrigerators to Eskimos. Good refrigerators, with ice-makers and upgrades. Self defrosting models with filtered water lines and stainless steel shelving. Sub-Zeros and GE Monograms. Expensive and stylish. Adam could arrange the financing as well.

"Winter's coming, Mr. and Mrs. Nanuck," you could hear Adam say in his smooth, charming voice. "Better pick up a freezer, too."

As the light finally flipped to green and Adam sped away, his pager went off. It was his private pager; the small, solid black one. He knew that he had to call the office immediately. If it was the office pager, the digital message pager, he could tend to it later. Those messages were standard inquiry calls. Someone wanting to list their condo, or someone wanting Adam to show them houses. Ordinary deals. His bread and butter.

But his private pager didn't display a written message. It blurted out one tiny chirp and that was the end of it. It would chirp every 60 seconds thereafter until he pushed the button on the side. It chirped big business.

It chirped raw land. It sang a quarter-second song about $3.8 million, or $7.4 million. It chirped about 34.23 acres with beach access, or a six-story bay-front multifamily with private boat dockage. The docks could be deeded individually and sold off separately. At a premium in this market. This was not a typical bread-and-butter deal that interrupted his leather-smelling bingo, this was filet mignon on the line.

Big, juicy porterhouses, tenderloins and medium-rare prime rib. Commission checks the size of Third World health care budgets. Checks that easily covered the lease on Adam's new Beemer. Checks that could buy three brand-new BMWs tomorrow.

Adam spoke out loud to no one. "Dial the office."

The voice-command car phone responded. Through the speaker he could hear it bring up the dial tone, punch in the numbers, and ring the office. Adam didn't lift a finger.

"Good morning, Shoreside Realty. How may we help you?" answered Betsy on the other end of the call.

"Betsy, get me through to Chris."

Betsy knew it was Adam. She had recognized his voice before he finished the second syllable in her name. She also knew that he was in his BMW. There was a hollow sound to his speaker phone that made it an easy read.

Betsy Owens had become a master at recognizing the voices of Realtors, customers and attorneys. She usually knew who was calling before they had introduced themselves. Adam was a no-brainer.

"Sure, Adam, hang on for a minute."

Betsy punched her little switchboard just as another line lit up. She knew Adam was working on something big, but she had yet to put all the details together. It might be a syndication of some kind? Maybe it was a new development? Within the next few weeks, over the course of patching together conference calls, typing in digital messages and piecing together who was talking to whom, Betsy would know everything about the upcoming deal. She would know the price, the location and the scope of the project.

Ironically, she would also have been the best person in the world to have asked if the project would fly. A $50,000 feasibility study was not as valuable as Betsy's one minute opinion of the project. But Betsy was just a switchboard operator, and no one would ever think to ask her.

"Chris, it's Adam. What's up?"

"Attorney Harris called a few minutes ago. I told him that I'd page you. He said that Boyle's getting cold feet again about the Sanderling deal. He thought that it might be wise for you to give him a call, or meet him at the Yacht Club tonight for happy hour."

"Damn, I had plans."

"Adam, you know when Charles calls, you've got to do the dance."

"Yeah. I'll do the goddamned dance. I just wish that Boyle wasn't such a pile of nerves. He's got more money than he could spend in ten lifetimes, what's the big deal about two million?

"Chris, call Boyle for me. Tell Boyle that I'm in a meeting now, but that I've got some great news on the Sanderling project and that I need to have a drink with him at 6:30 down at the Yacht Club. He'll love the invite, the way that man can soak up the Scotch."

"I'll call him right away, Adam. Do you want me to arrange those showings for Mr. and Mrs. Dudley tomorrow morning?"

"Oh shit, I forgot about them. Sure. What's their price range again?"

"They want something right on the Gulf, in the $450,000-$650,000 range."

"Be sure to include 544 Osprey Towers."

"It's already on the tour, Adam."

"I just can't figure out why that unit doesn't sell."

"It will sell eventually, Adam. They all do. Is there anything else?"

"No. Thank's a million, Chris, I'll talk to you later."

Adam pushed a button on the console and the phone went silent. He continued along Middle Gulf Drive on his way to his listing appointment, inhaling the smell of new leather like it was opium.

570-9514
Mildred Lee's Home Phone

It was midday, sunny and bright. Mrs. Mildred Lee had 27 fifteen-watt incandescent lights on in her little canal house on the north end of Shoreside Island. It was still dark in her two-bedroom house, as dark as burnt coffee.

"I'm glad poor Boots' smell is gone," Mrs. Lee mumbled to herself as she sifted through her real estate file.

Mildred was looking for her listing agreement with Coastal Realty. She was double checking the expiration date. The calendar hanging in her kitchen had the listing's expiration date clearly marked on it, but Mildred wanted to double check before calling Adam. She might have mismarked the calendar, being as forgetful as she was becoming.

"It's in here somewhere. It just has to be."

Mildred Lee was getting old. She was now well in her 80s and she sometimes felt as if she was never going to make it back home to Chicago. The house was taking years to sell and sweet little Mildred Lee, the widowed owner of this canal-front ranch, just couldn't understand why. It was such a lovely house.

"Having all the hurricane shutters up shouldn't make that much of a difference," Mildred thought to herself as her arthritic fingers painfully sorted through her listing file, which she had found readily.

The file was two inches thick. Over the years, Mildred had listed the house with just about every company on the island at least once. It seemed like half of the 200 agents working on Shoreside Island had tried selling it at one time or another. She had one offer during this time and it was too low to accept. Mrs. Lee hadn't even countered.

Adam will be able to sell my house. Adam's such a sweet boy, she thought.

She finally found her current listing agreement. Mildred picked it up and walked over to her calendar with it. The calendar was correct; the listing had expired two days ago. She was free to relist the house with Adam Bartlett at Shoreside Realty. She'd call him tomorrow with the good news.

Adam will be glad to hear that the smell is gone. Poor Boots, crawling under the bed to die like that. I didn't even know he was sick. I wonder what killed him?

Mildred had found her dead fifth cat, Boots, after five days of searching for him. His overwhelming odor eventually gave his hiding place away. The remaining four cats made the task of finding Boots that much more daunting. Always darting around, sneaking out from one piece of furniture to the other. Spooky, caged-up cats. It was a good three days before Mildred even realized that Boots was missing. She thought he might have accidently gotten outside. None of her cats knew that there was a world beyond the incandescent two-bedroom ranch they all lived in. None of them could survive outside for more than a day, once removed from their canned tuna and bowls full of warm milk.

After making a little note to herself on the calendar to call Adam in the morning, Mildred looked at the oversized hurricane tracking chart that hung beside it on the kitchen wall. The chart was a mess.

Mildred Lee had carefully charted and marked every tropical storm and hurricane that ran through the Atlantic and the Caribbean Sea last year, making countless notations and comments along the way. There were little memos as to the barometric pressure, wind speeds and average rainfalls scrawled randomly across the chart. She had noted ocean temperatures, the diameter of the eye on any given day and the death count, provided the storm had taken some lives along the way.

The chart looked like the work of a madman. It wasn't. It was the work of a mad woman.

It's coming. Dr. William M. Gray says that we're headed into that cycle again. The "Big One" is headed our way sooner or later. Dr. Gray knows his stuff. It'll be bigger than the storm of 1926 that hit Miami. Bigger than Hugo. Just look at all these close calls last year.

There were a few close calls. One tropical storm had brushed by Key West and was building into a Category 1 storm when it abruptly turned west toward Texas. It hit just north of Brownsville with no loss of life and only minor coastal flooding.

The other storm hit the east coast as a Category 3 hurricane and ran across the peninsula coming back into the Gulf just north of Shoreside. It was a backdoor storm, just like Donna was in 1960. The peninsula of Florida isn't wide enough to take the punch out of a good sized hurricane. Backdoor storms could be every bit as lethal as direct hits, reflected Mildred.

Only a matter of time until this entire island gets wiped out. There won't be anybody laughing about my hurricane shutters then. They'll be knocking on my door, looking for a safe place to hunker down and survive.

Mildred remembered that she had to call that television station and remind them to send her a brand-new tracking chart for the upcoming storm season. They knew Mildred Lee on a first-name basis. She called 50 times a year, minimum. Always asking for updated coordinates or the latest NOAA storm track predictions. She was the butt of countless jokes and wisecracks down at the local NBC affiliate.

"Hurricane Milley" was her nickname. The hurricane lady on Shoreside who wants the inside scoop on every storm within 1,000 miles of the island. Easy to make fun of for a bunch of local weathermen from a small TV station on the Gulf coast of Florida. Too easy.

312-354-8716
Cold Calling, a Chicago Number

"Hello."

"Hello, Mr. Carthwright? My name is Jason Randazzle and I'm with Shoreside Realty here on Shoreside Island, Florida. Our records indicate that you own a condominium at the Heron's Nest complex. Is that correct?"

"Why, yes, is there some kind of problem?"

"No sir, that's not why I'm calling. I've always felt that the Heron's Nest was one of the best condominium complexes on this island, Mr. Carthwright. The reason I'm calling is to see if you might be interested in selling your apartment? Season's coming up down here on Shoreside and we are in very short supply of properties to sell. So I thought I'd give you a little jingle to see if you are interested in listing your property with us."

"In selling my condo?"

"Why, yes sir, and for top dollar."

The telephone went dead. You could hear the mouthpiece hit the receiver hard just as Jason was saying "top dollar." Jason took Mr. Carthwright's action to mean, "No, not interested in selling at this time," and marked his bright red, college-style, $3.47 spiral notebook accordingly.

It didn't bother Jason to be hung up on like he just was. Customer rudeness ran off Jason Randazzle like water off a duck's back. It had no impact. He took out his yellow highlighter and drew a thin line through Mr. Carthwright, his phone number and his Chicago address. Yellow meant a no go, lime-green meant money and light blue highlighter stood for undecided. Jason went down the list to make the next call...412-658-2311.

"Hello."

"Hello, is this Mrs. Livingston? My name is Jason Randazzle and I'm with Shoreside Realty here on Shoreside Island, Florida. Our records indicate that you own a condominium at the Heron's Nest. Is that correct?"

"Yes, that is correct."

"How's the weather up there in Pittsburgh?" Jason thought that he might try the we-friendly approach this time. Try to break the ice a little before launching into his canned solicitation.

"The weather's fine. Is that why you called me long distance, to ask about the weather?"

"No, Mrs. Livingston, I didn't. I called because our busy winter season is fast upon us here on Shoreside and the available inventory of good condominiums is getting precariously low. Have you and Mr. Livingston ever considered selling your property at the Heron's Nest?"

"Mr. Livingston, my husband, passed away two months ago from kidney failure."

"I'm so sorry," replied Jason. But he really wasn't. Jason was, in fact, a trifle glad that Mr. Livingston had croaked. Maybe Mrs. Livingston would sell their condo now.

"Thank you. It was for the better in the end, with the dialysis and all. The children and I really haven't decided what we are going to do with the properties. You know, the Heron's Nest was Randy's favorite retreat. He just loved spending the winters at Shoreside."

"I can sure understand that Mrs. Livingston, the Heron's Nest is one of the nicest complexes here on Shoreside." Memorex.

"You can call me Martha."

Bingo! Number four, under the letter B, number four!

Jason felt like jumping up and shouting "BINGO" at the top of his lungs. When they gave you their first name, you were in. In, in, in! Unit 230, Heron's Nest, Jason noted while looking at his bright red notebook. He was thinking numbers now. Somewhere between $300,000 and $330,000. Maybe more. Widow. A full seven percent real estate commission. Co-broker it and I make around $8,000. My listing, my sale, and this call turns into $16,000.

Dialing for dollars. Jason Randazzle was a master at it.

"Well, Martha, would you like me to do a free competitive market analysis for you on the property? It might help you determine what course of action you should take now that Mr. Livingston is no longer able to come down and enjoy the apartment. Without him there, the place might never be quite the same for you and the children, don't you agree?"

"We're just not ready yet. We've got so many things to sort through right now. The estate taxes, the stocks, the bonds and all the endless details. Why don't you send me your card, and I'll get back to you in a month or two. You seem like such a fine young man. What did you say your name was again?"

"Randazzle, with two zz's. Mr. Jason Randazzle, but please, just call me Jason. I'll get that card to you this afternoon, Martha. Just let me verify your mailing address. My records indicate that you currently reside at 454 Baker Street, Pittsburgh, PA 12334. Is that correct?"

"Yes it is, Jason, and I look forward to hearing from you soon. Goodbye."

"Goodbye"

Jason took out his bright, lime-green highlighter and circled Mrs. Livingston's phone number and address. He was elated. A lead. And a damned good lead.

In Jason Randazzle's twisted world of real estate, deaths were good news. Deaths and divorces. Injuries weren't bad, especially if they were crippling in nature. Wheelchairs and hip replacements meant ground-level homes with wide hallways. Knee surgery could go either way. If the surgery went poorly, a move was probably just around the corner. If the surgeon knew his stuff, the patients rarely needed to relocate.

Divorces. Those were Jason's meat and potatoes. Husbands and wives at each other like junkyard dogs. "If she likes that property so much, then she can pay the fucking taxes on it!" "If he wants it so bad, let him pay the goddamned mortgage!" Court ordered dispositions and lawyers, lawyers and more lawyers. Divorces had a special place in Jason's contorted heart.

Another favorite, though far less common, were partnerships gone sour. They were similar to divorces in many ways. Partnerships, reflected Jason, were like marriage without sex. Eventually, most of them went south because of it. When they did, Jason Randazzle was ready to sell off the holdings, though he could rarely get more than a six percent commission out of partnership sales.

Estates, on the other hand, were simple. No one wanted the memories; the room where she collapsed on the floor; his favorite porch, you know, the one where he used to sit in that old rocking chair of his. Jason was glad that everyone eventually died. It meant change, and change meant new listings.

Jason Randazzle had been cold calling on this particular Monday morning since 8:15. He tried to make at least 50 calls a day. Most of his phone calls ended up in answering machines, or in hang ups like the one he just had in Chicago. That fact never slowed him down or stopped his relentless dialing for dollars. On a good day, Jason would actually speak with ten people. Of the ten, two might have potential. One might actually end up eventually listing his or her property with him. But all of the hang ups and rejections never bothered him.

Rejection was Jason's middle name. Jason R. Randazzle stood for Jason Rejection Randazzle. He had grown up being rejected and now he found that it turned out to be his strongest suit. He was making $250,000 a year being rejected by just about everybody he called. "Just about" being the operative words here. If he managed to hit just .02 percent of the number of calls he made in any given week, he was assured a quarter of a million dollars a year in income.

It was all right there, in plain old seventh grade arithmetic. The average number of calls to get a listing, the average days on market, average selling price, average commission split. He had worked through the numbers years ago and his dialing for dollars program had verified his math handily on his personal balance sheet.

Seventh grade math. How ironic, that was the grade when Jason started his long road down rejection. In the seventh grade, Jason's face broke out into a case study in acne. Through a magnifying glass, his cheeks looked like an unsuitable lunar landing site, with huge, pinkish-colored craters and miles of pimply mountain ranges. The NASA scientists would shake their heads in disbelief. They had never observed a more inhospitable terrain.

"We'll have to find a better place to land than this or the crew will assuredly crash and die," you could overhear the scientists remarking.

But there wasn't a better place for those fearless astronauts to touch down on the 13-year-old face of Jason Randazzle. The chin was broken out, the nose covered in blackheads, and the forehead...the forehead was a jungle of pimples, scabs and greasy ointments that never worked. Jason's young, teenaged face was an uninhabitable zitscape. In the end, he was rejected by NASA as a planet worth exploring.

The girls at Lincoln Junior High all giggled and pointed at him, while walking down the hallway with boyfriends whose faces had survived puberty. His friends, one by one, all gave up on him. Even his divorced parents grew standoffish. He withdrew into himself like a boat hunkering down for the storm of the century. He nailed down the hatches, sealed the doors and grabbed the helm for the long, bumpy ride ahead of him.

Jason R. Randazzle was still sealed in the stalwart lifeboat of withdrawal as he reached for his telephone to make his next cold call. His face, now 41 years old, looked much better, but it was still without promise. He knew full well that the person answering the phone up in..., where was it this time? Akron, Ohio, might slam the receiver down on his ear, but it didn't matter.

Jason was like one of those monsters in some cheap afternoon horror flick. Like the living dead, the owners on Shoreside just kept peppering him with machine gun fire and he would just keep walking forward. A real estate zombie making the next call, and the next call after that. Unstoppable. A quarter of a million a year income by dialing for dollars.

Death and divorce. Jason R. Randazzle. We all know what the R stands for. It actually stands for Roger.

773-2123
The Shoreside Conservancy

Scott Lindsey motored along Middle Gulf Drive. He was on his way to the office at the Conservancy. Running late. His Honda Civic didn't feel like starting again this morning. It was the solenoid, at least that's what a mechanic friend of Scott's kept telling him. After trying to jump-start it with an old battery charger he still had from his college days, Scott ended up push-starting his 1989 light blue Honda.

He needed to have it fixed, but it was out of the question until next week. That's when he would be getting his next paycheck from the Conservancy. Last week's check went to cover the rent and put some food in the refrigerator. Besides, he thought, push-starting his Honda wasn't all that bad. Florida was flat and his little four-door Civic was light. Scott appreciated the fact that he had a stick shift and not an automatic. You can't push start an automatic, he remembered. Not unless you're going 35.

As Scott drove along Middle Gulf Drive, he took note of the residential development along both sides of the road. When he had first come to Shoreside, 19 years ago while visiting the island with his parents, there were plenty of vacant lots left on either side of the street along this stretch. Not any longer. Row after row of condominium projects crowded the beach side of the road and house after house lined the inland side.

Along this one-mile section of Middle Gulf Drive, a portion of his short commute every morning before turning inland toward his office, there were only two vacant lots left. One of them had recently been staked by a surveyor. The pile drivers couldn't be far behind. Then there would be only one vacant lot remaining.

Everywhere on Shoreside Island, and throughout coastal Florida for that matter, it was more of the same story. Aside from the 15 tracts of land held by the Conservancy, two city parks and some decent acreage owned by the state, most of the island was developed. Shoreside was nearly built out, with only a handful of out parcels remaining worth trying to purchase for conservation. After that, the Conservancy could look to some of the mangrove islands still available in the bay that lay behind the island to the east, then on toward the mainland. There was always another old cow pasture to save from the hands of those who saw every square foot of the Sunshine State in terms of lot and block, who were at the ready with their bulldozers and golf course designers.

As Scott pulled up to the stop sign before turning right on Coquina Road, he glanced in his rearview mirror to see how his hair looked. Not that it mattered. Scott didn't have much hair left, and what little he did have he pulled back into a three-inch ponytail every morning before going out to argue with his Honda about starting. The top of his head was going bald, and if Scott had been concerned about it, he would have felt self conscious. He wasn't.

At 36 years old, with thick nerd-style glasses and a physique not unlike Ichabod Crane, Scott had bigger fish to fry than his vanity. He knew that his shirt collars were yellowed and pilled. Even his best shirt, the light gray one that he always wore to the board of directors meetings, had a button missing on the left sleeve. That's why he always kept it rolled up. No one knew.

Renting a tiny apartment on Shoreside for $800 a month, plus the car payments, the electric bill, the phone bill, the water and garbage bills and the cost of putting food on the table left little margin for error in his $24,000 annual salary. A defective solenoid could send his shoestring budget into a tailspin. One hundred and fifty dollars is one hell of a lot of money when you stop to think about it, which Scott did more than he should have.

But then again, working at the Conservancy wasn't about money. It was about something else.

Scott Lindsey had been the director at the Shoreside Conservancy for nine long years. His love of wildlife, his passion for nature had started long before that. As a child growing up in New Hampshire he was always tramping through the woods around his house looking for caterpillars and leopard frogs. In the eighth grade, his pressed-leaf collection had taken first prize at the Lancaster High School science fair.

He decided in his freshman year of college to take a major in ecology and a minor in biology. Scott had a lifelong love affair with the natural world. The money was just enough to get by. It was his passion and his dedication that kept him committed to preservation through the tough times. His zeal.

After kicking around in the Rockies for a few years, doing that standard, post-graduate ski bum thing, Scott decided to move in with his parents for a spell on Shoreside. He had run out of money and needed a financial pit stop to refuel with Mom and Dad. They had moved to Florida the year after he had gone off to Penn State. His father hated winter, and Lancaster, New Hampshire, being in the shadow of the White Mountains, had more than its fair share of winter.

Not expecting to like Florida, with its predisposition to amusement parks and over-development, Scott was surprised by how beautiful an environment it really was. At least what little there was left that had remained unscathed by heavy machinery and asphalt. He fell in love with the untouched places on Shoreside, charmed by the simple grace of a stand of cabbage palms and palmettos and enamored of the stately elegance of a forest of slash pines.

He decided to stay in the South. For a few years, he earned his living doing odd jobs around the island and volunteering at the fledgling organization known as the Shoreside Conservancy. Back then, it was little more than a handful of what people referred to as do-gooders and tree-huggers. The kind of folks that developers and real estate agents shy away from. Environmentalists. Troublemakers.

After operating the Conservancy on a volunteer basis for five years, the 501(c)(3), not-for-profit corporation, had grown to the point where they needed to hire staffing. Scott Lindsey was their first choice.

Over the years, Scott was always there for them. After getting off work as a bartender at midnight, he was always the first to volunteer for an all-night turtle patrol. He was the one they called when they needed an environmental assessment of a land parcel they were looking at, or the one they would ask when they needed an extra set of hands to stuff envelopes. They made him the executive director of the Conservancy by unanimous vote. The title was worth far more than the salary that came along with it. He kept his bartending job for the first three years.

Now it was different. The Conservancy's reputation had grown, and there were some people with deep pockets involved. Their membership stood around 1,000 and, financially, they had come a long, long way from their modest beginnings. They weren't exactly rolling in contributions, but they were solvent and gaining momentum.

The primary objective of the Conservancy was simple and straightforward: "The acquisition, restoration and preservation of environmentally sensitive lands on Shoreside Island." They wanted to save whatever acreage they could for the wildlife that had inhabited this barrier island long before some ingenious developer invented the condominium, long before the advent of time-share units or fee simple title, and long, long before the Niña, Pinta and Santa Maria set sail in 1492.

Saving the land from overdevelopment was 90 percent of what Scott did. Fund raisers, donations, estate contributions, membership drives, special projects and grants all pulling together to buy whatever they could afford. One acre at a time. Even less than an acre if it made sense. They had just bought a quarter acre last week that abutted one of their larger tracts. Anything and everything that would add to their holdings and offer a safe haven for God's creatures. Buy it, clear it of Brazilian pepper and a host of other exotic vegetation, and let it be.

Leave it as open space; unbuildable, untouchable and undevelopable. Leave it for the gopher tortoises, the indigo snakes and the red-shouldered hawks. Wetlands and marshes were even better. The list of animals that called these precious few marshes on Shoreside home was always longer. That list might include otters, herons, gallinules and the endangered woodstork. Dozens of species crowded into some of the remote sections of swamp that the Conservancy had saved from truckload after truckload of good, clean fill.

Scott took a right and headed inland toward his office. He had another mile to go. Here, further from the water's edge, he would drive by several of their tracts. There was the 30-acre Tipson Tract, and that wonderful 62-acre tract donated by the Solberg family five years ago. Nice properties, both of them. Aside from 20 acres of uncleared pepper on the Solberg piece, they were both coming along beautifully. Beautifully empty.

As Scott pulled up to his office in a low-rent strip mall just off Shoreside Drive, the main road that cut across Shoreside, he remembered to back his Honda in. The parking lot rose slightly from the grade of the road and he knew that if his darn solenoid decided to crap out on him again later, push-starting it would be a piece of cake. He had done it three times alone last week. He was getting good at it.

"Good morning, Scott," said Mary, Shoreside's part-time secretary, as he came in the front door. "Still having trouble with the Honda, I see."

"I'll get it fixed next week, Mary. It's the darn solenoid, or so I'm told. Cars. I wish we didn't need them."

Mary knew that if it were up to Scott Lindsey, Shoreside wouldn't allow automobiles over that two-mile-long causeway that brought residents and tourists onto the island. Scott would have everyone on bikes, or walking, or at the very worst, golf carts that ran on electric power instead of fossil fuel. That's just the way he was.

He saw cars as a necessary evil, just like he did 1,000 other inventions that made up the trappings of modern man: blenders, fax machines, jet airplanes and electric hamburger cookers. All of them as useless as asphalt in Scott's opinion. As useless as tar.

"Any news about the McKinzie parcel?"

"We got an e-mail from Roger in Tallahassee. No change. I've printed out a copy and put it in your box. Apparently Loggins has a meeting with the Army Corps next week. Word has it that his survey will come in averaging better than three feet above mean high tide.

"Roger said that if it does, the Corps will pull it out of a wetlands designation. Between that and their case for clearing out all of the exotic vegetation, he said that we don't stand much of a chance, Scott."

"We never did, Mary. The McKinzie parcel was a long shot from the day we made the offer. Too much money involved. When there's too much money involved and the boys in Tallahassee get wind of it, things get built in the Sunshine State. That equation hasn't changed since the twenties, and it isn't about to change for another hundred years, is it?"

"No, probably not. Well, take a look at the e-mail. I wish the news was more upbeat," added Mary.

Scott went into his small 8-by-12 office and started sifting through his e-mails and messages. There was a call from a guy over in Jupiter who owned a small lot near one of the shopping centers. It was a swamp. He had called twice previously trying to get the Conservancy to buy it off him but he wanted too much money for it: $35,000 for a 15,000 square-foot swamp. Way too much. Scott wouldn't return the call. He'd wait a few more months and see if some extra stalling might help to lower the asking price. It usually did. Scott felt that no one could possibly get a building permit on that particular lot, so taking a little more time couldn't hurt.

Then there was the e-mail from Roger. Hopeless. The Sanderling Condominium project, slated for the McKinzie acreage, was going to fly and Scott knew it. Sixty-four units sprawled across one of the last remaining freshwater marshes on Shoreside. Six hundred feet of beach that was the best remaining stretch of loggerhead turtle nesting site would be lost.

The board of directors of the Conservancy had already decided to file an injunction to stop the project as a fourth-quarter Hail Mary pass. Not that they expected to win that fight either. Scott already knew what the judge would say. He was a good old boy. Judge Sullivan owned a condo on Shoreside. That unit was built by TLD, Inc., and you could bet the farm that he got one hell of a good price on it. Not on paper. Just in fact.

Tom Loggins, president of TLD, Inc., wouldn't leave a paper trail for anyone to follow. He knew better. He had been developing Shoreside for years and he wasn't prone to clerical errors that might give a snooping reporter something to write an exposé about. Everything with TLD, Inc. was perfectly clean and perfectly dirty. That's how they do it downtown - perfectly clean and perfectly dirty.

Losing the McKinzie 13-plus acres tore Scott apart. Losing any land to development upset him, but this acreage was dear to him. Years ago, when he was working as a bartender at The Viscaya, on break he used to walk down the beach from the restaurant. Once there, in front of that darkened stretch of cattails and bulrushes, Scott would sit on the sand and listen.

He would hear the cries of the night herons and the croaks of the bullfrogs, the hoots of a great horned owl and the mating calls of the big bull alligators. Sometimes, when the moon was full and the night air was clear, he could catch faint glimpses of the wild animals of the night, the opossums, racoons and palm rats that worked the edges of the marsh. It had always been someplace special to him. Someplace sacred.

In a year's time, all of that would change. The bulldozers, the big trucks with their loads of sand, the construction cranes and the sounds of progress would soon lay ruin to this last remaining stretch of beachfront property. Out of the solitude of this pristine patch of wetlands would rise a half-dozen-plus condominium buildings complete with breathtaking views and garbage disposals.

There would be tennis courts where the gopher tortoises once wandered and an Olympic-size pool where the great white egrets used to wade after killifish and tadpoles. Driveways, dumpsters and drainage plans. The paving of paradise, the tireless march of progress.

But that wasn't the worst of it. The worst of it waited until after dark. That was when all the living rooms facing the Gulf of Mexico would be lit up brighter than fireworks on the Fourth of July. Brighter than the Vegas strip.

In the summer months, those lights would disorient and confuse the countless loggerhead turtle hatchlings. This once dark section of beach would then offer not one, but two directions for those three-inch sea turtles to crawl toward. One of those directions would be correct. It would lead them into the open ocean and give them a fighting chance to survive.

The other, the brighter lights coming from the newly built condominiums, would lead them into the freshwater swales that Loggins and his firm would be forced to dig as part of the overall drainage plan. The otters, snapping turtles, herons and alligators would make quick work of those hatchlings. None of them would survive.

Scott picked the phone up and forgot who he was going to call. In a way, it didn't matter. His heart just wasn't in it at the moment. He hated losing. Hated it with a passion.

570-9898 Ext. 1
The Sales Manager's Office

The young, attractive blond sat nervously just outside Elinor Braun's office. She held her 32-page company policy manual neatly on her lap while she surveyed the small foyer she was sitting in. These plastic palms need dusting, she thought quietly to herself. Jennifer was trying to avoid wondering why Elinor, Shoreside's sales manager, had asked to see her. I hope I haven't messed something up already, thought the anxious young woman.

In the foyer where Jennifer Willow was waiting, there were three nondescript chairs, a small coffee table and a large framed print hanging on the wall beside the door into Elinor's spacious office.

The print was a faded reproduction of a watercolor Jennifer had seen many, many times before. She remembered that they sold that very same print at the Decorating Hut. It was a reproduction of a watercolor of the old lighthouse that stood at the far end of Shoreside. The colors in this print had become lifeless and dry over time, like old bones. The lighthouse it depicted looked abandoned.

On the coffee table lay an impressive spread of real estate magazines. There were recent issues of *Home & Condo*, *Southern Living* and a half-dozen promotional booklets about the splendor and beauty found only on Shoreside Island. Those booklets went on to describe all the benefits of working with the *experienced professionals* at Shoreside Realty when it was your time to find your *place in the sun*.

Jennifer picked one of the booklets up and started glancing through it. It made her feel worse. She knew she wasn't one of those *experienced professionals* by any stretch of the imagination. She had just received her real estate license three weeks ago. It was so new that she dreaded taking it out of her wallet for fear that the ink on her signature might smear. Jennifer Willow was a real estate rookie, a neophyte.

Jennifer had barely passed her final real estate course exam and had scored a mere 77 on her state final. She needed a 75 to pass. It was so confusing to Jennifer, all those legal terms and descriptions. The fiduciary relationships, letters of estoppel, easements, nonconforming uses, accrued depreciation; they were all so complicated. What did any of those things have to do with real estate? Jennifer kept asking herself that as she sat patiently just outside Elinor's office.

Jennifer had her own reasons for getting into the real estate profession. Those reasons were as pure as the fine grain sands along Shoreside's beaches. Like the man in the tape loop inside the phone somewhere, Jennifer wanted to help people find their special place here on Shoreside.

To put it in her own terms, Jennifer Willow was a people person. To her, real estate wasn't about surveys, inspections and escrow accounts, it was about colorful family rooms and long walks along the beach. It was about helping people find their special place on the island.

Jennifer Willow was 31 years old, recently married and drop-dead gorgeous. She had long, luxurious blond hair, dreamlike green eyes and a face that could make the cover of *Vogue* on any given issue. She had been an assistant decorator at the Decorating Hut for the last five years and she knew all the Realtors on Shoreside, especially the men. They had an understandable tendency to bring their clients into the Decorating Hut even if its furniture wasn't exactly what their customers had in mind. Business had fallen off since Jennifer Willow had left the Hut to try her hand at selling real estate. It didn't take a rocket scientist to understand why.

Jennifer leaned forward in her chair to see if Elinor was still on the telephone. She was. She put the glossy, full-color booklet about Shoreside Realty down and opened her office policy manual. The manual reminded her of the test she barely passed a few weeks ago. It was full of graduated commission schedules, floor duty procedures and referral agreements. It was every bit as confusing as Jennifer's final exam. All she wanted to do was to meet some nice folks, find them a nice home, and help them purchase it. Why do they make everything so much more complicated than it needs to be?

While Jennifer was rereading the section of the manual on how the office settles questions of procuring cause, whatever that was, Elinor quietly hung up the phone, cracked open her wooden French doors and said, "Jennifer, you may come in now."

Upon hearing Elinor's deep voice, Jennifer was startled. She was mildly startled, like when a person hears a waitress drop a tray somewhere at a busy restaurant. It was a background noise startle. She quickly looked at Mrs. Braun.

"Oh, thank you, Mrs. Braun."

"Please call me Elinor."

The two women made their way into Elinor's office. Elinor took her seat behind her fine-grained mahogany desk and Jennifer sat in one of the two chairs that faced the desk. The chairs were similar to those in the foyer, but these were covered in genuine leather, unlike those vinyl ones just outside the door. Jennifer, with her years at the Decorating Hut, could instantly feel the difference.

"You're probably wondering why I called you in here this morning, aren't you?"

"Yes I am. Have I done anything wrong?"

"No, you haven't done anything wrong, Jennifer. I just wanted to go over a few new forms that the state has recently sent to us, to be sure that you understand them. I know that you're a "people person" and that all these forms seem to keep you from enjoying your job as a real estate agent, but, unfortunately, it's just a part of our profession."

Elinor took a little breath and continued. "Just as it's your job to go out there and make sales, it's my job to see that you complete all the necessary paperwork correctly. It's important to the staff and management at Shoreside Realty that you fill all the various forms out properly, and I just want to be sure that you're comfortable with that."

Elinor Braun was being unbelievably kind to Jennifer. Everyone at Shoreside Realty who had been with the company for longer than a few months knew Elinor Braun for who she really was: the "Form Nazi." If Linda Hinkle was sitting across the desk from Elinor, and Linda Hinkle had screwed up a form, Elinor Braun would have been verbally jamming bamboo slivers underneath Linda's bright red fingernails in a raging fit. Linda Hinkle would have been emotionally duct-taped to her chair, with her feet in a bucket of ice water and a fully charged 12-volt truck battery at the ready beside her. Elinor would not tolerate an improperly completed form, especially from an experienced agent like Linda Hinkle, or, God forbid, Adam Bartlett and his crew.

Fortunately, Jennifer Willow knew nothing of this.

In fact, you could not have had two women in the same occupation, in the same room, in the same company, be more polar opposites than were Jennifer Willow and Elinor Braun. Elinor knew it. She knew it the day she decided to hire Jennifer. She knew right after her first interview with the lovely Mrs. Willow that they had absolutely nothing in common.

Elinor Braun had been in the real estate business 39 years. Once, 38 years and 10 months ago, she had been like Jennifer. Sort of. Back then, Elinor was sincere, honest, forthright, genuine, concerned, caring, understanding and willing to go the extra mile for her customers. Those kinds of feelings existed in Elinor Braun four decades ago, although never at the same level as they did in Jennifer.

That was before the big fall. Before her first lawsuit. Before the house she sold to the Wilsons turned out to be infested with termites. Somehow, her sellers conveniently neglected to inform her or their listing agent about the infestation. Three months after closing, in an afternoon thunderstorm, the house had collapsed on her buyers, nearly killing their two children. Pinning them in their newly redecorated bedroom like hapless victims of some horrible Mexican earthquake.

It was before she discovered that the sellers had disappeared without a

forwarding address and that she had to forfeit her entire commission check and
then some to cover the legal costs. The two children were rescued by one of
those trained German shepherds, and had survived without serious injury. That
was the good news.

That was four decades ago. Twelve years of selling real estate in the
trenches, and the next 26 behind a desk just like the one that now stood between
these two ladies. Twenty-six years of listening to salespeople try to explain their
unbelievable, convoluted tales about deals that had fallen apart, houses that had
bats or competitors who had tried to steal her agents' clients, their cars and, on
occasion, their wives. Horrid, intricate stories that would send shivers down
Elinor's spine and have her reaching to speed dial the state legal hotline, or one
of Shoreside's attorneys or, if the situation merited, an exorcist.

Stories so improbable that Elinor would remain silent for hours listening to
the gory details as if in a trance. "Then," the agent would add, "I called the
Federal Express headquarters in Memphis and the man there verified the fact
that the closing papers were on that very same plane. You know, the one that
crashed." Or, "Well, I know that the listing had mentioned something about not
letting the parrots out, but when I opened the front door, this huge blue macaw
just flew right past me, knocking over my client, Mrs. Dugan, in the process.
When she landed flat on that concrete sidewalk, you could just hear her little
bones cracking. They say that after her hip replacement..."

Just as the fair skin of Jennifer Willow was soft and young, vulnerable and
impressionable, the skin of Elinor Braun was now impenetrable. Nothing could
get through it. It had become so hardened that it made Kevlar bulletproof vests
seem like delicate silk blouses. Alligator jaws, piranhas, screaming brokers,
threatening lawyers, even IRS agents, with their dark-blue suits and their federal
forfeiture and seizure paperwork in perfect order, rolled off Elinor's skin like a
soft summer rain. It wasn't even skin any longer. It was a combination of
unflappable durability and emotional titanium.

Nothing could surprise or amaze her at this point. It was all a new version of
the same unbelievable story. The house had caught fire the night before closing,
the sellers refusing to sign the deed, the bank electing to revoke the loan on the
morning of the closing, and 1,000 more variations on a theme.

Now, it was all a question of filling out the forms, and filling them out
properly. Forms that hopefully prevented the inevitable lawsuits. Forms that
acted as paper-thin shields against an onslaught of the lances, razor-sharp
arrows and the barrage of countless poison darts they would hurl at you - the
buyers, the sellers and their overpaid legal staff. Disclose, disclose, disclose!!!
That was Elinor's battle cry. Have the sellers sign a MATERIAL DEFECTS
DISCLOSURE and don't forget the ELEVATED HOME DISCLOSURE. How
about the REAL PROPERTY DISPOSITION DISCLOSURE. Those were just
the tip of the iceberg. It was always the form you accidently forgot that sank you

in court. It was the COASTAL CONSTRUCTION CONTROL LINE RIDER or the CONSENT TO TRANSFORM INTO A TRANSACTIONAL BROKER form that nailed you when the judge's gavel hit the bench.

There were hundreds upon hundreds of forms. There were places to sign, pre-sign, post date and initial. There were forms that were so confusing that no one, not even the chief justice of the supreme court, could comprehend them. But that never stopped Elinor from getting the buyers, sellers and cooperating brokers from signing them. There were forms that needed to be notarized, witnessed and signed in human blood, or so it seemed. It was Elinor's job to check and double check every listing and contract that came across her desk, but she wasn't to blame.

The state and federal government employees were to blame. They were the imps who had kept throwing these forms at Elinor until her heart and skin had turned to cement. Little goggle-eyed bureaucrats who had never seen the light of day. Like foreboding, medieval scribes, they sat hunched over in the basements of large rectangular buildings thinking of new forms to eventually send upstairs. New requirements pertaining to where the buyers bought their insurance, why they needed their insurance and when they bought insurance, provided there wasn't a named hurricane within 1,000 miles in any direction. Forms that were merely checklist forms to see if all the other forms were completed correctly. Duplicate and re-duplicate forms. Encrypted and encoded forms written in Egyptian legalese so impossible to understand that no one even guessed at what they meant any longer. Just get them signed.

No, the bureaucrats in Tallahassee just sat there, in those damp basement offices with their beady, red eyes and nervous, squeaky little voices, plotting and conferencing among themselves. Constantly thinking of new ways to confuse Elinor Braun and her counterparts in all the brokerage firms across the long, peninsular state of Florida.

It was a sickness that these hunchbacked clerics had succumbed to. They didn't trust anyone to think for themselves. No one was to be believed at their word or trusted unless it was initialed and witnessed. No one had the innocence of a Jennifer Willow in the pallid, flourescent universe these strange, gray-suited men existed in. The only way to protect people from themselves was by forms.

So they would crouch behind their tin desks and think of new forms. Forms they would work on for years and years.

Confusing, incomprehensible documents that, when completed, would be sent upstairs to be reviewed and approved by counsel. Counsel in this case being a bunch of "good old boys" who had helped the fine governor of the Sunshine State get elected. Graduates from Gainesville and Florida State who had just stumbled in from a three-cocktail lunch downtown. Half-in-the-bag attorneys who would passingly glance at the new forms stacked on their desks between making book over the phone on the Seminoles' next game, then sign off on the forms without so much as reading them. "The Seminoles are favored by seven over the Gators this week," their bookie would add.

"These look fine to me," the attorney would remark as he instructed his secretary to stuff all of them into brown, official-looking government envelopes and mail them to Elinor Braun and her peers throughout the state of Florida. Once received, Elinor would read them, try to understand them enough to be able to explain them to her hard-working agents, and insist that everyone get them signed, and signed correctly. If they were not signed where so indicated, the agent would have to come in to see her.

Only death scared the agents at Shoreside Realty more than having to come in to see the "Form Nazi." Sometimes, depending on how screwed up the form was, death scared them less.

Jennifer Willow, with her lovely green eyes gazing across Elinor's mahogany landscape, didn't know anything about the grim history of Shoreside's "Form Nazi." She didn't know about the torture, the memos or the reprimands. She was too naive and impressionable. Although only a few feet separated these two ladies, they were effectively on opposite sides of the universe.

"Are you familiar with the SEWER EXPANSION DISCLOSURE FORM recently sent to us from Tallahassee?"

"No, I've never heard of it. It was never even mentioned in my real estate classes. What is it?"

"I'll try to explain it to you, Jennifer. But since it arrived here just a week ago, I'm still trying to sort through the details myself."

Elinor was hedging. The truth was that the form was so confusing that Elinor was only guessing as to what the state had hoped to accomplish by it. You had to have a master's degree in sanitary engineering to understand it. But understanding something and getting it signed by all parties were two distinct agendas. Elinor didn't understand 70 percent of the forms she reviewed for signatures every morning. No one did.

"Well Jennifer," Elinor started in, "the State of Florida and the Department of Public Health have decided that all barrier islands, like Shoreside, are not acceptable locations for septic systems. Therefore, by the year 2010, the form says..." Elinor picked up the legal size form, put on her glasses and continued reading directly from it...

"By the year 2010, or sooner, all homes, multi-family or condominium developments having an occupancy of one person or more, shall be hooked up to a private or municipality operated sewer system licensed by the State of Florida and meeting all EPA standards for the year 2010 for the treatment of effluent and human waste. The cost of this expansion shall fall upon the current owners of the property at the time the assessment is levied unless that party has not been notified, in writing, prior to the purchase of a property that is not currently on a private or municipality operated sewer system.

"If the purchasing party, upon not having been given this form at the time of closing on a property with a septic system, of any design, or a private or municipal sewer system that fails to meet the future EPA standards, regardless of whether or not those standards are possible to meet, then the brokerage firm or firms, who were party to the sale, and the agents hereto a part thereof and knowingly and repeatedly violated the spirit of this agreement, will be notified, in writing, at least six days before the disbursement order, that they will have to reimburse the owner, or prior owners for the cost thereof."

"Oh."

"What they are trying to say here Jennifer, is that if your buyers don't sign this disclosure form, the State of Florida will make Shoreside Realty reimburse the purchasers any time between now and the year 2010 when they go to hook up to a sewer system. If we pay the state, you, of course, will have to reimburse us, plus any legal costs and interest we might have incurred. The point is, don't forget to get this form signed by everyone you sell anything to, even a vacant lot."

"But what if they're already on a sewer system?"

"That doesn't matter, because in the fine print on the opposite side of the form..." Elinor leaned over her desk and showed Jennifer the 69 standards set forth on the back side of the form. Standards that were written in print so small that Elinor felt she needed an electron microscope to read them.

"That any property connected to a sewer system that fails to meet the EPA standards for the year 2010, whatever those standards might be at that time, regardless of how stringent they might be, the brokerage firm will be held responsible if this form isn't fully executed and notarized by all parties."

"Notarized?"

"Rule of thumb in real estate, Jennifer: When in doubt, notarize!"

"But how can we be held accountable to comply with sewer system standards that are not even known yet?"

"Jennifer, if there is one thing I have learned over my three-plus decades of being involved in Florida real estate, it is this: Don't question these forms, just get them signed. Are we perfectly clear about this? Do you understand what I'm saying?"

Elinor was starting to get irritated. She didn't want to have to pull out any of her dental equipment or surgical tools on Jennifer just yet. She actually admired the vacuum behind her beautiful green eyes. Elinor wasn't in the mood to destroy this portrait of real estate innocence.

"Yes, I'll get it signed Elinor. Is there another form?"

"Yes, but this is a simple one."

"Oh, good."

"The state has revised the TRANSITION TO TRANSACTIONAL BROKERAGE FORM to exclude buyer's agents. Since buyer's agents cannot list property, they cannot in reality represent both parties to a transaction and therefore shouldn't be required to have their buyers sign this form."

"Oh."

"So when you have elected to represent the buyer as a transactional broker in a contract for sale and purchase not involving an agent from Shoreside Realty, you no longer have to get this form signed. However, you should still get it initialed."

"Okay."

Jennifer Willow looked confused. She looked confused because she was confused. Elinor Braun was equally confused, but she never looked confused. That would show weakness and from her perspective, any sign of weakness was unacceptable. It was part of her titanium wardrobe.

"So here, Jennifer, just take these two new forms home tonight and familiarize yourself with them. Please call me if you have any questions."

Elinor handed copies of the two forms across her broad desk into the well-manicured hands of Shoreside's newest agent. There was a slight tremor in Jennifer's right hand as she took hold of these two new, legal-sized forms. Elinor didn't notice it, but Jennifer did. There were butterflies in Jennifer's stomach and her mouth was dry as well.

Everything is so confusing, she thought to herself as she slid the two new forms between pages 23 and 24 of her company policy manual. Ironically, those were the pages that covered the various forms that the state and federal government presently required. Now there were two new ones added to that laundry list.

"Thank you, Elinor," Jennifer said while she rose and headed toward the door.

"You're welcome Jennifer. Have a nice day."

Jennifer walked quietly out of Elinor's office, through the foyer and past the faded print hanging on the wall. She headed down the long corridor, past the copier, the fax machine and the small kitchen area where the other agents hung out, joked and made small talk. She slid behind one of the three beige walls that encircled her small metal desk and sat down at her office.

She looked at her wedding picture, which was hanging beside her Certificate of Achievement for passing her real estate course. She felt like crying.

Everything in this business is so confusing, thought the young lady with the beautiful green eyes. She did cry. Just a little.

570-9898 Ext. 4
Mrs. Barbara Silberman's Line

Like a five-fingered cobra, Barb's hand struck the telephone before the first ring was completed. She was excited about getting a phone call. It had been a half hour since Barb had spoken with anyone and she was already beginning to think that the local real estate market was slowing down. She was worried about it.

The worry hadn't sunk in very far yet. It was a surface worry, like a cat's scratch, or a hangnail worry. Not a big worry, like the time she and her husband built the spec house off of Middle Gulf Drive and it didn't sell for seven months. That was a big worry. That was like an amputation worry. An incurable disease worry. When it finally sold they both insisted that they would never venture to build a house on speculation again. Five months later they put a lakefront lot under contract and started looking at floor plans. Worrying couldn't be avoided. Worrying was who Barbara Silberman was.

"Hello, I'm calling about your ad in Sunday's paper. The one about the two-bedroom home for $179,000? Could you get me some more information on the property? Where's it located?"

"It's a great little house. A real charmer. The price is great. Don't you think it's a great price? Where did you say you were from?"

Barb started throwing questions back at the caller faster than the caller could think of new ones to ask Barb. It was Barbara Silberman's tried and true technique, the porcupine close. Answer every question with another question. Catch them off guard. Confuse and conquer.

She was a master at it. Barb had already sold more than $11 million worth of real estate this year, and there were four months left of the selling season. "Sell, sell, sell." Why worry? Why not?

"Could you please tell me where it's located?" asked the woman who had called on one of Barb's ads.

"It's in Eagle's Landing subdivision. Are you familiar with Shoreside Island?"

"Yes, my husband and I have been coming here for years from Dayton. We love it here. But the prices have gone up so, I don't think we can really afford to buy now."

"Oh, sure you can. This little cottage is a great buy. When would you like to see it?"

Barbara was going in for the close. She did so instinctively. It was what she did best. Barbara always believed that since the market was probably going to collapse within the week, there was never any time to waste. You had to get what you could, before everyone in America was unemployed and put on welfare.

Barbara Silberman was short, tenacious and immensely neurotic. She was also worried. Mrs. Barbara Silberman had been selling real estate for 22 years. Before that, she worked as a reservationist in the rental division of Shoreside Realty. Real estate was her life's work.

She had worked with some of her clients for 20 years running. Selling them one house, then selling that house for them, buying a condo with them, then selling that condo; helping them to buy some land, then building a house on the land, then selling the house that they built on that land and on and on and on. Her customers loved her, although no one quite understood why.

Barbara Silberman and her husband, Stanley, had more than $500,000 in cash, mostly in jumbo CDs at an island bank and a laundry list of other assets that topped $3 million. It didn't matter. They both lived in constant fear of going broke by the end of any given day. She had dark brown, make that almost black, shaggy hair, brown eyes and thick, homely glasses. Barbara Silberman drove the largest SUV available at the time, a Lincoln Navigator. The leather smell had long since left the interior of her sport utility vehicle. It had been replaced years ago by the smell of chain smoking and spilled Diet Cokes.

Her cream-colored SUV was pockmarked with innumerable scratches and dents that Barbara had accidently caused over the past few years. The dings and dents were there because Barbara was always so preoccupied with talking to her clients that she paid very little attention to her driving. She had been in 37 fender benders with clients in her various vehicles during the course of her 22 years of selling. It might have been 38. Fortunately, no one was ever seriously hurt. They were just embarrassed.

Betsy, and some of the other girls who worked at Shoreside, were convinced that the only reason people ended up buying from Barbara was because they were afraid to go look at any more property with her. Her customers carefully weighed the thought of buying a property they didn't like against their apprehensions of spending another afternoon in Barbara's battered Navigator. It was the demolition derby school of real estate sales. Fear was the catalyst that made her clients decide to buy.

"Let's make an offer today," they whispered to each other on the way back to the office. After barely avoiding two head-on collisions, scraping a utility pole and jumping the curb three times in one afternoon, they felt, even though they both thought that the house Barb had just shown them was way too small, that it was the right thing to do. Which it was.

Barbara never believed the rumors about her clients fearing for their lives. She insisted that they wear their seat belts at all times when viewing property with her and Barbara felt that she drove carefully. No one had ever been taken to the hospital in one of her innumerable fender-benders. No one had ever died. "You can't sell real estate to dead buyers," she would silently remind herself while pulling out of the office parking lot, backing into a palm tree.

With the market about to fail, it was important to keep your clients alive. That's why she drove so slowly. If there was a collision, chances were that it wouldn't impair her clients' ability to sign a purchase agreement. Contingent only upon financing and a speedy recovery.

"We can probably pull ourselves off the beach for an hour or so tomorrow afternoon. Is that okay with you?" asked the prospective purchaser.

"Let me check my schedule," said Barb.

Barbara pulled out her schedule and saw that she had an appointment with an old customer of hers to do some shopping tomorrow afternoon.

"Looks like I'm wide open," she replied without hesitation. "Oh, I'm so sorry, I haven't even asked your name yet. Do you mind?"

"Mr. and Mrs. Skinner. Clark is my husband's name, and I'm Sylvia."

"Thank you, and I'm Barbara Silberman of course. But you've read the ad, and you already know my name."

"Should we meet you at the property, or come into the office?"

"It would be better if you would come in, that way we can get acquainted and I can get you some additional information on the development at Eagle's Landing."

"Fine, we'll be there at 3:30."

"See you then."

"Goodbye."

"Goodbye."

Barbara picked the phone up and called her old customer to cancel their plans for tomorrow afternoon. It would have been nice to spend some time with Mrs. Levinson, but she and her husband, Samuel already owned. They weren't planning to sell their place yet, either. With the market starting to tumble, Barbara knew that she had to prioritize her time. She dialed their number and the phone rang four times before the answering machine kicked in.

"Hi and thanks for calling. You know what to do. Wait for the beep and leave us a message."

"Mrs. Levinson, this is Barbara. I'm sorry but it turns out that I just have to show property tomorrow afternoon. We'll have to do a rain check on our little shopping spree. I'll call you later in the week to arrange something. Bye for now."

Barbara put the phone down and turned on her computer. Within minutes she was rifling through the computer's Multiple Listing System to see if there were any other properties she might add to her tour tomorrow afternoon. They might not like her little cottage. She had to find something that they liked. Like most of the renters at Shoreside, they were probably leaving on Saturday. She had to get them under contract before they left town. Time was of the essence.

The real estate market was finally picking back up. Thank God, she thought as her color printer started spitting out feature sheets faster than a Vegas slot machine stuck on jackpot. I've got to find them something by tomorrow! She knew she could do it, she would have to. It might be her last sale of the year, thought a concerned Barbara Silberman while grabbing at the printouts long before the ink was even dry.

570-9898 Ext. 12
Sam Goodlet's Extension

"Good afternoon, Shoreside Realty. How may we help you?"
Betsy picked line five up and responded in her automatic mode.
"I'd like ta speak ta Mister Goodlet ma'am. Is he in?"
"Please hold."
Betsy put Mr. Hazelton on hold and started laughing to herself. She knew who was calling immediately. His accent was pure Alabama. His accent was so thick you could use it to ford a good-sized stream. It was so southern that it was silly. Betsy chuckled out loud every time Mr. Hazelton called, and Mr. Hazelton called a lot.

Betsy knew that Sam was in, but she wanted to stop giggling to herself before she paged him. It was unprofessional. There were no other lines ringing for the moment and that was good. It gave Betsy some time to regain her composure. Within a few minutes she picked line five back up.

"May I ask who's calling?" asked Betsy, although she already knew who it was.

"Mr. Hazelton, Mr. Bartholomew W. Hazelton."

"Please hold, Mr. Hazelton, while I connect you to Mr. Goodlet."
Betsy pushed extension 12 and got Sam on the line.

"Guess who's calling?"

"Oh shit...."

"You guessed it. I'm patching you through. Good luck, Sam."
Betsy felt sorry for Sam as she punched a couple of switches on the keyboard and connected these two people. Betsy liked Sam Goodlet. Everyone liked Sam Goodlet.

Sam Goodlet was a short, rotund real estate agent who tried to make an honest dollar from an honest day's work. Sam was the kind of real estate agent who would come over to unclog a client's toilet at 3:00 a.m. if it needed it, even if he had sold the house to them four years ago. He picked his customers up at the airport, treated them to innumerable lunches, and was in the office every day from 9:00 to 5:00, rain or shine.

Sam Goodlet wasn't slick, or handsome or particularly clever. He wasn't a top producer and he never would be. In a great year, Sam might sell 17 properties and do better than $4 million in sales. In a bad year, he might sell 14 properties and end up selling around $3.8 million. If Elinor Braun, the office manager, had to say anything about Sam's performance, it was that he was consistent.

Betsy felt sorry for him because he was the kind of person who creeps like Mr. and Mrs. Hazelton took advantage of. Betsy didn't like Mr. Hazelton or his ugly wife, Delores. They were driving poor Sam Goodlet straight to the madhouse. Sam deserved better than this, but in his typical stick-to-itiveness kind of way, he was going to find them a suitable property if it killed him. The chances were good that it would kill him.

"Hello, is this Mister Sam Goodlet?" asked Mr. Hazelton in Alabamese.

"Sure is, Mr. Hazelton. What's up with you this afternoon?" Sam didn't want to know.

"Well, me and Delores here were just siften' through one of those fancy real estate brochures and we found a house that looked sort of interesten."

"Which brochure are we talking about, Bart?" Sam knew that he could call him Bart. It was a far cry easier than saying Bartholomew.

"This one here, with the bright red cover and a picture of some big, expensive mansion on the beach on the first page. Let me check with Delores." Bart pulled the phone away from his face and shouted over to his wife, "Honey, what month's issue is that?"

Sam could hear his wife's reply through the line. "March, it says March right on it, Bart."

"Delores says it's the March issue. It's on page 37."

"Hold on a minute while I get that issue from my files."

Sam's hands were visibly shaking as he hurriedly looked through his back issue collection of the four-color Showcase Magazine. He was certain that he had shown Mr. and Mrs. Hazelton every house on Shoreside by now. How could they have found one that he missed? It couldn't be.

Sam found the March issue, flipped to page 37 and said, "Well I'll be darned. That's the Grinstead place. I just can't believe that we haven't looked at that house yet. Are you sure we haven't seen it already?" Sam had his fingers crossed that they had seen it and they had simply forgotten about the showing.

"Delores and I have both checked our photos and our notes and neither of us can find anything on it. I think we must have overlooked it somehow. When would be a good time for you to show it to us?"

Never. Never, never, never, never, thought Sam to himself silently. He never wanted to show Mr. and Mrs. Bartholomew W. Hazelton another house in his life if he could help it. He had, by his conservative estimate, already shown them 57 houses. Those showings were spread across a six-week period of living hell.

Sam was completely fed up with Bart and Delores. Mr. Hazelton smoked huge, pungent cigars that smelled awful. He smoked them constantly, even in

Sam's Oldsmobile 88. Sam hated the smell of cigars, and now the interior of his car smelled like it was Castro's personal humidor. Mr. Hazelton swore, spat and always found the "fatal flaw" in every property they went through.

"The Achilles tendon, my son. There it is, big as the sun, the one reason why I'd never buy this house."

At first it was fun. He and his ugly, fruitcake wife, Delores, were such colorful characters that showing them property for the first week or so was a ball. They would all laugh and make small talk. They would pull away from the house and discuss its "flaw" over lunch somewhere while making plans for the next tour. Then the next tour. Then the next and the next and the next.

Sam Goodlet got to dreading Mr. Hazelton's phone calls, just like he was dreading this one. He knew that Mr. and Mrs. Hazelton were never going to buy a home. Sam knew that he was probably going to murder both of them if this kept up much longer. He had bought them 22 lunches over the past six weeks. He knew every "fatal flaw" imaginable.

"The kitchen's just too damn small..."

"Who the hell would want to take a crap in a yellow bathroom?"

"Floor plans, Sam, it's all about floor plans."

"The roof has too steep a pitch for this area. Way too steep. Downright dangerous to do any work on a pitch that steep."

"The roof's too flat. Can't have a flat roof in Florida. Too much rain down these parts. Too goddamned much rain. Cause ya all sorts of roofen' repairs."

"Don't like the curb appeal."

"Backyard's just too small"

"Too much yard to mow, way too much yard."

Sam realized that his car had just about rid itself of the three cigars Bart had smouldered through on last week's tour. He suddenly remembered that he had just spent $150 to have the carpets professionally detailed last Friday when he heard himself saying, "How about tomorrow afternoon at 3:00?" to Mr. Hazelton.

"Tomarah will work just fine, Sam. We all will meet you at the office. Should I bring you an extra cigar?"

"You know I don't smoke, Bart. You old kidder you. See you tomorrow."

"Goodbye"

Sam Goodlet put the phone down on the receiver and knew why Florida had a three-day cooling off period for the purchase of hand guns. He even knew the pawn shop where he would purchase the weapon. He had already planned what he would do with the bodies. There was that large culvert in Woodland Pines. There were plenty of alligators in that area and he doubted anyone would find the remains.

Then he came to his senses. It wasn't his style. He would show them the Grinstead place. Maybe they would buy it? No. They wouldn't buy it.

Acquisition

The bedrooms would be too big. Or too small. The laundry room would smell funny. There would be a dead cockroach in some obscure corner of the property somewhere and Bart would blurt out in his Alabama accent, "This joint's just crawlin with roaches." Delores, who dreaded the entire insect world, would bolt for the door.

That wouldn't be the end of it. Then they would wait. They would rifle through every real estate magazine ever printed on Shoreside in hopes of finding yet another unturned stone. They would call Shoreside Realty and ask for Sam Goodlet and he would succumb to his nice guy instincts and show the next house to them.

This could go on for years, thought Sam to himself as he dialed the other office to make tomorrow's appointment. Three days. That's all the state requires you to wait. Three days. It has to be .45 caliber, a Glock, or maybe a Beretta. Nine bullets. I'll want to empty the clip.

"Anderson Realty, may we help you?" said the telephone receptionist on the other end of the line.

"Yes, this is Sam Goodlet, is Dale in?"

"Yes he is, but he's on another line right now. Would you like to hold or can I take a message and have him get back to you later?"

"I'll hold."

As Sam sat on hold, waiting for Dale Anderson to get off the other call, Sam wondered whether or not you can charge handguns on your VISA in the state of Florida. Would it be tax deductible? No, the IRS would probably challenge the logic behind trying to write off a murder weapon. Besides, to avoid leaving any paper trail, Sam realized that it would be much better to pay cash. Cash at a gun show.

His daydream was suddenly interrupted by a voice on the other end of the line, "Dale Anderson here, what can I do for you, Sam?"

"I've got some folks who want to take a look at the Grinstead place tomorrow. Say around 3:00 in the afternoon. Can you set it up for me?"

"No problem, Sam. The house is on lockbox and I'll phone Mr. and Mrs. Grinstead to tell them to make themselves scarce. It's a mighty fine house, Sam. I'm sure your clients will love it."

"I'm not."

"Well, good luck to you, Sam. Call me if you need anything else."

"I will, Dale. Thanks a bunch."

"Bye now."

"Goodbye."

Sam put down the telephone and started thinking about the gun again. He was wondering where you pick up silencers. Where do you pick up silencers?

570-9898
Back at the Switchboard

Her long day on the phone lines was finally wrapping up. Betsy knew it instinctively. The pace of lines ringing and little red lights blinking on her switchboard was steadily falling off. Without looking at her watch, she knew that it was past 4:30. She took a few minutes between incoming calls and outgoing pages to eat a small bag of extra cheese Cheetos and to reflect on the day.

It's been a busy day, she thought. Busier than usual for this time of year. Usually October is slow on Shoreside. The snowbirds haven't flocked back to the beaches, the summer "family" crowd is at school and the tourists haven't even started booking their annual March reservations. No, for October, it was a busy day.

Nothing like mid-March, Betsy kept thinking. Mid-March on Shoreside is a switchboard operator's worst nightmare. The phone lines light up brighter than Times Square on New Year's night. They flash, they get forwarded, they get put on hold until the tape loop wears holes in the customer's eardrum. March is not for the faint of heart. And the pages!

Last year, just for the heck of it, Betsy kept count of the total number of pages she did on March 22, which happened to fall on a Monday. All totaled, Betsy sent off 139 pages, 41 percent of which went to extension 17, Adam Bartlett's office. She simply lost count of the phone calls, but it had to top 200. Actually, it was 259.

By the end of that day, all Betsy wanted to do was to go home, crack an ice-cold Miller Lite, fill the bathtub to overflowing with hot water and bubble bath, and soak for an hour. It was like crawling into the womb, a womb without a telephone or a computer. It was where Betsy could escape. She could escape from all the complaining owners, the curious buyers, the whining agents and the impatient tradesman. Sometimes, during the peak season, it was a two-beer bubble bath day. Sometimes she felt like downing an entire six-pack and sleeping in the tub.

October was much easier. The weather was cooling off, the calls were steady but not excessive and, overall, the tempo was manageable. On a night like tonight, Betsy would head home, crack a beer and watch some television.

Later that night, she might go out with some girlfriends to shoot pool or, rarely, go out on a date.

If there was one disappointment in Betsy Owens' life, it was her lack of a love interest. There were a few guys who asked her out now and again. There was that painter last August; he seemed nice enough. Then there was that adorable appraiser last spring. They must have gone out a dozen times before he met that other girl.

Betsy thought it was probably her weight that kept her love life from blossoming. Her 30 extra pounds that kept her prince charming from getting close enough to land that first gentle kiss upon her lips. She had tried to lose those excess pounds a dozen times. She had dieted, worked out and purchased every manner of supplement and miracle pill ever advertised. Nothing seemed to work. She was a "full-figured" gal and by this time she knew that she was going to stay that way. Someone would come along and love her for who she was and not for who she looked like. Someone.

"Betsy, do you have a minute?"

Betsy turned around and to her complete amazement saw Linda Hinkle poking her well-coiffed head in the doorway. It had been four or five months since Linda Hinkle had come to visit Betsy at the switchboard. Something was going on.

"Sure, Linda, the calls are slowing down a bit. It must be getting close to 5:00."

"It's 4:49, Betsy."

Betsy smiled. She appreciated Linda's exactitude. It was so typical. Linda had organized her life to match the spontaneity of an electronic metronome stuck on allegro. Nothing ever happened that wasn't meant to happen. She was no longer a person, she was a real estate machine.

"What brings you back here?" asked Betsy politely.

"It's about Mrs. Jensen. How did she sound?"

"Angry, Linda, she sounded pretty angry."

"Lawsuit angry?"

"No, not quite lawsuit angry yet, but getting there."

"Did she make any mention of the "A" word?"

"No mention of it yet, but I have a feeling it's not long in coming to that."

"I'll call her back. Thanks so much, Betsy. Have a great evening."

Linda headed down the hallway. Betsy could hear her heels clicking on the tiled floor as she walked away. Betsy knew that Linda wouldn't voluntarily call Mrs. Jensen yet. Not for just "angry." Linda was way too busy to bother with an old customer who was merely a little perturbed with her. She needed more motivation than that. Linda was going to wait for lawsuit angry before returning that phone call. She was waiting for Mrs. Jensen to mention the "A" word during one of her uncountable phone calls before taking some time off her nonstop schedule and returning the call. It was an office joke, the "A" word. It stood for "A"ttorney.

When Mrs. Jensen hung up the phone after saying something like, "Well, you can tell Mrs. Hinkle that I'm about to call my attorney!" or, "Just wait and see what my attorney has to say about all this!" Linda would take the time to call her. Linda would carve 20 minutes out of her hectic day to calm Mrs. Jensen down, convince her that this new roofer she found would be able to find that "little ole leak," and everything would return to normal. Whatever normal was.

Seeing Linda Hinkle in person reminded Betsy of why she never wanted to get into the business of being a real estate agent. All she could think to herself for the next few minutes was, "I hope to God I never end up like that lady."

✪

That lady, Linda Hinkle, was a single, divorced woman who found time for one man, and one man only in her life, Mr. Frank R. Estate. His middle initial stood for Real.

Linda woke at 6:15 every morning with him, went to work all day with him, got home at 7:00 and started making some phone calls to him, and crawled into bed with him at 9:45 sharp. The trouble was, Frank didn't give a damn about her. Frank had hundreds of women around the state of Florida just like her. Thousands upon thousands more of them scattered across the United States and Canada.

Mr. F. Real Estate seemed to attract them to himself with an uncanny consistency. Older, post-menopausal women with overzealous hairdos and closets full of mail-order business suits. Lonely, energetic women with long strings of initials after their names that no one cared about or understood. Linda Hinkle, GRI, CRB, CRS, CFP, CCIM, XYZ, who cared? Frank didn't care. He could find ten women just like Hinkle in a heartbeat.

Linda knew it, but she was in denial about the lopsided reality of their relationship. She needed him far more than he needed her. She had given everything she had to him during the last 20 years, and Frank was all she had left.

Linda Hinkle was 57 years old. She had earned enough money to retire in complete comfort 11 years ago. She owned more than $2 million in undeveloped land on Shoreside, two premium rental condominiums, had $812,941 in her personal IRA, $237,900 in the stock market, $54,765 in her savings account, $11,983.87 in her checkbook, and the thought of not going to work the next morning filled her with dread. Real estate was her life, her whole life and nothing but her life.

Her husband, Gary, had walked out on her nine years ago. He just couldn't compete with Frank. He was only human. He got tired of listening to Linda every evening after coming home from the office, hearing her go on and on about these clients, or that jerk, or this developer or that other cutthroat agent, until 9:45 p.m. sharp. He hated Frank. He wanted Linda to start slowing down when she hit 50. Maybe they could take some time off, take a world cruise or visit her family in Indiana?

Not Mrs. Linda Hinkle. She couldn't imagine being away for an entire week. Who would service her listings? Who would answer her phone calls, and show her clients around. She might miss a contract, God forbid. She might lose a sale!

When Gary Hinkle realized that his workaholic wife wasn't going to slow down until they brought her out in a plastic body bag, he packed two suitcases full of clothes, withdrew $5,000 from their joint checking account that held $23,468 at the time, left a nice note on the kitchen table held down by his wedding ring, hopped in his brand-new jet-black Dodge Sierra and drove off.

That was nine years ago. Linda filed for divorce the following month. Gary didn't want a thing. The money, the real estate, the condos - they were all her doing and undoing. Five grand was enough to get started, and that's all Gary ended up with. That and his black Dodge pickup.

Their only son, Albert, sided with his dad. Albert had long since graduated from college, and was living the ski bum life in Crested Butte, Colorado. Albert used to call his mom to try to convince her to relax, slow down and smell the roses. It was futile. Linda never eased up for a minute. The only smell Linda Hinkle slowed down long enough to enjoy was that of an overheated photocopy machine doing a lengthy set of condo docs for a sale at The Meadows. A cash sale.

So there she was, slightly overweight, graying steadily somewhere deep beneath the hair dye, wearing well-tailored suits and in love with a man that could replace her tomorrow with 1,000 women just as dedicated and foolish as she was. She took two long weekends off a year, one to attend the NAR State Convention and the other to attend the national convention.

Once there, in the air-conditioned comfort of those massive convention centers, Linda Hinkle would covey with a flock of women virtually identical to herself. They could reassure themselves that they were all having another great year with Frank. They could chat about market trends, new computer software, face creams and longer-lasting rinses. They were everywhere at these conventions, each trying to outdo the other. None of them daring to confront the sad, lonely reality of their personal lives. Successful losers.

That was Linda Hinkle. As a buyer, or a seller, you couldn't find a better agent to work with. She gave her clients 100 percent, leaving nothing for herself or her estranged family. She was the best the industry had to offer. Frank never even took notice.

Linda walked over to her spacious office, closed the door behind her, and decided that there was plenty of time left to squeeze in some phone calls before she headed home to feed her cats and catch a bite to eat. There were always a few more minutes for Frank.

✪

It was 5:03 p.m. Betsy shut down the switchboard and called the after-hours answering service to tell them she was knocking off for the day. She also let them know who the up person was for the evening. It was Vince Harding. Good old Vince.

The lady at the answering service had a nice voice, thought Betsy as she flipped off the fluorescent light in her office, picked up her bag and headed to her 1982 Pinto to drive home. She could almost taste that ice cold Miller as she pulled onto Shoreside Drive and headed toward the causeway to the mainland. Maybe two Miller Lites, she pondered. Maybe two.

870-2162
Bartlett's Cell Phone

Adam had just parked his *750 iL* between a Jaguar and a Lincoln Town Car. Junk, the both of them, he remarked to himself as he pushed the remote locking button on his key. They don't hold their value and they aren't built like a Beemer. The leather in either of those cars is good for three, maybe four months max. Junk.

Halfway across the parking lot, Adam's cell phone rang. He reached into his navy sport coat's right-hand pocket and pulled out a phone that was as thin as a Hershey's chocolate bar. Thinner, like a melted Hershey bar. He flipped it open and answered the call. There weren't that many people who had this number, and he was expecting this particular call all afternoon.

"Vanessa?"

"Hi, Adam, how did you know it was me?"

"I knew you'd call."

Adam continued on toward the entrance. It looked good for him to be walking over to the bar with his face buried in a cell phone. It made him look important. He would stand off in a poorly lit corner of the Yacht Club until the call was over. They wouldn't know if it was an important client, his eight-year-old son Danny, or Vanessa on the other end of the line. He would never tell anyone who it was either. Adam had learned early on the art of confidentiality.

"Are we still on for dinner?"

"Not tonight, Vanessa. Not for dinner. This important meeting has come up and I'll be tied up until around 8:00. Can I grab a movie and come over later?"

There was a silence on the other end of the line. Adam knew that the silence was bad. He had heard this kind of silence innumerable times before. It was a woman's silence, where time itself is slowly strangled. Where every second that elapses increases the severity of the crime.

Knowing that, Adam was quick to defend himself against it. His salesmanship sprang into action.

"Vanessa, are you still there? I think my cell phone is cutting out. Can you hear me?"

Vanessa waited another five seconds and answered in a calculated certainty, "I'm still here Adam. And your cell phone is working fine."

"Great. I thought I'd lost you for a minute."

He had lost her for a minute, but it had nothing to do with his cell phone. It had to do with Adam Bartlett's sense of priorities. Vanessa was ticked off. She was playing second fiddle to his passion for the deal. She didn't like it one bit and her long, dagger-filled silence made her feelings on this issue perfectly clear.

"I just showered, dressed and put on all my makeup for nothing, didn't I Adam?"

"I'm sorry." He really wasn't.

"What am I going to do now?"

"Maybe you can go out with the girls or something?"

Adam was knee deep in relationship quicksand and he could feel every word, every sentence pulling him further down. If he was going to save himself, this conversation would have to end soon.

Vanessa retreated into the fortress of her silence again. Every second on that digital phone ticked away like a week of cloudy weather. Wet, cold weather where people catch their deaths. Vanessa wanted Adam to be left standing in that rain, left there to shiver and drop from exposure. He felt a cold wind sweep over him as he tried again to break the silence. This time the bad connection ploy wouldn't work.

"I'm sorry, Vanessa, but I've got to meet with Boyle tonight about the Sanderling project. It's a big deal and it's important to me to see it through. How about a rain check for tomorrow night?"

"When?"

Adam gave a quick sigh of relief. He knew that she had conceded. They always do. Well, almost always.

"Say 7:00. We'll go out to the Viscaya. How does that sound?"

"Fine. But if you cancel one more time..."

"I won't. I promise. Love ya."

"See you tomorrow night, Adam."

Vanessa hung up the phone. Adam knew that he had to either show tomorrow night or cross Vanessa off his list of currently active girlfriends. That would leave only three, with that new waitress he met from the Pink Flamingo Bar a potential replacement for Vanessa. Four was his working minimum.

Six, he had learned, was his maximum. More than six active girlfriends and the situation became too confusing. Names, dates and arrangements became too scrambled. More than six and Adam needed to hire an assistant just to manage his personal love life. That was stupid. Assistants aren't cheap.

Of all of his current regulars, Vanessa was far and away his favorite. And to think that she was a redhead, just like his ex-wife, Peggy. He had promised himself not to get involved with another redhead that afternoon six years ago when he walked out of divorce court. But Adam was a salesman, and he rarely kept a promise for very long, even one to himself.

He slipped his candy bar telephone into the right pocket of his well-tailored sports coat and walked to the bar. Harris was already waiting for him, and reached out to shake his hand as Adam approached.

"Hey, Adam, great to see you could make it."

Charles was shaking Adam's hand as he spoke. It was one of those fake, attorney handshakes. Adam knew them well. They were too genuine and forthright to be either. Adam knew that so long as everything was going well, Harris and the developer he represented, Tom Loggins, and himself, were teammates. If everything went smoothly, these handshakes would continue. But if Adam screwed up, even for a moment, Harris' right hand could just as readily be reaching for Adam's balls. Adam knew the ground rules of playing with the big boys. He knew them by heart.

"You know me, Charles. When duty calls."

"Who were you on the phone with a minute ago?"

"Business, Charles, just business."

"Oh."

Adam loved answering Harris' question so enigmatically. He loved wallowing in the vast expanses of the gray areas that made up his career in real estate. He felt at home there, comfortable in his moral fog. A wonderful, wistful place where there was no up, no down, no east, no west and most importantly, no right and wrong. Just shades of gray, like an endless self-test on a new black and white photocopy machine. A thousand shades of gray.

He laughed to himself while ordering a drink from Harry, the Yacht Club's lifelong bartender. Vanessa is certainly business. Nice business. Vanessa had thick, curly red hair, brown eyes and legs that could stop a freight train. Vanessa was a prize, and Adam didn't want to lose her. Not for now, at least.

"So when's Boyle getting here?"

"Soon, I hope," answered Harris, taking a quick glance at his gold Rolex.

"Do you think he'll pull out?"

"No. He just needs some hand holding. Just like he did in the Water's Edge development two years ago. He made a bundle on that one. We just have to reassure him that his money's safe with us again this time. We have to sell him the Sanderling project from the ground up. He'll buy into it, Adam. They all will."

"What do you honestly think, Charles, does Loggins really stand a chance at getting the development permits from the city?"

If there was one person on Shoreside who could answer that question with any degree of certainty, it was Harris. He knew city hall better than anyone. His wife had been the private secretary for the city manager for years before marrying Charles. Harris and his wife, Alice, knew the maze at city hall better than anyone. They knew how to keep from heading down those costly dead ends. They knew the pecking order, and the politics of the city council. They knew all three major players in the planning department, and which of the three was the most likely to answer the big question with a yes when the time came.

"It'll take some doing, Adam, but Loggins can get the permits."

No one had been able to get the permits to develop the Sanderling acreage yet. Many had tried. The Sanderling project was scheduled to become 64 condominium units located on 600-plus feet of Gulf-front property. All totaled, there were just a bit more than 13 acres to be developed. The land had been owned by the McKinzie family for generations and the price was reasonable. They wanted $5.3 million for the property. Given the number of units it could support, it was a bargain.

It was the arithmetic of a gold mine. A little better than $82,000 per unit, land cost, and $30,000 to $40,000 per unit site improvement costs. Construction costs will run approximately $120,000 per unit. Marketing and brochure costs, between $4,000 and $7,000 per condominium. Sales commissions of 5 percent paid by the developer, the buyers pick up the title insurance and state documentary stamps. Asking price: $400,000 to $500,000 a unit. Bottom line: between $10 million and $14 million profit, depending on carrying cost and market time to turnover. The math of money. Serious money.

There was one problem with the Sanderling development, and that was why it was such a bargain. It was a swamp. It was "prime Florida swampland" in the classic tradition of the phrase. It was what the city had designated "lowland wetlands" on its ecological zoning maps. The acreage was covered with leather ferns, spartina grass and red, black and white mangroves. It was crawling with wildlife. There were a score of alligators on the property. There were green herons, blue herons, great white egrets, tri-colored herons, kingfishers and dozens of assorted ducks and gallinules.

In the northeast corner of the parcel, there was even a small rookery of yellow-crowned night herons. Rookeries, a developer's worst nightmare. Every summer, especially in July and August, all along Sanderling's stretch of undeveloped beach were a large number of loggerhead turtle nesting sights. They liked this section of beach because it was the darkest area remaining along Shoreside's nine miles of sand. In fact, it was the only large, undeveloped section of beach-front land left on the island. It was worth a fortune to the developer who could get the permits to build on it.

"So what's new with Tom?"

"He's working on it, Adam, and he's working hard. You know Tom, he's always way ahead of the game. He's been doing some field work on this project for better than two years now. He's not about to lose it. We've got a meeting scheduled with the Army Corps people next week in Tallahassee. They are going to give us the surveying criteria and elevation requirements for their approval for the development. They are also concerned about the proliferation of what they call "exotic flora" on the parcel. Seems like there's been one hell of a lot of Brazilian pepper sprouting up recently on this acreage. If we can prove that the parcel has already been substantially destroyed by this invasive, noxious plant, it'll go a long way toward getting our vegetation permits.

"But the elevations are another issue. If the land ends up being too low, we've got to try to bring in fill to build it up some. The fill thing could kill us. They'll only allow you so much trucked-in fill per site, and it will be nip and tuck all the way at Sanderling. It's not going to be a walk in the park, but I'm sure that we can swing it."

"And the Shoreside Conservancy? What are they up to?"

"Same old bullshit. Save the goddamned 'gators. Save the goddamned turtles, ducks, bugs. Who gives a shit? They're threatening to file an injunction to halt development if we do get the go-ahead from the city."

"Damn," remarked Adam.

"We can work around that. I've got some contacts downtown on the county level that can get the injunction overturned if need be. One thing you've got to remember, Adam, is that this county and the city of Shoreside both love their taxes. Sixty-four units at a half million apiece with the current millage rate of 19.66 means better than $600,000 annually in real estate taxes. Year after year, decade after decade, that money's going to flow into both of their coffers. That builds a hell of a lot of roads, schools and, most importantly, pays a lot of salaries to the good old boys who make the decisions.

"They like the Sanderling project downtown, Adam. They like the smell of it and they'll let the judges down the street know their position when push comes to shove."

Out of the corner of his eye Harris could see Boyle coming in through the front door. Harris liked Boyle. They both liked top-shelf Scotch and money. They liked the things that money could do for them. They met six years ago when Mr. Eugene Boyle came into Harris' office looking for some legal counsel on his first real estate purchase on Shoreside. He was buying a $1.3 million Gulf-front estate from a salesman named Adam Bartlett. Boyle wanted some reassurance that it was as good a property as this Bartlett fellow had said it was, and that all the loose ends in the contract were tightened up.

Mr. Boyle sold the entire estate last year for $3.7 million. It turned out to be even a better investment than either Adam or Charles thought it would be. Boyle was now a card-carrying member of the Adam Bartlett/Tom Loggins investor club. There were roughly 20 members in that club, and Boyle had some of the deepest pockets in the group. They weren't the deepest pockets in the club, but they were the easiest to slip your hand into.

Mr. Eugene Boyle was from Indianapolis, Indiana. He had made all his money in the paper business. He had a large manufacturing plant that produced labeling stock paper. The kind of paper that you see everywhere and never notice. It wraps itself around soup cans, sodas, green beans and firecrackers without drawing any attention to itself. Thin, high-gloss paper that rolled out of Boyle's plants by the trainload.

He still owned and ran the plant from his new penthouse condo on Shoreside but there wasn't anything for him to do. His managers oversaw production, his comptrollers oversaw the money, his sales staff oversaw sales. His accountant just kept a steady pipeline of profits flowing into his bank account and investments. All Mr. Boyle was left to handle was choosing where he and his wife, Maggie, were going out to dinner that night and what brand of Scotch to drink. Life was good.

"Hey, what the hell!" Harris greeted Gene as he sauntered over to the bar.

"How you doing, Charles?"

"Just fine, Gene, and you?" Eugene Boyle hated to be called Eugene.

"Couldn't be better. How's it with you, Adam?"

"Busy, Gene, busy as all hell."

"You're always busy, Adam. Tell me something new. You found yourself any new young things lately?"

Boyle loved hearing about Adam's private love life. He was a voyeur. One look at his wife, Maggie Boyle, and the reason was obvious. The Jacuzzi tub in their new penthouse had to be custom ordered to allow her to fit in. She was a big woman. "The big bitch" is how Harris described her whenever Gene wasn't around.

"No, Gene, just the same old escapades that I told you last week. I'll let you know if I come up with any new action. You can count on it."

Adam was sucking up to Boyle. Adam had spent his entire sales career sucking up to people like Mr. Eugene Boyle. Buying them rounds, dinners, fishing trips, tickets to the Shoreside Playhouse, the list was endless. Schmoozing with the players. Keeping his private cache of fat cats happy. If the fat cats were happy, Adam was happy.

He would dance their favorite dance and sing their favorite song. If they wanted to go on a duck hunting expedition in northern Manitoba, Adam was in. If they needed to find a mechanic to repair their brand-new Harley, Adam knew just the guy. If they wanted to talk about Adam's private life, about getting some action in an elevator, or in the back seat of his Beemer on the causeway, they got all the intimate details.

In return, Adam gained their confidence and, most importantly, access to that pipeline of cash that flowed through their lives like an artesian well in a tropical rain forest. The three of them, Tom Loggins, Charles Harris and Adam Bartlett, had found their calling. They owned Boyle and Mr. Levinson, Professor Meyers and both the Sander brothers, Dr. Bethel, Mr. Turlington, Mr. and Mrs. Harding and a dozen others. They were all herded up tight in their charming little enclosure. The three men kept a sharp eye on them and kept feeding them project after project, fattening them up for the next Shoreside real estate venture, and the next one after that.

They had made a killing on the Water's Edge development. Each investor signed a reservation agreement to buy a vacant lot in the project until it was 50 percent sold out to this loosely formed syndicate. With 50 percent in pre-sales, they could go ahead and get bank financing for the balance. The regional banks wouldn't touch a project that wasn't a proven winner, so without the 50 percent in confirmed reservations, the project would be left to flounder. It never dawned on the bankers to note that every development that Tom Loggins did was sold to the same individuals.

The truth being that the bankers involved really didn't care. All they needed to have was something on the books showing that it was 50 percent pre-sold and 100 percent bankable. They knew exactly what the bank's underwriters wanted to see, and that's what they provided. Nothing more, nothing less. No one asked any further questions.

With half of the project under confirmed reservation, the construction loan money started flowing. The land at Water's Edge was cleared of tons of Brazilian pepper, scraped clean and the pilings drummed into the sand like the sound of money being printed. The project was on its way.

When the subdivision was approved and the green light was given, the investors were asked to get their wallets out and show up within the week at the closing table. Wholesale pricing is what the investors received. Usually between ten percent to 20 percent more than the actual construction costs. Then the sales crew at Shoreside would start to sell, sell, sell that brand-new product. It was full retail price to the guy walking in off the street. If the market could handle it, more than 100 percent markup above actual purchase and development costs. When most of the retail units or homesites were under contract or closed, the investors were allowed to start selling their properties.

Generally, because the supply was now getting scarce, the investors got better prices than the developer did. Sometimes 10 to15 percent better. Eventually, everyone was out of the project completely, their wallets pregnant with profit and anxious for the next site plan.

It was the quintessential buy-low sell-high program, and everyone had made a bundle doing it during the last seven years. The Sanderling project was going to be the fourth one in a row for Boyle and he was both excited and nervous about it. That's why the three of them were at happy hour this evening. Bartlett and Harris were there to shmooze, to calm down Boyle's pre-project jitters, answer his questions, and, most importantly, help him suck down the Scotch.

"So, what'll you have, Gene?" Adam beat Charles to the draw on the first round of the late afternoon.

"Glenlivet. Glenlivet on the rocks."

Harry nodded, reached to the top shelf and took down the near-full bottle of

Glenlivet. He poured Gene a double over a full glass of ice and placed it in front of him. Harry didn't bother to put the bottle back on the shelf. He knew it would never make it back up there. With the certainty of death and taxes, that bottle was headed for the trash can before the night was over. Harry knew Boyle liked Scotch and he knew that he could make a bottle of good booze disappear quicker than a can of acetone spilled on a sidewalk in hell.

Boyle took a long, cold sip of the Glenlivet and dove right into the thick of it.

"So what do you think, Charles, can Loggins get the permits or not?"

"Sure he can get them, it'll just take some extra effort this time."

"Dr. Bethel called me yesterday and said that the Orion Group never even came close three years ago. He said that the Army Corps and the Department of Environmental Protection shot them right out of the water. Killed their plans for the McKinzie parcel before they even got to the first survey. Too low, they were told, too goddamned low to support that kind of density. What makes you think Tom will fare any better?"

"Tom's got some tricks up his sleeve."

"He damned well better have. And what is he going to do about the Conservancy folks? They're kicking and screaming already about Sanderling and we haven't even started clearing the parcel. Last week their boy in the *Shoreliner* rag wrote a lengthy piece about a family of otters that lives there. Just what we need, a family of fucking otters right where Phase II belongs. What're we going to do about those otters, Charles? I hate those fidgety little fuckers."

"Don't worry about those otters, Gene, we've got a new home all picked out for them," Adam interjected. Adam knew some of what Mr. Loggins was planning; he knew because he had sold him the mitigation islands.

"It's called mitigation, Gene. The state allows developers to mitigate environmentally sensitive lands, to trade them for similar sites. Tom knew this before we put the McKinzie property under contract. We went out a year ago and purchased three islands in the backwaters of the Sound to mitigate with. Those islands, all combined, give us 63 acres of wetlands to deed to the state, offsetting the environmental loss of the smaller McKinzie parcel."

"Well, I'll be damned. Why the hell have we never had to do this sort of thing before? We didn't do any of this mitigation shit on Water's Edge, did we?"

Boyle was smart. He didn't make his money by being a fool. He could play at being just another dumb old fat cat, but Charles and Adam knew better. He was as dumb as the fox.

Harris took over for Adam. "Water's Edge wasn't low, Gene. There wasn't a trace of wetland in those 165 acres. No wetlands, no environmental studies, no Army Corps permits needed. Not that we didn't have some problems with Water's Edge. We spent almost $100,000 clearing and burning out the pepper and the rest of the exotics. That wasn't cheap, but the land was high and dry for the most part. The Sanderling property is a whole different animal, Gene, and we've got to change our game plan or risk losing it."

Boyle would have more questions, tomorrow, next week and in the months to follow. Boyle stayed awake nights thinking of new questions. He might have had deep pockets, but he tried to make it difficult for TLD, Inc. to get into them without answering a question or two. They all loved it for the game it was. The development game.

As the amber colored liquid inside the Glenlivet bottle worked its way toward zero, the topics of conversations spilled out from the confines of the Sanderling Condominium project and across the vast flood plains of a typical happy hour. Football was eventually brought up, and this year, like the year before, the Colts sucked. Basketball came up, as it always does when you're drinking with someone born and raised in Indiana. Politics, Adam's sex life, some kind of bladder problem Maggie was having, and at least six dirty jokes from Harry the bartender all mixed together over melting ice and evaporating Scotch.

At 7:30, Adam mentioned that he had another appointment.

"Just one more drink for the road," insisted Boyle.

"Just one, and that's it," conceded Adam.

Adam knew the meeting had gone well. Charles Harris was drunk and had that look in his eye. He appreciated Adam's dedication to a long hard deal. They had already been working on the Sanderling project for two years since Tom had put that first $50,000 in option monies up and Adam Bartlett hadn't made a dime in commissions yet. Charles liked that kind of foresight and perseverance in a man. Adam was a great salesman.

Adam pounded down his last Scotch and said goodbye to Boyle.

"Call me in the morning Adam, we've got some details to sort through." Harris patted him on the back as Adam headed toward the front door of the Yacht Club.

"I'll call around 10:00 or so."

Just before Adam pushed open the front door he turned around for one last look at the two of them, Boyle and Harris. It was now dark outside but it seemed even darker in the bar. It was as if the lights inside the bar were inhaling their own incandescence, making the room darker than it would have been without them.

From the doorway, all Adam could see was the back of these two thick, middle-aged men. Harris was wearing an off-white sports coat and Boyle had on a dark green golf shirt. They were both melting into their stools, slouched over with cigarettes burning in nearby ashtrays. Their elbows were nailed to the edge of the bar. For an instant Adam saw them differently. They were neither rich nor poor. They were neither wise nor foolish. They were two drunks sitting at a bar sharing plans. Like all good drunks, these were big plans. They could have been in any bar on Earth. Maybe they were.

570-9898
The Main Office, the Following Morning

"Good morning, this is Shoreside Realty, how may we help you?"

Betsy hated the first phone call of the day. Her voice sounded a little like extra-coarse sandpaper at 8:45 a.m.. Besides, on this particular morning she just "wasn't in the mood."

Still, she knew better. Her Catholic sense of guilt kicked in and, 'mood' notwithstanding, Betsy threw herself into automatic and answered the call. If the roughness in her vocal cords was at odds with her telephone decorum, so be it. She knew it was all about keeping up appearances.

If a customer or another agent remarked, like they sometimes did this early in the day, "Is that you Betsy? It just doesn't sound like you," Betsy would handle it flawlessly with one of her three standard comebacks: 1)"I think I might be coming down with a cold." 2)"I have a touch of laryngitis." 3)"It's early and I was out late last night." The third response was rarely true, but it made her feel good to use it on occasion. Betsy, and her polite, unaffected telephone voice, had become very important to Shoreside Realty and its long-standing No. 1 position in the island real estate market. In reality, it was much, much more than that. Betsy Owens' voice *was* Shoreside Realty.

"Is Linda Hinkle in yet?" asked the woman making the call.

"I'm sorry, but she hasn't checked in yet this morning. Would you like to go into her voice mail? Or would you rather I page her for you?..Mrs ..," Betsy almost slipped. She almost said Mrs. Jensen. Betsy knew who was calling within her first three syllables, but she didn't want Mrs. Jensen to know that Betsy knew. When customers were on the warpath, Betsy had learned that it was better to remain anonymous. Otherwise, they had a tendency to tell you more about their particular problems than you cared to know. They could tie a line up for hours. She was lucky that she had caught herself. Hopefully Mrs. Jensen hadn't noticed.

There was a momentary pause in the exchange while Mrs. Jensen tried to decide between digital pager and voice mail. Neither would work. Betsy knew that but wouldn't dare tell it to Mrs. Jensen.

"Voice mail, please."

"Please hold for Linda's voice mail, ma'am. Thank you and have a nice day."

Betsy punched a couple of buttons on the console and Mrs. Jensen found herself at the other end of a short tape recording of Linda's happy, upbeat voice.

"Hi, this is Linda Hinkle's voice mail. I'm either on the other line or out showing some wonderful Shoreside property right now. You know what to do, wait for the beep and leave as long a message as you would like. I'll get back to you just as soon as possible."

Mrs. Jensen knew that the part about getting back to her wasn't true. It was the ninth voice mail message she had left about the leak. She kept a little notepad next to her phone in the kitchen. Mrs. Jensen was keeping track of all the calls, messages, pages and letters she had sent Linda about the roof problem. The notepad was covered in those tally style markings, four straight lines, with the fifth one crossing through the other four at an angle. Judging from the amount of marks on the notepad, it looked more like Mrs. Jensen was doing a traffic count on the Santa Monica Freeway during rush hour rather than simply trying to get Linda Hinkle to return a phone call. Eventually, when the "A" word finally did come into play, Mrs. Jensen knew that her little notepad would come in real handy. She started to leave a message...

"Hi Linda, this is Mrs. Jensen again. I don't know if you got my page yesterday, so I thought that I would leave you a voice mail message today. I just wanted to inform you that our roof is still leaking. Not today yet, because it hasn't rained. But when it rains this afternoon, it will probably start leaking again. Like it has for the last three months, Linda. Please, please give me a call. My number is 570-4232 in case you've misplaced it."

Mrs. Jensen hung up. She was angry. Not quite angry enough. Linda Hinkle would systematically note the level of anger in Mrs. Jensen's voice and postpone calling her until later. Much later.

Betsy was back at it. "Good morning, this is Shoreside Realty, how may we help you?"

"I was wondering if y'all could give me directions to the beach?"

"The beach?"

"Yeah. My wife and I are coming over to Shoreside Island later this afternoon and we've never been out there. We heard that the beaches are mighty fine. We'all figured you real estate people would know where the beach is? You do know where it is, don'tcha?"

Betsy was caught off guard. What do I do with this caller? Should I patch him through to the up person this morning? I'm not sure. Is asking directions to the beach in any way related to purchasing real estate? I don't think so. Should this go to Elinor Braun? No, she'll get pissed. The day is too young to get the sales manager pissed off. I'll handle it. Betsy was just about to give the tourist directions when two more lines lit up. Things were once again gearing up at Shoreside Realty. The buying/selling public was putting the pedal of the great real estate machine to the floorboards, one transaction at a time.

"Could you please hold?"

There, that was done. Betsy sent the hapless caller into the graveyard of Tuesday's Muzak renditions of Jimmy Buffet and promotional tape loops about the great beaches and lifestyle on Shoreside Island. Tape loops that told you everything about the beach except directions to it. Once sent there, into the nether lands of permanent hold, the caller would languish and eventually die, hanging up in frustration within the next two to three minutes, depending on his personal tolerance level. He would never call back.

Maybe I'll get to him in a minute or so, Betsy pondered.

Betsy was kidding herself. The switchboard was happening. Betsy was all over it like Vladimir Horowitz on a Steinway. She was paging, patching, holding and taking messages like a command performance at Carnegie Hall. Betsy saw line seven go dead and for an instant, felt sorry for the man looking for his little patch of beach. His personal afternoon in paradise.

If only he had mentioned real estate. Then Betsy would have known what to do with him. If only.

It was starting in again, the cacophony of it all, the pandemonium. It was going to be a great day, thought Betsy Owens to herself as three lines rang at once. Simply great.

570-9898
Later That Morning

The morning was growing old. The rough edges in Betsy's vocal cords had now been worn into a smooth, buttery demeanor that no one could resist. Like some tennis pro standing in front of an automatic ball machine, call after call had been effortlessly sent flying back over the net. Pages after pages had been sent, memos taken about appraisers arriving late, Orkin pest control finding termites and appointments being rearranged or canceled, depending on the whims of the nervous buyers or the anxious sellers. It was a thing of phone etiquette beauty, to hear Betsy Owens in action.

Her lunch break was coming and Betsy kept looking over toward the doorway for Doris Smothers to pop in. That's why Betsy was so surprised by the UPS guy. It wasn't who she was expecting.

"Hi, ma'am. Do you know where I might find a..." The good-looking UPS guy glanced at his small package and added, "a Mr. Randazzle? Does he work here?"

"Yes, he does. Is that package for him?"

"Yes, ma'am, it sure is."

Betsy was caught off guard. She was staring and she knew it. God, this guy was cute! She kept looking at his dark brown hair, his brown eyes and that adorable pencil-thin mustache. Errol Flynn, that's who he looked like. He looked like Errol Flynn in an army brown UPS outfit with an electronic notepad in one hand and a small cardboard package in the other. It should have been a sword and a dozen roses, imagined Betsy, but no matter.

"You can call me Betsy," she replied.

The UPS guy was staring. Unbeknownst to her, he was thinking along the same lines as Betsy. She was nice. A little overweight, he noted, but she had such a nice personality. Sort of plain looking, but mom always told me that those were the best kind.

"My name's Mark."

They both just stood there for a few seconds. Betsy didn't do anything by way of checking to see if Mr. "Dialing for Dollars" Randazzle's line was busy, and the UPS guy, unlike all the other frantic UPS guys in America, didn't seem to be in any particular hurry to deliver his package.

Indeed, there was a spark in the air. Like the smell the air has after a thunderstorm has passed and the first few shafts of sunlight meekly peer out from behind the dark clouds. A sweet, electric smell that invigorates the atmosphere. That's what it felt like as these two young adults cautiously inhaled each other, both of them secretly delighted at this chance encounter.

That's when Doris showed to relieve Betsy for her half-hour lunch break. Doris felt it immediately. She could sense the chemistry, looking around the room for a minute as if to check to see if it had somehow been soaked by the passing storm. Nothing looked wet, observed Doris. But the air, the air seemed different.

"Hi, Betsy, am I interrupting anything?"

Both of them blushed. Not big, self-conscious blushes, with glowing red cheeks and all the trimmings. Just those delicate, oops sort of blushes, like children being caught with their hands in the cookie jar.

"Oh no, Doris, I was just about to get Jason up here for Mark to get him to sign for this package he had with him and then, what time is it anyway?"

Doris picked up on it immediately. Betsy had just delivered a run-on sentence. Here was a gal who could return 50 volleys in a row in ten minutes' time without misspelling a name, misplacing a message, or mis-sending a page and suddenly she was fumbling for words. This wasn't chemistry, thought Doris as she looked again at the both of them. This was alchemy.

"Well, is he on his way here?"

"Ahhh, no, not yet. I think his line is busy."

Betsy was lying. Well, fibbing, would be the better way of saying it. She hadn't even taken the time to look at her switchboard to see if Jason's line was lit up. Which it wasn't.

Jason, for the moment, was off the phone. He was highlighting another name in flourescent yellow. Yellow meant a "no."

This particular owner, who was from Hackensack, New Jersey, had laid into him like there was no tomorrow. Talk about having a foul mouth. Wow! This owner could swear his way out of hell. Lucky that Jason's self-respect immune system was working fine. It was one thing to be hung up on, but quite another to be called "lower than a goddamned clam's asshole!!!" His pride unscathed, Jason was just about to make another call.

Betsy looked down and noticed that he was off his line. Darn it, she thought to herself, now I'll have to call him. Doris started making small talk with the UPS guy. She was quick to note, like Betsy had, that he was real good looking. He sort of looked like one of those old movie stars. What was his name? She couldn't quite recall. Doris was married, but, hey, no harm in flirting a little.

Betsy took quick note of the flirtation. Her female instincts kicked in as she looked at Mark and said, "I'm so sorry, but his line is still busy. Would you mind if I brought you over to his office? I was just being relieved for lunch and it's not really that much out of my way."

"No, Betsy, you don't have to. I don't want to put you through any trouble."

"Come on, Mark, it'll be my pleasure."

Doris shut up and smiled to herself. She walked behind the switchboard and sat down on Betsy's chair. It was warm. She looked at all the lines and quickly noted that Jason's line wasn't busy. She figured as much. She glanced at Betsy and Mark just as they were heading through the door and added, "Betsy, I don't mind if you run a little late today. I was a bit late getting here myself."

Doris chuckled as the two of them started chatting and carrying on as they headed down the hall, flirting as they did. She put on the headset and punched in Jason Randazzle's extension.

"Jason, are you in?"

The phones didn't have to be picked up for the intercom system to function. Jason answered his extension without bothering to pick up the receiver.

"Yes, is that you, Doris?"

"Yes it is. I have to tell you that Linda Hinkle wants to see you about something in her office immediately."

"Oh. Do you know what it's about?"

"No, but hurry, I forgot to tell you earlier."

"Thanks. I'm heading right over."

Linda Hinkle was out. Doris had just walked by her office not ten minutes ago and she knew that Linda was on a listing presentation until 2:00 p.m. Jason didn't know that. He would get to Linda's office, which was on the other side of the building from his, about the same time the UPS guy and Betsy would reach his office to deliver the package. The old, remodeled office of Shoreside Realty being such a maze of buildings and hallways, Doris knew they'd never cross paths in the process.

Doris smiled again as line six lit up. They'll be five or ten minutes longer trying to track down Jason. That much more time to get to know each other. And Jason, well, Doris didn't really care for him anyway. No one at Shoreside did. If Jason ever questioned Doris about it, she could just explain it away as a mixup. Mixups happen all the time at a busy office like this. No big deal.

As Doris turned to page one of the agents with another urgent message, she thought she caught a glimpse of something over in the far corner of the room. It couldn't have possibly been there, but she swears it was, if only for the briefest of instants. It was a rainbow.

Walk-ins
The Main Office

Betsy was still fantasizing about the UPS man as she came back to her desk after lunch. You couldn't blame her, with his cute, pencil-thin mustache and pleasant demeanor.

Will he really call me? No, they never end up calling me. Should I call him? No, that would seem too forward of me. I hope he calls. He's so darn good looking.

"Did you get his number?" Doris interrupted Betsy's mental deliberations as she walked into her small office.

"Whose number?" Betsy played coy.

"You know darn well whose number I'm talking about. The UPS guy's number. Did you get it?"

"It's none of your business, Doris."

"Baloney, who do you think made sure that Jason wasn't anywhere to be found?"

"What do you mean?"

"I called him out of the office for an urgent meeting with Linda Hinkle just as you two lovebirds headed down the hallway."

Betsy blushed. Lovebirds. She liked the sound of it. It was everything she ever wanted out of life. That and two children to fawn over. That was Betsy's real beauty.

"Thanks for being such a sweetheart. Yes, we did exchange telephone numbers Doris, but I don't think he'll ever call. They never do."

"He'll call, Betsy. That boy will call you within the week. I could see it in his eyes."

"Where did you go for lunch?" Doris continued.

"My usual spot. I just took some salad I made this morning and walked to my little bench on the bay. It's nice to find some quiet time, you know, with the constant phone calls and everything. Are you going out to eat today?"

"Elinor and I are going over to the Flamingo Bar for lunch. They have the best Caesar salad on this island. Today, I'll get it with the fried grouper strips," she said as though she had already ordered.

Doris grabbed her purse and her notebook and got up from Betsy's chair.

As she passed by Betsy she turned and added..."Don't forget, Jennifer Willow's on floor this afternoon. It's her first time being on floor, so go easy on her. Maybe you should direct all the Realtor calls over to Jason. I doubt that Jennifer could handle any of their questions."

"Thanks, Doris. That's a good idea. I hope she gets some up calls or walk-ins though, she needs to get started sometime."

Ups were what the real estate trade called buyers, sellers or anything in between. They might be dropping by for a free map of the island and end up buying a $750,000 house. They might be calling in to get a general idea of the value of their condo at Seagull Pointe and end up selling it three weeks later for $370,000 cash.

October's entire up schedule at Shoreside Realty had been set since the last week in September. Every agent who chose to be on the up schedule had three or four half days a month where he or she had to sit at the front desk and handle all general real estate sales inquiries. Most of the time the various walk-ins, phone inquiries and letters sent to Shoreside Realty asking about real estate on the island never amounted to anything. They were just tire kickers. Tourists who were curious about how much more expensive houses were on Shoreside than they were in Buffalo, or Louisville, or anywhere that was "back home."

But every so often someone would call, or walk through the door who was serious about buying or selling something at Shoreside. Every so often.

❂

Jennifer Willow sat at the up desk for the very first time this particular Tuesday afternoon. She was enduring a severe case of the butterflies as she clicked on the computer and straightened out the front desk.

What if someone calls about a property I haven't even seen yet? What if someone wants to look at property this afternoon? What will I do?

These and 1,000 other tiny fears were fluttering about her thoughts like a cage full of Mexican monarchs. There were far too many butterflies to keep track of. She was so nervous that you could sense it from across the hallway. Even the receptionist at the front desk, Kelly, could tell that Jennifer was apprehensive about her first half-day in professional real estate. The way the front office was laid out, if Kelly leaned forward a bit over her desk, she could just see into the up room. As she did, she tried to say something to Jennifer that would take the edge off.

"Aren't you excited about being first up this afternoon?"

Jennifer waited a second before responding. "No, I'm not. I don't think I'm quite ready for this. We still have three more weeks of training to do. What if I say something wrong?"

"Just relax. The people who come in here don't bite or anything. They're just curious about prices and what the island has to offer. You know the island, Jennifer, you've been living here for how long?"

"Seven and a half years, Kelly."

"Well, then just tell them what you like about Shoreside. Make small talk and enjoy yourself. They're just people."

With that, Kelly leaned back in her seat and continued typing some MLS information on four vacant lots Barbara Silberman had recently listed. More forms to trudge through on her long way to a paycheck.

Kelly Strong had been working the front desk for two years. She knew that, for the most part, the people who strolled into Shoreside Realty to ask about real estate opportunities were great folks. The vast majority of them were upper-middle class, suburban Americans with plenty of disposable income and friendly dispositions. Doctors, investment brokers, lawyers, engineers and businessmen. Most of them.

What Kelly purposely neglected to mention to Jennifer was anything about the occasional weirdos, kooks and quacks who showed up. Like the fellow on the bicycle they arrested last week. The pudgy, bald-headed guy who kept going to all the real estate agencies on Shoreside asking about any Italian restaurants being for sale. There were three Italian restaurants on Shoreside, and none of them was for sale. At any price. That never stopped this fruitcake from coming in week after week after week asking whoever was up the same exact question.

"Are there any Italian restaurants for sale?"

"No," the up person would answer.

Then he'd go outside, get on his rusty old bike and head over to the next real estate office and ask the same question. His T-shirt was dirty, he smelled like garlic and he had that lunatic glint in his eye. Kelly read in the *Shoresider* that they had arrested him last week at the local Eckerd Drug Store for shoplifting six bottles of Nyquil. Figures.

There were others. Belligerent couples from New Jersey wanting the up person to drop everything and take them around the island immediately. "Fuhget about making any appointments," they would insist. "We'll just peek in and see if we find anything we like." Indeed they would. Leaving a trail of complaining owners and disgruntled renters behind them in the scorched-earth tradition of common courtesy. Northern New Jersey. Fuhget about it.

Or worse yet, curious looky-Lous from Omaha who would spend their entire afternoon in the office asking irrelevant questions about properties all over Florida. Who want to know everything about Shoreside, from the Calusa Indians through the conquistadors, the early settlers, the exact year each and every subdivision was first developed and when the COs (certificates of occupancy) were issued for every one of the 79 various condominium complexes in the island.

Long, tedious conversations with folks who couldn't afford a square foot of island property, had no intention whatsoever of buying anything and wanted to keep talking to the up agent until the rain stopped. Sometimes it rained all day. Sometimes it seemed as though it would rain for weeks.

Eventually, the agent would have to feign epileptic convulsions to get them to leave. Even at that, the worst of them would hang around until the medics took the spoon from the agent's mouth just to squeeze in one more little question before leaving the office. They'd ask it just as they were loading the gurney into the EMS truck with the agent now looking fatigued and disoriented. The nerve.

Kelly had spared Jennifer all these gory details. She would get to know all of this in due time. For now, Kelly was content to tell her how great it would be and how much fun she would have sitting in the up desk, waiting for her first big customer to come walking through the front door. Hopefully with $1,000 bills falling out of their pockets from a recent inheritance and anxious to buy their own slice of paradise. Their private quarter-acre estate on Shoreside Island, Florida.

"Shoreside **is** the right choice," like the tape loop man had said.

That was when Dr. and Mrs. James Clifton opened the front door of Shoreside Realty's main office. It was exactly 1:35 p.m. Kelly made note of it on the walk-in log Elinor Braun required her to keep. Dr. Clifton politely asked if they could please speak with someone about Shoreside Island real estate. Not wanting to appear too informal, Kelly paged Jennifer rather than lean over her desk to yell.

"Jennifer," said Kelly though the intercom, "there are some people out front who are interested in some information about island property."

Jennifer, upon hearing Kelly's page, noted that the butterflies inside of her were all taking flight. She got up from behind the desk, walked over to the foyer and introduced herself.

"Hello. I'm Jennifer Willow, and I would be more than glad to help you. Please come into my office and have a seat. Can I get you anything to drink? A soda or some water perhaps?" Jennifer was clearly nervous, but trying her best to avoid appearing too nervous.

She continued. "Oh, before we get started, the State of Florida has requested that everyone looking at property here in the Sunshine State with a residential real estate agent must first receive a copy of this form." Jennifer took a single sheet of paper from the upper right-hand drawer of the desk and handed it to Dr. James and Marie Clifton. On that form it stated, in no uncertain terms, that the real estate agent they were speaking with didn't work for them until she did.

The Cliftons looked the form over briefly. They didn't understand it. No one ever did. With that, all the legal requirements were taken care of. Both parties were now equally confused about their relationship and, knowing that, they quickly forgot about the form and continued on.

"Thank you for this nice form and for offering us something to drink but we just had lunch."

"Oh. Where did you go for lunch?"

It was a great ice breaker, asking about a local restaurant. Through the years, Jennifer had gotten to know all the local eateries like the back of her hand. Especially before she became engaged. She had been taken to lunch by a different island salesman almost daily. She didn't know that much about real estate yet but Jennifer had the lunch menus down pat.

"We were over at that Flamingo place. They have such a great Caesar salad," answered Mrs. Clifton.

"The best on Shoreside. Did you order it with the grouper or the Cajun chicken breast strips?"

"The grouper of course."

"You can't beat the fresh grouper here in South Florida," added Dr. Clifton.

"So where are the two of you from?"

Things were starting to lighten up for Jennifer. The butterflies were settling down inside of her, lighting gently on the tall pines and trees of the Sierra Madre. This wasn't so bad. These were just people. Nice people, like the ones who used to come into the Decorating Hut. They just wanted some help finding a home here on Shoreside. It's just like finding them a nice sofa, only much bigger and 1,000 times more expensive.

The conversation went well. Dr. and Mrs. Clifton were from upstate New York, not far from Ithaca. As it turned out, Jennifer had a high school friend who went to Cornell University. Jennifer had visited Ithaca several times while her friend was at college. They kept finding more and more common ground. These were lovely folks, the Cliftons. After a while, she felt as though they could have been related.

Eventually, the conversation meandered back to real estate. Dr. and Mrs. Clifton were interested in finding a house on Shoreside, preferably on a golf course. They had already driven around some and they had jotted a few addresses down to see what the asking prices were.

"Thirty-two twenty-four Egret Lane?" asked Dr. Clifton. "Could you tell us what they want for that house?"

"Yes, and how many bedrooms does it have?" added Mrs. Marie Clifton.

"Oh, please give me a minute. I need to get the computer on line before I can answer you." Jennifer Willow clicked on the tiny icon that provided service to the MLS data base. She was concerned whether or not it would work for her. Jennifer was never very good at typing, and she knew that if you don't type in your password correctly, the server will automatically terminate your call.

Luckily, everything went smoothly and within a minute, Jennifer was on line. "Could you repeat that address?"

"Thirty-two twenty-four Egret Lane."

Jennifer typed in a few words, played with the mouse a couple of times and the computer quickly pulled up the MLS listing on the property. She scrolled down it to find the details. There, that wasn't all that difficult.

"The asking price is $435,000. It has three bedrooms, three baths and a large family room. It has a small office and a spacious screened porch overlooking the seventh green."

"No, I don't like having a place overlooking a green. You hear too much complaining. We used to have a place on the eleventh green in Ithaca and it wasn't a pleasant experience. Do you have anything with a lakefront setting? Something with a good view of the water?" continued Dr. Clifton.

"I'll put in a search for that. It might take a few minutes."

"Oh, no hurry," added Mrs. Clifton.

Jennifer typed in the search criteria and clicked the mouse several times. The modems discussed these commands in their typical high-pitched screech across miles of fiber optic cable until the search was completed.

Nothing came up. The last lakefront house had been put under contract a week ago. There were lakefront houses off the golf course but nothing on the golf course. No inventory meant no sale. Jennifer was unsure of what to say next. She looked at the monitor one last time, then looked sheepishly at her walk-ins.

"I'm afraid there aren't any lakefront homes available at Osprey Greens right now."

"Are you checking all the listings, and not just your own?" inquired Dr. Clifton, obviously somewhat familiar with the process.

"Yes, this computer is on line with the Multiple Listing Service of the Shoreside Association of Realtors. Every active listing is in here. There's nothing with a lakefront setting listed right now."

Kelly couldn't help but overhear parts of this conversation. Her desk wasn't 20 feet from the up desk. She could sense that Jennifer was getting herself further and further down a long, useless dead end. If she didn't think of something quick, chances were pretty good that Jennifer's first walk-ins would shortly walk out. Kelly had seen it happen before.

Looking at the four listings Barbara had just brought in, Kelly noted that they were all lakefront lots at Osprey Greens. Although she didn't generally interrupt meetings like this, she knew that Jennifer was losing ground quickly and that something would have to be done to save these customers from vanishing out the front door.

"Jennifer, can I see you for a minute," interrupted Kelly during a lull in their conversation.

The announcement came over the intercom but you could hear Kelly's voice at the same time. It startled Jennifer, but in a way she welcomed the interruption. Maybe it could give her a few extra minutes to think of something else. Jennifer excused herself and went over to see what it was that Kelly wanted.

"Jennifer, you might want to look at these four new listings Barbara just brought in. They are lakefront lots in the north section of Osprey Greens. Maybe your people would consider building?" whispered Kelly to Jennifer. Naturally, Jennifer realized that Kelly must have been listening, but for the moment she was glad that she was.

Building? The thought had never even crossed Jennifer's mind. Yes. That might work. They could build a house instead of buying an existing property. What a novel concept.

"Thanks, Kelly," Jennifer whispered.

Jennifer took the information sheet that Kelly had just prepared and headed over to the up desk to resume her conversation with the Cliftons.

"Have you ever considered building your home on Shoreside?"

"No, we hadn't thought of that. But we have built several homes over the years. Why do you ask?"

"Well, Kelly was kind enough to show me these brand-new listings that Barbara Silberman has just brought in. They are all cleared, spacious lakefront lots in the north section of Osprey Greens."

"Those sound interesting. Do you have a plat or a survey of some kind?"

"Just this information sheet, but I'm sure that Barbara has all the information you need on the property."

"Could you find some time to show us the lots? They sound interesting enough," said Dr. Clifton.

"I would love to but I'll have to get someone to fill in for me first."

Jennifer was floating. Her nervous butterflies by now had picked her up and she was drifting over the long, ambling mountain ranges of central Mexico. This was all a dream. It was this easy. You just sit here at the front desk for a little while, nice couples walk in to visit with you, you find them what they want, write up a contract and close. Nothing could be easier. It was the ideal occupation for Jennifer Willow. She was a real estate agent now, a professional. Soon, fantasized Jennifer, she would be making as much as Linda Hinkle does. Soon.

The rest of the afternoon went flawlessly. They got into Jennifer's white Acura and drove to Osprey Greens. Once inside the security gate, they wandered through all the curving, palm tree lined streets until they reached Palmetto Court. Up in the far northern section of the golf course, there were very few improved properties. The back nine of the golf course had already been completed but it was surrounded by undeveloped land. It looked peculiar, with the edges of the well-manicured fairways running alongside overgrown, empty lots.

The original developer of the golf course, Ralph Hardwick, was slowly releasing the remaining inventory. Barbara Silberman and Ralph had been friends for years. Aside from those properties that Ralph sold directly to builders, friends and relatives, Barbara ended up with most of his lot listings.

After wandering around a while longer, Jennifer and her clients finally found the four lots, all of them exactly 100 front feet by 125 feet deep overlooking a wide, beautiful section of an unnamed lake. Unfortunately, by the time Jennifer and her clients reached Palmetto Court, the skies had clouded. The low clouds, coupled with the winding roads, got Jennifer disoriented as to which lot on her photocopied plat was lot "A" and which was lot "D." She had to look at the plat several times to double check.

After looking everything over and making certain that she had her bearings straight, the three of them walked all four of the vacant properties. The only markers setting them apart were the four survey flags in every corner of each lot. Aside from the survey flags, lot "A" looked pretty much like lot "B." Lot "C" look basically identical to lot "D." All four were priced at $135,000 each. Lot "A" and lot "D" were both on the outside corners with a small curving green space along each edge that followed the curve of the road.

"Well, which one do you like the best?" asked Jennifer, trying her best to close her first clients.

"I like lot "A," the one to our right, the best," answered Mrs. Clifton decidedly.

"Well, if that's the one you like honey, then that's the one we'll buy!" concluded Dr. Clifton.

"Let's go to the office and make an offer," he added.

By 5:00 on her very first official day in the real estate business, Jennifer Willow was presenting an offer of $130,000 in cash to Barbara Silberman on one of her brand-new listings. It was a fairy tale come true for Jennifer.

✪

Needless to say, Barbara Silberman was shocked when she got the call from Jennifer around 6:15 that evening. She knew that Ralph would probably take the $130,000 offer but she didn't let Jennifer know that fact. Ralph had told Barbara the day before when he signed the listings that he was anxious to get one of the four sold. He and his lovely wife, Lila, were winding down their developer days and planning a world cruise that would take them out of the country for the better part of a year. Selling one of the lots right now would place Barbara on the top of Ralph's short, favorite real estate agent list. Very short.

Ten minutes after Jennifer called Barbara with the Cliftons' cash offer, outlining all the details - the $1,000 escrow check, the increase in deposit and the closing date, Barbara had Ralph on the other end of her telephone line.

"Ralph, you're just not going to believe this one."

Ralph was used to Barbara's hype. He remained calm.

"What's up, Barb?"

"You know that new gal at our office who used to work at the Decorating Hut?"

"The pretty blond, Jenny something?"

"Yes, Jennifer Willow. Well, she was in the up room this afternoon when a nice couple from upstate New York walked in and started asking about golf course properties."

"Yeah."

"Well, Ralph, she couldn't find them a house that met their needs, so Kelly, the receptionist, who just happened to be typing our new listings, asked Jennifer to tell the Cliftons about them and...,"

Ralph was getting bored. Barbara oversold everything. She didn't need to be telling him all these superfluous details. Ralph had been a developer for too long, he had grown completely immune to sales presentations. Time in the industry had inoculated Ralph against them, even the most virulent.

"And what?"

"And they went out, looked at the lots and made a $130,000 cash offer on lot "A." Can you believe it?"

"Shit."

"What did you just say, Ralph?"

"I just said shit, Barbara. Are you getting hard of hearing?"

"Ralph, I have a cash offer for lot "A" in my happy little hand. No contingencies, they aren't even requesting a survey, just 130K in your pocket within 30 days and you just said shit? Something's up, isn't it?"

"Barb, sit down. Now you're not going to believe my story."

Barbara Silberman sat down. She had spent her entire life on the roller coaster ride of real estate and she knew when it was time to sit down, double check all your seat belts and safety gear and quietly prepare to crash and die. That's what she was doing mentally as Ralph started telling Barbara the inevitable. The roller coaster was falling so fast that Barbara's cheeks were left flapping somewhere behind her ears. It was all a matter of bad timing and too much gravity. Way too much gravity.

"Around 9:00 this morning Lila's brother-in-law, Andy, called me from Panama City. I don't think you've ever met him, Barb, but he's a real character. His name is Andy Stoughton and his wife's name's Debbie, not that it really matters. Well, the two of them have been living in Panama City for going on ten years now. They don't really have a pot to piss in, mind you. Well, I should say, they didn't have a pot to piss in."

Barbara was listening. Her roller coaster had climbed to the top of the first huge drop of this fateful ride. She took one last look around the county fair of it all, glanced at Jennifer's contract and prepared for the rest of the downhill slide.

The other shoe was about to fall. Ralph went on.

"They live in a nice double-wide up there just outside Panama City and Andy's got himself a little bass boat and they're both happy as clams. They belong to two bowling leagues and fit in perfectly in the proverbial redneck Riviera. Like everyone in the Panhandle, Andy and Deb love to play the lotto. They spend about $40 a week at it, spreading their chances out between those stupid little rub-off cards they sell at all the convenience stores, the nightly cash four games and the big, winner take all lotto every Saturday and Wednesday night.

"One week ago, they hit pay dirt."

With that last line, Barbara's roller coaster had hit the bottom of its first big trough. Just as Ralph said "pay dirt," Barb could feel the left side of the roller coaster tipping. There were sparks shooting out and those screeching, metal-against-metal grinding noises. Derailment was inevitable. She said nothing. It would only hurt to talk at this point.

Ralph continued. "I know what you're thinking Barb, but they didn't win big. They didn't hit the jackpot. What they did hit was one of those cash four things, where they pay off all at once. They wouldn't give me an exact number, but I had a feeling it was around $200,000, $250,000 or so. Quite a chunk of change.

"Well, Andy went on to explain that it was always a dream of theirs to be able to move to Shoreside. With his job at the post office and Deb working part time at the local Walgreens, they weren't ever going to be able to afford a place here unless they did happen to hit the lotto.

"Well, when he called to tell us the good news, Andy went on to say that Deb really missed her sister, my wife Lila that is, and, now that they had some money, they asked me if I had any affordable property that might work out for them."

Barbara Silberman gripped the metal bar of her roller coaster car even harder. Just as her knuckles turned parchment white, all the intricate mechanisms that keep the cars on the track suddenly gave out. Her roller coaster car plummeted deep into the crowd. Bodies went flying in every direction. Jennifer Willow and the Cliftons, who only moments before were waving merrily to Barbara as she slowly ascended the ride, were now standing ten feet in front of a 35-foot roller coaster train going 60 miles an hour. No one would survive. Barb had been in a different version of this same terrible accident before. Too many times before.

"No," Barb said in utter disbelief.

"Yes."

"No, not lot "A?""

"Lot "A." I sold it to them this morning. I faxed him a contract around noon. He wired their $1,000 deposit directly into my account. Lila is thrilled. Andy and his wife Debbie are thrilled. It's sold, Barb. Lot "A" is under contract. Way under contract."

The runaway roller coaster hit Jennifer Willow first, sending her skyward into a high-flying, end-over-end flip. Dr. Clifton and his lovely wife were cut down next. The cars kept skidding along the midway. Barbara looked up and saw the "Haunted House" ride not 20 feet in front of her. Goblins, ghosts and screams awaited her racing cart. She was still going 45 miles an hour when she slid through the front door.

"Shit."

"I know how you feel, Barb."

"No, you don't, Ralph. It was Jennifer's first sale. She's going to freak out. I know what it's like, Ralph; it's like having your firstborn ripped away from your loving arms. Neither Jennifer, nor her clients, are going to like this situation one bit."

The telephone went silent. The telephone went into a catatonic state. It was a place where phone conversations go when they run out of options. That extended silence where negotiations fail, romances end and nuclear wars begin. It was a long, pregnant pause with no reprieve. The governor wasn't going to grant another stay. The roller coaster slammed into that haunted house like it was made out of butter. Boo!

Ralph broke the silence.

"I've got it."

"Got what?"

"The solution. I've got the solution."

"Well...,"

"We'll just get them to switch. I'll call Andy right now and tell him to switch lot "A" with lot "D." He hasn't seen either of them, aside from the plat I faxed him earlier today. They're both corner lots, they have about the same view of the lake and Andy's not planning to build for a year or so anyway. He and Deb need to sell their double-wide and get everything in order before they can move, so what's the difference?

"Give me 20 minutes, don't call Jennifer back yet and I'll call Andy with the plan. If he and Deb put up a stink, I'll knock another $5,000 off the price and they'll jump at it. What do you think?"

"I love it, Ralph. Can you reach him tonight?"

"What is it, Tuesday?"

"Yes, it's Tuesday."

"They'll be home. They stay home every Tuesday to watch *America's Funniest Home Videos*. Wednesdays and Fridays they have their bowling league and Saturday night they always go out dancing. But they're home tonight. I'll get back to you in a bit. Don't call Jennifer yet."

"I won't, Ralph."

"Bye now."

"Goodbye."

Barbara's roller coaster was now mysteriously back on track. The sparks and bloodshed were premature. Everything was probably going to be fine. Provided that Ralph could get hold of Andy before 9:00 tonight. That was when the "time for acceptance" clause ran out. That, and provided Andy and Deb were amenable to swapping the lots. That, and provided Ralph was willing to discount another $5,000 if Andy and Deb weren't willing to swap...

The provisos and complications of selling real estate were endless, and Barb, with decades of experiencing each and every one of them, knew it. As Ralph discussed all the options with his brother-in-law, Barbara Silberman played each and every scenario out to its illogical conclusion.

Thirty minutes passed. The roller coaster wheels were freezing up again. The deal was dead. Andy had probably gotten pig-headed about the whole thing and hung up on Ralph. It was over. Jennifer was going to be devastated.

The phone rang.

"Ralph?"

In her usual cobra-like quickness, Barbara picked her phone up before the first ring was finished.

"We've got it, Barb. Andy and Deb have agreed to swap lots. They'll take lot "D" and Dr. and Mrs. Clifton can have lot "A." And, not to worry you any more, I'll accept the $130,000 offer."

"Thanks a million, Ralph." Barb was elated.

"No, Barbara, thank you and all the pros at Shoreside Realty. It's been quite a day."

"I'll call Jennifer in a few minutes with the good news. I'm not even going to mention anything as to what went on between you and your brother-in-law. Jennifer just doesn't need to know.

"Did you have to do the deep discount to get Andy to switch the lots?"

"A little. I waived $2,500 at him and he jumped on it. It'll cover his water meter hookup when they move down to build in 18 months. Everybody wins, and I get to sell two lots in a single day. Not too bad."

"When are you and Lila heading on the cruise?"

"We leave just after the first of the year, Barb. I can't wait. I've been in the business too damn long. It's time to kick back and start smelling the roses."

"Well, I'll get all the paperwork over to you tomorrow, Ralph. Thanks for everything."

"Thank you, Barb, and have a great night."

"Goodbye."

"Bye now."

It was over. The roller coaster ride was over and no one was hurt. Just a few more gray hairs, a few more unexpected screams and scares. Nothing serious. Barb called Jennifer, and then Jennifer called her clients and everyone was happy. All's well that ends well.

570-9898 Ext. 12
Sam Goodlet and the Hazeltons

Kelly buzzed Sam's office. They were in the lobby. Right on time.

"Mr. and Mrs. Hazelton are here for their 3:00 appointment," said Kelly in a dry, professional fashion. Too professional.

"Tell them that I'll be right out," replied Sam. He wasn't at all surprised by their exactitude. Why is it that the people you wish would come in and view property with you never do, and people like the Hazeltons are as prompt as prime-time TV? As dependable as a bad sitcom, he pondered.

Sam picked the color flier up on the Grinstead house, took the key and stuck it in his pants pocket, grabbed his MLS book and headed for the lobby. He wasn't feeling well. The thought of spending another afternoon with this couple had him unsettled. He had a bad case of heartburn from the pastrami sandwich he had eaten for lunch, and he felt tired and distraught, like he had the flu. Maybe it was pneumonia. Hopefully double pneumonia.

Maybe I should tell them that I'm not interested in working with them after today, Sam thought to himself as he walked down the hallway. I could say that I've discovered that I'm allergic to cigar smoke? Or that I'm just too busy to keep showing them properties for weeks on end? Maybe I should take it a step further and let them know that I've been thinking about killing both of them. That I've been looking at handguns and checking out drainage ditches crawling with alligators. By this time Sam had managed to put a delightful smile on his face. He reached up to shake Bart's big hand.

"Well fancy meeting the two of you here!" said Sam Goodlet in his usual congenial manner.

"I reckon it is one hell of a coincidence," replied Mr. Hazelton.

"You two ready to go take a look at your new home?"

"We sure are."

"Well then, let's get started."

As the three of them headed out the door, Sam turned to Kelly and said, "Let Betsy know that I'm out and tell her to page me for the next hour or so. I should be back here around 4:00."

"I will, Sam."

Kelly felt sorry for Sam as she watched him through the front window.

He went around and opened the door for Mrs. Hazelton. He does that for all of his customers. He's the only agent who does, reflected Kelly. He's such a gentleman.

And to think of how long he has been working with those two kooks from Alabama. It's been almost two months now. Showing after showing after showing, and they haven't made a single offer. Betsy told me that he's a retired judge or something. His wife's a retired Southern belle, that's for damn sure. Any other agent in this office would have given up on these two losers weeks ago. Not Sam. He's just too good to be true, thought Kelly as she typed out some CONTRACT IN PROCESS forms for Elinor.

"Boy, your Oldsmobile smells like it's brand-new, Sam. Did you have it cleaned up or sumthin?" asked Bart as he made himself comfortable in the back seat.

"Sure did, Bart. I had it completely detailed last Friday morning in fact. Had it done at Terry's Car Wash. They do one heck of a job, don't they?"

Sam looked at Bart through the rear view mirror just as Bart was lighting an enormous cigar. As huge puffs of thick, aromatic brown smoke obscured his face, Bart replied in his thick, Southern accent, "They did do a mighty fine job."

Why did I drop that $150? Sam kept mentally kicking himself as they drove toward the showing. He watched the cigar smoke creep up and over the back of the front seat. He could feel it oozing into every crevice, every spotless nook and cranny of the car, slowly killing his new car smell, strangling it with the rotten, disgusting odor of tobacco smoke. Sam looked over at the glove box. He imagined for a minute that his shiny .45 caliber Beretta was lying in there. Ready to be put to the test.

Sam imagined that it was loaded. They would drive toward Woodland Pines first. Sam would come up with something. A new listing in the Pines, over near those big culverts. He would pretend to see something near the drainage ditch and pull over. He could tell them that he thought he saw a small, lost puppy. The Hazeltons would both get out of the car and walk down the embankment to the water's edge. He would follow a few yards behind.

As they walked to the water's edge, he would have just enough time to screw on the silencer. "Theeew! Theeew! Theeew! The strange, painless sound of the silencer would reverberate through the two large culverts as the victims fell face down in the swampy, stagnant waters in front of them. Sam, now completely committed to the crime, would empty the chamber into his clients. Madness would overtake him as he pulled the trigger repeatedly. This was your fatal flaw, Mr. Hazelton, you wanted to look at one house too many, he would say to himself as he fired the last round.

"Theeew! Theeew! Theeew!" He would be tempted to reload.

"Have you been in this house before, Sam?" Dolores asked, interrupting Sam's sick daydream.

"Yes, ma'am, way back when it was first listed. It was on our MLS caravan. Although I have to admit, it's been such a long time that I really don't remember much about it."

"It said in the ad that it had three bedrooms and a loft. Do you remember the size of the loft?" she continued.

"No, I don't, but we'll know how big it is soon enough."

Dolores didn't have anything to add for the moment. Sam returned to his daydream. He was now knee deep in the marsh, dragging Mrs. Hazelton's bullet-ridden body toward the culvert. He had already tossed the gun into the center of the lake. There were seldom any cars along this stretch of gravel road, so there was little chance of them being seen, even in broad daylight. He was just heading back to get Mr. Hazelton when they pulled in front of the Grinstead house.

"Looks mighty fine from the outside, Sam. Why's it been on the market so gull darn long? Must be overpriced?"

He was starting in again. Setting the stage for his "fatal flaw." Priming the pump. As Bart opened the back door of Sam's stinking car, his cigar smoke billowed out into the calm afternoon air. There was so much smoke pouring out that an unknowing neighbor might have been tempted to report a brush fire. Sam's detailing job was ruined. Sam looked at the glove box one last time as he got out of the car. He knew that there wasn't any gun in it. There were some island maps, his registration, some Dentine chewing gum and fuses in it. No Beretta. It just wasn't his style. Still, a man can always dream.

"It's a fine-lookin' property, ain't it," said Bart as he headed toward the house.

"Yes, it's a fine-looking home. Done in that Olde Florida style that the both of you seem to like. Let's go have a look at her," commented Sam as the three of them headed toward the front door.

They made their way up the front stairs of the elevated home and unlocked the front door. The Grinsteads had a security system but they had turned it off for the showing. Sam was glad. He never liked punching in those numbers on security pads when he entered a home. They always made him feel nervous, as if he was breaking and entering or something.

They all walked into the foyer and divided up from there. Sam wasn't one of those "tour guide" kind of agents. The kind that opens the door to the laundry room and says something insipidly stupid like, "and oh, what a lovely, spacious laundry room." Sam let the house speak for itself.

If there was a less visible feature that could be pointed out by him, then fine. If he saw one, Sam might mention the fact that the house had a humistat, which would help reduce summer electric bills. Or if he knew some things about the builder of the home. That this builder was known for putting together solid houses, or that his homes tend to leak over time, he might mention it.

Information that the buyers wouldn't be readily able to observe or gather from simply walking through the house. But opening closet doors and pointing to ceiling fans was out of the question. The Hazeltons could handle all that on their own.

Dolores went upstairs and Bart headed toward the kitchen. No one spoke. It was a calculated ritual that Sam was all too familiar with. They usually kept utterly silent as the two of them independently scoured the home. Silent as snakes.

If they liked the house, they might ferret through it a second time. One would head upstairs, the other down. One would be in the guest bedroom, the other in the master. One might flush a toilet in the powder room, the other might flick on the garbage disposal switch for an instant in the kitchen.

By this time, Sam knew that the Hazeltons were professional house lookers. They could have held degrees in it. Virtual Ph.Ds in how to look at houses but never finding one to actually purchase. Master's degrees at finding where the hot water tank was hidden, what kind of circuit breakers were in the electrical panel, and even going so far as checking the tops of the toilet tanks to verify the age of the home by noting the dates stamped under those covers and comparing those with the information listed in the MLS. They were good.

While they did all of these things, Mr. and Mrs. Hazelton never said a word. They were both stone-cold silent. They never showed or displayed an emotion or reaction of any kind. They were a real estate agent's worst nightmare. The quiet, unattached lookers that were impossible to read. Do they like the house? Sam couldn't tell. Do they hate the house? No way of knowing. They just walked around in a deafening muffle: checking, flicking switches, studying every hallway, every inch of crown molding, every cubby hole. Always in search of Bart's "fatal flaw."

Sam stayed out of their way. Early on, two months ago, he had tried to talk to them about the properties while they wandered through them. It didn't work. He would try to make pleasant conversation while they answered every query with a one-syllable response like, "yes," "sure," "smaller," "possibly," and the like. After the tenth house he gave up.

He either retreated to the kitchen to examine all the personal photos and notes on the refrigerator or he sat in the living room to look through the coffee table books. Provided, of course, that there were any. Sam's last default was to make use of the time to look over his MLS book. By now, he never said anything to the Hazeltons during their silent, looking phase. This was their special time.

Twenty minutes later they were both standing above him as he finished a beautiful coffee table book on *Whales: Their Secret Lives*. It was a great book, thought Sam. How do they take those fabulous underwater photographs?

"We're finished."

"Fine, do you want to head back to the office?"

"Maybe not right away."

Oh no. It was too late for lunch. Lunch was out of the question. What now? Sam told Kelly that he'd be back by 4:00. It was already quarter of 4:00. There was no time, nowhere for them to go, what was up? Early bird dinner? Not this early.

The three of them walked to the car and got in. Bart lit up what was left of his stoggie. By this time Sam didn't give it a thought. His detail job from Friday was ruined. He would just have to live with it.

"We thought we might stop by The Coffee Bean and have an espresso before going back to the office, Sam. Dolores and I want to talk about the house with you for a bit."

"Fine, we'll head right over there."

What's this? Did they actually like the house? No. It couldn't happen. They probably want to tell me that the loft is too small. That the disposal needs replacing. That the house smelled funny or it was way overpriced. There's no way that they would both actually like a house.

The three of them got to the coffee shop and ordered. Sam had a mocha java and they both ordered double espressos. Sam picked up the tab. They were already into him for several hundred dollars' worth of lunches, sodas and a detail job down the drain, what difference would two more coffees make?

"Well, where's the flaw?" Sam Goodlet threw himself right into the thick of it. No sense beating around the bush.

"We can't find one."

"We're both working on it, Sam, but we can't find one."

Sam took a long, painful sip of his mocha java. He could feel it scorch his tongue as he sipped it but it didn't bother him. The pain only added to his aura of disbelief. This couldn't be happening. House No. 58 was the charmer? Or was it No. 57?

"How much were they asking when they first listed the house?"

"Five hundred seventy-five thousand dollars."

"Overpriced," confirmed Bart.

"Overpriced," echoed Dolores.

"How much are they asking now?"

"Four hundred sixty-five thousand dollars."

"Fair price."

"Fair enough."

They both took a sip from their coffees. Sam's tongue was smouldering in a dull, steady pain as he heard the six words slip through the lips of Mr. Hazelton in a slow, melodic whisper. "We want to make an offer. Not right tomarah or anything too hasty, mind ya. But we want to make an offer."

Sam Goodlet was in shock. His heart stopped beating momentarily. His breathing became short and irregular. It could not be happening. It was happening.

No matter what it takes, even if I have to take my end of this commission down to zero, I am going to make this work. It will finally be over. The Hazeltons will have found a home. I will be free of them. Finally free of them!!!

After finishing their coffees and covering some fine points, they all headed to the office. Once there, Sam, along with the Hazeltons, sat in one of the conference rooms up front and drafted the offer. Sam was speechless. He would be willing to sell his soul to the devil to make this contract work, and the devil must have figured as much.

570-9898 Ext. 4
Barbara Silberman's Desk

Three-thirty-two rolled around and there is no word from Mr. and Mrs. Skinner. They aren't going to keep their appointment with me. I just know it.

Her customers were two minutes late and Barbara Silberman was already convinced that they were not going to show. She was being stiffed. Left in the lurch. Ditched, abandoned, ignored, slighted, deserted. Her career was over.

All that work for nothing, thought Barb. Four properties to look at, appointments set up and arranged, and a big fat "no show." Fellow agents going over and opening up their listings for her; turning on the lights, picking up, kicking the dead roaches under the appliances and making certain that their tired listings looked their best. All for naught.

Three-thirty-six rolled by and Barbara had rapidly descended into a deep blue funk. They seemed like such nice people, she thought to herself as she sank deeper and deeper into her private depression. How could they do this to me?

It wasn't the first time in over two decades of selling Shoreside real estate that Barbara Silberman had been stood up. She had been stiffed countless times before. No phone call to cancel, no reason given and never an apology offered. Just an insufferable 30-minute wait for customers that would never show. It was just the way real estate agents are treated by an indifferent public, thought Barbara to herself. We're treated like bums. Worse than a used car salesman. Way worse. It was the roller coaster ride again, but this time it was only the tiny one in the kiddie section of the fair.

Just then her extension buzzed. Kelly's voice came through the intercom. "Barbara, you have some people up front who just came in to see you. A Mr. and Mrs. Skinner, I believe."

"Tell them I'll be right up."

It was 3:39 nine on the button. They were here. They were such nice people, Barbara reminded herself. I knew that they would show. They probably just got hung up in traffic. Being nine minutes late isn't all that bad. I'm sure they have a good reason to be late. See, I knew that they would show all along. Her career was back in high gear. She was that resilient.

Barbara burst into the front room with her purse, her keys and a smile that could stop an ax murderer.

"Mr. and Mrs. Skinner, I'm Barbara Silberman. It's a pleasure to meet both of you."

"Thank you, Barbara, sorry we ran a bit late. Lunch was slow today at the Lazy Heron," apologized Mrs. Skinner.

"Oh, no problem. We've got only four properties to look at and we've got all afternoon to do it."

"Four properties? I thought we were just going over to see the cottage," queried a perplexed Mr. Skinner.

"Didn't I mention that I found some others that I thought you might like? I'm sorry, I just thought that there's never any harm in looking, is there?"

Close, close, close. Barbara didn't even have to think about it. There was the porcupine close, the puppy dog close, the take-away close and a dozen more. They were no longer a conscious effort. By this time, she closed out of instinct. She closed out of subliminal habits formed over decades of closings. "There's no harm in looking, is there?"

"Oh, I guess not," said Mrs. Skinner, actually a bit delighted that they were going to see some additional properties.

"Well, let's get in my Navigator and get right to it."

"Sounds good, show us the way," replied Mr. Skinner.

The three of them poured out the door and walked over to Barbara's battered SUV. Neither of her customers took note of the innumerable dents or scratches as they got in. Mrs. Skinner sat next to Barbara, while Mr. Skinner took the back seat directly behind her. Barbara turned to both of them after starting the car and said, "Remember folks, always wear your seat belt!"

They thought it was sweet of her to remind them like that. Little did they know what sort of ride they were in for. Had they the slightest inkling as to what they were about to experience, they would have come dressed like Mario Andretti, in fireproof racing suits and certified Bell racing helmets. They would have brought first aid kits and extra plasma. They would have stayed on the beach.

Barbara backed up without incident. She pulled up to the driveway and waited for a break in traffic to take a left toward the first showing. The cars just kept coming and coming and coming. After a 30-second wait, Barbara gunned it and squealed out between two cars that were way too close to each other for her ponderous Lincoln Navigator to squeeze through. The second car slammed on its brakes to avoid broadsiding Barbara. It stopped six inches short of her rear fender. The sound of the screeching brakes joined in with the sound of squealing tires to send shivers down the Skinners' spines. The only sound missing was that dull thud of metal hitting metal. Their tour had commenced.

Kelly watched it all from her front desk and said a silent prayer for the buyers. She always did when they walked out the door with Barb.

In the end, the near-hit right outside the office was the worst of it. Barb did scrape against some bushes that were planted too close to where she parked at one of the houses they viewed, and she did jump a curb, almost hitting a young boy on a bicycle, but other than that, to Barb at least, it was an uneventful ride. The Skinners weren't accustomed to Barb's horrific driving. They were nervous wrecks as they walked into the office an hour and a half later.

"Could I please use the restroom?" Mrs. Skinner immediately asked Kelly at the front desk.

"Sure you can, it's right down the hallway on your left."

Kelly knew that they would both need to go to the bathroom after touring with Barbara. They always do. She had the tendency to scare the urine out of you, so to speak.

"Can I get you anything to drink, Mr. Skinner, a Diet Coke perhaps?" asked Barbara.

"No, no thank you. Could we sit down somewhere? I need to relax a little."

"Oh, I know, looking at real estate can be so exhausting. Let's use the conference room."

There were two small conference rooms opposite the up office on the other side of the foyer. They were where the buyers and sellers generally sat to do the paperwork when a listing was being signed or an offer drafted. They were nondescript, with nondescript paintings of beach scenes that never really existed hanging on the walls.

The chairs were low and had rollers on them. They were upholstered chairs done in mauve. Pale mauve, meant to be soothing and calming to the customers. The table top was an eggshell-colored Formica. Nothing was disturbing or disruptive anywhere in the room. Fake silk flowers sat in the middle of the table, a telephone sat on one small desk to the side and four chairs encircled the oval table. More than a billion dollars in real estate had exchanged hands here and the entire room was furnished for less than $400, including the high-tech phone in the corner.

Barbara and Mr. Skinner sat down. They made small talk until Mrs. Skinner returned from the restroom. The minute she did, Mr. Skinner got up and excused himself as well. Only Barbara held out. She had taken her riveting car ride a thousand times before. She didn't need to go to the bathroom. She was used to fear.

"Well, Mrs. Skinner, which house did you like the best?"

It was a formality to ask. Barbara already knew it was the second cottage they looked at, the one that had the lovely lakefront view just north of Middle Gulf Drive. She knew within minutes that it was the property that they both took a shine to. Years of field work with clients not unlike these two had given her foolproof instincts as to which property was the one that was going to get the go-ahead and which ones were going to be dropped.

"Oh, I think Robert and I both like the second one. You know, the pretty one with the lake in back. It had such a nice view. And that big bird that walked by, what was it called again?"

"A great blue heron, Mrs. Skinner."

"Oh yes, that great blue heron. Well it was just wonderful to see it so close like that. What are they asking for that house again?"

"Three hundred and twenty-five thousand dollars, and there's room for a pool."

"Robert doesn't like pools. He feels that they're just too much maintenance. Do you like pools?"

Barbara smiled. She knew better than to answer that question. What difference did it make if she liked pools or not, and if she said the wrong thing it might take them off the trail.

"Sometimes." There, she didn't say anything.

Mr. Skinner returned from the bathroom. He looked tired. The car ride with Barbara had reminded him of his tour in Vietnam 30 years ago. In the midst of the ride, moments after Barbara just missed the kid on the bike, he suddenly remembered when his best friend stepped on that landmine. The horror of it all.

"We were just talking about the second house. Mrs. Skinner and I were discussing what we should do next. Maybe we should set up a time to go look at it again tomorrow?" suggested Barbara.

"No. No, that won't be necessary. Unless, well..," Mr. Skinner was fumbling for the right way to put it, "unless we could meet you there."

"Why not. Let's say around 3:30?"

"That would work just fine."

With the second showing set, all three of them found themselves with very little else to talk about. Mr. Skinner wanted to know what the utilities were running on an annual basis, and how long the house had been listed. Details. Barbara reassured them that she would have all of that and more put together for them tomorrow. In fact, unbeknownst to them, she would have a pre-drafted purchase agreement in her purse with her by noon tomorrow. Better to be prepared than to be sorry, she reminded herself once again.

The Skinners said goodbye. Barbara went to her office and made several more calls before the day ended. She still had some forms to get through with regard to the offer Jennifer had presented and needed to call the title company to set up the closing.

Business was good. Tomorrow she would sell that nice little house and wrap up the lot offer for Jennifer Willow. After these two contracts though, who knows? The real estate market on Shoreside might crash. Thoughts of a bleak future kept haunting her as she headed to her battered SUV to go home. Nothing was certain except death and taxes. Death and taxes, death and taxes. That thought kept running through her mind as she turned the ignition key and squealed out into the main drag, looking like a case study in reckless endangerment.

487-2314

Mr. and Mrs. Clarence Brown

"Hello, Mrs. Brown?"

"Yes."

"This is Linda, Linda Hinkle with Shoreside Realty. I was wondering if you have made a decision yet about the listing?"

Linda had just gotten back to her office after her hour-long listing presentation. When she smelled money, she kept on the scent like a mountain lion in a bad winter. By calling back right away, Linda felt that it showed her customers just how committed she was, how dedicated an agent they were listing their home with.

"Yes, we've decided, Mrs. Hinkle."

Not good. Very not good. Linda cringed, waiting for the other shoe to fall. They never use the formal, Mrs. Hinkle, unless you've lost.

"We're going with Loretta Snyder of Beachwalk Realty. We really appreciate your analysis and the effort you've put forth, but we bought our place through Loretta and feel that we owe her the listing. Thanks so much for calling."

"Well, Mrs. Brown, if things don't work out for you, keep my card handy. You know where to reach me."

"We certainly will, Linda. Bye now."

"Goodbye."

Linda gently put down the receiver. From all appearances she was handling the situation professionally. She calmly made some notes about the conversation in her computer's data base, tidied up the top of her desk and continued swimming forward, like a tireless shark wearing too much make-up.

But looks are deceiving. Deep within, Linda Hinkle was furious. She kept thinking to herself that Loretta Snyder couldn't sell her way out of a paper bag. She was a part-timer for godsake, with three young kids in school. Did the Browns want to sell their house, or just list it? If they wanted to sell it, hiring Loretta Snyder and those buffoons at Beachwalk Realty was the last thing on earth they should have done.

The fact was, Mrs. Linda Hinkle hated losing. She hated it with a passion. She knew that it was impossible to walk away with every listing, close every sale and get deposit checks from every buyer, but it never stopped her from trying. She had let Frank down this afternoon and she felt terrible.

"Tomorrow, I'll just have to work a little bit harder," Linda mumbled to herself while putting some files in her Italian leather briefcase to review after dinner. She continued with a silent monologue to herself as she got ready to head home.

"The house is overpriced anyway. Six months from now, when Loretta still hasn't sold it, the Browns will call me. I'll get them to drop the price $25,000 and we'll have a contract on the property within a month. It has an awkward floor plan. I didn't like the layout at all, and I'm glad I didn't get the listing. Loretta Snyder can try to sell it; it's probably riddled with termites. It may not even pass a home inspection. I was lucky to have lost this one."

Linda Hinkle was doing her best to rationalize away her defeat. She was angry with herself about losing the listing and whenever that happened, her very next move was to rifle through her Rolodex of reasons why she never wanted to list the house in the first place. It might be the floor plan, the lack of curb appeal, the price, the condition, or the attitude of the sellers.

All of these were just excuses. In reality, Linda was disappointed about losing. Losing was the pits. Losing sucked.

Had the telephone conversation gone the other way and she had received the listing, everything Linda was currently thinking would have been reversed. She would have felt sorry for a moment about Loretta Snyder not getting the listing, with the three kids in school and all. She needed the listing more than I did, but then again, I'm the better agent for the job. I'm the more dedicated. I'm the one Frank loves.

Her thoughts would have continued along those same lines. The price is a bit high, but with such a unique floor plan, it's worth every penny of it. The place has great curb appeal and I'm really looking forward to working with the Browns; they're such wonderful people. The property appears to be so well taken care of, I'm sure it doesn't have termites.

But Linda had failed, so none of these thoughts ever crossed her mind. Just before shutting down her computer, she made a note in her calendar program to call the Browns about their property in exactly six months' time. Linda assumed that their listing with Loretta would be six months' long. Ninety-nine percent of all listings are. If it hasn't sold, I can pick up the listing on the rebound, she reminded herself as she turned off her computer and headed home. It was 4:53 in the afternoon. She felt a bit guilty, leaving the office seven minutes early, but she had arrived an hour before anyone else had that day, so it was acceptable. Frank would understand.

After a nice salad and a turkey breast sandwich for dinner, Linda was planning on spending a couple of relaxing hours with Frank reviewing some contracts and making a half-dozen phone calls to clients up north. She would sip a nice glass of red wine, listen to National Public Radio, and savor this quiet time with the love of her life. She was looking forward to it as she pulled in her driveway and pressed the garage door button letting her into her quiet, completely empty house. A perfect evening, thought Linda. Another romantic night with Frank. Life was good.

An All-page:

"Reminder! All associates are required to attend the sales meeting tomorrow at 8:30 a.m. at the main office. Elinor Braun will be reviewing two new forms. Please plan to be there promptly."

Betsy highlighted every associate in the paging system and pressed the all-page button. Within three minutes everyone in the company would hear their Motorola pager chirp, or sing, or buzz or chime and the message would be passed along. It was 5:00 p.m. on a Tuesday afternoon and it was the last thing Betsy needed to do before turning the phones over to the answering service until tomorrow morning at 8:30 sharp.

What a day, Betsy thought as she closed up shop. I just hope he'll call sometime soon, he's so darn cute. I wonder if he'll have another delivery to the office this week. Jason orders a lot of catalogue items for his customers, pens and calendars, magnets and your typical real estate promotional junk; I wonder if he's got anything coming via UPS soon.

I'll ask him tomorrow. No, that'd be stupid. He would wonder why I would be interested. I'll just wait a week or two to see if he calls.

I hate waiting. I've spent too much of my life waiting for guys like Mark to call. Guys who say that they're going to call but never do. It's the hardest thing in the world to do, to wait.

Betsy started her tired Pinto and headed home. She unlocked the door to her small, two-bedroom apartment just off island and glanced at her mail. She didn't have any plans for the evening. Earlier, at the office, she had kicked around the idea of taking in a matinee but had decided against it. She wanted to be home just in case.

She fixed herself a Lean Cuisine microwave dinner and watched the evening news. After that, she turned off the tube, settled into her favorite chair and started reading a Jackie Collins novel. It was about a woman torn between three lovers. How ironic. Betsy would have given just about anything to have one.

At exactly 7:47 her phone rang. It was the UPS man, Mark. They talked until midnight. Small talk, mostly. Odds and ends. It didn't matter what they were talking about in a way. Betsy was thrilled. Yes, she thought as the hours drifted by, there is a God.

471-6900
Vanessa's Home Phone

"Hello."

"Vanessa, it's Adam."

"Oh, I was hoping you'd call. Are you in the car? Your voice sounds so funny."

"Yeah, I'm on my way to change and grab the Porsche, then I'll swing over to pick you up. We're still on, aren't we?"

"Sure, Adam."

"Well, by the looks of it, I should be there around 6:45 or so. We might end up running a bit late for dinner. Do you mind?"

"No, that'll be fine, but I want to get back to my apartment before 10:30 or 11:00 tonight though. I've got to work tomorrow."

"So do I. I just got paged a few minutes ago from Betsy. We've got a sales meeting in the morning at 8:30 a.m. God, I hate those things."

"See you in a bit then."

"Bye."

"Bye."

As Vanessa hung up, Adam's automated car phone system recognized the disconnection and terminated the call. Adam kept driving toward his house. It had been a long, tiring day and he was looking forward to an evening out.

Some days you eat the bear, and then again some days the bear makes quick work of you, Adam was thinking as he pulled in his driveway.

Throughout his long day, nothing had gone smoothly for Bartlett. At 9:00 a.m., while he was in the midst of organizing the Dudleys' condominium tour, Mildred Lee had called to ask him if he would re-list her house. No one had brought her an offer this past year, and she wanted to get her listing back with Adam and all the nice people at Shoreside Realty. Mildred Lee's house, reflected Adam, the listing from hell.

❂

Mrs. Mildred Lee, the elderly owner of the small, two-bedroom ranch that had been on the market for half a decade, hobbled over to her memo from yesterday and picked up Adam's telephone number. Time to give him a little jingle, she remembered.

I know you want to sell this joint before Shoreside gets clobbered by the "Big One," and Adam's the best darn salesman on this island. I'll call him in a few minutes, thought Mildred as she shuffled to her kitchen where her classic avacado-green rotary telephone hung on the wall next to her tracking chart.

The "Big One," Mildred knew, was only a matter of time. The geographic design of Florida, jutting down 700 miles into steamy, equatorial waters, seemed to say, "Come on then, hit me," to every Cape Verde storm ever born off the coast of Africa. At least that's how Mildred saw it.

The truth being, Mildred Lee never wanted to live on Shoreside. Her husband, Walter Lee, was the one who had convinced, or some would say cajoled her into moving down from suburban Chicago. They had bought the house nine years ago. Like many a spouse before her, Mildred arrived kicking and screaming to the Sunshine State. Mildred never minded the cold, long winters of her hometown. It afforded her time to knit and be there for her grandchildren. Winters were her special time. But it wasn't only the way she enjoyed watching the snow fall that made her want to stay in Chicago. It was her fear of hurricanes that made the move that much more agonizing.

Mildred Lee had a clinical paranoia about hurricanes. Hurricanes, and to a far lesser extent, alligators. From her safe haven in Melrose Park, Illinois, Mildred would take out her pencil and notepad every May and track the various tropical depressions, storms and hurricanes that pummeled the Carribean and coastal United States every year. She knew her Saffir-Simpson Hurricane scale inside out: Category 1) 74-95 mph winds, damage: minimal. Category 2) 96-110 mph winds, damage: moderate. Category 3) 111-130 mph winds, damage: extensive. Category 4) 131-155 mph winds, damage: extreme. Category 5) 155 + mph winds, damage: CATASTROPHIC!!!

Thank God they didn't live in Florida, she would remind herself throughout the hot summer months. Then, on November 30th of every year, the official end to the hurricane season, Mildred would sit down at her small desk in Melrose Park and solemnly review her horrific storm journal, its pages filled to overflowing with coordinates, death counts and estimated property damage for each and every tropical disturbance that particular summer. Noting every detail, from unnamed tropical waves to destructive monsters like Camille.

Walter Lee, on the other hand, paid no attention to hurricanes. He hated those long, Chicago winters. He hated going to work in mid-January, getting bundled up in 16 layers of wool and trudging through knee-deep snow out to his car. Once inside his ice cold automobile, he would put the key in the ignition, his back muscles all tensed up and shivering, only to have the car's starter make that dreaded, solitary "click." The click meant calling AAA and asking for them to put you into their jump-start rotation. That in turn meant waiting until 1:00 p.m. or later to get jump started and being hours late for work again.

No, winter wasn't his cup of tea. The grandkids could come down and see them in Florida if they wanted to. The day Walt retired, he was packed and ready to move south. Some friends of theirs told them about Shoreside Island and the rest was history.

When Walt passed away from pneumonia six years ago, Mildred Lee did two things upon returning home from funeral service. First, she put up all the inexpensive, corrugated aluminum hurricane shutters that were stored in the garage and next, she called Adam Bartlett to come over and list the house.

Mildred wanted to move back to Chicago to be with her four grandchildren in the worst way. Adam had sold them the house nine years ago. It was one of his very first sales with Shoreside Realty and in the long week that the three of them worked together, Adam had come to appreciate just how insane Mildred Lee really was.

With Walt no longer around to keep her hurricane phobia in check, the afternoon she got home from the cemetery she called a local handyman and had him zip her little house up tighter than a fascist bunker in the fall of '44. She wasn't going to be caught off guard!

Mildred had once read in one of those "Hurricane Preparedness" pamphlets, which all the local TV stations distribute every spring, *"that hurricanes had been known to hit Florida every month of the year."* It was mid-March when that local handyman was busy putting the shutters on. There wasn't a cloud in the sky and it hadn't rained on Shoreside Island in three weeks. An occasional cold front, with wind gusts to 25 miles an hour, were about the worst Shoreside might see for months and months to come, but that didn't stop Mildred.

She had her "alert radio" plugged in and ready to sound. She had her six-month supply of fresh water, canned goods, flashlight batteries, transistor radios, first aid kits and flare guns stockpiled in the pantry. She was ready to survive "THE BIG ONE." Everything was stacked up nice and neat. She and her five cats were not going to be caught off guard. When it came, and a hurricane could come any month of the year, she reminded herself daily, they were going to be ready.

Of course, having the hurricane shutters on all year round made selling the house considerably more difficult. When Adam stopped in for his initial listing presentation five years ago he diplomatically suggested that, at least until the summer hurricane season drew a bit closer, Mildred could probably take down the shutters.

"Over my dead body," was her terse reply, as she proceeded to get out her old, yellowed handout to show Adam the exact page that said that a hurricane could hit Florida any month of the year. The entire section was highlighted by a bright, flourescent green Magic Marker. It was also underlined in red. In fact,

Mildred had memorized the passage.

Adam tried to explain to her that it would be all but impossible to show the house properly with all the windows boarded up. He went on to describe to Mildred how the buyers wouldn't be able to see what a bright, sunny little home it was. Nor would the buyers be able to appreciate the wonderful views down the canal the house had from the kitchen and the living room. "Please reconsider," Adam added in his winning, salesman style.

Mildred didn't budge. She wanted to sell the house, but not at the expense of putting her and her five felines at risk. It was simply too dangerous to take the hurricane shutters down, even for a day.

Adam reluctantly took the listing. He took it more out of his allegiance to Mildred's dead husband Walter than anything else. He had regretted taking it for that first six-month period ever since.

Now, half a decade later, no one on Shoreside wanted to list Mildred's house. Their position was understandable. Not only did Mildred refuse to leave the house during the showings, for fear of someone accidently letting out one of her precious cats, but she kept talking a blue streak to the prospective buyers about the awesome power of hurricanes throughout the entire showing. That and the dangerous, lurking alligators in all of Shoreside's freshwater lakes. "Big alligators," said Mildred. "The size of Egypt!!!"

Eventually, the only agents that Mildred was able to convince to list her house were the novices and the kind of agents that have a hard time saying no. Adam had taken the first stretch five years ago and had skillfully managed to dodge Mrs. Lee's calls ever since. The listing had bounced from firm to firm, agent to agent through the years like some kind of real estate virus. Like a listing influenza. No one wanted to list Mildred Lee's little two-bedroom CBS anymore. Why would they?

By now, the island's agents all dreaded bringing their customers into a small, dingy house that reeked of cat urine and had about the same amount of sunlight pouring into it as a New Orleans crypt. While throughout their showing, a strange little old lady with a heavy Chicago accent followed them around the house talking about the destructive power of Hurricane Donna or the terror of Hurricane Andrew.

Mildred would follow the prospective buyers around the house quoting various death counts from the big storms.

"Like the 'Big One' that hit Galveston at the turn of the century. That one killed over 6,000," she would add while the purchasers nervously inspected the master bedroom. "Half the houses in town were wiped out by the 15-foot tidal wave!"

As they reached the guest bedroom she would be explaining how the "Great 'Cane" of '28 made Lake Okeechobee overflow its banks and wipe out over 2,000 in Belle Glade, Florida. "There were so many bodies that they ended up having to burn the dead!"

By the time they reached her little kitchen, they would hear Mildred's predictions of 20-foot storm surges sweeping over Shoreside like massive tsunamis, destroying everything in their wake. Tornados, wind gusts in excess of 200 miles per hour, pounding surf, all communications knocked out and the local 'gators feeding on the carrion after the storm. Gorging themselves on the bloated bodies of the dead.

As the buyers timidly said, "Thank you for allowing us to view your lovely house," to Mildred, the salesman could sense their newfound apprehension. Tours would abruptly end at Mildred Lee's house. Prospects from Pennsylvania would have a sudden "change of heart" and unexpectedly mention to their real estate agent that they were also considering Arizona or California. Anyplace but Shoreside, the island, as Mildred Lee had put it, "historically, smack in the center of hurricane alley."

Mildred Lee had gotten to them. The dark, smelly house with the spooky cats darting from under the couch to under the table to under the bed while Mildred went on and on about falling barometric pressure and the fury of the eyewall could scare off the most dedicated of buyers. Now, no one dared to show the house and fewer still dared to list it. It was worse than the listing from hell. To a real estate agent in south Florida trying to make a living selling barrier island property, it was hell.

❂

That's how Adam's morning had started. One of his new assistants, not knowing anything about who Mildred Lee was, had accidently patched her through to Adam as a standard "listing inquiry" call. Adam recognized her voice immediately.

"Mildred, is that you?"

"Why yes it is, Adam, how could you tell?"

"How could I forget such a sweet voice?"

"Oh, Adam."

Adam knew why she had called. He noted that her listing had expired with Coastal Realty three days ago. He knew that she might be trying to reach him, put prayed that Chris would field the call. Mildred would never have gotten though Adam's first line of defense if Chris had answered. Chris would have been polite to Mildred, told her that he was out of the office, and taken a message. Adam would never have seen the message. Over time, Mildred would give up. Someone else would end up with the listing. Someone who didn't know.

Adam went on to explain to Mildred in his cordial manner that he would love to re-list the house, but with his new project and all, he was just too busy to do the kind of quality job that Mildred deserved. He asked if the hurricane shutters were still covering all the exterior windows, and Mildred confirmed to Adam that they were.

He asked how the cats were doing, and Mildred replied that "Buffy" had died about a week ago. She had found him under the bed yesterday.

Adam mentally added "strong dead cat odor" to the list of buyers' objections and politely turned down the listing. However, he did tell her that he would give some thought as to who at Shoreside might have the time and expertise to handle the property. He said that he would think about it and get back to her later that afternoon. Adam realized that a 25 percent referral was better than nothing.

Mildred was disappointed that Adam couldn't take the listing himself. She reminded Adam that he could show her house any time, "no appointment needed." Adam reminded himself to never do anything that stupid as he politely said goodbye. Mildred had friends with houses that he possibly could sell someday, so there was never any point in being rude.

❂

After Mildred's unwanted phone call came the Dudleys. Their scheduled tour began at 1:30 p.m. sharp. Mr. Dudley was an accountant, a CPA with a fixation on factoids and figures. Their two-and-a-half hour condominium tour was reduced to numbers. How much were the maintenance fees? What were the taxes running? What were the taxes last year? What year was the complex built? What is the average rental occupancy rate? How much does insurance run?

Adam hated numbers. They got in his way. He would point out the beautiful view and Mr. Dudley would ask, how far is the pool from the coastal construction control line? What is the FEMA minimum flood elevation here? How many residents are full-time residents and how many rent? By the time they reached 544 Osprey Towers, Adam knew that a sale to this couple wasn't going to be easy. He wasn't going to sell Mr. Dudley anything. Not today. Not ever.

Mr. Dudley was retiring from Ernst and Young in two years' time. Mrs. Dudley wanted them to have a place on Shoreside to come down and enjoy. She wanted her husband, Roger, to kick back and enjoy himself for a change. Adam knew better.

He knew that Mr. Dudley would probably decide to stay on with the firm another five years and retire by being wheeled downstairs in a body bag. Retired for good.

Besides, Roger Dudley was the kind of buyer who would put their so-called "investment" condo through the numbers crunch. There, on an even playing field with zero-coupon bonds and blue chip stock, the $450,000 rental condominium they were considering didn't fare very well. Take away the sunshine, the beach and leave just the numbers and it made about as much sense as standing in a cold shower tearing up $100 bills all day. Roger Dudley would discover that in his first glance at the massive negative cash flow on Adam's hurried pro forma.

Adam knew it. He had worked with people like the Dudleys before. Sharp CPAs who calculated the net return from the 16 weeks of rental you might or might not get each year. They would analyze the property's potential income against all the expenses: the mortgage, the monthly maintenance fees, the taxes, utilities, flood insurance, telephone, wear and tear on the furniture, appliances, carpet and the value of your 20 percent down payment over 10 years and invariably realize that they were better off with their money in a certificate of deposit paying a negative 7.5 percent. If they returned to Shoreside at all, they came back as renters. Or worse still, they would buy a week or two of timeshare on the island to pacify their wives.

To make the sale, Adam Bartlett would have to ignore the husband completely. Halfway through the tour, he literally dropped Roger Dudley off the face of the earth and concentrated all of his efforts on his wife, Shirley. Shirley loved the views and kept asking Roger to stop talking about all those facts and figures. It sounded like he was back in the office.

Adam had used this technique uncountable times before. Divide and conquer. Adam and Shirley were now in one camp, walking down to the beach on every listing, talking about seashells and sandpipers, while Roger was left in the utility room, checking to see the number of amps coming into the main electrical panel. It was two to one.

By the end of the afternoon, Shirley had picked out the condominium they were going to buy. It wasn't 544 Osprey Towers, which was the one Adam had pushed for, but a new Island Shores listing over at Gulfside Reach. Roger didn't suspect a thing. He had convinced himself that the only way to enjoy Shoreside from an economic perspective was from a rental apartment.

Adam let them head home, promising to call them by Friday. There wasn't anything left for him to do but to let Shirley start working Roger over. Adam Bartlett knew the drill. There would be the tears, the pouting and no physical contact or sex whatsoever until Roger conceded. By Friday, Adam would call Roger and he would be willing to buy three properties from him, just to make Mrs. Dudley happy. By the following Monday they would have their Gulfside Reach unit under contract.

Refrigerators to Eskimos. Nice refrigerators, with those little doors in front to store their walrus blubber. Stainless steel shelving. Lots of extra features. Piece of cake.

✪

By late afternoon Adam had come up with a plan for Mildred Lee's house. He would refer it to Sam Goodlet. He had Chris check back five years to make sure Sam had never taken the listing. Chris confirmed that he had not. Great! Sam was the perfect candidate for the job. Nice guys finish last, thought Adam to himself as he phoned Mildred Lee with the news. He would interoffice memo Sam in the morning that he might expect the call and that the referral would cost him 25 percent. Sam wouldn't turn Mildred down. It wasn't in his nature to turn anyone down. Sam was such a sucker.

With that last bit of business done, Adam rifled through a couple of old files, made a half-dozen phone calls and told Chris he was knocking off for the night. He would have his two pagers and his cell phone with him if anything important came up.

"Vanessa tonight?" asked Chris as he headed toward the front door of his office suite.

"Vanessa," confirmed Adam. Tonight, Adam Bartlett was in the perfect mood for a double martini, an imported cigar and Vanessa's legs.

After showering, Adam put on a nice pair of slacks, a white shirt with tiny blue stripes running through it and an argyle sweater. He looked in the mirror and he thought that for 38 years old, the boy he saw still looked pretty damn sharp. His hair wasn't thinning much, his eyes still had that sparkle to them, and his waistline was still there. The workouts, the racquet ball and the long swims were paying off. Life was good.

He grabbed the keys to his new Porsche Boxster and went downstairs to take off the cover and fire it up. He loved his Porsche. It was British racing green, a custom paint job. He loved driving it after a hard day at the office. It made him feel like it was all worth it, putting up with the Boyles, the Dudleys, the Lees and all the rest of them. He owned the Boxster free and clear. No lease and no car loan. It was the only thing his accountant had given him the go ahead to pay for in cash. There were no tax breaks for owning a two-seater Porsche. It was a luxury item that the IRS would instantly red-flag if they tried to slip it past them. That was just fine with Adam. It was his toy to enjoy.

He got in, pulled out of the driveway, and floored it. He knew that this dark green speed machine attracted tickets like a magnet, but he didn't care. Going fast worked for Adam Bartlett. It worked well.

He made it over to Vanessa's apartment around 7:00. A bit late, but not late enough to set her off. You have to be careful with redheads, Adam reminded himself. He knew that because he hadn't been careful enough with his ex-wife six years ago. The memory of that still hurt somewhere deep inside of him. Somewhere he avoided going.

"Be right there, Adam."

Adam could hear Vanessa shout to him through the thin wooden door of her apartment. He could picture her already. She was probably wearing some razor tight black shift, with her hair curled and her face painted in delicate tones of light-blue eye shadow and dark red lipstick. Vanessa was a fox, a stone-cold fox.

Adam heard her unlocking the deadbolt to let him in. He stepped inside, noticed that the shift was dark blue tonight and quickly swooped her up, smothering her with a long, wet kiss. Vanessa Swenson was candy to Bartlett, beautiful, red-haired candy.

"What a day!" He added as he slowly released her and walked toward the white sofa. "What a day!!"

"That bad?"

"Worse."

"Then let's not talk about it, okay?"

"Fine with me. Are you ready to head out?"

"Just give me a minute or two, I want to put on some mascara."

"You look gorgeous."

"Thanks, Adam. I'll be right out."

Vanessa vanished into her bedroom. Adam grabbed the remote and flipped on the TV. He quickly pushed the mute button and rifled through the stations silently. He gave every station no more than 15 seconds. There were 61 channels, including the fringe channels near the top of the rotation. Like channel 57, the Roman Catholic channel. Or channel 59, the public access channel. He never paused long enough to get involved in any of them. He never took the television off mute. It was like watching silent blips of some cathode reality that never had time to stabilize or give any reason for its existence. To Adam Bartlett, a high energy salesman, it was relaxing.

Vanessa came out in five minutes and Adam flipped off the TV. He hadn't learned, watched or heard anything. Just flashes of colored lights in the shape of people, buildings, cars and situations. Five minutes of nothingness.

They headed out and hopped into the car. Vanessa looked like the perfect accessory to his dark green Porsche. She should have been in all of their promotional material. She belonged there, in the seat next to him, just like the black coral necklace Adam had bought for her belonged around her neck.

They drove straight to the Viscaya. The valet parking attendant couldn't help but notice Vanessa as they pulled up. Adam made note of it and laughed to himself. Eat your heart out, he thought as he stepped from the car and walked around to take her hand. The attendant took one more savoring look at Vanessa's exquisite ass as the two of them walked up the seven stairs and into the restaurant. What a wonderful ass it was.

Once inside, Renee quickly came and greeted them in his thick, contrived, European accent. "Adam, Vanessa, what a pleaszure to 'ave you come out tonight and join us. Smoking or nonsmoking tonight, monsieur?"

"No cigars tonight, Renee, but thanks for asking," said Adam.

Renee had their favorite table waiting. It was a picture of ambiance. There was a single long-stemmed rose set in a dark blue vase as the centerpiece. A brilliant halogen beam settled on the rose from directly overhead, making every bead of water on the rose petals sparkle. The beam was so small that it stopped at that dark red rose, leaving the rest of the table smouldering in soft, semi-darkness.

The background music was Baroque recorder music: Vivaldi and Bach. The white linen napkins were folded to resemble shells and the silverware was perfectly placed to the centimeter on the pale blue tablecloth. It was what the clients who frequented the Viscaya expected when they came there to dine: romance, elegance and a substantial dent in their American Express cards. It was worth it.

Adam slid Vanessa's chair in and took the one right beside her. He knew that he could slide his left hand down along her thigh, stroking it softly as they sipped their Merlot and enjoyed their dinner. She loved it. It was just naughty enough to add some excitement to a lovely dinner.

Their favorite waiter, Brian O'Shaunessy, brought them menus and in his practiced, soft spoken voice, read the evening's specials to them.

"Tonight we have a fillet of venison, slow roasted with braised apricots and pears, complete with just a dash of chestnut puree, honey Porto jus and juniper berries; or if you prefer seafood, this evening's choice is a shrimp royale, sautéed with garlic, sun-dried tomatoes, fresh oregano, imported white wine and risotto cake."

Adam and Vanessa listened casually. They appreciated Brian's attention to detail, but no sooner had he completed his careful monologue than Adam looked at him and said,

"Thanks Brian, but we'll have the usual."

"And the Merlot?"

"Of course Brian, Ferrari Carano, 1995."

"An excellent choice! I'll be right back with your wine."

Excellent choices. That's what it came down to at this stage in the game. Outstanding California wines, Long Island duck, Black Angus beef, Rolex watches, Armani sports coats, German sports cars, beach front developments and beautiful redheads with a penchant for sex in public places. All of them excellent choices.

After Adam took a brief whiff of the cork and a small sip of the Merlot, he nodded and smiled to Brian. Brian filled both wine goblets about halfway and told them that he had already placed their order. He asked how Vanessa would like her fillet done and made sure that Adam wanted his blue cheese dressing on the side. Adam was having the duck. Brian knew this before he had read them the evening's specials. He was just being a good waiter. Adam tipped well, and Brian was going to do all the dance steps necessary to get his hands on that 25 percent. He always did.

"Here's to a lovely night together, Vanessa," said Adam Bartlett as their two wine glasses discreetly kissed beside the solitary rose.

"To us," added Vanessa with a wink.

Dinner was, as expected, exquisite. The salads were cold and crisp, the duck tender and the fillet melted in Vanessa's beautiful mouth. Halfway through the meal Adam ordered another bottle of wine, and by the time Brian was bringing their check, they were both feeling no pain. Adam was glad that his small pager had not made a single annoying chirp throughout the evening. He was glad that Boyle was home watching television and not in a panic about Sanderling. Glad to have some time off.

After dinner they split a soufflé for dessert. Renee came over to them just before Brian arrived with it.

"And how was eberyting?" he asked in his pseudo foreign accent.

"Delicious, as always," replied Adam.

"You are too kind, Mister Bartlett. And how was your fillet, Vanessa?"

"It was done to perfection, Renee. How has business been?"

"It's October. A little slow for us dis time of year, but that's usual." Renee turned and directed his next question to Adam. "Mr. Loggins tells me that you and he are werking on dis...Sanderling project. How does it go?"

"Slowly, Renee. Like your business in October, very slowly."

"Well, the best of luck with it, Mister Bartlett. Enjoy the rest of your ebening."

With that, Renee glanced briefly around the room and made off toward another table of regulars. Renee was the ultimate maître d', always drifting from table to table, answering questions, making sure the wine was served at the right temperature and the steaks weren't overcooked. If anything wasn't just right, he was always at the ready with a free cocktail or a complimentary dessert. Or, if the situation merited, dinner was on the house. In a bad year, he might have to hand out half a dozen free dinners. Renee understood that in the gourmet restaurant business, reputation is everything.

Adam and his shapely redhead walked over to the bar for a nightcap. Tom Loggins wasn't at the bar tonight, which was a welcome relief for Adam. Tom owned a piece of the Viscaya, just like he owned a piece of everything on Shoreside. Adam didn't feel like talking about business tonight.

Aside from Vanessa's thin, curving legs, he didn't want any distractions.

They each ordered aperitifs. Vanessa had a well-aged tawny port and Adam had a cognac. With the alcohol slowly eroding his willpower, Adam was half tempted to ask for a cigar. But he resisted. He knew that if he chose to go with the cigar, Vanessa wouldn't kiss him later on. It wasn't a momentary debate, an imported cigar or Vanessa's tongue? Adam let his urge for a smoke pass without ever mentioning it to her. The tongue had won.

Finished with the after-dinner drinks, and now both feeling very light headed, they finally left the restaurant. It was just after 10:00. The valet was about to fetch Adam's Porsche when Adam turned and asked Vanessa if she would be interested in a walk on the beach.

"Sounds delightful," came Vanessa's quick reply.

On the way to the beach access, which was 100 yards from the restaurant, Adam stopped and grabbed a blanket from the trunk of the Porsche.

"What's the blanket for?" asked Vanessa.

"Oh, I thought it might be nice to have if we decide to sit down by the surf for a while."

"Sure, Adam."

Vanessa knew better. She had been dating Adam for months and she knew that he never did anything without a plan. Everything was calculated and on a "things to do" list with Adam Bartlett. Vanessa didn't mind. She had been on that blanket a half-dozen times before. In town one night at a local park that was closed for the evening. Just off the ninth green at the Osprey Greens Golf Course. There were others.

Vanessa liked making love outdoors. She loved the added risk of the thought that someone might accidently find them there, in that park just off one of the foot trails, along the edge of the beach. It made everything a little more exciting to her.

"Let me show you where we're planning to build the Sanderling Condominiums."

"Is it far?"

"No, not very. I think it's about a half a mile north of here at most. Do you want me to carry your heels?"

"Thanks Adam, that would be nice. I love walking in the sand barefoot."

They started walking along the sand, just above the breaking waves. It was a superb night. The wind was light and the air was still humid and warm. It was still the summer air of Florida. It quickly enveloped them in its dark, moist arms as they strolled quietly along the beach.

Every so often, they would stop. Adam would take Vanessa in his arms and kiss her. These were long, luscious kisses under a waxing moon. They were wine-inspired kisses, full of tongues and sex. They were wonderful.

They finally found themselves in front of a long, dark stretch of sand. As they looked toward shore, all that they could see was the low profile of mangroves and cabbage palms. The wind rustled the leaves of the palms and beyond, they could hear frogs and an occasional bird squawking in the darkness.

"Here it is."

"It's so quiet here."

"Yes, it is."

"How far back will the condos be?"

"Not too far. I would think about 100 feet from here, depending on how the fill permits go. We'll need to fill in most of those wetlands that lie just beyond the beach."

"It's a shame, in a way."

"What is?"

"Changing the land. Making condos where there is quiet. Developing this nice stretch of beach."

"It's 64 units, Vanessa. Sixty-four units at $500,000 each, give or take a few thousand depending on the location and view. That's $32 million at sell out. If all goes well, I end up with a little better than two percent of that number. That's over a half a million dollars. Sooner or later, someone's going to get permits to develop this land. It might as well be Tom Loggins and us."

"I thought the conservation people were trying to buy it?"

"They are, but we've got our offer in first position, and they just don't have the money. I don't think they can afford a Gulf-front property like this one."

"Well, Adam, I suppose you're right," conceded Vanessa. She had always loved nature, but not as much as she did money.

"Do you want to sit down and rest for a few minutes before we head back?"

Adam spread out the blanket and they both sat on the beach. It was late and since the tide was up there weren't any beachcombers out shelling. On their long walk they had passed only one elderly couple walking the other way. All that shared the beach with them now were the ghost crabs and the sound of the surf.

For a brief moment Adam was thinking about Boyle. He knew that in a few weeks, over drinks at the Yacht Club, or an afternoon out on Tom's 46-foot Bertram, he would tell Boyle all about this evening. He would tell it slowly, giving him all the intimate details. The drunken, wet kisses along the shoreline, the walk toward the edge of the beach, the blanket and the hour that followed. It was business. It helped to keep Boyle in the corral. Vanessa would never know that her lovemaking was a small part of Adam's real estate career.

Adam leaned over and kissed Vanessa once again. It was a long, tender kiss that spoke silently of his intentions. Vanessa knew what was happening and had no intention of stopping him. She knew it from the moment Adam had reached into the trunk to take out the blanket.

They both fell back onto the large cotton blanket. They were kissing passionately now while their hands were looking for more. The wind was kicking up a bit, rustling the sea oats that surrounded them along the place where the sand and the native vegetation meet. Someone walking right along the shoreline wouldn't even see them unless they looked toward the empty acres beyond. Nobody would have any reason to look that way.

"Let me help, Adam."

Vanessa slid her panties down and rolled up her tight dark-blue skirt. Adam could see her smooth, well-rounded ass in the dim light of the half moon. It was so inviting.

He unbuttoned her blouse and took off her bra. She had young, firm breasts that begged to be caressed and kissed. As the ghost crabs danced across the sand, searching for coquinas, they made passionate love. It was the ideal ending to a perfect night. It was all about choices at this point in Adam's illustrious career. Excellent choices, he thought as the night wind rode atop the sea beyond them. Excellent choices.

The Sales Meeting
8:30 Wednesday Morning

Babylon. Betsy could hear the salespeople down the hall and, from a distance, it sounded like a branch office in Babylon. The din of 27 real estate associates all talking at once was deafening, and Betsy couldn't make out a single conversation clearly. It sounded like everyone was speaking in their own private dialect, their own confusing language. It was what happened every Wednesday morning. The nervous chemistry of combining too many salespeople, chocolate donuts and way too much coffee.

This is what the construction site at the tower of Babel must have sounded like, thought Betsy quietly to herself. No wonder they never finished the darn thing. Elinor must still be in her office, she'd never tolerate this racket if she were there.

Betsy was right. Elinor was running a few minutes late. She was trying to decipher the two new, encrypted forms she had recently received from the state. Her presentation had gone fairly well with Jennifer Willow, but Jennifer didn't have enough experience to question or challenge these new forms. Linda Hinkle, who had been wrestling with these convoluted documents for nearly as long as Elinor had, would be the first to question these two new ones. Elinor wanted to be ready when she did. The best defense is a strong offense, she reminded herself. Still, reflected a confused looking sales manager, these things are incomprehensible.

Back down the hallway from Betsy, in the small open space just off the day kitchen where she sometimes took her lunch, 27 real estate agents were getting fired up on fresh pastries and coffee. It was a scene. Everyone was blabbering on and on, trying to impress upon every other agent how lovely his or her new listing was, what a pain in the ass their new buyers were, how she had just heard about so and so filing for divorce and so and so having that gall bladder operation and on and on and on like the sea. Only larger than the sea and a lot saltier.

The office coffee machine was working overtime trying to keep up with the conversations. The donuts were disappearing faster than clay pigeons at a skeet match. It was a verbal feeding frenzy down that long, narrow hallway. It was a salesman's idea of what heaven must be like.

As Elinor Braun walked in, a silence swept across the pandemonium like a solar eclipse on a bright, sunny day. Conversations ended mid-phrase, people stopped chewing their custard-filled long johns, and quickly found seats. Elinor disliked meaningless and idle conversations, and everyone knew it. The business of Wednesday morning sales meetings was business. Enough chatter, already.

"Good morning, everyone."

There was no reply. Everyone had found a seat and everyone was as silent as Stonehenge. Only the faint, internal sound of a few associates quietly chewing and swallowing their Danishes could be heard. They knew the drill and they knew it instinctively: Elinor Braun demanded your full attention.

"Well then, let's get started."

Elinor Braun went into her well-rehearsed weekly agenda. First, she covered the monthly statistics to date, what the competition up the street was doing, and what her own office's monthly sales goal was. Then she brought out the charts. Her charts were graphic thermometer-like displays showing where her associates were in sales and listings and where they should be for this time of year.

No one said a thing. They were never where they should be, nor had they ever been in the six years since Elinor took over as sales manager. Business was up 128 percent from that time, but it didn't matter. Shoreside Realty's goals were up 143 percent. No matter how great a year they were having, even if every sales record on Shoreside had been shattered, Elinor's thermometer graphs proved that everyone still had a long, long way to go. Proved so indisputably.

It was a fact of life for the two-dozen plus associates at Shoreside Realty that they would never, never reach their sales goals. Management had it planned that way, and Elinor Braun never deviated from a plan. The sales goal strategy at Shoreside Realty was just like the mechanical rabbit at the greyhound track. Management felt that if you ever let your salespeople actually catch the rabbit, they would all stop selling. Keep the rabbit in overdrive and let the sales force drop dead trying to catch up to it. All that mattered was that Shoreside Realty remained No. 1 in the market. It was sound thinking in a bent way.

Sam Goodlet looked at Elinor's big thermometer and thought it reminded him of one of those United Way charts. Sam hated goal setting. He never changed his goal. It had been $4 million a year for the last ten years. He looked at Elinor again, then at her big thermometer. Sam knew where he would like to put that three-foot thermometer. Elinor Braun suspected as much.

Jennifer Willow sat nervously in the back of the room. She was hoping that Elinor wouldn't single her out for the sale she and Barbara put together late last night. She didn't want to be singled out. She wanted to go back into her silent cubicle and disappear.

Everyone was in attendance: Vince Cricket, Linda Hinkle, Jason, Andrew, the two Daves, the two Susans and the rest of the sales force. Everyone had to be there. Although they were all employed as independent contractors, and theoretically not subject to the tyranny of a time clock, everyone at Shoreside knew that they had better not miss a Wednesday morning sales meeting. Elinor Braun wouldn't be happy with you if you did. If Elinor wasn't happy, ain't nobody happy.

There were a few acceptable excuses. Open heart surgery was one of them. Another qualified excuse was the unexpected and tragic death of your spouse. Short of those two, all other excuses failed, and they failed miserably.

Elinor finally got through all the charts and mentioned that next week they were going to have a guest speaker.

"You had better not miss next week's meeting," she went on to say.

"Next week, we have Mr. Larry Barter from the County Tourist and Convention Center speaking on upcoming trends in Florida tourism. Larry is always so much fun. I've asked him to stop at Publix to pick up some extra donuts for the meeting."

The donuts helped. They helped to deaden the pain. The donut count ran close to a three to one ratio. If all 27 associates showed, Doris would pick up five dozen donuts to divide among them. There were bear claws, éclairs, chocolate covered donuts, sugar-glazed donuts and more. There were jelly-filled Danishes, custard-filled Danishes and sometimes Doris would throw in a dozen chocolate chip cookies for good measure.

The donuts counteracted Elinor's dry presentations and statistics. They were like sugar-based heroin to the junkies having to make each and every Wednesday morning's mandatory sales meeting. In fact, many of the sales force present this particular meeting were just nodding off on their rush of sugar and fat when Elinor brought them all back into reality.

"And now, I want you all to PLEASE PAY ATTENTION!"

Everyone's head snapped like they had just been rear-ended by a garbage truck. Over years of attending sales meetings every Wednesday, they all recognized the nuances of Elinor's stern voice. When she asked you to "PLEASE PAY ATTENTION," Elinor meant it. No matter how deep a somnambulistic trance a sugared-up salesperson had fallen into, those three words meant that you had to pull out of it immediately or face the consequences. The consequences were drastic and painful, to put it mildly.

"The State of Florida recently sent us two new forms that we need to begin using by the first of November. I've got copies of these forms to hand out to everyone this morning."

Elinor took two large stacks of legal-sized forms and gave them to Jason, who was sitting in the front seat. He silently passed them to the associate beside him and so on and so on until all the agents had the two new forms held tightly in their little hands.

"The first one is a bit confusing, so please bear with me while I go through it with you."

Elinor once again pored over her well-studied monologue about the upcoming changes in barrier island sanitation requirements and regulations. She read some passages from a form letter that had arrived with the disclosures. It discussed the failures of septic systems on barrier islands such as Shoreside, and how the forthcoming changes would be good for the overall environment. It went on to state the requirement for all barrier island communities to meet the new EPA standards by the year 2010. Elinor spoke without interruption for 15 minutes.

As she spoke, she couldn't help but look up on occasion to take note of how her sales agents were handling her presentation. She felt like a fifth-grade school teacher at times like this. Her classroom consisted of 27 overgrown children, some of them with incomes pushing $500,000 a year. Most of them were hyperactive and had various learning disabilities: attention deficit disorder, dyslexia and worse. A few of them, like Jason Randazzle, were ethically challenged. Severely.

For the first few minutes of her presentation, everything appeared to be going well. Her students were bright eyed and ready to learn. During the middle section however, a few faces appeared puzzled by her presentation. But by the time Elinor delivered her summation, Elinor looked across the faces of her sales force and realized that she might as well have been trying to teach them nuclear chemistry. They were lost.

Their looks had long since gone beyond puzzling and soared straight to befuddlement. It was obvious to her that no one understood the form or any of its innumerable conditions. How could they? The chances of anyone understanding this form in 15 minutes were equal to the chance of understanding gravitational field theory in the same amount of time.

"Does anyone have any questions?"

She hated ending her presentations like that. It was a trap. Of course someone would have a question. Elinor prayed nobody would raise their hand. She prayed in vain. Linda Hinkle's hand shot skyward.

"What are the EPA standards for the handling of effluent in the year 2010?"

"They haven't been drafted yet."

"Elinor, do you mean to tell me that you are asking us to tell our clients to sign a form stating that they are willing to comply with sewer systems standards that don't even exist?"

"Yes."

"That's ridiculous."

The murmuring started in. Elinor hated the murmuring. She knew that it meant dissension, disillusion and rebellion. While her sales force was busy mumbling and whispering to itself, she skillfully devised a different tack. As she thought about it, she could overhear some of the salespeople up front.

"Linda's right you know, this is not a good form," someone mentioned to another agent quietly.

"Bad form, really a bad form."

The murmuring never helped. It made everyone bitter and angry. Elinor realized that she had to put a quick stop to it.

"PLEASE PAY ATTENTION!!!" Elinor had to shout to be heard over the rumbling that had built up in the last 45 seconds.

"If you fail to get your clients - both your buyers and sellers to sign this new form, and the house's septic system or sewer system fails to meet the new standards, the state requires that the real estate agency, henceforth, the real estate agent, will pay for any and all capital improvements, connection fees and septic removal costs incurred at the date of enforcement. That will be including all penalties, accrued interest and fines imposed."

A silence fell over the crowd. It was an intense silence. Now we were talking money. Some of the female agents reached down and picked their purses off the floor. Some of the men took their hands and reached around to feel for their wallets. They wanted to be sure that no one had secretly entered their bank accounts during the night. They wanted to recount their stack of $20s. The thought of paying for their clients' wastewater treatment connections sent shivers through both their souls and their individual retirement accounts.

"Well, that's different," remarked Linda Hinkle, suddenly no longer concerned about comprehending the form.

"If that's the case, we'll make sure that everyone signs it."

The murmuring started in again, but this time the tone was good. The comments centered on what a well-thought out form it was. How the State of Florida should be commended. Anything that protects us from liability is a good thing, whispered one of the agents, who only minutes before was dead set against this new form.

"And remember to get the signatures notarized!" concluded Elinor.

She went on to cover the new TRANSITION TO TRANSACTION BROKERAGE FORM in considerably less detail. No one really understood the laws of agency or fiduciary relationships in general so there was no reason to belabor this new form. The issues involved were just too complex for most salespeople to get a handle on.

Elinor realized early on in her career as a sales manager that most of her salespeople didn't work for their buyers or sellers, or for Shoreside Realty, or for a builder or developer for that matter. They worked for themselves. They worked to get the sale put together and to get the transaction closed. Paper relationships were confusing.

The fundamentals were simple: when the property closed, the salesperson got paid a substantial amount of money and went looking for the next deal.

Real estate agents worked for themselves, like most professionals. Some were sincere, great agents like Goodlet who would literally give you the shirt off his back to help out. Others were young, enthusiastic people who wanted to be of service, like Jennifer Willow. And then there were those who were in it for the money, or the game, or 1,000 other reasons. In the end, the 27 agents who sat quietly in front of Elinor Braun that morning were a cross section of everyone who works for a living. Some loved the people, some loved the cash, some were as honest as the day is long, and some were not. They were just like all of us: all too human.

But the fact remained that sub-agents, buyer's agents, selling agents and everyone in between didn't mean much to the associates seated before her. Elinor knew that it didn't make any difference which side of the fence they were supposed to be sitting on when they got in that car with their customers. The end result was the same. Sell them the house or sell the house for them. The rest was all lawyerese, all that *heretofore* and *theretofore* garbage. The rest was bullshit.

Elinor had spent her life defending her sales people from their own mouths. They were always saying something that would put them in legal harm's way. Things like, "Oh, that roof doesn't leak all that much," or "Sure, you can put a pool in," or "No, I don't think we need an inspection."

Infamous one-liners that would end up in the court records, dutifully taken down by the court reporter and ample evidence of negligence, breach of contract, misrepresentation and worse. Ultimately, all their one-liners could be reduced to simple cash equations. The roof repair ran $12,000. The pool that wouldn't fit costs $28,500. And the inspection that wasn't recommended: try $247,800, with talk of further litigation.

It was a trap, trying to sell something expensive in a world full of thirsty lawyers. There were just too many loopholes and far too many things that could go wrong. In the end, you had to rely on the goodwill of people and as many forms as they could sign in a given afternoon. The system itself was dysfunctional. In a world where her sales force thought that ingress and egress were two different kinds of small white herons that lived on Shoreside Island somewhere, lawsuits were inevitable. Elinor just prayed to God that her associates had gotten everything notarized and witnessed along the way.

No one had any questions about the new transition form. No one understood the form, so why bother questioning it? Her associates would get their clients to initial it and be done with it. They would slip the form in about halfway through a stack of forms that rose a quarter of an inch high by the end of a deal.

There, right at the bottom of the new TRANSITION TO TRANSACTION AGENT FORM would be a cute little pink fluorescent sticker pointing to a short line for their initials to go. If the customers asked what it was they were initialing, the agents would recite some standard rhetoric they had memorized about agency relationships and leave it at that. If the clients wanted to know more about it, the agent would generally confess to the fact that they didn't understand it either but that it was impossible to buy the house if this form wasn't properly initialed. Since they were there to buy the property, the clients would initial it.

Then they would sign the next two forms, initial the next one, sign the seven after it, date and sign the next three, and after 20 minutes and a bad case of writer's cramp they would leave the office excited and bewildered, ready to buy and collapse at the same time.

Many times throughout his long career, Sam Goodlet was half tempted to insert a personal promissory note for $100,000 payable to him about three-quarters of the way through a stack of forms. The customers would sign it. They would look at that little pink sticker that said sign here, smile like happy little consumers always do when they're signing their lives away, and put Mr. and Mrs. John Doe right at the bottom of a $100,000 personal note payable to Mr. Sam Goodlet. Payable in cash within 90 days.

Sam never did insert one of his promissory notes, but he knew they'd never catch it if he had. When you finally got your buyers to make an offer, they seemed to go into some kind of daze during the form signing stage. Like they were numb to it by that time, ready to sign whatever you put in front of them. In the end, it wasn't just about real estate, it was all about trust.

Elinor wrapped up the meeting by asking everyone if they had any new listings, or if they had any buyers looking for a specific property. A few new listings were brought up, and Barbara announced that Jennifer Willow had made her first sale.

"I would like to thank Jennifer for selling lot "A" in the newly listed north section of Osprey Greens. Let's all congratulate her on her first sale with Shoreside Realty."

The associates all cheered and clapped enthusiastically. Jennifer was now an official member of the club. She was a real estate agent. She blushed coyly and smiled as they applauded her.

Elinor dismissed the meeting and wished everyone a good upcoming week of selling and listing properties. She ended the meeting by reminding everyone that if they ever needed help with anything, that her door was always open.

It was true, her door was always open. The agents were always welcome to come in and sit down. The trouble was that most of them wouldn't dare.

Part II
Construction

773-2123
The Shoreside Conservancy

Scott Lindsey bent over to pull a single Brazilian pepper sapling out of the ground. It didn't pull out easily, its ball of roots clinging desperately to the sandy loam of an old beach ridge. As Scott added his second gloved hand to the effort, the sapling released its stubborn grip on the soil. He tossed the young tree in the nearby swale, glad to have destroyed it.

God, how Scott hated Brazilian pepper. How, over the years, he had watched it transform acre after acre of prime wildlife habitat into a matted jungle of sprawling branches creating a desolate, lifeless understory. When they were still young, like the three-foot high specimen he had just uprooted, they were easy to remove. But when a pepper forest matured, reaching heights of 30-plus feet with the larger trees having trunks two feet in diameter, they were damned near impossible to eradicate.

It had become an unending battle to keep them off Shoreside Island, a long, protracted war between the Conservancy and a ruthless exotic. Sadly, Scott admitted to himself as he stood atop this low beach ridge, the pepper was winning.

It all started ages ago, in the '20s, when some unknowing physician in Punta Gorda thought that its bright red berries made a lovely, decorative spray when they appeared on the female trees around the Christmas holidays. A colorful addition to the dining room table. The amateur horticulturist named it "Florida holly." He collected the seeds, grew countless saplings and distributed them freely amongst fellow gardeners from Sarasota to Naples. It soon became a popular addition to front yards from Tampa to Miami. That was more than 70 years ago. Little did that doctor realize what a nightmare he was nurturing.

Wintering robins, mockingbirds and a host of other creatures soon discovered that the bright red berries were delicious. The native wildlife was delighted that the doctor had imported this new Brazilian delicacy into south Florida. What no one realized at the time was that the seeds were capable of passing through the bird's digestive systems unscathed and still fertile. It was a recipe for disaster.

Within a decade, Brazilian pepper was sprouting everywhere. All it needed to survive and take root was moderately fertile soil, a fair amount of rain and ample sunlight. It was a perfect match for the vast open savannahs and hammocks of south Florida. Within a few more decades, it had run rampant. It suffocated everything beneath it, becoming an expansive monoculture of twisted, brown branches and an evergreen canopy of dark green leaves. Every Christmas the immense pepper forests would once again bear their bright red berries. Only now there were not enough living rooms in all of Florida to handle the billions of sprays that stretched across the landscape.

"Florida folly," Scott mumbled to himself as he looked down the beach ridge covered in pepper saplings. "An environmental catastrophe!"

Scott Lindsey had long known that the Florida pepper infestation bore sad testimony to mankind's misunderstanding of the delicate balance of nature. Like the introduction of the mongoose to Cuba, or the feral pigs that decimated the bird populations of Hawaii, Brazilian pepper was just another environmental blunder in a long string of well-meaning mistakes. If that doctor in Punta Gorda were still alive today, or had he known of the devastation his pretty red sprays would cause, Scott would have been tempted to drive there and slug him. But the good doctor couldn't have known.

In Brazil, the pepper tree had a host of natural controls that held it in check. There were beetles, caterpillars, mites and mold that kept the pepper in its environmental niche. In Florida, like the invasive punk trees and Australian pines that came before it, there was nothing to stop it. So it spread like a malignant melanoma across the skin of peninsular Florida. It inhaled the beautiful spartina marshes and devoured the West Indian hammocks of the everglades. The pepper forest marched right to the edge of the beaches along the barrier islands that hung like a string of sandy pearls along the western edge of south Florida.

Now it was everywhere. It covered thousands of acres on Shoreside and it was all but impossible to remove. Scott reached over and pulled out another sapling in disgust. Ornamentals. Who could have known what havoc they would eventually bring to the land and to the native environment.

Nothing seemed to curtail the spread of this noxious weed. Bulldozers, backhoes, poisons, volunteers and bonfires that burned for days were all employed by the Conservancy to keep the pepper at bay. It was an unending battle, with a clear-cut victory impossible.

Still, this outbreak on the McKinzie parcel was unusual. It was perplexing to both Scott and the biologists who consulted with the Conservancy. They had never before witnessed such a rapid outbreak of Brazilian pepper on a single parcel before. Five years ago, when Scott Lindsey first walked the McKinzie acreage with a group of potential benefactors, there were only a few scattered clumps of pepper. They could have counted the number of Brazilian pepper trees on two hands. True, they were large, mature trees with plenty of berries to offer to the local winged fauna every winter, but no one would have expected this kind of infestation in such a short time.

Now the pepper trees were everywhere. Most of them were young trees, all standing three to five feet tall. But there were thousands and thousands of them. They were quickly reaching skyward among the native buttonwood, cabbage palm and the red and black mangroves. Scott had never seen such a rapid spread of pepper in his 14 years with the Conservancy.

It must have had something to do with all the redwing blackbirds and warblers that thrived amongst the wetlands of the property, reasoned Scott. It was a shame. A damn shame.

As Scott threw down yet another dislocated sapling, he looked over at the pneumatic pile-driving machine a hundred yards away. The Conservancy had lost. Not only had they lost this parcel to the Brazilian pepper, they had lost the property to Tom Loggins and his development group, TLD, Inc. The huge pile driver, with each and every blow on those 60-foot cement pilings, reminded him of their defeat. The noise of that mechanical monster turned his stomach in disgust. It was the rhythmic thud of progress.

"The Florida state bird," Scott mumbled to himself as he watched the construction crane at work. It was a long standing joke around the hallways of the Shoreside Conservancy Nature Center and all the conservation groups throughout Florida. They all knew it to be true. The Florida state bird wasn't the mockingbird, although there was a certain element of irony to that bird being the official choice. The real Florida state bird was the crane; the construction crane. That was the bird that held the rhythmic pile driver in place as its pneumatic hammer shattered the afternoon silence.

Purchasing the McKinzie property was a long shot from day one. Scott and the board of directors at the Conservency knew it. It was too valuable and too expensive for their shoestring budget. Five million dollars to purchase a mere 13 acres made for a hopeless equation. Still, it was a shame.

They had put up a damn good fight, but to no avail. Their back-up offer consisted of a $50,000 option and a year of praying for the balance. Everyone knew that had Loggins failed to get the permits on the first round, the Conservancy didn't have the cash on hand to close on the property. They would have to try to raise the money through donations and fund-raisers. (That's not a problem when they are trying to buy a 25-acre tract of uplands for $200,000. But Gulf-front acreage on Shoreside Island? It was always a long shot.)

Then, when the final elevation survey showed that there was just enough upland ecological zone to pull it out of the hands of the Army Corps of Engineers and the Department of Environmental Protection, Scott knew it was over. In that final survey, 53.4 percent of the land turned out to be sitting higher than three feet above the mean high tide. Loggins needed anything more than 50 percent to make it. Had they ended up just a few inches lower, Scott and the Shoreline Conservancy might have had a chance. The parcel would have been treated as designated wetlands. Permits would have taken years. Development might have delayed TLD, Inc. long enough for the Shoreline Conservancy to find someone, anyone, willing to help finance the purchase.

Help like they had with the Pratt Parcel, the Duncan Tract and the hundreds upon hundreds of acres they had saved from those relentless pile drivers over the years. Saved from the long, mechanical neck of the unofficial Florida state bird, the construction crane. Saved for the real birds: the purple gallinules, crested mergansers and the yellow-crowned night herons. Saved for the soft-shelled turtles, alligators and the otters. Saved forever.

Now it was over. Scott stood atop the long, dry stretch of beach ridge and watched from a distance as trucks full of fill lumbered back and forth across the temporary construction driveway. From a distance he could see foremen standing beside their white Chevy Blazers looking over blueprints and pointing to where the pile driver sang its rhythmic lament. Scott couldn't hear the men speaking but he knew what they were talking about. He had worked construction as a young man during his summers in Colorado.

They were talking about pile caps and stress loads. They were deciding where to stack the pre-fab concrete floor sections and when they might expect to finish the first floor of Phase I. They were looking over site plans showing where the retention swale would be located and how the drainage plan could be landscaped. They were boys again, building with full-sized Lego kits, using bulldozers and steel instead of their fingers and pieces of molded plastic. Boys.

Scott knew that they wanted to have most of the units completed before the start of next season. It was March, and unless heavy summer rains held up construction, they could get the CO for the Sanderling Condominiums before November. Loggins was famous for making deadlines. Just as Loggins was famous for making money.

Just before the final CO, the City of Shoreside would make them remove the Brazilian pepper and relocate the remainder of the wildlife. The truth was, by then there wouldn't be any wildlife left to relocate. The hammering of the pile driver and the roar of the dump trucks would send most of the wildlife running. The developer had already trapped the family of otters and relocated them to one of those islands they had used for mitigation with the state.

"They don't stand much of a chance there," Scott said to himself. "There's not enough fresh water for them to make a go of it."

They would use heavy machinery to scrape off the pepper when the time came. Everything else would be stripped off the land along with it: the hundreds of cabbage palms, the scattering of red and black mangroves, the buttonwood, the strangler figs and the imported Australian pines. The entire parcel would then be re-sculpted into retention areas and asphalt, tennis courts and guest parking slots. The landscapers would arrive with truckloads of ornamentals and imports. Palms, shrubs and trees from other continents that looked the part:

Canary Island date palms, Hong Kong orchids, Norfolk pines and hibiscus. Plants from every corner of the world. Plants that don't belong here any more than did the malignant Brazilian pepper they were replacing. Lessons never learned.

Scott took one last look across the construction site. He would write his report for the board of directors on Monday morning when he got back into the office. TLD, Inc. appeared to be in compliance with its development permit. There was nothing left to do about the Sanderling project except to watch it go up. The courts wouldn't even listen to their objections at this point.

As Scott Lindsey sat behind the wheel of his Honda, he paused for a minute before starting the car. Tears were welling up in his eyes. They were tears not just for the otters, the herons and the wildlife of the world, but for the men who labored under the hot Florida sun to displace them. Men who thought that it was a good thing to develop the land, to change it. He felt so sorry for them, knowing that they needed their wages to raise their children and families in town.

Development; it was never simple. Never. He turned the key and started driving home, deciding it was just too late in the afternoon to head back to the Conservancy office on this particularly depressing Friday. The radio played some sad country western song about losing a lover in a car accident. It made Scott think about those 13 acres of wetlands he had lost. Lost them to development. Forever. He didn't look forward to writing his report come Monday. Not this report, at least.

570-9898 Ext. 12
Sam Goodlet's Line

Sam's telephone was dead quiet. He was ecstatic. All morning Mr. Goodlet, as they often referred to him, had been fielding calls from unpaid home inspectors, frustrated pest control companies and a furious listing agent. Not to mention the relentless Mildred Lee. He had developed a nervous twitch every time his extension rang. Like one of Pavlov's dogs, the ring of his phone made him break out in uncontrollable ticks and twitches. Conditioned response. Sam Goodlet was not having a good day. Make that year.

"I should have shot them," Sam kept mumbling to himself as he sorted through his Hazelton file. "Left them to the 'gators in that drainage ditch like I had first planned. It would have been easier doing hard time in Florida state prison than going through this shit now. A lot easier."

It was shit. Chin deep and gaining on him. It hadn't started out badly. For a few weeks earlier in the year, Sam felt like he was on a roll. First, he finally got Mr. and Mrs. Hazelton to write an offer on the Grinstead home. After nearly two months of, "We're still thinking about it," neither Bart nor Dolores could find a fatal flaw. So they decided to make an offer.

It was a good offer. It was all cash and within $10,000 of the asking price. The Grinsteads were pleased as punch to finally get an offer on their property - so pleased that they didn't even counter. It was signed, sealed and delivered in fewer than five hours. Closing was set for mid-January, just after the Christmas holidays, allowing ample time for the standard list of inspections. The Hazeltons and Sam quickly lined those inspections up: the home inspection, the septic inspection, roof inspection and, as always in south Florida, the standard termite/pest inspection.

It was now mid-March and they were no closer to closing than they were in late November when the purchase agreement had first been signed. Nerves were frayed, patience was running thin and there were lawyers sniffing around the edges of the deal like a pack of hyenas on the scent of a mortally wounded wildebeest. If things weren't resolved soon, blood was sure to spill.

Then, there was Mildred Lee. The listing from Hades. At first, Sam wanted to add Adam Bartlett to his hit list. It was going to be Sam's way of thanking him for the referral. After Sam had walked through the house, the house that reeked of cat urine and came complete with Mildred's continuous hurricane seminar, he reminded himself to pick up an extra clip for the handgun he didn't own. Sam figured the additional nine rounds would take Bartlett out handily, and there was plenty of extra room in that culvert for the bullet-riddled corpse. The 'gators could handle the rest of the problem.

Sam never considered killing Mildred. She was just a misguided, sweet little old lady who needed some help selling her house. Sam had a soft spot for little old ladies like her, a psychological holdover from a great aunt he had growing up as a child in northern Michigan. She used to give him peanut butter cookies and warm milk whenever she came over to baby-sit him. Great Aunt Claire Goodlet, but Sam always called her Auntie C.

Sam couldn't think of plugging Mildred Lee with hollow point bullets. It would have been like shooting Auntie C. Unimaginable.

Early on in the season, Sam was on a roll. First, he figured that he would close on the Grinstead house and rid himself once and for all of those two weirdos from Alabama; secondly, he would convince Mildred to take her hurricane shutters down, leave the house for every showing and purchase a dozen of those little plug-in air fresheners to place strategically around her little ranch. Strategically being defined as a minimum of two air fresheners in every room. Three in the bedroom where the olfactory memories of Boots still lingered.

With the hurricane shutters gone, Mildred unavailable to recite her monologue of killer hurricanes, and the house smelling as fresh as a year's supply of Glade, this cute little ranch would be under contract before the holidays.

That was his plan. Sam had been in the real estate business long enough to know that things seldom go as planned. This plan was to be no exception.

Things started to skid away from him after the first inspection of the Grinstead home. The inspector, who worked for a company called Nuts & Bolts Home Inspections, noted that there appeared to be some slight cracking, running alongside the drywall by the pilings, underneath the house. The observant inspector also noted that the same settling cracks appeared upstairs just above the same row of pilings, and once again on the vaulted ceilings in the living room.

"Structural damage," was the very first comment to come off of Mr. Hazelton's lips when he looked over the report.

"Damn it," was the very first thing that Sam mumbled under his breath as he braced himself for a long, complicated closing.

Shortly thereafter, Bartholomew Hazelton himself contacted a structural engineering firm by the name of Baker, Baker & Strong to do some additional inspections and testing on the pilings of the Grinstead home. To start their inspection of the framing, they needed to have all the sheet rock removed that covered all the floor joists underneath the home. That meant bringing in contractors to do the demolition.

Baker, Baker & Strong was a huge engineering firm in town and they were tied up with the design and construction of a 30-story building downtown at the time. The Grinstead piling problem immediately sank to the very bottom of their priorities. Their take on the 30-story bank building was $285,000. The best they could hope for out of the Grinstead inspection was $2,000. With those numbers in mind, their field inspector took five weeks to show. The first set of extension forms were drafted and signed. January came and went.

Along with the apparent piling problem, a bad pest control report had come in. They didn't find any termites, and that was welcome news to Sam. They did observe ants though: both carpenter ants and small red sugar ants were cited in the report. The pest control firm recommended tenting the home. They were willing to take on that task as well for a fee of $1,500. A convenient coincidence.

"Bugs!" was the second word to roll out from Mr. Hazelton's lips as he looked over the pest control inspection report. "Bugs!!" He made a point of repeating it, knowing how much his homely wife, Dolores, hated insects.

"Fuck," was the only word that Sam Goodlet muttered under his breath as Bartholomew handed him his copy of the report. Sam didn't feel like repeating it.

Since carpenter ants can inflict considerable damage on wood-frame structures, and the report noted seeing them in not one, but two distinct areas, further inspections were needed. "We've got to look into this ant problem, Sam. We've got to get this resolved before we can close on this house. You know how Dolores feels about insects, she's deathly afraid of them. Roaches, grandpa bugs, mud wasps, fire ants - you know she can't even stand the thought of them. Now that we're darn near certain that this joint has an infestation of various species of ants, well, that puts another clinker in the closing, Sam. Doesn't it?"

Sam didn't bother to reply. The pilings were collapsing into the sand while the carpenter ants and sugar ants made whoopie with the rest of the house. His original plans weren't going well.

A second inspection was ordered, to try to determine the extent of the problem. The second pest control inspection stated that, "Although several areas of ant infestations were noted, the problem did not appear serious enough to merit tenting of the home and localized poisoning should suffice."

"Bullshit!" barked Bartholomew after looking over the report. "Pure bullshit. If there was ever a house in the state of Florida that needed tenting, it's this ant mound owned by the Grinsteads."

Mr. Hazelton promptly phoned "Dead Bug Doug," the fellow who did the second inspection, and fired him. He let Doug know that hell would freeze over solid before he'd ever pay him for such a slipshod report.

Dale Anderson, the listing agent for the Grinsteads, had his own copy of

Doug's report. Needless to say, he agreed with the second report and felt that the $1,500 tenting job recommended by the first pest control report simply wasn't necessary. The Grinsteads agreed, since under Paragraph "D" on the back of the contract, it was their responsibility to take care of the problem. Localized poisoning would run $300, tops. The Grinsteads were responsible either way, and the $300 figure looked a hell of a lot more attractive to them than did the tenting estimate.

A third, tiebreaker pest control firm was now brought in. It was late January and the odds of this house ever going to settlement were running about the same as winning the Florida lottery. Those odds are 14 million to 1. Sam was sinking into a dark blue funk.

The third pest control company, Orvin Pest Control, agreed with the first report. Since there was no way of knowing how much damage the carpenter ants had done without removing most of the vinyl siding, it was easier to simply tent the entire house. All the while Mr. and Mrs. Grinstead were waging their own private chemical war on the ants. They had bombed the house several times with those small six-ounce foggers available at any local hardware store, left little piles of Andro poison around the baseboards, and had run through an entire case of Terro ant poison in an attempt to wipe out the sugar ants.

Mrs. Grinstead, who was of frail constitution, was starting to have a reaction to all the toxins. She started complaining of nausea, aching and general malaise. Her doctor felt that her symptoms resembled those of the Gulf War syndrome. She started looking weak and acting disoriented.

The ants didn't respond to the first assault, and Mr. and Mrs. Grinstead were soon engaged in a personal war against millions upon millions of six-legged insects. They were spraying, fogging, injecting and handling more neurotoxins than the Iraqis had ever dared to throw at the allied forces. Saddam never went as far as these two homeowners had gone. The trouble was, the Grinsteads were losing the battle, and Mrs. Grinstead was fast becoming the first casualty.

Because of her rapidly deteriorating health, Mr. Grinstead had now decided that tenting the home might land his wife in the hospital. Fumigation was no longer an option. Instead, he decided to remove all the vinyl siding to prove to Mr. and Mrs. Hazelton that the damage from the carpenter ants was of no consequence. The cost to remove all the siding and put it back on was $5,950.

The money didn't matter at this point. It was the principle that mattered. His wife couldn't handle any more exposure to toxic chemicals without endangering her life, and he wanted to prove to everybody that "Dead Bug Doug," was right.

By early February the beautiful Grinstead home looked like it had been the target of a right-wing militia bombing. All the sheetrock had been torn out from under the home to enable the structural engineers to inspect the pilings, and all the vinyl siding had been ripped off the exterior. It was scattered in large piles around the yard. It had rained on the sheetrock and the white chalk from it had run all over the yard, killing most of the lawn. The homeowners association had contacted Mr. and Mrs. Grinstead about possible legal action if they didn't clean things up within 30 days.

Two days ago, Sam had been informed that Mrs. Grinstead had been hospitalized. The stress of the sale had made her break out in shingles. That, and her continuing reaction to all the ant poisons, had sent her into an intensive care unit. Dale Anderson had called just yesterday saying that her prognosis wasn't good. The death of Mrs. Grinstead would, of course, complicate the closing further. There would be her last will and testament, and then, possibly probate to deal with.

On top of the Grinstead fiasco, after weeks and weeks of phone calls and cajoling, Mildred Lee had agreed to take only one of her hurricane shutters off. She also refused to leave her house during the showings, fearing that some careless real estate agent might accidently let one of her cats out.

Sam was about ready to admit himself to the local mental health facility. The one shutter Mildred did take off overlooked a privacy fence, her air conditioner and her garbage cans. She only agreed to take it down because, according to all her data, it was located to the north, and that was the least likely direction for a hurricane to approach Shoreside Island from. She told that fact to everyone who dared to show the house.

She did put in all the air fresheners, but they could hold their ground only a week or two against the powerful stench of regurgitated furballs and cat urine. By mid-November the smell of old air fresheners somehow mingled with the odoriferous mementos of Boots in some sick new odor that reminded Sam of a dying evergreen forest. The house would never, ever sell under these conditions. Worse still, Adam had convinced him to take the listing for a year.

That's why Sam sat there praying that the phone wouldn't ring. He didn't want "Dead Bug Doug" calling him asking when he might expect to get his $75 inspection bill paid. He didn't want to hear from Baker, Baker & Strong telling him that it was going to be another month before their report was completed because of some new job they picked up in Tampa. He didn't want to hear from Mildred Lee, asking why her morgue wasn't being shown today, or having someone from the hospital calling telling him that Mrs. Grinstead was as dead as Boots.

Sam was wearing out. He was threadbare and frightened. He had put together only three deals since the first of the year and he felt lucky at that. He was even thinking about trying to find where Vince hid his bottle of vodka. Vince, now that was an agent you had to admire, thought Sam.

"Sam, I've got a call for you on line three," said Betsy in her congenial manner. "Sam, are you there?"

"I'm in, Betsy. I'm just not feeling very well."

"Oh, neither am I. My voice is going. Here's your call."

"Thanks," said a twitching Sam.

Betsy patched the call through and Sam's line rang for a bit before Sam picked it up.

"Hello, this is Sam Goodlet, how may I help you?"

"This is Mr. Strong, of Baker, Baker & Strong Engineering. We've just wrapped up our inspection report on the Grinstead house. You'll be glad to know what we discovered."

"And what is that?"

"Your clients are going to have all new pilings and a few new floor joists when they move in. They all need to be replaced."

"All of them?"

"All 32."

"Do you have a ballpark estimate of the cost?"

"Sure we do. We do this sort of thing all the time."

"And that number is...?"

"Thirty-eight thousand dollars."

Sam didn't say good bye. He simply hung the phone up and put his head down. He knew that this figure would end up killing Mrs. Grinstead. He could see her sweet little blue eyes rolling into her head now as her husband read her the final report. Sam could hear all the monitor alarms going off as her feeble heart gave out.

Bart would be pleased. He knew that there was a problem. He knew it was more than just those "mere settling cracks." It was this house's fatal flaw. That and the goddamned bugs. They all have them you know. Every house has them.

Sam sat there in a quiet, motionless stupor for five minutes. He wondered if it wasn't too late to get into another occupation. Clerking at the local 7-11, and driving a beer truck both seemed appealing to him. Just then the phone rang for a second time.

"This call's for you Sam, it's Jennifer Willow," said a worn-out Betsy Owens.

"Thanks, Betsy," replied a contemplative Sam.

Sam picked up the line and started talking to Jennifer. She wanted to show Mildred's house on Monday. She had never shown it before and wanted Sam to set things up for her. In a way, Sam felt just a twinge of revenge as he listened to Jennifer say, "Would 2:00 p.m. work?"

Sam Goodlet was getting even with a world that had been dumping on him for the last few months. As he replied, "2:00 p.m. is perfect, you don't even need a key. Mildred will be expecting you," Sam knew that he was now dumping on lovely Jennifer.

She even thanked him for setting up her showing.

Wait 'til Monday, thought Sam as he put the receiver down. She won't be thanking me then.

570-9898
March; the Main Switchboard

"Shoreside Realty, may we help you? Please hold."

Betsy's voice was gone. It was Friday afternoon, peak season, and her vocal cords were down for the count. She sounded rough and raspy, like a professional wrestler after a nationally televised match. A losing match. There were two hours left and Betsy wasn't sure that she was going to make it. It had been an ugly fight.

Another line lit up.

"Shoreside Realty, please hold."

Betsy looked at the switchboard and realized that she had seven lines on hold. The chaos and calamity of Florida peak-season real estate was fast upon her. Betsy looked down again and couldn't remember where any of the blinking calls were supposed to go. She knew that one of them belonged to Vince, another to Jason, and two were supposed to somehow get over to Bartlett and his crew. Betsy didn't have the faintest idea as to where the remaining three calls were headed and an eighth line started ringing.

Betsy did the unthinkable. She shut the system down. It was a trick she had used only half a dozen times in any given year. She picked up each of the remaining four open lines and put them on hold. No incoming call could now get into the system. A caller would get a busy signal and have to call back. It was a desperate, bottom of the ninth measure, but it was her only way out.

After shutting down the incoming phone lines, Betsy methodically picked up each of the eight people on hold that were beeping and flashing away, and proceeded to find where each caller belonged. If she had to take a message and a line opened up again, she immediately placed it on hold with all of the others. No one would ever know.

If Elinor Braun knew about Betsy's drastic telephone maneuver, or even suspected Betsy of doing something like this, she would fire her on the spot. In the real estate industry, creating an intentional busy signal is a first-degree felony. Damn near a homicide.

But the week had been a living hell for Betsy. The avalanche of phone calls had started before 9:00 on Monday morning. By late Friday afternoon it had buried Betsy Owens beneath 30 feet of snow. There was no hope that the well-trained rescue dogs or the search teams would ever find her. Betsy was cold, disheveled and her voice was shot. There was nothing left of that bright, uplifting girl everyone knew and loved. She was gone, and her voice was a gravel pit. She picked line six up, determined to dig her way out of the avalanche.

"Sorry to keep you holding, how may I help you?"

"Is Vince Cricket in?"

"Yes he is. May I ask who's calling?"

"Mrs. Sophie Doren."

"One moment please."

Betsy punched in Vince's intercom.

"Vince, line six's for you. It's a Mrs. Sophie Doren."

Vince picked up the intercom line to let Betsy know that he was in and about to take the call.

"Thanks Betsy. What's with your voice? You sound like hell."

"It's shot Vince, completely shot," said Betsy.

"Go home and have a beer."

Betsy looked at the clock just above her desk. "I will Vince, in one hour and forty-three minutes. Now pick up line six, please."

It was the only thing that kept her hanging on; the thought of that nice warm bubble bath and an ice-cold six pack of Miller Lite. She couldn't wait. Then, around 8:00 or so, Mark was coming over with a video.

He hadn't told her the name of the flick he was bringing over, but it didn't matter. They would order a pizza, kick back on the couch and snuggle. The movie didn't matter to Betsy. It could be anything from *Godzilla* to *The Godfather*. What mattered was that they could spend some time together. What mattered were the tender kisses, the laughing and the companionship. The feeling of loving someone and knowing that they, in turn, loved you. They were going steady now, and Betsy had never been happier.

What started out as a package of real estate garbage being delivered to Jason Randazzle was now a full-fledged romance. They were months beyond that first awkward date and those initial first few weeks of finding out about each other. They were now settled in. About three weeks ago they had started sleeping together. Making love together.

Sometimes Mark would spend the weekends at Betsy's apartment, and sometimes Betsy would spend a weeknight at Mark's place. Absolutely perfect.

As Betsy daydreamed about that first can of Miller, line nine lit up.

Damn, I must have forgotten to put that line on hold when Chris hung up. I'll have to answer it. Betsy cleared her raspy throat for the call.

"Shoreside Realty, how may we help you?"

"Is Linda Hinkle in?"

It was that attorney again. Betsy had forgotten his name. Normally she wouldn't have, but she had been so damned busy this week.

"I believe she is in, may I ask who's calling?"

"Bruce, Mr. Bruce Strunk, attorney for Mr. and Mrs. Larson."

"I'll put you through right away, Mr. Strunk."

Something ugly was going on with the Larson deal, but Betsy wasn't sure what it was. As she made all the electronic connections, she kept hoping that Mark's movie was a comedy. I need a good laugh about now, she reflected.

Linda Hinkle picked line nine up. Betsy was hoping, praying that the calls would start tapering off. One hour and 32 minutes to Miller time. Friday afternoons are all the same, thought Betsy. As if God has intentionally added 25 seconds to every minute. I hope it's a comedy. Or at least something romantic and sweet, like *Sleepless in Seattle* or *The Way We Were*. Something nice.

570-9898 Ext. 9
Linda Hinkle's Desk

"Hello, Linda speaking."

"Mrs. Hinkle, this is Mr. Strunk. I'm calling about the closing of unit 801 at Osprey Landings. You know, the closing we currently have scheduled for Monday. My understanding is that you are representing the buyers in this transaction, is that correct?"

Shit. Linda didn't want to take this call.

"That's correct."

"You are, of course, well aware of the seller's position regarding this closing, are you not?"

"I am aware of it, but it still doesn't make any sense to me."

"And why is that?" asked the attorney in that tone attorneys love to use.

"It's just a paint-by-number watercolor, Mr. Strunk. It can't be worth over five dollars."

"What the watercolor is worth or is not worth is not at issue here, Mrs. Hinkle. We are talking about the painting's sentimental value, not its monetary value. The Larsons' daughter, Rose, painted this particular watercolor when she was only five-years old and gave it to her mother on her 35th birthday. You will note her signature on the bottom left-hand side of the painting. Since Rose, who is 26 and now lives in Hawaii, rarely gets to see her parents any longer, they both have become very attached to her childhood painting.

"That paint-by-number is a treasured family heirloom. It is either struck from the inventory or the closing will not take place this Monday. Do I make myself perfectly clear?"

"Yes, Mr. Strunk, you do."

"Then I will expect you to advise your clients, and their attorney, of our position in this matter. We want to close, we are willing to close, and we are going to close, provided the painting is struck from the inventory and personally delivered to my office by 11:00 Monday morning, March 23. Because of prior commitments, Mr. and Mrs. Larson will not be able to attend the closing. But I will be there, awaiting the delivery of the watercolor."

"I'll see what I can do."

"Thank you, Mrs. Hinkle, and have a nice day."

"Goodbye."

Linda Hinkle leaned back in her leather chair and shook her head in disbelief. How in the world could this be happening? How did I get into this mess in the first place? And, more importantly, how on earth am I going to get out of it?

As she had a hundred times before, Linda went through the comedy of errors that had created this particular real estate nightmare. She kept hoping to find someone to blame, someone to pin the crime on, but there really wasn't anyone. It was like a train wreck that took place over six long weeks. Human error had caused the wreckage, but there were just too many humans involved to blame any one individual. Her sale was going to end up in court, and Linda felt totally helpless to prevent it.

Six weeks ago, Linda Hinkle received a phone call from two of her old clients, Dr. and Mrs. Asp. They had sold their unit at Shell Pointe Condominiums two years ago and had disappeared into the woodwork of Linda's enormous mailing list. They lived in suburban Chicago. He was a heart specialist and his wife, well, his wife was a spoiled bitch.

His wife, Mrs. Nancy Asp, had decided that they really, really missed their place on Shoreside. All totaled, they probably spent little more than a week a year in their Shell Pointe apartment, but that didn't matter. What Nancy really missed was being able to tell all her socialite friends in Wake Forest that they had a place on Shoreside. The fact that they never used it was moot. It was a pleasant luncheon topic. Something to chat about during their Wednesday bridge games.

Her husband, Dr. John Asp, didn't care either way. He was so busy doing quadruple bypasses and angioplasties that they could have had a condominium in Papua, New Guinea, and he wouldn't have objected. When they did come to Shoreside, he spent his entire vacation in the guest bedroom sending e-mails and faxes to his clinic in Chicago. Nancy shopped and went down to the beach all week. The only time they actually saw each other was when they went out to dinner.

When Nancy suggested they buy another place on Shoreside, John, on his way into the office, turned to her and said, "Fine." That was that.

Mrs. Asp had called Linda to let her know that they were coming down to "look around." Linda knew better. She was on them like a roll of brand-new flypaper. The good doctor made more money than he could spend in ten lifetimes and Linda knew that Mrs. Asp wanted the right address to talk about during her afternoon bridge games. They wouldn't fly all the way to Shoreside and head back to Chicago without a signed purchase agreement. It was a slam dunk.

Linda queried Nancy as to what sort of property they might be considering.

"Oh, nothing too fancy," said Nancy.

"You still want to be on the top floor, don't you?" queried Linda over the long-distance line.

"Of course. You know how I simply hate those noisy condominiums."

"You'll want three bedrooms, right?"

"Or four."

"Do you have a price range?"

"We would like to keep it under a million. But if you have anything just a trifle over that, we'll take a little peek at that as well."

"Furnished or unfurnished?"

"Definitely furnished. With John's schedule, we simply don't have the time to go shopping for furniture. We'd like it completely furnished, right down to the silverware, if possible. And, as always, it has to be directly Gulf front. I want to be able to hear the song of the surf at night."

"I know that, Nancy. Let me throw a few listings together and fax them to your husband's clinic. Should I call him before I fax up the listings?"

"Oh, don't bother."

Linda knew that she didn't have to call first. Nancy wanted everyone on staff at the clinic to know that they could afford a penthouse unit on Shoreside. It was all for show.

"Well thanks for calling, Nancy. I'll see what I can find for the both of you."

"Thank you, Linda, and thanks again for keeping us on your mailing list."

"My pleasure. Goodbye."

"Goodbye."

That was how it started. God, if Linda had only known then how it was ending. How all hell was going to break loose at 11:00 Monday morning if she didn't walk into Strunk's office with that watercolor. That $2.99 watercolor.

The painting in question was 12 inches high and ten inches wide. It was a picture of a solitary palm tree along a stretch of beach with the surf breaking. It couldn't have taken the Larsons' five-year-old daughter an hour to paint. There were only ten colors in it. When she looked at it closely, Linda noted that the daughter had done a terrible job. She had hardly stayed within the lines and some of the colors were smudged. What could you expect? Rose was in kindergarten at the time. Her mother must have helped.

But it was all coming down to this one item and this one item alone. A $1,245,000 transaction was hanging on whether or not the purchasers, who had a signed inventory, were willing to give a $2.99 paint-by-number back to the sellers on the day of closing.

Mrs. Asp, the bitch Linda represented, was adamant. The painting was included in the inventory. The inventory was signed by all parties and the answer was no. The painting matched the color of both the bedspread and the drapes in the second guest bedroom and it clearly belonged with the unit.

The sellers were furious. Their Realtor, Loretta Snyder of Beachside Realty, had accidently included it in the inventory. She had also accidently included Mr. Larson's golf clubs, some antique Hummels and her grandmother's waffle iron. Mrs. Larson had struck all these items when they reviewed and signed the final inventory.

But she had missed her daughter's paint-by-number. Amid the hundreds of items included in the sale - the three sofas, the cutlery, the blenders and wall decorations - it was an easy oversight. Nobody reads inventories very carefully. Mrs. Larson had told Loretta to exclude the watercolor and Mrs. Larson trusted Loretta to do what she had asked.

Loretta had meant to exclude it, but she had simply forgotten. She had offered to replace the paint-by-number with a lovely, signed and numbered print of a similar beach scene by a renowned local artist. That framed print cost $975. It was not a paint-by-number.

Mrs. Larson, who was also quite adept at doing the bitch thing, said no. If her daughter's watercolor went with the sale, then the sale was off, contracts or no contracts. Off, off, off. Linda knew it had become a cat fight.

Mr. Larson, who was somewhat ambivalent about the whole thing, was the CEO of a large insurance firm in Connecticut. His firm had a legal staff the size of a banana republic's death squad. If his wife, Violet, was ready to go, his SWAT team of lawyers were at her command. Personally, he felt that it was a pretty silly issue to go to court over, but he had advised his entire staff that come Monday, if Strunk didn't have the watercolor in his hand by 11:00 a.m. sharp, they were going into battle. All 46 of them, not including the nine in Strunk's firm. Well-trained attorneys, dressed in army fatigues, instructed and trained to shoot the wounded.

Elinor Braun, in this particular disaster, was powerless. Linda had explained everything to her a few weeks ago when she first noticed how deep the trenches were getting. Elinor had called everyone to try to head off the inevitable. She called Dr. and Mrs. Asp and pleaded with them to reconsider. She had offered to buy them a beautiful, signed and numbered print by a renowned local artist of a similar beach scene and pay for it out of Shoreside Realty's side of the commission. That print, beautifully framed by the way, cost $975. It was the same painting Loretta had offered to the Larsons. It wasn't that great a painting. It could have been a paint-by-number, just a professionally done one.

Nancy Asp said no. No, no, no. The watercolor came along with the condo on Monday or they'll sue. Impasse. Rich people with attitudes, a Realtor's worst nightmare.

Dr. Asp, with his mountains of open heart surgery money, had already called in his own personal hit squad of lawyers. It was going to get ugly. Really, really ugly.

Elinor, in a noble attempt to avoid the legal slaughter, had phoned Loretta Snyder, attorney Strunk, Mr. Larson, Dr. Asp and everyone else who was party to the battle. It didn't matter, they were all dug in deep with their gas masks on and fire power in place. All of them waiting for Monday.

Linda Hinkle didn't understand why Frank, her one and only love, had done this to her. It wasn't like him. Thus far her year had been nothing short of spectacular. Linda was already pushing $9 million in sales. At her current pace, she would probably be giving Bartlett and his crew a run for their money if it wasn't for the Sanderling project closings scheduled for the fall. She and Frank had been getting along fabulously.

Now this mess. She had run the numbers a hundred times. She was going to lose her 78 percent split of a 3.5 percent pass through on $1.245 million. Linda knew that she was going to relinquish a $33,988.50 real estate commission because of a $2.99 paint-by-number. It was maddening.

Linda took a long, deep breath and picked up the phone to start making some appointments. She was showing property tomorrow to a nice young couple that were referred to her from the Petersons. She didn't mind working on Saturdays. Or Sundays either, for that matter.

Still, she kept thinking, there has to be a solution. There just has to be. I'll think of something. I always do.

570-9898 Ext. 21
Vince Cricket's Call

"Vince here." He answered the call in a short, terse manner. Vince was being rude again. He didn't care.

"Hello, Mr. Cricket, this is Mrs. Sophie Doren. Do you remember me?"

"Sort of." Vince had the rude groove going.

"I bought the Landley place from you two years ago. Remember, that run-down canal house that you had listed over on Beachside Drive?"

"The one with the cracked swimming pool?"

"Yes, but the crack was only cosmetic."

"I thought you sold that place already?"

"Oh, yes I did, almost a year ago. It sold right after I fixed it up. You remember me now, don't you?"

"I guess."

Vince Cricket didn't remember Mrs. Doren. But then, Vince didn't remember much these days. He was hung over and tired. He was always hung over and tired.

He continued. "What can I do for you now, Mrs. Dornell?"

"Mrs. Doren, Sophie Doren."

"Well, why'd ya call me?"

Vince was on a roll. It was more of a tumble than a roll. It was a long, drawn-out tumble, like falling off the far side of Everest. Vince Cricket had been falling down his personal mountainside for years, end over end. At this juncture in his long-tarnished career there wasn't anything graceful about the fall. His shirt collars were pilled and stained, his breath smelled like cigarettes and his long-abandoned charm was layered in rust. It was hard to imagine that he once stood at the top of the real estate market on Shoreside. That he had once planted a flag on the K2 of island sales.

Ten years ago, Vince Cricket was the boy wonder at Shoreside Realty. He was top listing agent, top selling agent and top producer. Unlike Adam Bartlett, Vince didn't have a team of assistants to help him attain the summit. Back then, no one had assistants. You scaled that precipice alone, and no one looked better than Vince did at the top.

A decade ago, Mr. Vince Cricket wore Brooks Brothers suits, gold chains and a platinum Rolex. He started every morning with a three-mile jog and a cup of herbal tea. Time has a way with people. A cruel way.

Vince didn't jog any longer, his beautiful gold chains and his Rolex had long since been traded in for cases of Skol vodka and his Brooks Brothers suits left dangling in his musty closet, their once fashionable cuts looking as dated as zoot suits. The herbal tea had become coffee. Black, and too much of it.

Today, Vince Cricket looked like a Salvation Army poster child. He had gained 40 pounds. The weight had all gathered in his belly, which protruded out as though Vince was about to give birth to a bowling ball. On some days, he looked as though he might have been carrying twins. His teeth were suffering from years of neglect and his eyes had that glazed look to them. Like the eyes of the homeless.

He was almost bald. He had one long clump of graying black hair he tried to swirl around the top of his head to cover his enormous bald spot. To keep it in place, he used Brylcream. He was the last person on Earth still using Brylcream. Vince's present condition wasn't a well-kept secret on Shoreside. Everyone on the island knew him for what he was: a has-been.

Mrs. Doren completely ignored Vince's rude behavior. She remembered him from the Langley sale. She knew that he was in tough shape but she didn't let it distract her from her agenda. Her agenda never changed. Mrs. Doren looked to find distressed properties, steal them by any means possible, and get them back on the market the day after closing, or sooner, if possible. She was damn good at it. She could zero in on troubled properties like a peregrine falcon diving for tethered pigeons. God help the real estate agent who got in her way.

She continued. "Yes, you can help me. I'm calling about the Simpsons' place, 948 Siesta Lane. Do you still have it listed?"

"Sure I do."

"Well, I've heard through the grapevine that the two of them are in an ugly divorce. Is there any truth to that?"

"That's confidential information, Mrs. Dorling. I owe it to my clients not to reveal anything personal about them that might negatively impact the sale of their home. I'm not really at liberty to discuss their private matters with you."

"Would you rather I call another agent at Shoreside Realty and ask them? I am a cash buyer, Mr. Cricket, and I'm prepared to close in a week's time. If you would prefer, I'll call Mrs. Hinkle or Adam Bartlett right after I hang up the phone with you. Either way, I'll eventually find out what's going on."

Mrs. Doren was giving Vince the full-court press. She was gathering speed for the final blow. Vince listened carefully as the shadow of a diving falcon descended. Mrs. Doren delivered the ultimatum.

"It's your listing, Vince, and it could be your sale if you just give me some sort of idea of what's going on between them. Am I making myself clear to you? Do you want to make some money or not?"

Vince was stuck. He hadn't had a sale in months. He couldn't even remember the last time he had a double-dip, that being a sale where it was both his listing and his sale. The house was on the market for $385,000. With a full seven percent commission and Vince's 65 percent plateau, he was looking at better than $15,000.

Even if I cut the commission to five percent to make the deal work, I'm looking at over $10,000 take home. That's a hell of a lot of vodka, marijuana, cocaine, cigarettes and past- due mortgage payments. It was food for thought.

Still, Vince hesitated for an instant. He had promised Mrs. Simpson not to spread around the news about their divorce. It would hurt her chances of getting fair market value for the property if any buyers knew that they were in financial trouble. The truth being that Mr. and Mrs. Simpson were in a shitload of financial trouble. Mr. Simpson had stopped making the mortgage payments out of spite five months ago. The bank was proceeding with foreclosure and the electricity had been shut off twice in the last month. Mrs. Simpson had to hock her wedding ring just to cover the utility bills. It was a mess.

The fact was that almost everyone knew about the divorce by this time, thought a waffling Vince Cricket. It was part of the public records, provided someone wanted to go over and search through piles of divorce court proceedings. Hell, Mrs. Dorling will probably find out anyway, reasoned Vince in his final moment of rationalization. With that he opened the floodgates willingly.

"Promise not to tell anyone, or mention to my broker that we ever had this discussion. Because if you do say anything, I'll deny it."

Fifteen thousand dollars was just too much money to pass along to Hinkle or Bartlett. At this point in his career, Vince Cricket needed this sale more than he needed the self respect. It was never really an issue.

"I won't say a thing to anyone, Vince."

"Good. You're right, Mrs. Dorling. They are divorcing. Mr. Simpson's already moved out. He's taken an apartment in town."

"Are they behind in the mortgage payments?"

"Hell yes, months behind."

"Will they take a low-ball offer?"

"Mrs. Simpson's still holding out for $370,000 or $375,000, but Ernie, her husband, is willing to sign anything at this point. He just wants the damn thing to be over. Rumor has it that he's in love with some gal he met at work."

"Offer them $300,000 cash and get back to me ASAP."

"Are you serious? Three hundred thousand dollars is a ridiculous offer. They had an appraisal done for the court and it came in at $365,000. I can't offer them $300,000, they'll be insulted."

"Then insult them for me. I can't make any money buying property if I pay market price, now can I?"

"Are you going to make it a written offer?"

"Only if they accept my verbal one."

"When can you close?"

"Next Thursday will work. No inspection, no financing contingency, no questions asked. Three hundred thousand dollars cash and they're out the door."

"What about the furniture?"

"Five thousand for all the furniture. Get back to me tomorrow. I'm at 570-7230. It's best if you call in the late afternoon."

"Thanks."

"No, Vince, thank you."

Vince hung up the phone. He felt like shit. He had double-crossed his clients and he knew it. When he sold Mr. and Mrs. Simpson their canal house ten years ago, he would never have imagined having a conversation like the one he just had. He wouldn't have needed to.

At the top of his career, Vince was turning $10 million a year in sales. He was driving a brand-new Lincoln Town Car and wining and dining his clients all the way to the bank. He was "the man" at Shoreside. The Golden Boy of his era.

Somewhere along the line he started having one more martini than he should have at those dinner parties. Just one last cocktail for the road. Then he started having them at lunch as well; extra dry, with an olive. A few years thereafter, Vince started having three martinis at lunch and a half liter of Stolischnoya vodka at his house after work.

His wife warned him that he was drinking too much. Her comment just pissed him off. He was the top producer at Shoreside Realty, the most prestigious firm on the island, and he knew how to handle his liquor.

Vince kept drinking and sliding. Two years ago his production fell to under $2 million. By this time, everyone on the island knew that Vince Cricket was a drunk. His wife, Kathy, was still with him but their relationship was ice cold. Luckily, Vince and Kathy had never had any children. If they had, Kathy would have taken them with her and moved out years ago. Instead, she put up with him. She was either a fool or a saint for doing so, and no one could tell you which it was.

Vince's latest vice was smoking marijuana. Too much marijuana. Way too much. He was going through a half ounce a week at times. Designer pot when he could afford it. Cheap homegrown when he couldn't. Vince would light up a joint on the way home almost every night. When things were really looking grim, he would burn one on the way into the office. If Vince could have afforded it, he would have started doing coke again, but his income stream couldn't support a coke habit at this point. If he got this Simpson sale, a gram or two was inevitable.

Drunk, stoned and willing to sell out his brother for a dime - that was Cricket. At 52 years old, pot bellied and short fused, he was a total washout. Vince was

40 miles of bad road with no road map. He forgot telephone numbers, missed countless appointments and kept a small flask of vodka in the top back corner of his file cabinet. Kept it just behind the hundreds of folders that held all of his closing documents from ten years ago. Folders where the name tags were yellowing and falling off. Folders full of memories and customers before the fall.

"I'm an asshole," Vince mumbled to himself as he picked up his phone to call Mrs. Simpson. "A total asshole."

570-9898
The Main Switchboard; 4:45 p.m. Friday

Fifteen minutes left. At this point, every minute was a struggle. Betsy's voice was hanging on by a thread. She was waiting for the bell to ring at 5:00 p.m. sharp. Then she could turn the system over to the answering service, hop into her Pinto, and drive home.

Miller time. She would set her purse next to the door in her small, one-bedroom apartment in town, go directly into the bathroom, pour half a cup of bubble bath liquid into the tub, and turn the hot water on. Then she'd walk over to the refrigerator, take out two or three ice-cold Miller Lites, putting them carefully in a small cooler she had purchased last year just for evenings like this, and smother them in crushed ice.

When the tub was just about filled, Betsy would add just enough cold water to make getting into the tub possible, and slide in. She would lie down, using a washcloth as a pillow and, while listening to the millions of foamy bubbles popping and crackling around her, reach over and take out a can of Miller. She could hear the crack of that ice cold can as...

Line four lit up.

"Good afternoon, Shoreside Realty. How may we help you?"

The caller, Dr. James Clifton, was quick to react to the sound of Betsy's voice.

"Excuse me, ma'am, is there something wrong with your voice?"

"Laryngitis," said Betsy.

"If it doesn't clear up soon, you should have that looked at by a doctor," advised Dr. Clifton, totally in character.

"Thanks, I will," said Betsy, trying to keep her words to a minimum.

"Is Jennifer Willow in?"

"Yes, I'll put you through."

Betsy had taken the system off of hold just after 4:00 p.m.. She knew that the incoming calls always fell off late in the day on Friday. Everyone starts kicking into their weekend mode and, even though she could barely speak, Betsy felt that she could field the last hour of incoming phone calls. Besides, if she used her private put-them-all-on-hold technique too often, there was always a chance that Elinor might find it out. That wouldn't be good. Betsy would have one hell of a lot of explaining to do. Shutting down the business of uncertain buyers sort of wanting to buy and unreasonable sellers wanting too much for their properties wouldn't sit well with Elinor. No, that wouldn't be good at all.

Betsy looked at the switchboard again just to take note as to who was still in the office and who had already gone home for the weekend. She could tell by her switchboard. Sam Goodlet was gone, his extension line hadn't lit up once since 3:00. Vince was still in, and he was on his line. Randazzle was on the phone, but Randazzle seldom left the office before 6:00. His line was permanently lit up. He was relentless.

Bartlett was on the phone, as was Chris Taylor, his top assistant. Elinor wasn't on the phone, but Betsy knew she was in. Elinor left at 5:15 every day. You could set your watch by it. She was methodical, if nothing else.

One of the two Daves was still in the office and on his line. But that was it. All of the others had called it quits. Some were showing property tomorrow, some were sitting open houses and some were hanging out for the weekend with company from up north. Betsy had plans.

Friday night, Mark Thurston, her boyfriend, was coming over with a movie. Saturday night they were going out to dinner and after that, if Betsy felt up to it, they were going to hear a band in town. Two of the other UPS drivers played in the band. They called themselves "The Brown Truckers." Betsy had heard them before. They weren't too bad. They played old rock'n'roll and some classic country western hits. They played in the cocktail lounge at Stadium Lanes Bowling Alley. "The Brown Truckers." The name could use some work.

Sunday she and Mark were going on a boat ride in the bay with some friends. Mark wouldn't expect Betsy to talk to him much over the weekend. He knew that her voice would be tired after a long week of fielding calls at Shoreside Realty. Her pretty brown eyes could speak for her. Her smile could say 1,000 words.

All he wanted was to spend time with her. That was worth more than all the words in the world. They were falling in love; Betsy Owens, the full-figured girl who answers the phone all week on Shoreside Island, and Mark Thurston, the UPS guy with the Errol Flynn mustache, were getting serious about each other. Life, even without a voice, was good.

Betsy patched Dr. Clifton through to Jennifer's extension. Fourteen minutes left and counting. Miller time.

570-9898 Ext. 22
Jennifer Willow's Desk

Jennifer heard the phone ring. She had been expecting the call all afternoon. It had to be Dr. Clifton calling. With his busy schedule, thought Jennifer, it must be hard for him to break away and make a call down here to Shoreside. She picked up her telephone.

"Jennifer Willow here, how may I help you?"

"Hi, Jennifer, it's me, Bruce. Sorry I wasn't able to return your call sooner, it's been another crazy day at the clinic."

"I understand, Dr. Clifton. Did you receive the overnight package yesterday?"

"We sure did, Jennifer, and the photos were great. We still haven't had time to watch your video yet, but we'll get to it soon enough."

"It's really coming along, isn't it?"

"It sure is. Right on schedule and not too much over budget. When did they say they would get the roof completed and start in on the drywall?"

"Well, Chuck Olsen, the site foreman, said that they should have the roof on and be dried in within two weeks. After that come all the mechanicals. You know, the plumbing, the electrical, the air conditioning and all that stuff. Then comes the drywall. Chuck said that would be a couple of months at least. So we're still about four months from your CO."

"Just keep us posted. We hope to be able to get to Shoreside in the next month or so, but things have been pretty hectic at the clinic lately. We'll count on you to update us as to how the construction is going, Jennifer."

"I will, Dr. Clifton, you can count on it."

"Well, I've got to run. Thanks again for the package. Bye now."

"Goodbye."

Jennifer Willow gently put the receiver down. She was glad that she had taken the time to go shoot some photos and a short video of the house for her clients. Elinor Braun had suggested it during their last little get together. It was a great idea.

Jennifer Willow was having the time of her life. Her real estate career had flourished. From that lucky encounter with Dr. and Mrs. Clifton on her very first afternoon of floor time, to her most recent condominium sale of Adam Bartlett's

544 Osprey Towers, Jennifer was on a roll. She had put together nine transactions in the last six months and had three or four likely prospects in the works. Island real estate was going fabulously for Jennifer.

True, there were a few small bumps along the way. She had ended up in her sales manager's office more than once in the past six months. She needed some help with how to word an addendum that had some owner financing terms in it. Then she needed to learn how to handle the refurbishing credit the purchasers of 544 Osprey Towers wanted on their contract.

That was her best sale to date, Osprey Towers. Only a former decorator could have sold that condo. It had the original lime-green, low shag carpeting, a floral print rattan living room set and harvest gold appliances. The entire interior of the condominium could have been donated to the Smithsonian as a museum-quality representation of early '70s Florida kitsch. Osprey Towers needed a complete redo, right down to the dark brown Formica cabinets.

Luckily, Adam Bartlett, who had it listed, was on Jennifer's side right from the get go. The original owners had both died in the apartment; Mr. Smits had passed away first, followed by his wife, Arlene Smits, three years later. Their grown kids had inherited the property and none of them had so much as a passing interest in the condo. No one wanted to put any money into it, so it sat and sat and sat.

Next to Mildred Lee's canal-front ranch, it was the dog of Shoreside. The only redeeming quality was that the apartment had an outstanding view of the Gulf. The trouble being that you needed to walk your customers through this repository of tacky furniture, worn linoleum and acres of lime-green shag carpeting to get to the view. Very few buyers made it as far as the screened lanai. Most turned around when they got to the horrid dining room chandelier. It was one of those tin floral chandeliers that were popular in the seventies. It was painted lime-green and urine yellow with about a dozen little nightlight-sized bulbs in it. It was hung by a swag chain and on an inexpensive dimmer.

Not to forget the dark brown dining room set it dangled over, complete with tube steel chairs and brown plastic seats. The rest of the decor was equally abominable. It was no wonder both owners had died.

But Jennifer Willow knew better. She could see past all of it. Decorating this place was going to be fun. She dashed her clients quickly past all the vintage Salvation Army furniture and showed them the outstanding view from the lanai. They didn't spend five minutes looking at the interior of the unit. Instead, she grabbed a key to Mrs. Carlson's unit one floor below. Jennifer had redone Mrs. Carlson's apartment about a year before she had left the Decorating Hut, and it showed like a dream.

It had pickled ash kitchen cabinets, an off-white patterned Berber carpet and leather furniture. Jennifer's clients spent over an hour looking at Mrs. Carlson's interior, taking copious notes and a complete set of photos.

The rest was easy. Jennifer brought her buyers to the office and told them that they could redo 544 Osprey towers at ten percent over cost. She would help coordinate the entire renovation. They submitted an offer contingent on a refurbishing allowance of $30,000 from the sellers at closing and the deal was done.

Adam literally railroaded the heirs into signing the deal. The listing was over two years old and it had to go. Adam was sick of making excuses to their trustee in Urbana, Illinois. The tactic worked.

By this time, Jennifer was well on her way. She was helping to oversee the construction of the Cliftons' new house on Palmetto Court, coordinating the redo at 544 Osprey Towers and soon to get her first listing from one of the owners at the Decorating Hut.

Dr. and Mrs. Clifton's house was scheduled to be completed in four months. That was about the same time the developer and his wife, Ralph and Lila Hardwick, were to return from their luxurious world cruise. It was also about the same time Andy and Deb Stoughton were supposed to come from Panama City to get things started on their house plans on lot "A." Or was it lot "D?" Well, on the lot that they had purchased the same day the Cliftons had purchased theirs. Jennifer was still a bit sketchy on details.

Jennifer looked at her watch. It was 5:00 p.m. and time to call it a day. Jennifer had planned to sit an open house at one of the two Daves' new listing along Middle Gulf Drive tomorrow. She packed her bag, careful to throw in some extra free maps of Shoreside to hand out tomorrow, and headed through the back door of the office. It had been another great week of real estate, thought Jennifer as she started her Acura. Another great week.

570-4318
Peggy Bartlett's House

"I can't make it by 6:00."

"You have to. This isn't a negotiable item, Adam. This isn't a real estate deal. This is about your son, Danny," said a frustrated Peggy Bartlett.

"Peg, I just can't. I've got a closing at 5:30 that will take at least an hour, then the drive over to your place...7:00 is the earliest that I can pick him up."

"Seven's too late. Ken's arriving here at 6:15 and we'll be on our way to Orlando for the weekend. You have to be here by 6:00."

Same old shit. Same old, same old. This was why mankind invented divorce, to save me from having to deal with a lifetime of shit storms just like this one, thought Adam. There had to be some way out of this particular mess.

"I'll have Chris come over at 5:30 to watch Danny until I get there."

"That'll work fine," said Adam's ex-wife, Peg. There was a momentary pause, then Peg started in again, "God, Adam, you always act like it's such a chore. You're the one who wanted the visitation rights. You're the one who demanded at least one weekend a month with your son. But when that weekend comes, you always act like it's some major imposition. What is it, Adam, you want to see your son but not if it means actually having to fit Danny into that busy schedule of yours? You can't have it both ways, Adam. No one can."

"It's March, Peg, and you know damn well how busy I get in March. I've got the Sanderling marketing presentation on Monday morning, three closings next week and tours scheduled every afternoon," complained Adam.

"Well, Adam, schedule some time for Danny now and then. He needs you a lot more than those rich assholes you love working with."

The anger was surging back into Adam's veins. That was the ironic beauty of calling Peggy, his ex. Within a few minutes he could be reliving all six of their miserable years together. All the shouting matches, the arguments and the labeling could come returning into his bloodstream in 30 seconds or less. To Adam, Peg had become the quintessential bitch.

Early on, their marriage was good. That was when Adam was still waitering. Those were the good times, the party times. It was in the early 80s. Plenty of after-hours parties, complete with an open bar and line after line of nose candy. They were young, stoned and in love.

Adam was a different person then. He lived day to day. It wasn't until Peg started listening to her biological clock that their romance started faltering. She knew that if he kept on being a waiter, and the parties kept on ending in somebody else's hot tub every Sunday morning, they would never have children. That was when Peg suggested to Adam that he might give selling real estate a try.

Why not? He knew scores of people from waiting on them at the restaurant through the years. He was young, good looking and sharp. If he was successful at it, which Peg felt certain he would be, they could buy a house on Shoreside and raise a family. Unfortunately, Peg's plan had worked far better than she ever could have anticipated. Adam took his real estate exam, passed it with flying colors, and was soon making money hand over fist.

Adam was thrilled. He and Peg started house hunting and found a small, affordable three-bedroom bungalow off Shoreside Boulevard. Peg got off the Pill and not long afterward, Danny was the newest addition to the Bartlett family. Peg, who had been working part time at a local boutique, decided to stay at home for a few years to be with her son, and Adam became increasingly engrossed in his real estate career. Life was good. Too good.

The dream didn't last very long. Adam changed. As a waiter, Adam had a devil-may-care attitude. He was fun loving and carefree. But as the money started rolling in, Adam became serious about it - serious about work and serious about the things that money could buy. He started spending too much time at the office and very little of it at home with Peg and their newborn son. As the years went by, the situation steadily worsened.

Adam was always showing property, going on listing appointments, going out to dinner with clients, arranging rentals, picking people up at the airport and scheduling inspections, repairs, fishing charters and golf outings. The commission checks kept getting larger and arrived more and more frequently, but his family time dwindled to zero.

One day, Adam told Peg that they needed to get a new car and find a larger home. They needed, as Adam put it, "to look the part." He insisted that his wealthy clients would expect him to live in a big house, drive the finest automobiles and know the first names of all the maître d's on Shoreside.

Peg didn't particularly like being an accessory to Adam's flourishing career. She was happy in the home they had. It became an issue. Peg liked living simply and inexpensively.

They started to fight. Adam would insist that she find a sitter for Danny almost every other night to allow the two of them to take Adam's wealthy clients to dinner. Peg was sick and tired of all of Adam's fat cats and wanted nothing more than to stay home with her boy. They started digging in.

The situation deteriorated. It finally got to the point where Adam, frustrated with Peg's unwillingness to join him in his move up the gilded ladder of success, simply packed and moved out.

Peg filed for divorce a month later and hired one of the best attorneys in town to represent her. The divorce was short and bitter. Luckily, Danny was too young to remember much of it, being just over two when the divorce was finalized. When it was all over, Peg was set for years to come. Adam was pulling down more than enough money to satisfy her simple needs. She kept the house on Shoreside Boulevard and he took all the toys. "Good riddance," was all Peg mumbled as he backed his BMW out of her garage for the last time.

Now it was just one weekend a month, and Peg was fine with it. No more pleasant conversations over an exquisite Merlot with some old doctor and his new-found trophy wife. No more social engagements with lawyers, developers and investment bankers. Just her son, her long-term boyfriend, Kenny, and two days a month dealing with Mr. Fucking Superstar.

Twenty minutes later the doorbell rang. Chris Taylor had arrived to baby-sit Danny.

"Hi, Chris, how are you doing?" Peg liked Chris, Adam's assistant.

"Just fine, Peg. And you?"

"Ken and I are heading to Orlando for the weekend. We'll probably take in Sea World tomorrow."

"Sounds like fun. Where's Danny?"

"He's still in his room playing some new CD on his computer. That boy could spend all of his time on that darn thing if I would let him. He's just crazy about his new computer."

Adam had bought him a new computer for Christmas; top of the line. It had everything possible on it: DVD, CD-ROM, plenty of RAM and enough hard drive to archive the Library of Congress. It was what his father did in lieu of spending any time with his kid: He showered him with gifts.

"Do you mind if I look in on him?"

"Not at all, Chris, go ahead. Ken should be here any minute. Tell Adam to bring Danny back around 5:00-ish on Sunday afternoon. He'll need to take a bath and get ready for school on Monday. And tell him not to buy Danny anything, he's got too dang much stuff already, okay?"

"Sure, Peg. Have fun in Orlando."

Chris walked to Danny's room down the long hallway. As always, the little house was as neat as a pin. She opened the door to Danny's room and peeked in. He was sitting at the computer, completely absorbed in some space ship game. Things were exploding, catching fire and vanishing into space in a constant barrage of laser flashes and cannon fire. Danny was having a ball. Chris knocked quietly between battle scenes.

"Oh, hi, Chris," said Danny as he turned around, glancing at her for a second.

"Hi, Danny, what's going on?"

"Dad got me this really cool game last month. It's called the *X-Force*

Invasion. Do you wanna play?"

"No, Danny, I'm not very good with lasers. You know, it's that girl thing. I'll just watch if you don't mind."

Chris could hear Ken arrive and both of them depart in the distance. Chris had met Ken only once and that was a year ago. He seemed like a nice guy. He worked with Mullins Electric on Shoreside. He drove a late-model black pickup, made a steady income and loved Peg with all of his heart. It was an uncomplicated relationship, completely the opposite from Bartlett's confusing agenda.

Chris looked at Danny and she liked what she saw. Danny had blue eyes, just like his father. His hair, once almost blond, had turned light brown as he grew taller. He had it cut in that funny bowl-cut style that's popular with kids today, but it looked good on him. Like his father, Danny could be quite the charmer. Danny knew when to turn on that charm and because of it his teachers adored him. Peg was doing a fine job of raising Adam's son, and she could be proud of that.

Chris sat on Danny's bed and watched him shoot down what seemed to be a never-ending onslaught of aliens and mutants. Time vanished.

At first, Chris didn't even hear the doorbell. Danny turned around and told her that he thought that he had heard the doorbell ring. Chris looked at her watch. Six fifty already! It must be Adam.

She went over to let him in. The door wasn't locked, but Adam wouldn't dare enter Peg's home without ringing the doorbell. Peg would flatten him if he did.

As Adam walked into his boy's bedroom, Danny put the computer game on pause, turned around and jumped into his father's waiting arms. Chris could feel the tears well up in her eyes as she quietly slipped out of the bedroom. God, that boy loves his dad.

Danny released his father from his long, wonderful hug and returned to the computer.

"Dad, Dad, Dad, just look at how supercool this game you bought me is. See, look, that's the aliens' gigantic mothership. If I can blow it up, I get one thousand bonus points and I can move up to the next level. Watch me, dad, watch me try and nail it."

"Well, guess what I have for you?"

"What is it, Dad?" asked Danny, stopping himself just before taking the game off pause.

Adam reached into his navy blue blazer and pulled out a small, square package. It was obvious to Danny that it held three or four CDs in it. Danny was too sharp a boy to miss that.

"More games?"

"No, Danny, these are three opera recordings. Aren't you excited?"

"You're teasin' me, right, Dad?"

"I'm teasin' you. Here, open them."

Danny grabbed the gift-wrapped package from his father's hand and tore it open faster than a piranha could devour a slice of head cheese. Inside the package were three brand-new games: one was another outer space game, complete with ugly mutants; the second was a Duke Nukum update; and the third was a program that taught typing. The typing program was quickly set aside. Adam knew Danny wouldn't use it, but he bought it to appease Peg. She didn't like the fact that he gave so much to Danny and the educational game was just to keep her off his back about it.

"Thanks, Dad, these are really cool! Can I play this one?" Danny asked, holding up the one with all the mutants and space monsters on the cover.

"Just for a few minutes, Danny, we've got tickets to a hockey game and we're going to be late as it is."

"Ahhh, come on, Dad."

"A few minutes and that's all."

"OK."

Chris poked her head in the door and said her goodbyes. Danny never even looked up. He was too busy putting his new CD in and hitting the install keys. He wanted to start blasting those ugly monsters as soon as possible.

"Thanks a million for helping me out again, Chris."

"Any time. You've got a wonderful boy there, Adam. Have a great weekend together."

As Chris headed out the door she knew that Adam wouldn't be spending any time with Vanessa this weekend. Vanessa didn't want any part of Adam's baggage. Vanessa liked fine dining, meaningless conversations and clean satin sheets. Kids, to Vanessa, were not what weekends were designed for.

Vanessa would likely spend the weekend out with the girls or cleaning her apartment. Adam would spend it with his boy. Whereas Vanessa was glad that it was only one weekend a month, Adam wished that he had time for three of the four weekends a month. But he didn't have the time, and he wouldn't make the time either. The truth being, Adam liked those clean satin sheets just as much as Vanessa did.

As they drove toward the hockey arena Adam kept looking over at his nine-year-old son. He could see that Danny was growing up. Adam found himself forgetting about Vanessa, about the Sanderling project and about his failed marriage. He could think of only one thing as they hurried toward their weekend together. It was how much he loved his boy.

570-9493
Linda Hinkle's Home Phone

Linda Hinkle couldn't sleep. It was 11:00 on a Saturday night and Linda lay tossing and turning in her empty bed. Wide awake. Monday's deadline was just over 36 hours away and the image of that little watercolor hung over her head like a well-honed guillotine. A $2.99 guillotine. It was an inevitable disaster, and Linda felt helpless.

She had made one last volley of calls earlier that evening but to no avail. Loretta Snyder had informed Linda that her clients were no longer even returning her calls. It was not going to close unless the watercolor was personally delivered to Strunk's office on Monday by 11:00 a.m. sharp. Ultimatums, a real estate agent's worst nightmare.

Linda decided to go make herself some toast and try to get to sleep. Staying up all night wasn't going to help matters any. She was exhausted and completely out of solutions. She needed some rest.

As Linda was smearing on the strawberry jam it came to her. Maybe it was the painting-like motion of covering her whole wheat toast in that dark red raspberry jam that triggered the idea. It just might work, she thought. A bit risky, but better than losing $30,000. After all, it was only a paint-by-number we're talking about. Who could really get that upset over a $3 painting? It wasn't as though we were talking about a Picasso here. Who's to know once it's closed, anyway? Who would care?

But today was Sunday, and Linda couldn't remember if Billy's craft store was open on Sunday. Was it?

She remembered seeing an ad in the local paper for Billy's craft store and began flipping through last week's issue looking for it. She finally found the ad and it said that Billy's was open Sundays, 12:00 noon 'til 5:00. Now the only remaining question was whether they still carried that particular paint-by-number: the island beach scene with the single palm tree in it.

There was no way of finding out without going over there. Linda knew that Billy wouldn't be staffing the place personally on Sunday, and the part-time weekend help barely knew how to unlock the front door. Calling would prove futile. Linda would have to head over right after noon and look for the paint-by-number kit herself. It was a long shot but it was the only thing she could think of. It was worth a try.

    She finished her toast and glass of warm milk and fell back to sleep around midnight. She dreamed of being with her husband and child somewhere in the mountains. It must have been a long time ago, since her boy was still young and her husband was still with her. It was a good dream, better than the one she now lived when she was awake. Far better.

495-0097
Adam Bartlett's Home Phone

Adam leaned over and kissed his sleeping child. It was an act of love. They had spent all Saturday having fun together and Danny had fallen asleep within minutes of hitting his bright blue pillow. The morning swim in Adam's pool, the drive into town to get to the water park, the dinner at Arby's and the movie afterward had taken their toll. Sleep was a welcome recess for a little boy after a long, super fun day with Dad.

Adam wasn't far behind. It was 11:30 and Adam was winding down. He thought of calling Vanessa but decided against it. Besides, she's probably out with the girls at some dance club, driving the rest of the men on Earth mad. Vanessa wasn't out, but Adam couldn't have known that. She was watching *Breakfast at Tiffany's*. She had seen that movie 22 times, not including this latest viewing. Her bright red hair notwithstanding, Vanessa was Audrey Hepburn.

After his tender kiss, Adam paused for a moment beside his son's bed. He looked longingly at his boy, knowing that he would have to get him back to Peggy by 5:00 Sunday afternoon or she would read him the riot act. It was fair enough, with school the next day, homework to catch up on, showers to take and dinner to wolf down. Five o'clock Sunday was too soon, but it was fair.

Adam knew that he wasn't raising his son. One weekend a month wasn't raising a child. It was more like having a little buddy you could become a child with again for 48 hours. There were trips to Disney World, snorkeling trips to the Keys, sojourns to Busch Gardens and a hundred variations on this fun-until-you-drop theme. There were plane rides, boat rides, trips to the county fair and the Ringling Brothers Barnum and Bailey Circus.

Adam wasn't stupid. He realized that his wife was the person who was raising Danny, and he knew that she was doing a damn fine job of it. Danny's grades were good and his manners were a delight. Adam knew that inasmuch as his two nights a month were a tumble in fantasy land, Peg's 28 nights with his son were all about dishes and homework. She was the one who washed his underwear, tended his scrapes and bruises and took him to the dentist. She was the one Danny needed.

It was a bitter pill to swallow, but Adam had what he wanted. The Porsche, the long-legged redhead, the Bang and Olafsen stereo system and the pipeline to the land of plenty. It all helped, but he still felt empty at times. As he looked at his son, hearing each and every tiny breath as the boy slept, the emptiness was that much larger. The space between the stars that much farther apart.

Adam turned and slowly walked out of the guest bedroom. He wanted to read through his presentation one more time before hitting the hay. Practice makes perfect. Monday morning at 10:00 sharp Adam knew that he had to be 100 percent prepared. Harris would be there listening to every detail. Tom Loggins and Elinor Braun, his sales manager, would both be in the front row. Up to a half-dozen of the investors in Sanderling would show, as well as most of the big players at Shoreside Realty. They were all invited to attend and most of them wouldn't miss it for the world. Come Monday morning, Adam was going to unveil his marketing plan for the Sanderling Condominium project.

After the presentation, there would be a host of questions, and Adam wanted to walk through most of them before the meeting. Being blind sided by a question he may have overlooked was unacceptable to him. Adam couldn't afford to have anything missing or lacking in his presentation. He was going to hard-sell this idea and the last thing he wanted was to have some well-heeled investor come up with an objection he didn't have the answer to. It wasn't Adam's style.

Adam went over to his den and sat at his computer. It was paused on one of Danny's innumerable computer games.

Do I save it or just reboot? Adam wasn't sure if Danny had saved the game or not. On the bottom right hand of the screen there was a little display that told him that Danny B. was on the 27th level. He had 84 percent health and a vast array of weapons still at his command, lasers, blasters and weapons whose names Adam didn't recognize. But it didn't say anything about whether or not the game was saved.

"Well, he can always reconquer Mars tomorrow if need be," said Adam to himself quietly.

With that Adam pressed control, alt, delete and the computer quickly rebooted. Once back to Windows, Adam clicked on Microsoft Power Point and pulled up his presentation. He read it through once more and made a few revisions along the way. No real changes, just the minor tweakings of a well-studied piece.

When he finished reading through it, he just sat there for a minute, mentally trying to punch holes in his idea. What could go wrong? What if this happened? What if that happened? But Adam couldn't find any chinks in the armor. The concept was brilliant and unless something completely unforeseen happened, it should kick off the Sanderling Condominium sales with a tremendous bang.

It was well past midnight when he shut off the computer. Adam was tired. Tomorrow he and his boy were going to the beach and then off to a go-cart track before heading home. It had been a long day and sleep would be welcome.

Adam reminded himself to phone Tom Loggins in the morning to let him know that he couldn't make the fishing trip that they had planned a few weeks ago. He had forgotten that this was his one weekend a month with Danny.

Adam knew that they'd be ticked at him but not enough to matter. They understood the situation. They were both fathers themselves, although their children had long since flown the nest.

Adam brushed his teeth and settled back into bed. He flipped on the television and watched five minutes of *Saturday Night Live* before turning the show off. It wasn't as funny as it used to be. Not since John Belushi had died. In a way, nothing was.

870-2629
Tom Loggins' Cell Phone

Loggins flipped the paper-thin cover of his cell phone closed.

"That was Bartlett. He can't make it. He's got Danny all weekend. He'll take a rain check on the fishing. That leaves just us two," said Loggins to his attorney.

"Fuck," complained Harris.

"It isn't worth taking the boat out for just the two of us, is it?" asked Loggins.

Charles Harris didn't answer. He took a long, calculated sip of his gin and tonic and waited.

"Well, is it?"

"Let's just have another drink and think about it."

Loggins knew that they'd never fire up those two turbo-diesels sitting just below the fantail if they had another highball. It was after 10:00 already and getting too late to make it offshore far enough to hit their favorite grouper holes.

They were going to drink this fishing trip away. A half-dozen shots of Tanqueray and a couple of Cuban cigars and to hell with it. By noon neither of them would give a shit. They could buy some fish fillets on the way home and tell their wives that the fishing was great. It was easier.

They had both gone on this kind of fishing trip 100 times before. A bottle of good gin, the cool winter sun rising slowly in the east, and Loggins' 45-foot Bertram Sportfish tethered securely to his private slip. The bait remained frozen solid in the freezer, the rods neatly stored. The only things they used were a half bag of ice to keep their gin and tonics nice and cold.

Loggins was sitting in the fighting chair on the rear deck and Harris was at the helm, occasionally grabbing hold of the wheel for no apparent reason. They were getting hammered. It was their favorite way to fish.

Tom Loggins looked strange in that huge fighting chair. He was too small a man to fill it. Short, with a dark complexion, he looked more like a deck hand than the owner. His mother was Greek and he had that olive-colored Mediterranean skin. Rich, curly black hair and dark eyes made Loggins look more like an old Greek fisherman or a character out of a Kazanzakas novel than a Florida developer.

He was built tough and durable, ready to stack cinder block all day in the hot sun if need be to make a deadline. Despite his 52 years and train loads of stress, there wasn't a gray hair to be found. Loggins was the kind of man who was made for rough seas.

Charles Harris, his longstanding attorney, completely looked the part. Well-dressed, balding, with glasses and a desk-job pot belly, his looks said attorney from the get-go. He was sitting there behind the wheel overlooking a huge cockpit full of instruments, displays, nobs and switches. All of them as silent as the ice in their drinks. It was only a matter of time before the conversation drifted back to business.

"So tell me, Harris, how much does Bartlett know?"

"He doesn't know shit about the Sanderling project, Tom, and he never will."

"Good. The tighter the loop, the less chance we run of getting strangled by it. Has he ever asked how we managed to finally get all the permits?"

"He hasn't, but that asshole Boyle has. Every chance he gets he breaks out with another laundry list of questions. You'd think that son of a bitch worked for the state attorney's office or something."

"What does Boyle want to know?"

"He can't figure out how our surveys came out better than anyone else's ever did."

"You didn't tell him that I own the goddamned survey company, did you?"

"Hell no."

"Did you tell him that Ralph and I went out one night and dug up two of the government's geodetic survey markers and set them down three inches lower? Boyle would understand that it makes everything in that section quite a bit higher than it was the day before. That's the quickest way in the world to get 13 acres out of the wetlands. Three inches of extra fill covering 13 acres in four hours of digging. Not bad.

"If you sit down and think about it, that's like bringing in 400 truckloads of fill in a couple of hours. Not too bad for our budget either, figuring the cost of trucking in all that fill would run $50,000 or better."

"Come on now, Tom, I'm sure Boyle would love to know that his $2 million rested on your construction manager's ability to work a hacksaw and a spade. Neither Bartlett or Boyle know anything about our changing the survey markers any more than they know a thing about the Brazilian pepper."

"Shit, I forgot about the pepper."

Harris leaned over and freshened up his drink. Harris knew all about how they had gotten the development permits. There were only three people on earth that knew: himself, Loggins and the man who actually did most of the work, Ralph Galano.

It was Ralph who filled three gunnysacks full of Brazilian pepper the week they did the final clearing for the Water's Edge Development. Loggins had told him to do it. After that, they rented an air-conditioned storage Merlot in town and placed the three gunnysacks of seed right in the middle. Cool, dry and the only thing sitting in this spacious ten-by-ten storage unit.

At the time, Ralph hadn't a clue as to why Loggins wanted all that pepper seed, but Ralph was a yes man. When Tom said jump, all Ralph said was, "How high?" About two months later Loggins called Ralph and told him what to do with the pepper seed.

Ralph had been Tom's right-hand man for 15 years. He was the only person on Earth that Tom trusted without reservation. Ralph was the kind of friend who would take a bullet for him if it came to that. Loggins never trusted Harris like he did Ralph. Loggins always felt that if Ralph did end up taking a bullet some day, that chances were pretty damn good that it would come from Harris's gun. Harris was an attorney. A damn good attorney. That said it all.

The night before Loggins was to sign the option agreement Bartlett had negotiated for the McKinzie acreage, Ralph became the Johnny Appleseed of Brazilian pepper. He drove over to the storage facility and took out all three of those sacks of seed. Each one must have weighed 100 pounds. The bright red berries inside made the brown gunnysacks look auburn.

Ralph threw the sacks into the bed of his Chevy Blazer and headed toward Shoreside and the McKinzie parcel. That night, between 10:00 p.m. and 6:00 in the morning, Ralph Galano planted hundreds of thousands of pepper seeds. The moon was half full and he worked all night despite 100 mosquito bites and a deadline of daybreak. It was difficult going, with barely enough light to stay on the beach ridges, but he kept at it until all three sacks were empty.

No one saw him. A few early morning beachcombers came by but it was easy enough to crouch over for a minute until they passed. No one came by to check on the property or to take note of all the newly planted pepper. Why would they? It wasn't developed. No one patrols 13 acres of marshy Gulf-front land.

The Brazilian pepper planting went as smoothly as the resetting of the two geodetic markers. The markers, one set on the north side of the acreage 50 years ago, and the other inland and to the south a half mile, would each have to be lowered exactly 3 inches to make it work. The long copper rods that held them in position would have to be cut and welded back together perfectly for the scheme to work.

Loggins had to have help on this one. The cement footings that held the brass benchmarks were heavy. Too heavy for one man to handle.

They did them one at a time, just a few weeks before the survey crews were sent out to do the final elevation shots. Tom had his chief surveyor do some preliminaries early on to give him a rough idea of how much they might need to lower the markers to make his ploy work. Two inches would probably have done it, but Tom added another inch just to be certain.

When the survey crew headed out to do the final cuts and calculate the average elevation, they would use the two closest U.S. Geodetic Survey markers to benchmark their instruments. Raise the markers and the surrounding land is lower than it really is. Sink them 3 inches each and the surrounding land is higher.

The trick is to sink more than one marker. If the City of Shoreside should decide to cross reference your survey, they'd use a second nearby benchmark to do so. If there was a discrepancy between the two closest benchmarks, all hell would break loose. But if they were both exactly 3 inches lower than all the rest on the island, no one would bother cross-referencing a third or a fourth. Two would suffice. It was like bringing in hundreds of truckloads of fill in two long nights with a spade, a steel tripod and a come-along. It was all they needed.

"Adam and Boyle both think it was dumb luck and mitigation," said Harris.

"You mean those 50 acres of swamp land we traded off?"

"I think it was 63 acres in all, Tom."

"Whatever. That was just for show. If we hadn't been able to pull the McKinzie land out of its lowland-wetlands designation with that survey, 1,000 acres of mitigation couldn't have helped us."

"I know that."

"So what the hell has Adam got planned for us on Monday morning?"

"Some marketing idea he's been working on. He won't tell me much about it, just that he thinks it will really put our new project on the map when we finally get CO'd come October. I think we'll like it, whatever the hell it is. You know Bartlett, that son of a bitch can sell anything. All I know is that he's making sure all the units are furnished as soon as possible. Not that we mind that request."

"Yeah, that's Adam all right."

"Can I get you another one, Tom?"

"Might as well, Charlie, we don't stand much of a chance of getting seasick this afternoon now, do we?"

"We sure as hell don't."

The sun had climbed one notch higher as Harris walked to the cockpit and took Tom's plastic glass from him. He poured another stiff one just as a 30-foot Ocean Master came into the harbor. The waves rocked Loggins' boat briefly while one of the crew on the other boat held up a big gag grouper for Tom and Charlie to admire.

"Maybe we can buy that fucking fish from him," blurted an inebriated attorney.

"Yeah, but let's have him clean it first," added Loggins.

They did end up buying some grouper fillets off that angler. At $25 a pound, there wasn't an angler on Shoreside who wouldn't have sold them a portion of their catch. The fisherman who sold the fillets to him laughed as he watched them walk down the dock. He knew it was how rich developers like Loggins liked to fish. With cash.

594-1611
Billy's Craft Store

"Billy's Craft Store, Len speaking. How can I help you?"

"Do you still carry all of those paint-by-number kits?"

"We sure do, ma'am."

"How late are you open today?" Linda asked, trying to confirm the schedule posted in the newspaper.

"We're open until 5:00 on Sundays, but if it's slow, we sometimes pull out of here around 4:30 or so," said Len.

"I'll be there in half an hour."

Linda didn't bother to say goodbye, she just put her cell phone down and continued driving across the causeway toward town. Had she taken a minute to look across the Intercoastal Waterway as she crossed the single high bridge that separated Shoreside from the mainland, Linda would have seen a pod of dolphins swimming in the morning sun, their graceful flukes always the last to disappear into the channel. She would have seen terns and gulls diving for glass minnows and pelicans flying in perfect formations toward the open waters far to the west.

But Linda looked straight ahead and drove. The beauty of the natural world surrounding her went totally unnoticed. She had pulled her Jaguar to within six feet of a minivan full of tourists who were intentionally driving slowly, watching this wondrous scene to their north. Linda Hinkle, always on an agenda, wished that they'd get their asses in gear. Nature sucked if it meant doing 20 mph.

Linda Hinkle was hot on the trail of money. She started honking. The minivan accelerated and sped off down the highway, eventually heading north to Kentucky.

It was 12:15, and it would take her another half an hour to reach Billy's Craft Store. Linda kept thinking to herself along the way, "Oh, I hope they still carry that watercolor. I remember seeing stacks of them there two years ago when I went to get some poster board for my open houses. An entire aisle dedicated to paint-by-number watercolors. Who in the world has time for such a stupid hobby?"

Billy's Craft Store was huge. It was located between a retirement center on one side and the largest mobile home park in the county on the other. Wedged between thousands of Florida retirees like a holy Mecca of needlepoint, wood-carving tools, crochet hooks, colored beads and jigsaw puzzles. Every Wednesday morning Billy offered ten percent off for anyone over 60 years of age. There wasn't a soul under 60 years of age within a square mile of his craft store. The aisles would be filled to overflowing with little old ladies buying brightly colored yarn and feeble old men using walkers picking up balsa wood and model airplane glue.

It was like a geriatric craft feeding frenzy. Everyone moved at a steady, glacial pace. Billy's Craft Store was a gold mine. An ancient, venerable gold mine.

There was only one car in the parking lot when Linda arrived. All of the old folks were having cookies and coffee after church or doing those slow-motion aerobics in one of the local pools. They were all waiting for Wednesday.

Linda walked in and headed straight to Lenny. He was idly reading the Sunday paper at the cash register.

"Which aisle has all the paint-by-numbers in it?"

"You must be the gal who called a while back, ain't you?"

"Yes I am, now could you please tell me which aisle holds your paint-by-numbers?"

"Aisle five, just over there to your right."

What a bitch, thought Lenny to himself as Linda's high heels clicked their way along the cement floor. Linda found aisle five and started praying to herself as she meticulously checked each and every paint-by-number on the shelves.

God, there must be 500 different sets in here.

Linda's estimate was low. There were 647 to be exact. Paint-by-numbers was a hot-selling item at the retirement center. The center's activity director was getting a ten percent kickback from Billy under the table. Every two weeks her class had to complete a new painting. Billy was nothing if he wasn't sharp.

After 20 minutes of meticulous searching, Linda spotted it. There were three of them left. Linda reached in her purse and took out one of her photos of the original and double-checked the kit to be certain. It was the identical paint-by-number set as the one in the Larsons' condominium. Same ten colors, same size and the same insipid palm tree. Only the price had changed. They were now $7.95 each. Inflation.

Linda grabbed all three and headed to the checkout counter and Lenny.

"Going to be doing some painting, I see," said Lenny. He was giving Linda one more shot at idle conversation. His specialty.

"They're for my niece." Linda lied, not wanting to spend any more time than she had to at Billy's.

"Cash or charge."

Linda's legal mind snapped into action. I should pay cash. I don't want to leave any kind of a paper trail should my plan go awry. Credit cards leave trails. Big trails.

"This will be cash."

Lenny scanned the three identical paint-by-numbers and didn't say a word. He hoped that her niece wasn't as bitchy as this gal. He did note that it was odd for her to be buying three identical sets. Maybe her niece was retarded?

Lenny put all three of them in a large plastic bag and watched as Linda turned tail and headed out the door. No time for a simple thank you, no time to even say goodbye. Bitch, reiterated Lenny to himself as he settled back and dove into the sports section.

Linda pushed the remote on her key chain and the Jaguar unlocked itself. She put the paint-by-numbers on the seat next to her and headed to her apartment on Shoreside. She kept trying to remember the last time that she had held a paintbrush in her hand.

It must have been when we painted the porch deck, she reflected. Albert was still in high school. That would make it nine, no, maybe ten years ago. But that was a big brush and there was only one color. Deck gray, we painted the whole porch deck gray. The last time I held an artist's paintbrush in my hand was in high school. Wow, that was a while ago.

Just then she remembered that she had forgotten to buy paintbrushes. I hope these sets come with paintbrushes included, she prayed. They did.

When Linda got home she immediately cleared the kitchen table and covered it in newspaper. She put on a pot of coffee and opened the first paint-by-number set. Her intentions were simple. Linda Hinkle was going to paint a forgery.

Once the copy, as she liked to refer to it, was completed, Linda would then take the original off the wall of the condo and deliver it to Mr. Strunk's office tomorrow. Replacing it with an exact duplicate. She would tell her clients, who were closing by mail, that the Larsons had finally given in and the watercolor was theirs to keep. No one would ever know and no one would be harmed by her little deception. It was the only way out from a box canyon full of gun-slinging lawyers.

There was only one problem, and that was replicating the signature and unmistakably bad painting techniques of a five-year-old. That was not going to be easy. Luckily, her purchasers had seen the actual painting only once. They hadn't even taken that good a look at it. The only picture they had of the watercolor was the tiny photograph Linda had taken for Dr. Asp's attorneys. The photo was very small, and because of it, all the details were lost. Linda felt certain that she could pull it off.

It was 2:30 by the time she dipped her brush in the lukewarm water and brought it nervously to the numbered paint board. Her hand was shaking like a maple leaf in a tornado. She was on the verge of panic as the light green paint touched down on the clearly outlined palm frond.

The next frond went on easier. Likewise the next after that. Ten minutes later Linda found she was enjoying herself.

This isn't half bad. It's sort of relaxing, actually, she kept thinking to herself as her perfect strokes carefully followed each and every well-marked contour and number on the painting. It's kind of fun in a way.

An hour later it was completed. She was proud of herself. The lines were crisp and clear and the play of sunlight and shadow came out beautifully. She reached into her purse to hold her photo of the original beside it to compare the two.

Shit! It's too damn good. My painting's too damn good.

Linda looked closely at the photo and then at her work. The five-year-old had made the trunk of the palm tree too fat, the leaves were far more blotchy and the sand looked like it had more dark brown in it. Linda's painting looked exactly like the one on the cover of the box. The girl's painting, by comparison, looked pathetic. As Linda carefully studied the child's sloppy work, she noted that Mrs. Larson's daughter had signed the piece in the lower right-hand corner. It was signed R.L. for Rose Larson.

I might as well use this one to practice Rose's signature. I can't very well put this in the guest bedroom. Mrs. Asp will certainly recognize it as a forgery. It's too well done to have been painted by a little girl.

Before she decided to open the second box and try her hand at it again, Linda took a break. It was nearing 6:00 and she needed to take a breather and grab dinner. She had already skipped lunch and she was famished.

Linda fixed herself a Lean Cuisine and poured herself a tall glass of Merlot. As she sat in the living room, watching television and enjoying her dinner, she felt that the second painting would go a lot smoother. She wouldn't need to be so careful this time.

As 7:00 rolled around, Linda started in on her second attempt at the forgery. For a while, it did go better. She wandered off the lines quite a bit and kept the photo of the original right beside her fraud, carefully smudging and smearing each and every stroke. She decided to have a second glass of Merlot to help take the edge off.

By 9:00 she was finished. It looked much better. It was done in the same sloppy style and the sand was way darker. That little girl must have mixed some of the dark green in with the light brown to come up with that color. It's an interesting mix. With the interplay of light and shadow I think it works better than the original #6 they've got stamped all over the sand. Much better.

Linda had finished off her second glass of wine and was working on her third when she mixed the last drop of dark green and steadied her hand for the final initials. That's when it happened.

While reaching over to paint Rose Larson's initials, Linda accidently tipped her glass of wine over. Before she could lift the painting out of harm's way, the blood-red Merlot hit the upper right hand corner of her painting. The effect was both interesting and disastrous. It added an element of surrealism to the painting. The Merlot immediately reactivated the watercolors and blended quickly with the greens, browns and sky blues. It looked as if the sun had been shot. The painting was ruined beyond any hope of redemption.

Linda felt like crying. It was almost 11:00 p.m. Linda was now quite tired, quite drunk and very concerned. Billy's had closed six hours ago. Even if she broke in, there weren't any of these particular paint-by-numbers left. No one else in town carried them. It had come down to one last canvas. If she botched the next one, it became a $30,000-plus mistake. A very expensive paint-by-number.

Linda decided to take a breather and finish off her bottle of Merlot. She was throwing caution to the wind. It was all or nothing at this point. It was very uncharacteristic of her. It was the tried and true combination of lack of sleep and too much wine that allowed her to unwrap that last paint-by-number. It was midnight as her right hand went to make that first imperfect stroke.

Passion had overcome her. Van Gogh himself would have been proud of Linda Hinkle. It was the artist in her finally coming out. The drunken artist.

579-2327
Mark Thurston's Home Phone

Betsy slipped Mark's arm from behind her head and quietly got out of bed. It was late. It was sometime after midnight, but the exact time didn't matter. It was just late.

Their weekend had gone as planned. Friday night was spent at home, watching a video starring Julia Roberts and Hugh Grant. It took place in England and it was sweet. They spent the night at Betsy's place.

Saturday night the two of them had gone to dinner and then to listen to some live music at the bowling alley. Dinner was delicious. Betsy loved Chinese food and no one puts out a better sweet and sour chicken than does the Golden Dragon. That and their wonton soup. The word delicious doesn't do it justice.

Mark would have preferred a T-bone over at the Outback Steakhouse but he never mentioned that to Betsy. Mark would have gladly eaten Mongolian fondue just to be with Betsy. That's the kind of guy he was, the kind that likes to see his girlfriend happy.

After dinner they both hopped into Mark's new Saturn and drove over to the Stadium Lanes Bowling Alley to hear the first set of "The Brown Truckers." When they arrived, a bit before 9:00, the band hadn't yet started. Two of the guys in the band came over and had a quick drink before playing. The lounge was pretty empty but the two guys Mark knew from work kept insisting that it would get busier later. They seemed a little embarrassed by the lack of a crowd.

Betsy didn't mind. Her vodka Seven tasted just fine and she looked forward to hearing the band. Mark had told her that they were pretty good.

They finally started playing around 9:30 and, given the fact that all five of the guys had day jobs, they were pretty good, reflected Betsy. Most of the songs sounded more or less like the records they had copied them off of. Most but not all. They could have used a better lead singer, was Betsy's final criticism of the band. She would never say anything about it to Mark though, fearing it might get back to one of his friends at UPS. Betsy was like that, sweet beyond measure.

By 11:00 the crowds that Mark's friends were looking forward to still hadn't shuffled into the cocktail lounge at The Stadium Lanes, but half the tables were taken. The bowling league play had ended around 10:30 and that helped to make the joint seem a little less empty. Betsy and Mark slipped out during the first song of the second set and drove home. It was a dark and chilly night, not atypical for March in south Florida.

When they got home, they both undressed, giggling a little as they did and slipped into Mark's waterbed. They knew what each other's plans were, but their romance was still young and awkward at times, like young lovers tend to be.

Mark owned a small house near the edge of town. It was situated on an acre of land, nestled quietly amidst an old stand of slash pine and saw palmettos. He had bought the house a few years ago, having grown tired of the singles scene at the various apartment complexes he had lived in over the years. It was a modest house. Modest, but charming.

Although it was far from the floodplain of the coast, the people who originally built the house in 1976 had decided to build it on pilings. They had wrapped the place in a small, elevated porch that ran completely around the two-bedroom home. Betsy liked having all the porches surrounding the house. She felt that it gave it more of a country feel.

They awoke late on Sunday morning and packed a picnic lunch for their boating excursion that afternoon in the sound. Island hopping and drinking beer all afternoon with some old friends of Mark's made for a fitting ending to a glorious weekend. Mark and Betsy had hardly spoken a word to each other throughout; Mark not wanting to put any extra wear and tear on Betsy's exhausted vocal cords. Whenever they did talk, Mark tried to keep their conversations to whispers. Young lovers like to whisper.

On Sunday night, although Betsy knew it meant getting up at 6:00 a.m. and getting over to her apartment before work, she decided to stay at Mark's place again. They had their leftover Chinese from the night before for dinner and went to bed just after 9:00. It had been a fabulous weekend and they were both ready to snuggle and cuddle a while before going to sleep.

After making love and falling asleep in each other's arms, Betsy woke unexpectedly. She was thirsty and decided to head into the kitchen for a glass of water. It was probably from all that salt spray from the boat ride, she thought, as she put on her favorite robe and walked as quietly as possible into Mark's small kitchen. Being on the ocean always makes me thirsty, she remembered.

Betsy poured herself a glass of water and took a long, refreshing drink. It was cold. Mark's tap water, because it was on a well, had that funny taste to it. You got used to it after a while. But it was always cold, and that made the funny taste seem palatable.

Before climbing into bed, Betsy decided to sneak out the kitchen door for a minute and take in a breath of fresh air. As she slipped outside into the chilly night air she was amazed at how gorgeous an evening it was. The moon was only a sliver of itself and the stars were thrown across the sky like a paint splatter from the brush of God.

Below her, a thick ground fog had wrapped itself around the trunks of the slash pines and mahoganies, covering all but the very tops of the numerous thickets of saw palmettos that encircled the house. Crickets and the cries of nighthawks filled the air, mingling with the songs of tree frogs and noises unknown to Betsy. A winter's night in southern Florida, beautiful and serene.

For the longest while Betsy just stood there. She looked up to that spray of stars a million light years away and thanked God for sending Mark to her. She thanked God for mistakenly sending him into her tiny back office with his UPS package for Jason R. Randazzle and she thanked God for Mark's sweet, tender disposition. It was a lover's prayer that Betsy prayed amidst the slash pines and the solitude. A prayer from a girl who had fallen madly in love with a man who seemed to be falling in love with her.

Everything she had ever wanted was now laid out before her. Maybe we'll be married someday, she added to her prayer. "Maybe we'll have children together," she whispered to God, hoping that he was up there somewhere, listening.

After a while, she noticed that she was starting to get goose bumps. She was naked beneath her thin robe and the night air was damp and penetrating. It was time to go back inside.

As she reopened the bedroom door, Betsy saw that Mark hadn't moved. He worked hard all week and when he slept, he slept hard. Nothing woke Mark once he was asleep.

Betsy looked at him and wanted to pinch herself. Anything to be sure that it wasn't a dream. That this was real. That the weekend had been perfect. That her sweet and sour chicken was cooked to perfection, that "The Brown Truckers" were okay, but not all that great, and that the man of her dreams was snoring ten feet in front of her. Snoring sort of loudly, Betsy noted. Not that it really bothered her.

It wasn't a dream, and Betsy smiled again because of it. It was real.

Betsy climbed quietly into bed and fell fast asleep. Her lover sleeping beside her. In the distance, a great horned owl hooted somewhere deep in the forest beyond. The ground fog settled and the constellations made their slow parade across an unwatched heaven. Life is beautiful.

570-9493
Linda Hinkle's Silent Home Phone

Linda's home phone was utterly silent. No one ever phoned anyone after midnight unless they were drunk or delivering bad news. When a telephone rings after midnight it's when you find out that your mother has died, or that your sister was in a terrible accident. Either that, or some old, drunken friend calling from the other end of America. Calling to reminisce. The vodka doing both the dialing and the talking.

But neither event happened. The phone just sat there, as silent as the rest of the furniture in the house. No one was going to interrupt Linda as she made her midnight run at her 3.5 percent deception. No one at all.

Ironically, she was no longer nervous or concerned. She was half in the bag. Make that two halves in the bag. The bottle of Merlot was now in her recycling bin, the last of its precious fluids in a glass on the kitchen counter. To take a sip she would have to walk away from the table, making sure that its deep red hues were a safe distance away from the last remaining paint-by-number kit. The previous painting, now that the wine had permeated most of the poster board, looked more like abstract expressionism than paint-by-number. It was actually quite pretty looking she thought, almost pulling it out of the garbage can when she set the bottle of Merlot next to it. The colors reminded her of early Chagall.

Linda had put on a Johnny Mathis tape and changed into her nightgown. It was a scene worth noting; this drunken, middle-aged woman listening to *Misty* at 1:00 in the morning as she intentionally mis-painted a ten-color paint-by-number. This was a bizarre facet of real estate never mentioned in Jennifer Willow's real estate courses. It was never in any of Shoreside Realty's policy manuals or job descriptions either for that matter.

Painting forgeries in the middle of the night, bombed on a choice Merlot. No, this was an advanced, postgraduate real estate course. It was right up there with slipping in an occasional missed set of initials, postdating some checks now and again and hedging about when the second deposit actually arrived.

This was real world real estate. Buying a gallon of KILS paint to cover the leaky roof stains on the ceiling, setting off a dozen cans of Raid just before the showing to keep the fleas temporarily at bay, or turning off the main water line outside to keep all the toilets from running while you presented your "well cared for home." Real world real estate.

Linda Hinkle, even in her wine-induced stupor, knew it and loved it. Postgraduate real estate, complete with Johnny Mathis and his lovely, liquid voice.

As she worked, Linda kept glancing back and forth between her painting and the small snapshot beside it and saw that it was going well. The colors were identical, the liquor induced sloppiness in her technique mimicked that of a five-year-old like nothing else could have. It was better than a perfect fake, it was fast becoming an identical match. Linda was ecstatic.

It was 3:00 in the morning as she lifted her brush from the work. The initials came out marvelously. The copy was every bit as bad as the original. All that was left was for her to try to get some rest, head out to make the switch at the condominium by 10:00 and deliver the original to Mr. Strunk's office by 11:00 a.m. sharp. It was the perfect solution to an imperfect problem. It had to work.

✦

When Linda's alarm went off at 8:30 the next morning, she wanted to die. Her eyes were red and swollen from staring for hours on end at that absurd beach scene, and her head felt as if it had been filled with some of that same auburn-colored sand that made up the #3 on her masterpiece. Heavy, wet sand that weighed in at 95 pounds.

She was exhausted, still somewhat drunk and very, very hung over. Not that it mattered. She had taken the plot this far and there was no turning back now. Her dogged determination kicked in and, whatever her condition, even if it had involved arterial bleeding or multiple stab wounds to the chest, Linda Hinkle was going to be standing in front of Mr. Strunk at 11:05 this morning handing him the original watercolor. This condo was going to close this afternoon unless Linda was hit by a train between now and then. A big train. One carrying iron ore.

Linda got up and walked into her bathroom. She looked in the mirror and just as quickly, she looked away. There was a stranger in the mirror, someone who had broken into her house last night, drunk an entire bottle of her fine California merlot and then slept in her bed. She didn't look at all like the woman in the mirror. She had better check her jewelry. No doubt this vagrant had stolen most of it.

Linda didn't look in the mirror again until she climbed out of the shower and had a few cups of coffee to neutralize the residuals of the wine. Both remedies helped. At least now she was vaguely familiar with the face that stared back at her. A double hit of Visine, cake makeup, lipstick, perfume and a host of other cosmetics followed. By 9:15 she was covered in so much makeup that it could have made the bride of Dracula look like Cindy Crawford. If Linda Hinkle were to accidently sneeze, no doubt half of her face would have blown off in the process.

She got into her Lincoln Town Car and headed to the condo. She had purchased a cheap matching frame for the watercolor at Eckerd's Drug Store. That ran her another $3.95. All totaled, including the bottle of Merlot, Linda figured that she had just under $30 into the forgery plus ten hours of her time. It was worth it. If she pulled it off, it was worth over 30 grand in commission monies to her. A good return by any standard. All this for a watercolor painted decades ago by a five-year-old.

While driving down Gulfshore Drive, Linda thought of her ex-husband. Maybe Gary was right. Maybe Frank does ask too much of me. I wonder where Gary is these days. The last time I got a postcard from him he was working with a logging firm in Oregon. I miss him. I never think about it, but I miss him.

Linda pulled in front of Osprey Landings and parked in one of the guest parking slots. She checked her purse to make certain that she had the key and the alarm code with her. She did.

The ride up the elevator to the top floor seemed painfully slow. She was glad that no one else had seen her thus far. Linda had been careful to hide the 10-by-12 watercolor in an oversized folder just in case. She wanted to slip in and out of the vacant unit as unnoticed as possible. It was important not to leave any blood trails for the legal hounds to follow should something go wrong later. Stealth was important.

She punched in the alarm code after opening the front door and headed straight to the guest bedroom where the original painting hung. Taking it off the wall carefully, she brought the original and her forgery over to the dining room table to set them both down side by side.

As they both lay there, almost touching each other, Linda was astonished to see how accurate her duplicate was. The copy was slightly different from the original but only in that some of the smudges were in different places. The colors were the same, the frame the same and the sloppy, poorly executed techniques identical. Apparently, a drunk and a five-year-old have the same level of talent. I should say lack of talent, thought Linda to herself.

Just then her cell phone rang. She had left it in her purse next to the kitchen sink in the other room, so she had to quickly run out of the dining room and dig it from her overstuffed handbag.

"Hello, Linda Hinkle speaking."

"Linda, this is Elinor. Are you planning to attend Adam's presentation this morning at 10:00?"

"No, Elinor, something's come up and I just can't make it."

Linda looked at her watch. It was 9:45. Adam's presentation on the marketing plan for Sanderling was beginning in 15 minutes. It would be over by

11:00. Linda had to be at Strunk's office by 11:00. She wanted desperately to make the presentation but knew that she couldn't possibly fit it into her schedule. The closing of 801 Osprey Towers this afternoon took a $33,988.50 priority. She could read about Adam's proposal in the office memo later that afternoon.

"Oh, that's too bad, Linda. Adam really wanted you there, especially since you sold so many of his Water's Edge properties a few years ago. Why can't you make it?"

Shit. That's what Linda hated about Elinor. She always had to go the extra mile. Ask the extra question. Interrogate the prisoner to the breaking point.

"Oh, nothing really. I just have to do a quick walk through this morning for Dr. and Mrs. Asp at their new penthouse in Osprey Towers. We're scheduled to close this afternoon."

"Did you finally get that little painting thing resolved?"

"I think so."

"Well, Linda, we'll miss you this morning. Everyone else will be here but you. But you can get brought up to speed by reading the memo we'll have out this afternoon about the marketing plan. Then we can start taking reservations for the units. Be sure to look for it."

"I will, Elinor. I promise."

"Bye for now."

"Goodbye."

Linda folded her little cell phone shut and gave a sigh of relief. She was damn glad Elinor didn't pry any further into how she had resolved the so-called "little painting thing." She didn't want to answer any more questions than she had to at this point. It was best to let sleeping dogs lie. No one would ever know about the forgery. The buyers would have their cute watercolor hanging in the guest bedroom and the sellers would have their daughter's paint-by-number hanging up north somewhere within the week. No one would ever know.

Linda went back to the dining room table after taking a drink of water. Her mouth was thick and dry from the hangover. She felt terrible. As she walked toward the two paintings a terrible feeling overcame her. She looked at the watercolors and her stomach instantly tied itself in a knot. Panic followed.

Good God, which is which? She couldn't remember if the original was on the right or the left. I'll check the photograph. She ran over to her purse to take out the photograph she had of the original. She found it and immediately took it into the living room with her. She squinted to look at it, comparing it carefully to each of the full-sized paintings on the table.

It was useless. The photo was just too small. The tiny smudge differences were too minuscule to give her any guidance whatsoever. One of the two paintings was the original, and one was a fake, a fraud, an imposter. She realized that she was now caught in a snare of her own design. It was a craps shoot, a 50/50 guessing game as to which painting was hers and which was little Rose Larson's.

Linda stood over the dining room table for the longest time, trying to think of some tiny detail that could tip her off, help her choose the original. But it was to no avail. She had gotten too drunk last night to remember much of anything and ironically, she was now too hung over to care.

She reached down, picked up the painting on the right and brought it into the bedroom and hung it there. What difference does it make? Linda thought to herself as she walked back to put the other one in her oversized folder. They both stink.

She set the alarm upon leaving, took the elevator back downstairs and got into her Jag. It would take her half an hour or more to get to Strunk's office in town. There might be just enough time to stop by the 7-11 for a booster shot of java.

By 3:00 this afternoon the property would be sold and closed and the whole nightmare would be over. Everyone would walk away happy. Linda was glad it was coming to an end. All's well that ends well, she remembered as she drove across the two-mile causeway toward town. All's well that ends well.

570-9898 Ext. 30
The Conference Room

Adam flipped down the visor mirror in his BMW and double-checked his hair. It looked good. He smiled and his teeth looked perfect. He had taken an extra 15 minutes this morning getting ready for his presentation. Everything had to be perfect. His dark red tie had to be tied just right, his blue sports coat lint free and his penny loafers polished to the letter. It was his moment in the sun, and Adam didn't want anything to take the shine off.

He pulled up to his reserved parking spot, grabbed his leather briefcase and headed into the office. It was exactly 9:30. His presentation was scheduled for 10:00 a.m. sharp in the large conference room just off the front lobby. If everyone showed, there would be 20 people present to see Adam unveil his marketing proposal for Sanderling. Adam couldn't wait.

"Good morning, Chris," said Adam as he headed toward his office.

"Big day, Adam," she replied.

"Damn big. Could you get me some coffee?"

"Cream this morning, or black?"

"Black, Chris."

Adam closed the door and sat behind his mahogany desk. He flipped open his briefcase and took out his notes. He was excited. He had been working on his marketing plan for two months and this morning was to be its unveiling. Two months' worth of phone calls, lunches, appointments and estimates were coming down to a 40-minute Monday morning presentation. Adam was thrilled.

He loved moments like this. He lived and died for them. It was when he could stand there and be the king. Everyone's attention would be focused on Bartlett. Everyone would be anxiously awaiting his ideas. His last big marketing presentation was four years ago, for the kickoff of the Water's Edge development.

That subdivision sold out in record time, in large part due to Adam's fantastic concepts: the full-color brochure, the creative aerial shots and the fabulous copy. Sanderling would be even better.

Chris brought in the coffee and suggested to Adam that he should get out to the lobby in the next few minutes. There were some investors already showing up and it was a perfect opportunity to mingle. Adam agreed.

"Well Chris, it's 'SHOWTIME!' "

"Good luck, Adam. You look sharp."

"Thanks, Chris. You'll be taking notes this morning, right?"

"Absolutely, Adam."

Adam grabbed his presentation copy and his coffee and headed down the hallway toward the lobby. He was floating on an extraordinary high of adrenaline and caffeine. He said good morning to Kelly and grabbed half a Danish. Elinor had picked up a fancy assortment of donuts and fresh fruit for the meeting. She knew that the Sanderling Condominium project meant 64 sales to Shoreside Realty, not to mention years and years of resales. Everything had to be done right. And it was.

Charles Harris, Tom Loggins and his project manager, Ralph Galano, all walked in together. Sam Goodlet, Barbara Silberman and Jason Randazzle were already there. Linda Hinkle was supposed to attend but she was on her way to Strunk's office with a paint-by-number watercolor. Vince Cricket wasn't out of bed yet. No one had asked Vince to attend anyway. No one had asked Jennifer Willow to attend either. It was a major players only presentation. Rookies and washouts could read the memo later that afternoon.

The investors were slowly filtering in. Mr. Levinson had arrived, but only one of the Sander brothers, Gregory, was there. Dr. Bethel was in the lobby, enjoying an orange juice and a glazed donut. Mr. Turlington, both Mr. and Mrs. Harding and a few of the others were there for the presentation as well. Eugene Boyle was the last investor to arrive. He didn't look good. Perhaps last night's bottle of single malt Scotch hadn't agreed with him. His wife, Maggie, had stayed home, not that anyone would miss her.

People were chatting, patting Adam on the back and adding their own opinions and ideas to how they would kick off the Sanderling Condominium sales. The lobby soon filled to near capacity. As the conversation crescendoed to an unintelligible din, Elinor Braun clapped her large hands several times and instantly drew everyone's attention.

"It's 10 after 10:00, and I really think it's time we all find a seat in the conference room. We promised all of you in the invitation that we would be out of here before 11:00, and you know how I am about schedules."

They all knew how Elinor was about schedules. Ruthless. Just like she was about everything else at Shoreside Realty. The "Form Nazi," the schedule fanatic, it was all the same to Elinor. Exactitude gone awry.

Everyone made his or her way into the large conference room just off the lobby. Elinor had told Kelly to bring in some extra chairs for the presentation but they were still one chair shy after everyone was seated. Elinor didn't have to say a thing. By the time she had noted that they needed an extra chair, Kelly was standing there holding one just outside the double doors into the conference room. There were 21 people sitting around a large Formica table when Elinor stood.

"Good morning, everyone. It's so nice to see such a great turnout for this morning's presentation. I know that Adam has been working on these kickoff plans for the Sanderling project for quite some time now and that he has to be excited about finally unveiling his plans to you. I would appreciate it if you could all turn off your pagers and cell phones for a few minutes while Adam tells us what he has in mind. And now, here is Mr. Adam Bartlett, Shoreside Realty's top producer for the last three years' running!"

A small round of applause followed as Adam stood. After clapping briefly, half a dozen people reached around in their pockets and belt loops to disarm their digital pagers and cell phones. It wasn't out of respect for Adam that they did so. They just didn't dare disobey a direct request from Elinor. Life was too short for that. Way too short.

Adam walked toward the far end of the table. He didn't have any charts or photographs with him like he had on the Water's Edge development project five years ago. He felt that they weren't needed. He had taken a totally fresh approach to the Sanderling project, one that no one had ever used before.

As he stood there, in front of this room full of millionaires, lawyers, developers and the best salespeople in the firm, Adam felt exhilarated. The black coffee was rushing through his veins as his pulse raced and his confidence intensified. For the moment, Adam Bartlett was the man who would be king.

He was standing there, before his loyal followers in all of his glory. Shoreside Island was his fiefdom, these then were his humble subjects, and this was his decree. He began his presentation.

"Good morning, everyone. It's great for all of us to be finally gathered here together this morning. After years of surveys, permits and waiting, it's a wonderful feeling to be getting to the point where we can ultimately talk about the Sanderling project in terms of sales, rather than in terms of whether or not we'll ever see those pilings being driven into the sand.

"I had the opportunity to make it to the site yesterday to see how things are coming along and, Ralph Galano here," Adam pointed over to Ralph, "gave me the royal tour. The project looks fantastic. The pilings are in for all seven buildings. Six of the buildings will hold ten units each and the seventh will have only four units in it. One of those units will be retained as an onsite manager's quarters and the other three will also be available for purchase at a discounted price. Those four units are the only ones that have only a limited view of the Gulf. All the rest have outstanding views.

"Four of the buildings under construction are almost roughed in, and the construction schedule, thanks in no small part to Mr. Tom Loggins here, is once again ahead of schedule."

Adam took a sip of water and continued reading from his notes. All eyes were upon him. It was up to Bartlett to sell the Sanderling project from this point on.

As soon as the remaining 32 units that were not pre-sold to the investor group were CO'd, they would be listed with Adam and Shoreside Realty. This coming winter season would make or break the project. If sales were steady and brisk, the investors could start turning their units over as early as next spring. If sales were slow? Well, Adam didn't even consider it. He continued.

"At the present pace, we should have everything but the small four-plex building in the rear completed by late October of this year. The landscaping might still need some work, and the remainder of the Brazilian pepper and the mangrove trees might need to be removed, but for all intents and purposes, the Sanderling Condominiums will be ready to sell.

"As all of you know, the Sanderling project is probably one of the last condominium projects on Shoreside that will still allow weekly rentals. That's one of the reasons we have kept these units as two-bedroom, two-bath apartments. If these were monthly rentals, chances are that the density would have been lowered and the size of the apartments increased dramatically. The cost per unit would have gone up in the process.

"But that isn't the case with Sanderling. We have weekly rentals written into the development permit and I felt that this feature should be the focus of our marketing efforts. Since the day isn't that far off when the city of Shoreside will no longer allow weekly rental complexes to be constructed on this island, I felt that this unique feature should be the focus of our marketing efforts."

Tom Loggins liked what he was hearing thus far. He and Harris had gone to great lengths to keep the weekly rental provision in his development permit. He had to scale the number of tennis courts back from four to two to cut back on his developed area. He was required to berm and swale the entire project as part of an extensive drainage plan. The two smaller pools originally slated to be a part of the site plan became one large one instead. All of this in an effort to keep Sanderling weekly instead of monthly.

Weekly meant that buyers could get a return on their investment. It increased the potential market dramatically from the high-end luxury condominium market. It meant more buyers and a quicker turnover. Tom liked where Adam was going thus far. He liked it a lot.

"With this in mind, I thought that what we needed to kick off Sanderling Condominiums was something totally distinctive, totally fresh. For Sanderling, color brochures and glitzy artist's renderings were never going to capture the charm and the natural splendor of this project. We needed something new, something exciting."

Adam was on a roll. He was completely intoxicated with his own ego and it was beginning to wear on Elinor Braun. She disliked Adam Bartlett. She loved Adam for all the business he and his crew brought into Shoreside Realty but she thought he was just another golden boy on his way to the fall. Another Vince Cricket before he sealed himself into an oversized bottle of vodka. She had seen too many of these superstars climb to the top of their ladder of success only to nosedive off it in the end. Hitting the concrete below with a familiar splat. She wished that Adam would just get on with it.

Adam's soliloquy continued. "For Sanderling, we are going to make everyone an intrinsic part of the program. We're going to have a grand opening unlike anything ever done before on Shoreside.

"Over the past few months I have been having meetings with all of the managers of every rental company on Shoreside. Naturally, I started with our very own Shoreside Executive Rental Company and the present manager, Colleen Lawton. But I didn't stop there. I met with Margaret Hyde over at Beachwalk Realty, Stacy Sheen from Ocean Crest Realty and a number of other managers from the smaller firms on Shoreside. What they have in common is that they control nearly 90 percent of the weekly rentals here on Shoreside.

"But who makes these reservations? Who ends up selling Shoreside Island over a trip to the Bahamas, or Martinique for that matter? The reservationists do. The girls and guys who answer the telephone day in and day out. They are the ones who make the difference in the end. They book the winter months and develop their rental relationships with their customers over the years. We want Sanderling Condominiums to have the best rental track record on Shoreside.

"So how can we make this happen? I asked myself. We have to sell it to the folks who sell it to their clients: the reservationists!"

Loggins was thrilled. Bartlett was once again showing his stuff. Great looks, smooth presentations and a veneer of cool beyond reproach. God, that man could sell shit to a sewage plant, thought Loggins as he listened to him. It was a talent that came totally naturally to Adam. Sanderling was a given, reflected Loggins as he sat there taking in Adam's presentation. A done deal, Loggins mused. I had better start looking for some new acreage to develop.

"Because of that, Tom Loggins Development, Inc. has agreed to let me offer the top 32 reservationists on Shoreside an invitation to come out to Sanderling Condominiums on opening weekend and stay in the units for two wonderful evenings, free of charge, enjoying all the many amenities that the project has to offer. We have contacted the managers and they will announce all the lucky recipients of this free weekend at Sanderling this afternoon in their respective offices.

"Since only 32 of the units have been sold to date, most of them to many of these fine people I see before me here today," Adam was always good for a well-placed stroking, "...we can make this offer only to the top reservationists. If there are any cancellations, some of the units may become available to other members of Shoreside's staff. The purpose is to get this project kicked off with a bang.

"Every apartment will be beautifully furnished. The views will be outstanding, the pool and tennis courts in perfect condition and the entire tab will be covered by myself and Tom Loggins Development, Inc. Included in the package will be a free barbeque party Saturday afternoon for everyone staying that night at the project. We'll have an open bar at the party and, most importantly, Sanderling Condominiums, the finest Gulf-front development ever built on Shoreside, will be on every reservationists' lips first thing the following Monday morning.

"The plan is to have the island reservationists completely sold on Sanderling. Once they start booking the 32 pre-sold units for the upcoming winter rental season, sales will be as easy as cake. Of course we will have the usual brochures, photos and marketing tools, but these will only be the icing on that cake. Sanderling Condominiums, my friends and co-workers, is a natural. Let's get out there and start selling!"

Their was a round of applause. Loggins and Harris glanced over at each other and nodded. If Bartlett was a king, there could be no doubt who had helped him ascend to the throne. Who had hand fed him project after project, client after client and commission after commission. Loggins and his attorney had. They were the two Rasputins behind his climb to power; they were the king makers.

Adam took another sip of water and opened the floor to comments or questions. Several of the investors asked if it would cost them any additional out-of-pocket expenses. Adam explained that the actual closings would occur the following week and that TLD, Inc. was going to cover any and all expenses. The only thing that the investors needed to do prior to the kickoff was to purchase their furniture package from Citation Home Furnishings by mid-October.

They had all been contacted by the decorators from Citation and knew that the package would run them each an additional $37,000 per unit prior to closing.

Loggins owned 35 percent of Citation Home Furnishings through a holding company that he and Harris had set up nine years ago. Harris owned 20 percent. No one, except Ralph Galano and their personal accountants, knew that the two of them controlled Citation Home Furnishings. It might have appeared to be a conflict of interest to some people, building the complex with one of their companies and then arranging that property to be equipped, at full retail by another, so they kept their ownership in Citation quiet. In fact, it was a conflict of interest, but since no one knew, it was an invisible one. They picked up an additional $320,000 along the way. For them, it was a very profitable conflict of interest.

At exactly 11:05 a.m., Elinor Braun clapped her massive hands one more time and wrapped up the presentation. She wanted her sales force out of that conference room and on the phone, or showing property, or sending follow-up letters. Anything productive would work. Enough of this speech making.

Loggins and Harris asked Adam if he would care to join them for an early lunch at the Flamingo. They wanted to go over some additional details and discuss the logistics of the plan with Adam in private. Adam quickly accepted, remembering that Roxanne, the new waitress Adam had his eye on, usually worked on Mondays.

Perfect, thought Adam. Just like my marketing plan for the Sanderling project: perfect.

They walked across the street together making small talk about a million little details. The coronation had gone well. Very, very well. Adam was successfully enthroned. Life was his oyster.

212-965-7780
Randazzle Calling

Randazzle left the Sanderling presentation more fired up than usual. Having a new project gave him the excuse he needed to make the next 1,000 calls. Now there was actually something to talk about when the party on the other end of the line foolishly picked up his phone. There was news from Shoreside worth discussing. Change was exciting.

He got to his office after checking with Betsy to see if anyone had called him while he was in Adam's hour-long presentation. Betsy told him that no one had called. Clients rarely called Jason Randazzle. His telephone line sometimes appeared to be a one-way system. He called out and no one hardly ever called him back. Just like high school.

Once comfortably seated in his nondescript desk chair, he immediately reached for his bright red college-style $3.47 spiral notebook. He had, as always, marked the last call on Friday with a bright yellow Post-it. He remembered that particular call, at 5:28 Friday afternoon. The lady answering - where was it? - in Paducah, Kentucky, seemed to be drunk when she got the call. Really drunk in fact. She was slurring her words and after starting the conversation with your typical standoffish reaction, actually began to describe the nightgown she was wearing by the time the call was over.

Not all that bad a call in the end, although the drunk in Paducah knew absolutely nothing about the house her boyfriend owned on Shoreside. The nightgown sounded sexy though.

Jason looked at his notebook and punched in the next number. He was working an older subdivision on Shoreside known as Eagle's Ridge. Jason never understood why anyone would have called a subdivision on Shoreside something so misleading as Eagle's Ridge. There weren't any eagles left on Shoreside and there certainly weren't any ridges to speak of. The highest point on the island was 12 feet above mean high tide. You wouldn't exactly name that the Shoreside Ridge Mountain range. Flat as a pancake, that's what this barrier island is, thought Jason as he punched in a New York number. Flat as my desktop.

"Hello, is this Mr. Blum?"

"Why yes it is. To whom am I speaking?"

"Mr. Jason R. Randazzle, with Shoreside Realty here on Shoreside, Florida," said Jason in a very formal tone.

"May I ask what this call is regarding?"

God this guy is formal, thought Jason as he listened to the speech mannerisms of the man on the other end of the line. He almost sounds British.

"Well, Mr. Blum, I'm calling for two reasons. First off, I'm calling to let you know about our new, upcoming condominium project here on Shoreside. Located on the beautiful former McKinzie property, these 64 apartments will all have a lovely view of..."

Mr. Blum abruptly cut Jason off. "Not that 20-acre stretch of swamp along the beach?"

"Yes, that's correct. But I wouldn't call it swamp. I might call it lowland, but swamp doesn't do that beautiful stretch of sand justice."

"Swamp, lowland, slough, swale, quagmire, you call it what you want sir, but it's a swamp. A rose by any other name is still a rose."

Jason weighed his options. This particular owner was well educated, probably a professional of some kind. His address put him on Manhattan Island, Upper East Side. Possibly a college professor at NYU, or, even worse, Columbia. Jason disliked smart people. He had never gone to college, having gone to a local vo-tech for two years after high school studying to be a computer programmer. By the end of his two years of training, Jason hated computers, too. They were just like smart people, in a way. Better than him.

He ended up taking a job selling cable TV packages in Scranton, Pennsylvania, for a few years before relocating to Florida because of the climate. He had spent his entire lifetime on the telephone. Now this jerk from Columbia University saying nasty things about Sanderling. Normally, Jason would have shut up and let it slide. But he was in a mood this Monday morning and instead of retreating, he advanced.

"Well, I wouldn't exactly call your home over at Eagle's Ridge the Himalayas, Mr. Blum. There aren't any ridges and there sure as hell aren't any eagles flying around. Have you ever seen an eagle in Eagle's Ridge?" Jason was taking his gloves off.

"Excuse me, sir. There used to be eagles there; before they developed it in the '60s, there was a nesting pair not 100 yards from my property," replied a defensive but determined Mr. Blum.

"Well, they're long gone now, with the entire 40 acres being wall-to-wall homes. I just thought that you might want to sell your little house and get a reservation on one of the new Sanderling condos the very first day they came on the market. But I can tell from your comments about it being a swamp and all that you're not interested."

"I don't know who you are, Mr. Randazzle, but I would appreciate it if you hang up this moment and never call me again. I'm perfectly content with my lovely home at Eagle's Ridge and you could not convince me to buy a place in that mosquito-infested stretch of marsh if it was the last development on Earth."

Mr. Blum, who actually was a retired college professor from Bernard M. Baruch College in Manhattan, was now on a roll. He and Jason Randazzle had become a classic telephone oil and water conversation. These two men didn't mix, and despite that fact, they were both willing to go an extra round for good measure. Jason and Mr. Blum let it fly.

"Besides that," continued an inspired ex-professor, "you and all of your cohorts down there in Florida want to develop every square inch of that state, don't you? You don't see trees, or swamps, you see nothing but townhouses and golf courses. I'm a long-standing member of the Shoreside Conservancy and it breaks my heart to see you turn the McKinzie property into still another condo project. You people will stop at nothing.

"You won't be satisfied until the last patch of green is paved over and the whole of Florida is one big subdivision and parking lot, will you?"

Jason Randazzle thought that Mr. Blum's thinking was sound. The more development, the more phone calls to make. Death and divorce were always just a numbers game. The more numbers, the better the odds. Perhaps Jason should add development to the double Ds. Development, death and divorce, the triple Ds. It has a nice ring to it.

"Is that all, Mr. Blum?"

"That's all for now, you imbecile."

With that Mr. Blum slammed the receiver down. Jason smiled and went to the next number on the list. Let's see, this looks like a St. Louis exchange.

Water off a duck's back. He just kept dialing. Jason was excited about the new project; he knew he'd be mailing out a half-dozen brochures on Sanderling by the end of the week. He was excited as his fingers hit the telephone keypad.

Triple Ds. A very nice ring to it.

570-9514
Mildred Lee's Home Phone

"Hello."

"Mildred, this is Sam Goodlet. How are you this fine Monday morning?"

"Fine Sam, just fine. Except I can't seem to find Buffy. I sure hope nothing's happened to her."

Sam remembered the story of Boots and felt a little nauseated. He wondered where Mildred might end up finding Buffy. Stuck in some corner of Mildred's small, two-bedroom ranch. Maybe behind the fridge, dehydrating. Becoming slowly mummified from the warm air of the compressor. Dead. Sam shook the morbid thought from his mind and snapped back into their telephone conversation.

"I'm sure Buffy will show. She's probably just hiding under the bed."

"I hope so, Sam. Why did you call me?"

"Well, Mildred, I just phoned to remind you about our showing this afternoon. You do remember, don't you?" Sam figured that Mildred had long since forgotten about the appointment he had arranged for Jennifer Willow on Friday. Mildred seldom remembered anything overnight, let alone an appointment set three days ago. To Mildred, three days was an eternity.

"What showing?" Mildred replied, true to character.

"Jennifer Willow has asked me to set up showing your property this afternoon. Will that be okay with you?"

"Sure it would, Sam. Who's Jennifer Willow? I don't seem to remember that name."

"Jennifer's one of the newer agents here at Shoreside. She used to work at the Decorating Hut. You'll just love her."

Sam knew that Mildred Lee had never been to the Decorating Hut. There wasn't a snowball's chance in hell that Mildred would buy any new furniture for her place. Her house was a case study in shag carpeting and a hundred different uses for Formica. If anything, it was anti-decorated. It was the black hole of decor. New furnishings would have been sucked into it without hope.

"About what time will she be coming by, Sam? I'll try to pick up a little."

"Expect her between 2:00 and 3:00, Mrs. Lee."

"Thanks for calling, Sam. I must have completely forgotten." She had completely forgotten. Chances were pretty good that when Jennifer showed later in the day, Mildred would be surprised by the ringing doorbell. Her memory was slipping. No, her memory had fallen and could not get up.

"Thank you for letting us show the house again, Mildred. Have a nice day."

"Goodbye."

"Goodbye."

Sam was half tempted to remind Mildred to stay out of Jennifer's way when she was showing the house later that day but he didn't bother. It wasn't any use. The only people Mildred ever talked to were her two daughters in Chicago and the infrequent Realtor who accidently showed the house. Mildred would inevitably get into her well-studied hurricane monologue with Jennifer's unsuspecting clients. It was hopeless.

No one at Shoreside Realty had taken the time to forewarn Jennifer Willow about Mrs. Lee and her boarded-up CBS. It was a rite of passage for rookie agents on Shoreside, like a bizarre initiation ritual or a college hazing. They had to discover the horror on their own. Sam himself wouldn't dare interfere with Jennifer's forthcoming nightmare. It had to be.

❂

At precisely 2:34 p.m. that Monday afternoon Jennifer Willow and her two clients, Mr. and Mrs. Ringly, pulled up to Mildred's two-bedroom ranch. Jennifer had already shown the Ringlys a plat of the subdivision, explaining how this particular house should have wondrous canal views. It did have wondrous canal views, at least on paper.

As Jennifer approached the home she thought it peculiar that all of the hurricane shutters were on. It was still March and the official hurricane season in Florida doesn't begin until June first. Maybe they are just making certain that they all fit properly or something, thought Jennifer to herself as she rang the doorbell.

Within a minute the front door opened slightly. Mildred had put the chain across the door like she always did. She had the chain shortened by two links to be sure that none of her overfed cats could squeeze through the front door by accident. As she opened the door to her humble abode, the first few wafts of cat urine made their way to Jennifer and the Ringlys. All three of them, trying not to embarrass each other, politely ignored the odor.

"Who is it?" asked Mildred as her frail blue eyes peeped through the slit in the door into the overwhelming sunlight outside. She had, of course, totally forgotten about the showing.

"It's Jennifer Willow from Shoreside Realty. Didn't Mr. Goodlet arrange an appointment for us?"

Mildred hesitated for a minute, trying her best to remember her telephone conversation with Sam earlier that day. She couldn't remember anything about a showing, but to make herself look good, Mildred said, "Of course he did. I just have to check to be sure. You can't be too careful these days."

With that, Mildred closed the door and started fiddling with the door chain. Because she had taken the two extra links out as a precaution against runaway cats, undoing the chain had become a daunting task. The chain was now almost too short to remove and Mildred's wrinkled, feeble fingers only exacerbated the problem.

Minutes passed. As the three of them stood outside waiting they could all hear Mildred fumbling around hopelessly with the chain. Like the door chains in cheap motels, it was obviously not working properly. More time passed.

Jennifer didn't know what to do. She had no idea that the best thing she could have done was to quickly round her two clients up and forcibly escort them into her car. The best thing for her to do was never to step foot in the crypt she was about to show to two ready, willing and able buyers. Of course Jennifer Willow had no way of knowing that. Sam knew it, though. Sam Goodlet who was sitting at his office looking at the clock on his computer thinking that Jennifer was probably arriving about now. Chuckling to himself while thinking about the next 15 minutes of Jennifer Willow's real estate career. Her christening into the cult of Mildred Lee avoidance.

"Is everything okay, Mrs. Lee?" Jennifer broke the long silence.

"It's just fine, ma'am. I just have a real hard time getting this darn chain undone. It's too tight or something."

With that comment, they all heard the final click as the chain fell off the holder on the inside of the door. Mildred Lee opened the front door inward and stood there in all of her glory smack before them. It was difficult to tell which of the two senses were more overwhelmed: the visual or the olfactory.

The first blast of the cat urine stench slammed into Jennifer and her clients like the initial shock wave of an atomic blast. Their eyes watered. None of them dared to look at each other. They were too afraid of how their faces might appear. Like an atomic bomb, the shock wave made it about half way out to the car then doubled backed on itself, causing the three of them to unexpectedly step inside the blast zone itself. As their eyes cleared they all looked point blank at Mrs. Mildred Lee.

Mildred was short. At the apex of her tallness, Mildred Lee had stood proudly at five feet two inches. Age had now reclaimed many of those inches and, because of that, it was hard to say just how tall she actually was. The question was one of protocol.

Sam Goodlet had debated the question with himself a dozen times. Do you measure from the floor to the top of the hump in Mildred's back, or do you then bend the tape and continue on to the top of her head? Depending on her posture at the time, her head and her hump seemed to vie for top position. Sam never could decide. In any event, neither pinnacle now approached four feet ten. Mildred Lee wasn't just short, she was shorter.

Mildred was still in her nightgown. Although no one but Mildred knew it, she was always in her nightgown. It was one of those willowy, sheer nightgowns that are apparently made out of old curtains. The gown was originally white but that was years and years ago. The white had turned a muted yellow over time, like old newspapers tend to do when left in a damp basement. A musty, damp basement.

Mildred looked at the three of them, temporarily lifting the top of her mop of thick gray hair above her hump and said, "Well, don't just stand there, come on in and look the joint over." You can take the Chicagoan out of Chicago but you can't take the Chicago out of Mildred Lee.

They didn't say a thing. The three of them just walked inside of the house as silent as prisoners are the morning of their execution. They were in shock. Little did they realize that the firing squad that had been hired to shoot all three of them that afternoon was using pellet guns. There was much, much more shooting to follow.

"Don't mind me, I'll be in the kitchen watching television. Make yourself at home and look around. If you have any questions, I'll be glad to answer them if I can."

"Thanks." It was all Jennifer could think to say.

Mildred shuffled off toward the kitchen in her slippers and antique nightgown as the three of them headed toward the other side of the house, where the two bedrooms were located.

The house seemed darker than it should have, with all of the innumerable light bulbs burning. Jennifer leaned over one of the lamps to check the wattage. Fifteen-watt light bulbs, she discovered. That's why it's so dark.

Mildred didn't want to run up a big electric bill. She liked all the 15-watt light bulbs scattered throughout the house more than she liked a single 100-watt bulb here and there. It made it more peaceful, as if she were lighting her house with hundreds of oversized candles. It made it more festive, thought Mildred. Festive.

"I think that this must be the master bedroom," said Jennifer sheepishly to Mr. and Mrs. Ringly.

"It's nice," replied Mrs. Ringly.

"Nice," added her husband quietly.

As they stood there in the dark, smelly master bedroom, several of Mildred's cats darted from underneath the bed. They were those nervous, paranoid house cats that no one but their owner ever sees. They crouched and slithered as they ran, acting more like oversized rats. In the dim light of the bedroom, it was hard to see much of them except their red, glowing eyes. The cats helped. They added another "e" to eeerie.

The three of them backed out of the master bedroom and walked down the short hall to the guest bedroom. Once again, silence overwhelmed them. Jennifer was about to point out the ceiling fan when she noted a new addition to the overpowering bouquet of unchanged kitty litter boxes and cat pee. She couldn't quite place this smell. Was it the passing aroma of road kill?

Little did Jennifer know that this was the room where Boots had passed away. Poor Boots.

Jennifer didn't say anything, let alone dare to turn on the ceiling fan. She could only imagine what sort of windstorm of stench the fan might kick up. They quickly left the guest bedroom without so much as a comment.

The dining room and living room were nondescript. Jennifer wanted desperately to say something about how cute she could make it, recalling her earlier sale at Osprey Towers, but she was concerned that Mildred might somehow overhear her. She didn't want to insult this sweet little old lady.

The furnishings were appalling. The coffee table, the two end tables, the bookcase and the dining room table were all made out of Formica. Brown, meaningless Formica. The rest was done in some sort of brown-green plaid that escaped definition. The couches and chairs were all threadbare and sagging, the lamps all dusty and dim. It was the house of horrors. The Salvation Army would have passed on picking up a single piece of Mildred's furniture. The county landfill would have said no to the garbage truck it was in. Turn around, we don't want this crap dumped in here.

As the three of them left the dining room, they opened a small swinging door that separated the dining area from the kitchen. The kitchen was the only room where a dash of outside light was spilling in. That was the one shutter Sam had convinced Mildred to remove. It looked out over the trash cans and the air-conditioning unit. The unit was on at the time but neither Jennifer nor her clients noticed. They couldn't hear the noise of the running air-conditioning compressor over the din of the 12-inch television that Mildred was watching.

It was one of those combination TV/VCR units that people buy when they are going on long trips with their children. Mildred, because her hearing was beginning to fail, had turned the volume up on her little television set as high as it would go. That, in and of itself, wasn't all that bad. It was the tape that proved to be the *coup de gras*. The name of the tape, which was Mildred's favorite tape by the way, was titled *Hurricanes: Nature's Wrath Unleashed.*

Just as Jennifer was trying to catch a glimpse of the canal, to point the views out to her clients, roofs not unlike the one above them were being ripped off homes in Mildred's horrific video. It was incredible footage, and Mr. and Mrs. Ringly were instantly transfixed. They proceeded to do the unthinkable. They both found an empty kitchen chair and sat beside Mrs. Lee. They were mesmerized by the fury displayed on that tiny, 12-inch screen. Hypnotized by it.

Jennifer leaned way over the kitchen sink, and by pressing her face against the glass, could just peek past the six-foot privacy fence that encircled the trash cans and the rusty air compressor. There it was, a view of the canal. She turned to ask her clients to come over and catch the pleasing view but it was useless. They were now both comfortably seated beside Mildred, watching a ten-foot tidal surge in the Florida Panhandle wash over a used car lot. The proverbial clean low-mileage cars were tossed around like toys. The narrator, his deep voice penetrating the sounds of the screaming wind, said that over 40 lives were lost in Panama City alone. The damage caused by the storm exceeded one-billion dollars.

Just as the same narrator started describing the torrential rains of hurricane Mitch, Mr. Ringly leaned over and tapped Mildred on the shoulder. With the pounding rains falling on Honduras, Mr. Ringly spoke. "Excuse me, ma'am, where might we buy a copy of this tape?"

"Do you like hurricanes?"

"Why, yes, in a way. My wife and I are from Wisconsin and we've never seen anything quite like this before."

"I'm originally from Chicago ya know."

"No, we didn't know."

"My husband and I moved here years ago from Orchard Park. He's dead now."

"Oh, I'm sorry."

By this time the torrential rains had inundated Honduras. Streets were washing away along with the squalid Third World homes that lined them. The death count was mounting. Entire villages were being covered in catastrophic mud slides. The dead numbered more than 20,000 when Mildred leaned back and said, "You can get them at MacToshes Bookstore and Video on Shoreside Drive. I paid $21.95 for it. It's my favorite tape. I've probably seen it 100 times."

Mr. Ringly was caught off guard. He thought that 100 viewings of a tape like this was a bit excessive. Obsessive-compulsive was a better description. Between shots of Red Cross workers trying to throw up makeshift sandbag dikes and people being rescued from rooftops by helicopters, Mr. Ringly glanced around the room. When his eyes discovered Mildred's hurricane chart, he quietly got up from his seat and walked over to it for a closer inspection.

Jennifer was leaning against the kitchen sink with her face buried in her beautiful white hands. She was weeping. She kept hearing the narrator go on and on about Hugo and Marilyn, Andrew and Floyd but none of it mattered. Her tour was now running late and this showing was a complete disaster. Mrs. Lee and Mrs. Ringly were engrossed in some conversation about the video while Mr. Ringly was transfixed by all the detailed notations on Mildred's hurricane chart. Assuredly this lady was obsessed with hurricanes and their precursors, tropical storms.

Twenty minutes later the tape ended. Mr. and Mrs. Ringly applauded. Jennifer was sobbing off in the corner. Mildred asked if they would like her to rewind the tape in order to see the part they missed.

"It has some great footage of transformers exploding and some spectacular reconnaissance shots done by one of those hurricane hunter planes," said Mildred, trying to get them to stay.

"Thanks, but we really must be going," answered a polite Mr. Ringly.

"We'll buy our own copy this afternoon," said Mrs. Ringly.

The three of them, Jennifer and her two clients, once again thanked Mrs. Lee for allowing them the privilege of showing her home, and made their way toward the front door. As they headed out into the fresh air they all once again recalled just how awful Mildred's house smelled. The sun nearly blinded them.

Jennifer's stunning green eyes were now puffed up and red from crying. No sooner had they climbed into the car than Mr. Ringly asked the inevitable.

"Has a hurricane ever hit Shoreside?"

Jennifer pretended not to hear him. She didn't want to deal with it. But Mr. Ringly simply had to know, so he repeated the question slightly louder, thinking that Jennifer hadn't heard him the first time.

"Has Shoreside ever been hit by a big hurricane?"

"Not since the '40s," said Jennifer.

"What was the name of that storm?"

"They didn't name them back then, Mr. Ringly. They just called them hurricanes."

"How bad was it?"

"Bad enough."

The tour was over. Jennifer showed them two more island houses but she knew that they were simply patronizing her at this point. They were anxious to go and buy that video, *Hurricanes: Nature's Wrath Unleashed*, and take it to their condo for further study. Buying a place on an island like Shoreside was no longer a consideration. Perhaps they would just buy a lake cabin near Solon Springs, Wisconsin, or a place in Arizona somewhere. Shoreside Island was no longer even a remote consideration.

Jennifer Willow, the novice, was now a full-fledged member of the Mildred Lee fan club. She would never set foot in Mildred's house again.

570-9898 Ext. 4
Barbara's Desk

"Build out," mumbled Barbara to herself as she looked over some HUD statements for Thursday's closing. "We're fast approaching build out."

Barbara Silberman had left Adam's presentation earlier in the day with mixed emotions. Instead of being elated about having a new project to sell, Barb was disturbed by the notion that Shoreside was fast approaching build out. In a few more years, she reasoned, there wouldn't be any vacant land left. What am I going to do then? Barb pondered.

Thus far her sales for the year had been phenomenal. She had closed on better than $3 million, had $5.3 million pending and $4.8 million in unsold listings. In all likelihood, Barb would hit $20 million in sales for the year.

That's not how Barb looked at it, though. Barb was dead certain that she was through. She kept looking for a mistake on the HUD statement that would scuttle the closing this Thursday. The listings would probably all expire without selling and she hadn't received an inquiry call in ages. Technically, since last Friday morning. Like Mildred Lee, three days was an eternity to Barb.

Last year was a good year, she reminisced. Last year the Skinners bought that cute little house from me, most of my listings sold and everything went well. Not this year. This year's going to be the worst.

That's how Barbara Silberman approached every morning, with the cup being half empty. Instead of jumping for joy at the thought of having a ton of brand-new condominiums to sell at the Sanderling project, Barb was focusing on the inevitability of build out on Shoreside. Once it was built out, what's there to sell?

Of course she didn't even consider resales. Most of what she sold, and all the other agents sold on the island, were resales. People traded up, traded down, moved to other locations, jumped from a home to a condo, or a condo to a home and, as Randazzle knew, there was always death and divorce. Always.

But Barbara Silberman was slipping again. Sinking into that blue funk that seemed to hang around her like a personal fog. She started thinking that it was over. The good years are behind me, she thought as she double-checked the commission due Shoreside on her HUD closing statement. Behind me.

Just then Betsy put a call through. It was someone asking about a two-bedroom rental condominium Barb had just listed.

Well, thought Barb as she picked up her telephone, things aren't all bad. And they weren't.

570-9898 Ext. 12
Sam Goodlet's Phone

"Oh, Jennifer, I'm sorry that your showing went so badly."

"You don't understand, Sam. It didn't go badly, it was the worst showing of my life," said Jennifer between sobs.

"Maybe Mildred's house wasn't what they had in mind. I'm sure that you can find them something else here on Shoreside. How about Linda's new listing on Sandy Lane? That's a sweet little house."

Sam was patronizing Jennifer. He had allowed her to enter the listing from hell without so much as a whisper as to what she was about to encounter. Now he was feigning concern. He felt terrible when she started crying. He was glad that Jennifer hadn't come in to confront him in person about the showing. Her tears would have reduced him to rubble.

"My customers are leaving in the morning. I drove them over to MacToshes Bookstore to pick up that horrible video Mildred had on, and then back to their condo. They told me that they were now considering a lake place over in the Wisconsin Dells. They thanked me for taking them around. They had that look in the eye. You know the one. Oh, Sam, it was dreadful."

Jennifer started crying again. Long, pitiful sobs that Sam found very disconcerting. He should have forewarned her. But that wouldn't have been fair to all of the other rookies that had to run the Mildred Lee gauntlet. Even with her sparkling green eyes, her long, sensuous blond hair and *Cosmopolitan* features, Jennifer had to undergo the baptism by complete submersion. She had to show Mildred's house alone.

Not that she hadn't heard rumors. Shoreside was way too small an island to keep Jennifer off the rumor net. She had heard that the house smelled awful and that the hurricane shutters were up almost all the time, but Jennifer felt invincible. If she could sell that fixer-upper at Osprey Towers last year, then she could sell Mildred Lee's house. Wrong.

That condo didn't have a hurricane chart covered with last year's body count. That condo might have been poorly decorated, but it paled when compared with the Formica-filled vacuum that Jennifer walked into. A two-bedroom ranch that seemed to suck the word "decorated" right out of the English dictionary. Mildred's house was the *piéce de résistance*. The *blitzkrieg* of all showings.

"You'll get over it, Jennifer. Everyone in real estate has shown a dog or two during their career. Mildred's was just a little worse than you expected. That's all. You'll get over it."

"Thanks, Sam. Thanks for talking to me about it. It helps."

"Anytime, Jennifer. Anytime."

"Goodbye."

"Goodbye."

Sam hung up and smiled. Mildred Lee's house wasn't a dog. It was a kennel full of dogs. Dogs that never stopped barking. Not even when they slept.

Unbeknownst to Jennifer Willow, she was now a card-carrying member of the Mildred Lee initiation club. She, like all of the other agents who had dared pass through that darkened threshold, would never show Mildred's house again. Ever.

Sam knew that his only chance of finding a buyer for Mildred's house was to wait it out. In a few more years, the land beneath Mildred's two-bedroom ranch would be worth more than the improvement sitting upon it. Then no one would need to go inside. They could just walk the perimeter of the lot, back out the demolition cost of taking down the house and make an offer. It was known as redevelopment, and as Shoreside approached build out, it was sure to come more and more into play.

Mildred's house, the shutters and the cat urine would all fall prey to the wrecking ball. One long morning and 15 truckloads later, Mildred Lee's bunker would end up in the county dump. Probably where it belonged, thought Sam.

It was a gamble, but it was the only payoff Sam could think of. He had done all of the calculations after first accepting the listing and doing his standard walk through with Mildred. The average island appreciation, the remaining homesites, the current value of the lot if Mildred's house didn't exist on it and the projected time that would pass before the two values crossed. The numbers worked.

Demolition made sense in 27 months. It was either that, or, and Sam smiled one more time before calling Mr. Hazelton about another inspection, either that or a hurricane would take it out.

Part III
Collapse, Begin To Fall

473-8782
Eugene Boyle's Home Phone

"Goddamned right I'm concerned. Why the hell shouldn't I be, Adam? This storm could ruin our grand opening plans for the Sanderling project. Three years of effort down the toilet all because of some tropical storm named Kandee. I've got a right to be concerned." Eugene Boyle was a pile of nerves. He had been following the storm's development for the past few days and it didn't look good.

"Don't worry, Gene, I just called my contact over in Coral Gables at the National Hurricane Center and he assured me that Kandee will be somewhere near Jacksonville by Friday night. The storm is heading north, northeast, Gene. Aside from a few inches of rain and some wind, we won't feel a thing."

Adam was hedging. Boyle was fast becoming a basket case and Adam had learned that it was better to hedge with the old man than come clean with him. His contact in Miami didn't say a few inches of rain. The National Hurricane Center's forecast put the projected rainfall total closer to a foot of rain, perhaps as much as a foot and a half. That much water could create some real problems with the kickoff party for the Sanderling project. Nothing insurmountable, just some unwelcome complications.

"That's not what I'm hearing on the local news, Adam. I'm hearing that they expect this storm to dump a foot of rain on Shoreside within the next few days. What the hell is going to happen to that site when Mother Nature hits it with a foot of rain? We built the project in a swamp, Bartlett. The assholes down at City Hall made us put up all those retention berms and dig out all those goddamned swales, but who the hell knows how much water that site can handle? If we get all the rain they're predicting, it'll look like we built those condos in the middle of a lake."

"Calm down, Gene. You always get yourself worked up for nothing. It's just a little tropical storm.

"The maximum sustained winds are expected to be only 45 miles per hour at the most. The state required us to build the Sanderling units to withstand winds of up to 130 miles per hour. This storm isn't going to change a thing. Saturday will be bright and sunny. Those reservationists will have the weekend of their lives. Just take a deep breath and stop worrying.

"Are Maggie and you coming to the barbecue Saturday afternoon?"

A skilled salesman at work, trying to change the subject. Bartlett wanted to get Boyle off the rain issue as soon as possible. Bringing up the wind, or focusing on the party, reasoned Adam, would both be a good distraction. As solidly as the Sanderling Condominiums had been built, the winds from Kandee wouldn't be a factor.

But beneath it all, Adam, like Gene, wasn't at all sure what a foot of rain would do to the Sanderling site. The entire project was built in a very low-lying section of the beach. The surrounding higher ground would drain into it and there might be some localized flooding. If Kandee did dump more than a foot of rain on the island, the old McKinzie parcel would become a lake, Lake Sanderling.

Anticipating that, Adam had already ordered some large commercial pumps from Tampa. He would use them to drain the swales in the event they filled to overflowing. The plan was to pump the excess fresh water across the beach and into the ocean.

The pumps were huge, oversize units driven by big diesel engines. Adam had ordered them from an industrial rental firm in the Tampa Bay area and arranged for them to be trucked in on Thursday to be on site just in case. No one in town handled pumps of that size and Adam wanted them to be at the complex at first light Friday morning. Bartlett, with the help of Ralph Galano, had calculated that pumps of this size could drain Lake Sanderling in less than a day. Planning ahead, that's what Bartlett was famous for.

Gene took the bait and, for the moment at least, dropped the rain issue. "Sure, Adam, Maggie and I will be down around 4:00 in the afternoon on Saturday. You're sure that we shouldn't postpone this thing until the following weekend?"

"I'm sure, Gene. It's hard enough getting everything arranged for 32 of the island's top reservationists to get away for the weekend. Changing the grand opening date at this point would be an even bigger disaster. We'll stick with it and hope for the best. I've got some contingency plans just in case. Everything will go just fine."

"If you say so, Adam. I just pray that it goes well or it will be your ass on the line."

"It will."

"Goodbye."

"Goodbye."

It was Bartlett at his finest. Selling and reselling. Everything will go just fine. That was how it always was with Bartlett. No matter that the sky was raining chickens or that tropical storm Kandee was making a beeline toward Shoreside Island, everything would come out smelling like roses in the end. Bushels full of roses. Thorns removed.

Adam's contact at the National Hurricane Center had agreed with Adam that it would be advisable for him to truck in those pumps just in case. Kandee was going to be a rainmaker. The storm wasn't expected to strengthen before making landfall and that was the good news.

If it did strengthen, there could be trouble, but conditions were unfavorable. It was a typical late-October storm. A mild cold front had swept across Florida the week before and stalled over the central Gulf of Mexico. As the rain and clouds hung over that 85-degree water, the system started its slow counterclockwise spin in an effort to become a hurricane. But it wasn't going to make it to hurricane strength.

Tropical storms like Kandee were common late in the hurricane season. The water wasn't quite warm enough and there was too much wind shear around to allow the big thunderheads enough headroom to build. They weren't at all like the storms that arrive in August or September, when the water temperature is still high and the westerlies haven't started blowing off their ponderous tops.

Kandee would probably drench the island Wednesday night, all day Thursday and head through central Florida toward Daytona Beach sometime early Friday morning. After that, the computer forecast indicated Kandee would exit over the Atlantic and continue north, northeast along the coastal United States.

On the back side of the storm, the counterclockwise winds would pull down some colder, drier air behind it. By daybreak Friday morning the forecast was for blue skies and breezy conditions. Nothing they couldn't handle. By Saturday afternoon the winds were expected to diminish to under 15 knots. Sunny, cool and a light wind out of the north. Great barbecue weather.

"An ideal forecast," Adam said to himself as he hung up the phone and headed to the office on a clear but windy Monday morning. "Simply ideal."

570-9898
The Main Switchboard

"Shoreside Realty, how may I help you?"

Betsy was in gear. It was Monday morning and she was shifting through the gears of her phone console smoother than a Formula One at Monte Carlo. She was burning rubber at the telephone Grand Prix. Her voice working as effortlessly as a well-tuned V-8.

"I'm an owner down there on Shoreside. I think we bought from a lady named Barbara Silverberg or something like that about two years ago."

"Yes, and?" Betsy wanted this caller to get on with it.

"And I was wondering, 'cause we're back up here in Ohio, well, I was wondering if that there storm, Kandee, is expected to cause any harm or anything to our condo?"

"Where's your condo located, Mr...?"

"Mr. Breeze, Mr. Randolf Breeze. Our place is over at the Promenade, you know, near the Publix grocery store."

"That's fairly inland, isn't it?"

"Sure is, ma'am; Molly and I couldn't quite swing those beachfront prices. But we love it there. They've got the nicest shuffleboard courts on the island."

Betsy was getting the picture. These were working-class owners from somewhere in the industrial heartland of America. Simple folks who spent their entire lives working alongside some assembly line in Dayton or Akron. Three kids who made it all the way through community college, complete with one golden retriever and a Ford Bronco. Americans on a budget. The salt of the earth.

Betsy knew that the Promenade Units sold for under $100,000. They were at least a half-mile from the gulf. Unless it rained buckets and buckets, they were unlikely to suffer any real damage, reasoned Betsy. Then she continued.

"Oh, I wouldn't worry about it, Mr. Breeze. Your condo is well away from the wind and the waves. Unless your roof leaks, I shouldn't think you'll have any damage. Kandee is just a tropical storm at this point. Not too much worse than a big thunderstorm."

"So you think we'll come out okay?"

"Sure you will. Give me your number and I'll give you a buzz if things take a turn for the worse."

"Thanks, ma'am. My home number is 208-722-9772 and my work number, and you can reach me here at work any time after 4:00 p.m., is 208-722-7976. You promise to call me if it looks bad, right? I've got a brother-in-law in Sarasota that could come over and get all of our personal belongings out if need be."

"I promise to call."

"Thanks, and goodbye now."

"Bub-bye."

Working-class all the way. Still working and pulling the night shift on top of it. These are the people that make America what it is: a great nation. His wife probably works as an LPN somewhere while he assembles widgets until midnight. They've probably been married 34 years. Happily married. What a beautiful country we live in, thought Betsy. What a beautiful country.

Betsy jotted Randolf's number down on a Post-It and stuck it on the outside edge of her computer monitor. She doubted that she would find it necessary to call him, but wanted to hang on to his telephone number just in case. She liked people like Mr. Randolf Breeze. They had a common bond in that if Betsy ever wanted to own a place on Shoreside, it would likely have to be at the Promenade or at the Palms. These were simple, two-bedroom condominium complexes that offered little more than a view of some palm trees and a heated pool. That and shuffleboard courts that were the envy of the island. If the word envy is allowed when describing shuffleboard courts.

It's ironic, thought Betsy to herself while waiting for another call to light up her switchboard, that Mr. Breeze's $85,000 condo was far safer than the penthouses at Osprey Towers, or the first-floor units at Shoreside Cove, or any of the expensive units that sat along the edge of the ocean. It didn't make sense if you really sat and thought about it, pondered Betsy as she worked the phone lines.

People were willing to pay hundreds of thousands more to place themselves in harm's way. The better the view, the nearer to the sand and the surf, the higher the sticker price. Having money must make you stupid, she concluded. Lucky for me, I'll never have that particular problem.

As that final thought rolled around in Betsy's head, two more lines lit up. Betsy was on them in an instant. She was in overdrive. Ready to handle anything they could throw at her. Ready to page, to say "Repeat that spelling please," ready to forward, "I'll try to get this message to him as soon as possible," ready to stand on the front lines of Shoreside Realty and take the flak.

With Kandee twirling in the Gulf of Mexico, and Adam's big kickoff planned for the weekend, Betsy knew there would be plenty of flak coming before the bell rang at 5:00 Friday afternoon.

570-9898 Ext. 22
Jennifer Willow's Desk

"Jennifer, line five's for you. I think it's Dr. Clifton," said Betsy through the intercom system.

"Thanks, Betsy," replied Jennifer, expecting this particular call all morning.

"Hello, Jennifer Willow here. How may I help you?"

"Jennifer, this is James. How are things?"

"Well, I'm sure you've heard about Kandee by now."

"Yeah, it's all over the news up here. But it doesn't look all that bad and, from what we're hearing at least, it looks like you're in for a ton of rain. What are the local forecasters predicting?"

Dr. Clifton and his wife, Marie, had been following Kandee since the National Hurricane Center named the storm Saturday morning. With the scheduled walk-through on their new home Friday afternoon at 4:00 for the final certificate of occupancy, they had reason to keep an eye on Kandee.

"They're saying the same thing here. Kandee is expected to drop around 15 inches of rain on us. It's a slow-moving storm, and that's the problem. She's supposed to make landfall sometime Wednesday afternoon, and hopefully move inland sometime Friday night. I sure hope that those forecasters are right this time.

"Are you still booked to fly down Friday morning?" asked Jennifer.

"Unless the storm takes a turn for the worse, we're still planning to be at the airport at 7:15, bright and early. We should arrive in town around 10:30. We're planning on seeing you there, right?"

"Of course I'll be there, James. You're my very first clients, and I wouldn't even think of letting the two of you take a cab from the airport. I've got your room booked at the Holiday Inn and I thought we could all head to lunch over at The Oyster Bar. How does that sound?"

"You know how I love oysters, Jennifer."

"Then we'll head over to the property around 3:45 or so. They say that it will be pretty windy on Friday, but the rains will have stopped. Windy and sunny, that's what to expect. That doesn't sound too bad, does it?"

"No, Jennifer, that sounds just fine. How does the house look?"

"Great; they're still working on the sprinkler system, but most of the landscaping is in. The house looks just great, Doc; I hope that you and Marie will like it."

"We'll love it, Jennifer. You've done such a terrific job. Finding us that great lot, helping us find a good builder, sending all the photographs and videotapes over this past year. We really appreciate it, Jennifer. Unless you hear from us, or Kandee takes a turn for the worse, we'll see you at the airport Friday morning, right?"

"I'll be there, James. Say hello to Marie for me. Bye now."

"Goodbye."

Jennifer hung up the phone and smiled. She had reason to smile. Her very first customers were flying in Friday afternoon to do a final walk-through, then close on their gorgeous four-bedroom home on Palmetto Court. Over the course of her first year in real estate, Jennifer had closed on $2,875,000 in sales.

She had just leased a brand-new Toyota Camry, bought a brand-new laptop computer and was sitting on top of the world. She had finally found her niche. Jennifer Willow had arrived. No longer that starry-eyed rookie, her business was growing in leaps and bounds. Aside from the imposition of having to deal with this tropical storm, Kandee, she was having the time of her life.

570-9514
Mildred Lee's Home Phone

Steve, the Sears repairman, was having a hard time breathing. He had always been mildly allergic to cats and Mrs. Lee's house was not the best place in the world for him to kick off his Monday morning work week. Understatement.

Mildred had called Sears last Friday to have them come and take a look at her ice maker. It had gone on the fritz Thursday. The reason Mildred's ice maker broke was obvious. Two huge, 72-quart coolers sat in the kitchen beside the refrigerator, filled to overflowing with stockpiled ice. Mildred was getting ready for the "Big One."

On Tuesday, when the National Hurricane Center first identified Kandee as tropical depression No.14, Mildred Lee began making ice. Ice. She had purchased the coolers five years ago and every time, without fail, that the National Hurricane Center issued a statement that a new tropical depression had formed, Mildred immediately dragged the coolers out of the garage and began stockpiling ice.

"You can never have too much ice after a storm," she would repeat slowly to herself every time she dumped whatever ice had accumulated in her ice bin into one of the coolers. Ice saves lives, she added silently. With the electricity knocked out from the downed trees, ice keeps your meats and vegetables from spoiling, cools your drinking water, and makes an excellent compress for any bruises or wounds a person might have received during the cataclysm heading toward Shoreside Island, Florida.

It didn't matter to Mildred that the storms were off the coast of Nova Scotia or a 100 miles inland of Brownsville, Texas; she was dumping tray after tray of ice into her clean white coolers. She wasn't going to be caught unaware.

Naturally, her ice maker eventually failed. It wasn't designed for commercial use and couldn't keep up with the sheer volume of Mildred's incessant stockpiling. It gave up the ghost. Kaput. Defunct. Shot.

This wasn't the first time that it needed replacing. In fact, it was the fourth ice maker Mildred's overworked fridge had seen. The others had collapsed from exhaustion as well. From May through the end of November there were always storms somewhere in the vast Atlantic, doing their graceful pirouette, cooling down the vast equatorial seas. Mildred would drain her ice machine six times a day, dumping the frozen cubes into her coolers methodically every four hours. When the ice makers were fresh and new, she could expect about a quarter of a binful every four hours. As they aged and tired, that amount dwindled to a dozen cubes. Last Thursday, her worn and weary ice maker had coughed out two undersized ice cubes and dropped dead.

It was glad to have died. It was a haggard and emaciated ice maker that had coughed out those last two ice cubes. It had looked forward to its own mechanical failure all summer. No ice maker in the world deserved this kind of cruel treatment. Had they known how hard Mildred Lee worked her ice makers, Sears would have had their repairman bring them sympathy cards when he came over to install the new one. They would have given them a nice burial by the canal. Right next to Boots. Mildred's ice makers deserved it.

Steve, the Sears repairman, presently hacking and wheezing in the kitchen, had never been to Mildred Lee's house before. He was the new kid at the local Sears service center. When the call came in the shop foreman took one look at the roster and went directly to the rookie. Like Jennifer Willow before him, Steve needed to be initiated into the strange world of Mrs. Mildred Lee, cat hair notwithstanding.

So there he was, standing in her darkened kitchen at 11:30 on a Monday morning with his tool kit in one hand and a replacement ice maker in the other. His eyes were watering, his nose was running and his breathing was labored. He was totally mesmerized by the large hurricane tracking chart that was nailed on the wall beside Mildred's telephone. It had so many notations on it that the Caribbean Sea had vanished beneath an avalanche of black Magic Marker. The Atlantic was rapidly following suit. There were barometric pressure readings, projected paths, wind gusts and, as always, death counts scrawled across the chart like some kind of twisted geriatric graffiti. Steve took one more long look at the chart and one more studied look at the hunched-over Mildred Lee and knew. She was fucking nuts.

"What seems to be the problem?" asked Steve.

"The ice maker crapped out on me last Friday. They all do. They just don't make things like they used to," said Mildred in her classic Chicago accent.

"Well then, let's have a look."

Mildred's freezer was on the bottom of her refrigerator and as Steve bent over to take a better look at the ice maker, Mildred couldn't help but notice the crack of his butt poking out from his dark blue Sears uniform. It was kind of sexy, thought Mildred. Not that she really had any idea of what sex was any longer.

After tinkering around with the ice maker for a few minutes, Steve got up and said, "She's a goner."

"Told ya that already. Can you replace it?"

"Sure can, ma'am. I'll need to pull the fridge out and disconnect the water line.

But first, I need to turn off your main water supply. Do you know where that is?"

"It's out back by the garbage cans. But I've got the hurricane shutter over the kitchen door, so you'll have to go through the front door and come around."

As Steve opened the front door he was nearly blinded by the intensity of the morning sun. His eyes had become adjusted to the dimly lit catacomb Mildred lived in. He had to stand there and wait for his eyes to adjust before heading to the back of the house to shut off the main water supply or risk running into something in his state of near sun-blindness.

The fresh air though, it smelled glorious, thought Steve, like the first breath of air a newborn takes in. Glorious, and filled with life.

He went around back, turned off the main water supply and reluctantly headed into the house. As he closed the front door behind him you could see his lips silently saying, "That son-of-a-bitch," about his boss at the warehouse. He knew now why they were all standing around laughing as he pulled out of the barn on his way to Shoreside Island. Mildred Lee and her house of cat hair. That's why they were laughing.

"So what do you think of this here Kandee?"

"Oh, you know, it's just a little tropical storm. It isn't going to amount to much."

"Don't bet on it!" countered Mildred with that lunatic tinge in her quivering voice. "That's what they said about the storm of '35 that ravished both Upper and Lower Matecumbe keys. They called it the great Labor Day storm. Came on September 2, 1935. It was just a little tropical disturbance two days earlier. Nobody even saw it coming."

Mildred, the hurricane lady, kicked into high gear.

"Things can change fast out there. When that unnamed storm slammed into the Florida Keys that Labor Day weekend, it had sustained winds that topped 200 miles per hour. It wiped out Flagler's entire train route to Key West. Hundreds perished in a storm surge that went 25 feet. Rail lines high above the ocean were twisted and bent from the fierce winds and the flooding waters. During the height of the storm, one man had a two-by-four driven straight through his chest.

"When they found him the next day, he was still alive. They gave him a shot of whiskey, pulled that two-by-four out of him and watched him die. Must have been awful gruesome, don't ya think?"

But Mildred didn't bother waiting for the Sears man to respond. She continued, "Bodies were found weeks later in Florida Bay, bloated and stinking in the subtropical sun. It was disgusting. The Labor Day storm of '35 turned out to be one of the worst hurricanes to ever make landfall in the United States. Next to that monster hurricane Hugo back in 1989. In Hugo, the barometric pressure dropped so low they say people's ears started bleeding.

"Don't count on this here Kandee being anything less than that. That's why I'm stockpiling ice. You can't be too careful when it comes to hurricanes.

They're the most powerful force in nature, ya know."

Fucking nuts, thought the Sears repairman as he struggled to pull the refrigerator out from the wall to disconnect the supply line. When he finally worked it far enough out to be able to get his wrench to the connection, he saw it. At first he thought it was the largest pile of cat dander in the universe. It looked like a massive clump of dark gray fur. It resembled a pile of malignant lint.

Then he saw the two empty sockets where the eyes once were. He knew it wasn't a pile of cat fur. It was a dead cat. A dehydrated cat, like a sun-dried tomato cat, or a beef jerky cat. He got up and stood there, tears running down his face from his allergies. He didn't quite know how to break the news to Mrs. Lee.

"Ma'am, I think that there's a..., well, um, ma'am...,"

Mildred was over by her hurricane chart, making some new notations in the upper right-hand corner. She was trying to calculate how long Kandee might have before making landfall, still looking for similarities between the killer that hit the Keys in '35 and this weak tropical storm that was 400 miles to the southwest of Shoreside.

"What is it?"

"Are you missing a cat?"

"Buffy! Did you find Buffy?" Mildred exclaimed.

"Sort of, Mrs. Lee. But I'm afraid she's, um, well, she's...,"

"Dead." Mildred had a way with words. It was that blunt Chicago upbringing that made her cut to the chase. She knew damn well Buffy was dead. She hadn't seen hide nor hair of Buffy in four months. She had a hunch that Buffy might be behind the fridge because she always used to crawl there to enjoy the warm air blowing off the air compressor.

"Poor thing," Mildred went on. "She must have crawled back there to get warm and gotten stuck somehow. Can you reach back there and get her for me? She should have a proper burial next to Boots by the canal.

"Please try to reach her for me," pleaded a smiling Mildred Lee.

Steve bent over and reached to pick up Buffy. As Steve bent over again, Mildred took one more long look at his butt crack, although she hadn't the faintest idea as to why. He leaned way over and finally managed to get hold of Buffy.

As he handed the dead, dehydrated cat to Mildred, Steve's eyes, because of his allergies, began watering profusely. Mildred mistakenly thought he was crying. In her tough Chicago accent she tried to console him.

"Oh, now don't be getting all sentimental on me. Buffy had a good life and she was getting up there. She was happy when she died, as warm as a baby kitten behind that air compressor."

Steve looked confused by what he was hearing and handed the mummified cat to Mildred.

"Why, she's just as light as a feather, ain't she? That air compressor must have slowly cooked all the juices out of her these last few months. And look," Mildred grabbed the hind legs of Buffy and held the dried cat straight out, "she's as stiff as a textbook, too."

Steve wanted to leave everything where it stood and bolt for the front door. But he needed this job and, to get it, he had just completed nine months of refrigerator repair school. He desperately fought off his instincts to flee, and remained there in Mildred Lee's dark, twisted kitchen.

"I'm sorry," said Steve.

"Don't be. We all gotta go sometime."

Mildred set the dead cat on the kitchen table and shuffled over to her chart. She would have her errand boy bury the cat later. Bury it beside Boots by the seawall where they could have a nice view of the canal for all eternity. Next to the seawall where all of her dead ice makers should have been entombed as well.

A half-hour later, Steve wrapped up installing the replacement and pushed the refrigerator back into place. His eyes were now puffy and swollen, as if he had just gotten out of the boxing ring with Muhammad Ali. It was a bad match from the get go. Muhammad, in the form of a ton of cat hair and a little old lady, had kicked the living shit out of him.

"We'll send you the bill for this ma'am. Is that okay with you?"

"Fine," answered Mildred, not even bothering to turn away from her chart. "That'll be just fine."

Steve packed up his tools and headed toward the door, anxious to make it back into the world of oxygen. Just as he grabbed the front doorknob, he could hear Mildred call him from the kitchen.

"Mr. Sears man, Mr. Sears man!"

He put his tool box down and walked into the kitchen, waiting for that one last slug from the feeble, bent-over heavyweight champion of the world. "Yes, ma'am?"

"Could you take Buffy outside and set her on top of the garbage cans for me? My errand boy won't be coming over until tomorrow and I don't want to leave her on the kitchen table. Ya know, all those germs and stuff. Could you do that for me?"

"Sure, ma'am. I'll put her out back when I turn the main water line on."

Kapow! That left jab landed. He had to take the dead cat into his swollen hands.

"Thanks."

"Thank you, Mrs. Lee. Good luck with your new ice maker."

"Bye now."

"Bye."

Steve picked up the evaporated cat and walked toward the front door. He picked up his tool box and opened the front door. Once again, the brilliant sunlight seemed to burn his eyes as he walked into the yard. His whole face was reacting to his allergies. The champ had been merciless. He needed an entire bottle of Benadryl and he needed it now.

At that very instant, Steve swore that he would quit if his boss ever asked him to return to Mildred's house again. Every repairman ever sent to Mildred's house had made that same oath. Knowing that, his boss wouldn't ask Steve to ever go again. It was an honor reserved for the new kid on the block. It was baptism by fire.

Steve walked around and placed the dried cat on top of one of Mildred's two plastic garbage cans. The cat looked bizarre lying there like that, straight out and as stiff as a tennis racket. Steve bent over and turned on the main water supply. Little did he realize that Mildred was watching him through the kitchen window.

As he bent down Mildred could just catch one last glimpse of his butt crack. Mildred felt a tingle somewhere deep inside her. The tingle she felt was now totally foreign to her, but now, she vaguely remembered something about it. The third time was the charmer.

Well, no matter, she concluded.

As the Sears repairman walked to his truck, Mildred took the cap off her black Magic Marker and shuffled back to her hurricane tracking chart. Kandee was on her way. Kandee, the killer 'cane, thought Mildred with her fingers crossed.

773-2123
The Shoreside Conservancy

It was dawn, Tuesday morning. The sun had recently finished illuminating the urban sprawl that stretches across the eastern seaboard of Florida. The sun had already passed over the morning rush hour that jammed all 12 lanes of I-95. It had slowly made its way across the western suburbs of Ft. Lauderdale, West Palm Beach and Miami. Suburbs that were already pushing hard against the dark green skin of Marjorie Stoneman Douglas' river of grass.

A half-hour earlier, the morning sunlight had spread across those savannahs of sawgrass and hardwood hammocks, awakening the egrets and warblers from their evening roosts. That very same sun was now rising over the west coast suburbs that pushed equally hard against the Everglades from the other direction, slowly closing in on the vast, open interior of the Sunshine State. Development after development methodically creeping, walking across the state toward each other. A long, dreadful walk at that.

Now, as Dee and Scott sat quietly in the old Jeep they used to patrol the beach, the first rays of sunlight lit the back sides of the seven buildings soon to be known as Sanderling Condominiums. The certificate of occupancy had been issued late last week. The day after that, the lights were switched on. That was the problem.

Dee and Scott had been up all night looking for the last few remaining nests of hatchlings to break out of their sandy nests and crawl to the ocean. It was late October and the loggerhead turtle season was drawing to a close. With tropical storm Kandee 300 miles to the southeast and headed toward southwest Florida, both Scott and Dee knew that this would possibly be their last run. It had been a good year for the loggerheads and the occasional, but rare, green turtle. The midnight volunteers of the Shoreside Conservancy's turtle patrol had discovered 451 nesting sites.

Every nest held about one hundred eggs. Of those, maybe 80 percent of the hatchlings would dig their way out of the sand. Most of them would eventually die long before they grew into breeding adults. The seabirds would eat their fair share, as would the snook and sea trout that patrolled the beaches this time of year. Beyond those threats there were a million other hurdles for these tiny creatures to overcome. There were sharks and octopuses, shrimp nets and pollution. The list was endless. Only one in a thousand would survive.

But as the two of them pulled the Jeep in front of the Sanderling project and sat there quietly, only one thought came to mind. The lights. For years and years running, this 600 feet of shoreline had been the loggerheads' favorite nesting site. In a good year, they would count as many as 30 nests along this solitary stretch. That was double the average along developed parcels.

The reason was simple. The McKinzie tract was dark. Darkness, for an expecting female loggerhead, was an ally. Darkness, for the hatchlings that were digging their way out of the sand-covered nests, was essential. When they first opened their tiny eyes after tunneling out of their sandy nests, those scores of tiny, three-inch sea turtles were lost. Their instincts told them, in the darkness of it all, to crawl toward the light. With nothing but the blackness of unbroken vegetation behind them, the only light they had found for the last million years was that of the open sky over the Gulf of Mexico. Starlight and moonlight. That, for countless generations, was where they had learned to crawl.

Not any longer. Thomas Edison changed all that one hundred years ago. Tom Loggins and TLD, Inc. now had brought Edison's invention right to the shoreline of the McKinzie tract. As Scott and Dee looked over at one of three staked nest sites that had yet to hatch, they knew what would happen.

"It's a shame, isn't it?" said Scott.

"Yeah," replied Dee in a quiet voice that you could barely hear over the rumble of the idling Jeep.

"How many do you think we'll lose?" asked Scott.

"Half. Maybe more. It's really hard to say. The hatchlings along this stretch have never had condominium lights to confuse them before. The beach here is low and there isn't really a beach ridge to slow them down any. If they crawl toward the condominium lights instead of the ocean, many of them will end up in that swale over there," Dee pointed toward the first beachside swale that was created as part of the general development and drainage plan. It wasn't 50 yards from where they were parked, running between the front two buildings.

"If they end up in that swale, which is mostly fresh water, the egrets, alligators and herons will make quick work of them. We'll lose at least half of these nestlings, maybe more," concluded Dee.

"Why do they need all those lights on? There isn't going to be anyone in the buildings until this coming Saturday night. I should call Loggins and ask him to turn them off for the next few days as a favor to these last few hatchlings," said Scott.

"Scott, get serious. Loggins will give us his standard response. Once he's CO'd, his insurance company will require that all the stairway lights in the project be left on every evening for insurance purposes. It's a liability issue. The insurance companies don't give a damn about some three-inch sea turtles who happened to get lost along the way. They're trying to avoid some last-minute subcontractor missing a step after fixing a leaking drain, or some decorator falling down a stairwell after hanging some drapes.

"Loggerhead turtles can't sue, Scott. If they could, they'd have one hell of a case against TLD, Inc. They would have one hell of a case against us.

"They could make a good argument that this project will kill more of their brood than all the seagulls, snook and sharks combined. That those bright fluorescent lights mean that hundreds and hundreds of hatchlings will turn the wrong way when they first open their eyes. They'll accidently head east instead of west, finding themselves swimming in fresh water and not in the salty ocean where they belong.

"If loggerheads could sue, Scott, they'd win. But what's the point of dreaming about it. Loggins and his group have won this one. We did the best we could, but we can't win them all."

Scott didn't respond. He was tired. Dee was supposed to have a volunteer ride along last night but she canceled at the last minute. One of the rules of the turtle patrol was that there always had to be two people on each patrol. It made sense.

The patrols sometimes went on all night long. Anything could happen at 3:00 in the morning. Most of the people patrolling were volunteers. Most of those volunteers weren't accustomed to staying up half the night. They were used to getting to bed at 10:30 and not spending the better part of their night being awake in the darkness. Taking turns driving these deserted beaches of Shoreside looking for huge creatures to be crawling out of the ocean to lay their eggs in the sand. A single person could easily fall asleep at the wheel and end up in an accident. End up hitting one of the very turtles they were trying to save as she crawled to dig her nesting cavity.

When Evelyn Gardner called Dee at 6:30 to tell her that her husband had come down with the flu, and that because of it, she wasn't going to be able to make patrol that night, Dee called Scott. He was always there for backup. Scott was like that, dedicated to conservation to a fault.

So Scott tried to get in a little sleep before Dee came over in the Jeep and picked him up at midnight, but it wasn't enough. He had already put in a full day at the Conservancy and now, as the sun headed off to illuminate the east coast of Mexico across the broad expanse of the Gulf, Scott was completely exhausted. He would have to sleep some before heading into work, and Dee knew it.

"Let's go, Scott. You're beat and there's not a darn thing we can do about Sanderling at this point. It's all in God's hands now."

Dee took the Jeep out of park and started driving the beach toward their short tote road that brought the Jeep back on paved roads again. As Dee drove Scott to his home she couldn't help but think of the fate of the last three nests. All of them were right in front of the new Sanderling complex. The bright new

Sanderling complex.

She knew that most of the hatchlings would turn toward the fluorescent trademark of 20th-century man instead of the simple starlight of God. Turn east instead of west. It was a shame that their mother waited so long to lay her eggs. No, that wasn't fair.

The fault wasn't with some 70-year-old turtle who was only doing what her instinct told her she must do. The fault was with us. The fault was in wanting a room with a view, a stairwell that was bright and safe, a private getaway on the beach. We were to blame, always invading the natural systems with our upscale shelters and our white Berber carpet.

As Dee pulled in front of Scott's house, his two boys came and greeted him on the way to catch the school bus. Tears were pouring down Dee's cheeks as she said goodbye to Scott and hello to his young kids. They all said goodbye and Dee sped off toward her apartment.

"Why's Dee crying, Dad?" asked Matt, his youngest.

"She's crying for the turtles."

"Oh."

But Dee wasn't crying for the turtles. She was crying for the entire world.

212-984-7472
Cold Calling to New York

"Hello. Mr. Stanislaaaw...sky?" Jason wasn't sure if he was pronouncing it correctly. It was his tenth call this morning. At his present rate, he could hit 50 calls before noon.

"Yes, that's correct, I'm Mr. Stanislowski."

"My name is Jason R. Randazzle from Shoreside Realty here on lovely Shoreside Island. Our records indicate that you own a spacious three-bedroom canal house over on..."

"Didn't you call me last year?"

"I might have." Jason knew that he had. There were 18,000 property owners on Shoreside. He tried to average 75 calls a day. During the course of a year that meant he would make 19,500 calls. For Jason R. Randazzle, Shoreside Island was an 18,000-card personal Rolodex. He kept all of his notes and numbers in his bright red $3.47 college-style ring-bound notebook. That inexpensive notebook was his lifeline to dialing for dollars. In it, Jason had every number to every owner on the island.

Jason went to great lengths to keep it updated and accurate. If a number was unlisted, Jason would call the condo or homeowners' association pretending to be an appliance delivery man, or a cable repairman needing to reach the owners of the property. He used every available means to acquire Shoreside's owners' home phone numbers: the Internet, telephone books, directory assistance, neighbors, everything short of private investigators. Four years ago he had actually hired a private eye to try to find a particularly difficult home phone for a Mr. Robert Caprianni from Trenton, New Jersey. The PI ended up taking a bullet in his left shoulder. Mobsters like to keep their personal phone numbers on a short list. Luckily, the private investigator lived.

After his hospital stay, Jason did get the number from the private eye. But after thinking about it for two weeks, Jason decided not to call this particular owner about selling his penthouse. Probably a wise choice, although Jason kept a close eye on the local obituary column for Mr. Caprianni. Mobsters had a tendency to die, and death, even murder, was good.

Over the years, Jason Randazzle's notebook became his ticket to prosperity, his personal El Dorado. Without it, he was lost. Apparently, it was Mr.

Stanislowski's turn to come up on rotation again. Jason waited for Mr. Stanislowski's angry response.

"Might have? I'm damn sure you called me last year at about this time. I've got the exact time and date written down right here in my telephone log. I've also written a notation next to it with my express wishes to be permanently removed from your phone solicitations. Or don't you remember any of that?"

Jason did remember but he never paid any intention to owners who requested that he stop calling them. His reasoning was simple if not perverse. They might die, divorce or become hopelessly incapacitated over the course of a year. Their loved ones might need Jason to call, to help them through their time of crisis. Help them sell off the assets and settle the estate. Removing someone from his college notebook, even when the person requested that removal, was unthinkable to Jason.

"No sir, I don't recall that conversation at all. You have to understand that I make over 50 calls a day and it gets very difficult to keep track of all of them."

Jason was lying. He kept meticulous records and right beside Mr. Stanislowski's phone number, Jason had noted that he had asked last year to have his name and number removed from the rotation. It even stated, in Jason's tiny handwriting, that Mr. Stanislowski was a registered member of the United States government's official non-telephone solicitation list.

Jason sheepishly continued, "Then might I assume that you are not interested in selling your property at this time?"

"Selling!!! Why the nerve. I'm thinking about suing, not selling.

"What is it with you people anyway? Are you totally nuts? I told you last year when I hung up on you that if you ever called me again I'd sue you. I'm already on the government's non-solicitation list but what the hell good is that. The world is full of assholes just like you Mr. Randazzle. Short of pulling my goddamned phone right off my kitchen wall, nothing stops you."

Mr. Stanislowski was on a roll. Jason quickly checked the time on his watch and waited for the rest of the verbal attack. He had been kicked in the ear before by dozens of irate owners. It now became more of a question as to how much time this particular assault was going to take. After all, time was money.

The pissed-off owner of that spacious three-bedroom canal house resumed his onslaught, "I'm sick of it. I'm sick of gold VISA cards, sick of phony cruise line offers, sick of firefighters, whale savers and soul savers. I've gotten to where I'm afraid to answer my phone any longer. I've gotten to the point where I can't sleep at night, knowing that it might ring at any moment. Knowing that it will be some shithead just like you asking if I want to change long distance companies or buy Christmas wreaths to support the mentally challenged or the physically handicapped."

Jason was withdrawing. His instincts were impeccable in this regard. Mr. Stanislowski was a basket case. He had crossed the line. Jason wanted to hang up on this kook but it was a firm policy of his never to hang up. Instead, he tightened his grip on the phone and hung on. It was going to get real scary, real soon.

"Do you know what I'm saying?"

"Sort of," Jason sidestepped. He knew damn well what he was saying. In Mr. Stanislowski's mind, Jason Randazzle was part of the conspiracy of telephone callers who were secretly plotting to drive the great middle class of America completely mad. They were all card-carrying members of a sick group of people hell bent on destroying the United States of America one telephone call at a time.

It was a cult. A demented telephone cult that always called mid-morning or around 7:00 p.m., just after dinner. Called to ask the unsuspecting consumer for a donation, an opinion, a subscription, a free evaluation, or anything and everything that they were paid to call for. The sect of the phone solicitors. Worse than Moonies.

Mr. Stanislowski went on, the pitch of his voice growing higher and higher. "Don't lie to me you worthless piece of shit. You know damn well what I'm saying. You know damn well that you're ruining this country of ours with your Touch-Tone phones and pseudo-friendly monologues. I've had it. Do you understand that Mr. Randazzle? Do you understand the fact that I can't take it anymore? That I haven't had a decent night's sleep in a month just thinking about it. Thinking about the next call, and the call after that!"

Jason understood it. He knew that the other shoe was going to fall in a few more minutes time, but he didn't want to think about it. For Jason, it was like being in a car wreck. He saw the brick wall 50 yards out, heard the snap of the tie rod, felt the steering wheel break free and even as Jason slammed on the brakes as hard as possible, he realized that the vehicle would not stop in time. His hand clenched down one notch further on the phone. Jason was holding his telephone so tight that his skin was slowly peeling off the back of his pure white knuckles.

Jason made a break for the exit, "Well, I'm sorry for calling, Mr. Stanislowski, but I really must be going."

"Going where? Going to make another call just like this one. Probably to some unsuspecting widow who's unsure of what to do with her property, or someone going through a horrible divorce trying to decide what to do with his or her condo there on Shoreside. That's how you operate, isn't it Mr. Randazzle? You're sick. You worthless piece of trash.

"Well, I've got news for you."

Jason's face turned as chalky as a bottle of Wite-Out. He felt faint and dislocated. One of the bullets was finally going to penetrate his rhino-like skin. Jason realized that it was about to get expensive. Very, very expensive.

"I know my rights, Mr. Randazzle. No doubt you know them too. The fine for calling someone on an official non-phone solicitation list is $10,000. That's a hell of a lot of money, even for a slime ball like you.

"And don't even think about hanging up. Just put me on hold and patch me through to your sales manager, so we can get the paperwork started. If you do hang up I'll simply call your office back. I've got Caller I.D. and your telephone number is sitting here in front of me as big as Alaska. How does that make you feel?"

Jason didn't say a word. He just watched the car he was driving smash against the brick wall as if he wasn't inside. He heard all those sounds that car accidents make; the grinding metal, the shattering glass and then the sirens approaching from a distance.

He thought of Mrs. Martha Livingston for a moment before putting Mr. Stanislowski on hold. They had just closed on her condominium two weeks ago. She was that uncertain widow Mr. Stanislowski had just mentioned. He did manage to double-dip that sale. He cut the commission $500 to help her out. That brought his commission down to $17,230. Now he would have to further reduce that by $10,000 to cover this action. Still, that's a $7,230 profit, thought Jason. That's not too shabby.

"Please hold while I connect you to Mrs. Braun, our sales manager."

Jason R. Randazzle was already bouncing back. He was now calmly climbing out of the passenger window of the car and walking away from the incident unscathed. That's how resilient he was. It was as if he were made from some kind of human Silly Putty. Stretch him, snap him, stomp on him with high heels and it didn't matter. He would reshape himself within minutes and pick up the phone as if nothing had happened. Rejection was his forte. Jason was unsinkable. Unstoppable.

Next time, he pondered, I'll think about crossing Mr. Stanislowski off my list. Well, maybe not. He's so stressed out that he might not make it another year. Jason made some notations next to his phone number.

He wrote, "Mr. Stanislowski sued me for $10,000, might consider not calling when he comes up on my list next year at this time. I'll wait and see. He seemed very stressed out, and might not make it another year."

Nothing could stop Jason Randazzle. Nothing. He picked up the phone and called Mr. and Mrs. Lewis Bradley, who, unbeknownst to Jason, were thinking about selling their place on Shoreside this year. Life was good, so long as it came with a dial tone.

570-9898 Ext. 1
Elinor Braun's Office

Linda Hinkle sat quietly in one of the two chairs just outside Elinor Braun's office. Elinor was still on the phone. Linda had already been waiting five minutes and during that time she had glanced at her Gucci watch three times. She had an appointment at 9:30 that she really didn't want to be late for. Whatever the reason Elinor had for requesting this 9:00 a.m. meeting with her, it had better be a good one. Linda hated small talk when there was money to be made.

Maybe it has something to do with that tropical storm, thought Linda to herself. I know that we won't be able to close on the Wilson home this week because of it. You can't close on a home when there's a tropical storm anywhere within 800 miles of Florida. It's because the home buyer can't get insurance. The state's insurance companies have a policy making it impossible to write flood or windstorm insurance when a named storm is inside this enormous box. Maybe that's why I'm here? Elinor just wants to be sure that I've done an amendment to the closing date. Elinor and her damn forms. Figures.

But Linda Hinkle still wasn't exactly sure why she had been called in to see Elinor. It was a rarity for Elinor to call a senior agent into her office. Sometimes it was to reprimand them for missing a disclosure, or overlooking an initial on some obscure addendum, though Linda Hinkle was rarely guilty of either of those infractions. Sometimes it was to discuss a particularly difficult closing. Whatever the reason, it didn't happen very often. Linda couldn't even remember the last time she was in Elinor's office.

Maybe it had something to do with the Jensens' leaking roof? That mess has certainly gotten out of hand. Mr. and Mrs. Jensen were now suing Shoreside Realty for the entire cost of a replacement roof, plus new carpeting. That bill was coming in just under $25,000. They were still in the midst of getting the dispute over to arbitration. Shoreside's attorneys had recommended splitting the cost 50/50 with the purchasers. It sounded fair enough.

The Jensens' attorney, Mr. Bruce Peterson, wanted all of the money for the repairs and replacement to come out of Shoreside Realty or he was going to go to court. Once in court, the Jensens would seek punitive damages for their pain and suffering over the last 18 months of toothless roofers tracking tar all over their house and endless phone calls to an agent who might as well have moved to Tasmania. It could get pretty costly if the court-appointed arbitrator didn't find some middle ground. Which, as fate would have it, he wouldn't.

Linda couldn't think of any other reason why Elinor might call for a special meeting with her. The Jensens' leak was in the hands of the lawyers at this point and, aside from some meetings last week, there was nothing new with that case. Maybe their roof had collapsed? No, Linda could only guess at the reason she was to be sitting here at, what was it now? Nine-twelve on a Tuesday morning.

As she sat there and pondered the purpose of this visit, Linda looked idly around the small foyer. There were your typical glossy magazines: *Southern Living, Gulfshore Living*, and an old *Newsweek* lying on a glass-top coffee table. There was also a small pamphlet designed by the company's marketing firm that explained to the general public the benefits of working with the "experienced professionals" at Shoreside Realty. Linda didn't bother to pick it up and look it over.

She knew why the public should choose to work with Shoreside Realty and Linda Hinkle in particular. She had already closed $18.3 million in sales this year and there were two months of selling left. She was an experienced professional. A damn good one and a damn rich one, at that. These pamphlets are good for my business, she decided.

Across from Linda, hanging on the wall, was the famous beach scene painting she had seen in a hundred homes and condominiums on Shoreside. The sea oats, the sand and the Shoreside Island lighthouse in the background all combined to create a perfectly generic depiction of the Florida lifestyle. This particular painting had become old and faded. In a way, so had the Florida lifestyle it depicted, although Linda Hinkle would have been the last person in the world to admit that.

As Linda casually glanced over the details of the painting, the pristine beach stretching off into the distance, the breaking surf and the flock of seagulls above the lighthouse, she remembered her brief career as a painter. That was seven months ago.

Linda remembered that this same lighthouse scene was the painting both Elinor and Loretta Snyder had tried to buy to replace the Larsons' daughter's watercolor. Linda looked at the painting and thought that it was strange that neither of them wanted this lovely beach scene over that stupid paint-by-number. People are impossible, reflected Linda Hinkle as her Gucci watch ticked by 20 past 9:00. Impossible.

Just as she thought that, Elinor Braun opened one of the two French doors that led into her office.

"Linda, thanks so much for waiting. You may come in now."

"Oh, not a problem, Elinor. I hope that we can make this quick; I've got a listing presentation at 9:30 that I just can't be late for."

Elinor didn't respond. That was bad. Elinor's instincts for money were as keenly developed as Linda's. If Linda was going to be late for her appointment, then this was trouble. Both ladies knew the age-old real estate axiom by heart: "WHOEVER CONTROLS THE LISTINGS, CONTROLS THE MARKET!" These two ladies might as well have had it tattooed on their forearms, given how ingrained it was in their respective psyches. If Elinor wants me to postpone a listing presentation, then this is trouble, thought an anxious Ms. Hinkle. Big trouble.

As Elinor sat down she picked up her desk phone and turned it around to make it easier for Linda to make the call. "I think that this might need a few minutes, Linda; why don't you phone your clients and let them know that you'll be running a little late."

Linda had already sat in one of the two leather chairs that faced Elinor's immense mahogany desk. Linda was nervous. Like Dustin Hoffman in *The Marathon Man,* she had already started looking for the dental tools Elinor was soon going to be starting in with. Linda's mouth was dry and her hands were trembling ever so slightly. This was bad.

"Oh, that's a good idea, Elinor. Let me find their number."

As Linda took out her Day Timer and looked up the number, Elinor picked up her notepad and reviewed the memos that she had taken during her phone call a few minutes earlier. The notes were in shorthand. Elinor had learned shorthand years ago when she was a young attractive secretary at a small legal firm. She didn't stay there for long, but over the years the shorthand had come in very handy. Her extensive notes were as thorough as a court stenographer's and many a lawsuit had been settled post haste due to Elinor's shorthand. Paper trails, said Elinor Braun at her sales meetings - it was all about leaving paper trails.

Linda found the number and phoned her clients. It wasn't a problem. They would simply wait for Linda to arrive. The only conflict was a luncheon appointment that they had with their financial adviser. They were thinking about moving the house into a trust before listing it. The house was worth $2.8 million and they had been advised that there might be considerable tax advantages to forming a trust prior to the disposition of the property. Rich people have a way of staying rich.

"Then look for me around 10:30 at the latest," wrapped up Linda.

"That will be fine," answered Mrs. Grace Boland. "We'll keep the coffee warm."

"Goodbye."

"Goodbye now."

Linda hung the receiver up and Elinor quickly picked the entire phone up and turned it back around. She punched in the intercom and told Doris, her personal secretary, to hold all calls. Linda was now extremely apprehensive.

Like all the agents at Shoreside, she dreaded being stuck in a room with the "Form Nazi." Now that the doors were shut, and all the calls were held, Linda felt completely confined.

In Linda's anxious mind, Elinor's well-appointed office was now a windowless room beneath some Third World presidential palace. Her comfortable leather chair instantly became a stiff wooden one, to which Linda was bound and gagged. The duct tape had come out.

Elinor became three, no, make that four ruthless henchmen. They were all putting on black leather gloves and smiling that sick, sneering smile henchmen are masters of.

There was a single electric bulb hanging over Linda. A tray full of various instruments was being wheeled alongside her. Exacto knives, brass knuckles, black leather batons and a hypodermic needle were all neatly arranged on the tray. As the largest of the four henchmen leaned over and picked up the foot-long billy club, Ms. Elinor Braun looked straight at Mrs. Linda Hinkle and said, "What do you know about a paint-by-number watercolor, Linda?"

Wham!!! The thug's first blow shattered Linda's jaw. The pain shot through her like someone shooting rivets though ice-cold steel. It was excruciating. Worse than anything imaginable. Linda knew instantly that the torture session had just gotten under way.

"What paint-by-number?" Linda calmly replied.

"Linda, don't bullshit me. I just got off a 30-minute phone call from an attorney by the name of Mr. Bruce Strunk. He represents Mr. and Mrs. Larson. They have recently discovered through a friend of theirs who still owns a condo at Osprey Landings that there appears to be not one, but two original watercolors of a certain paint-by-number that their daughter Rose painted when she was five years old. Now how in hell can there be two paintings when their daughter painted only one, Linda?"

The second blow came in lower. The leather baton made a dull, crunching sound as it hit Linda's left knee. She could feel the kneecap explode beneath the impact. The single incandescent lightbulb flickered above her as she tried to cry out in pain through the gray piece of duct tape covering her mouth. One of the other deputies had seized the Exacto knife. The other two were smoking cheap, unfiltered cigarettes and making small talk. They were used to torture. They enjoyed it.

"It was only a $2.99 watercolor, Elinor. I had, no, I should say we had over $30,000 in commissions coming and it was all falling apart over this stupid little painting that hung in the guest bedroom. Don't blame me on this one, Elinor. Given the same set of circumstances you might have done the same thing."

Linda Hinkle was going on the offensive. This was a conversation between two equals. There wasn't an ounce of anything resembling Jennifer Willow left in Linda Hinkle. She wasn't going to take the rap without a fight. Real estate commissions were important to Elinor and the owners of Shoreside Realty, and if an agent had to fudge now and then to get the job done, well then, so be it.

"I want the truth, Linda. I want the who, what, where and why from beginning to end. If I find out later that you lied to me, or left out even the tiniest of details, I'll never forgive you for it. Just tell me everything that happened and we'll go from there."

Elinor got out her legal notepad at the exact same moment the thug with the Exacto knife stood in front of Linda. He looked awful. There was a long, deep scar across the left side of his face and an eye patch over one of his dark eyes. He still had a cigarette in his mouth as he leaned over Linda. With his face not more than six inches from Linda's he took his right hand up, the same hand that was holding the knife, and brought it close to Linda's face. With his right eye he winked. It was a wicked, foreboding wink.

Linda waited in terror for the first long cut across her face. She could almost feel that razor knife slicing into her when the henchman ripped the duct tape off her mouth and said, "Start talking or I'll cut you up like a frying chicken." It was a horseshit metaphor, but what could she expect from an uneducated, right-wing thug.

Linda knew it was over. She didn't know how her little scheme had come undone, but it had. In a way it didn't matter. The big dogs were on her and it would only be a matter of time before they would run her down.

It was a stupid thing to do, thought Linda, to have purchased and painted the fake. But it was too late for that now. All that was left was the firing squad and the six-figure settlement.

After 20 minutes of Linda spilling the beans, Elinor was numb. She thought that she had heard every preposterous real estate story in the universe and now she realized that the universe was larger than anyone expected. The universe is endless, as are the variations on how Florida properties wind up at the closing table. This tale took Elinor beyond our solar system and on toward the distant galaxies. It was totally unbelievable.

Near the end of her twisted soliloquy, just after Linda Hinkle explained how drunk she was when she finally finished her last watercolor, Linda asked Elinor the question she had been wanting to ask from the onset.

"How did the Larsons find out?" said Linda.

"Their neighbors, Mr. and Mrs. Waterman, were invited to dinner one night by Dr. and Mrs. Asp. Naturally, Mrs. Asp wanted them to look around and see all the lovely little additions and bric-a-brac she had added to the condo. When they reached the guest bedroom, Mrs. Waterman couldn't help but notice Rose's watercolor hanging in the exact same spot it had always hung.

"The trouble was that Mrs. Waterman had just had the nicest conversation with Mrs. Larson not two days prior to that. During that conversation, Mrs. Larson had told Mrs. Waterman that they had just found the perfect place for their daughter's paint-by-number at their new lake place near Oswego. Now Mrs. Waterman knew that there simply couldn't be two originals, so she quickly surmised that one of these paintings had to be a fake. She had remembered all the fuss about it back in March when it closed, so her discovery was quite the event.

"She didn't say anything to Dr. and Mrs. Asp at the time because she thought that it would have simply ruined their dinner. Which it would have.

"The next morning she was on the phone to Mrs. Larson just after sunrise. The rest is pretty obvious. The Larsons got in touch with their attorney immediately and now they are demanding to know which is which. Once we get that straightened out, you can have the honor of calling your customers and telling them about the forgery. Now tell me, and tell me honestly, Linda, which is which?"

Linda wanted the needle. She looked straight away at the scarfaced thug with the bad metaphors and said, "I'm not talking, give me the goddamned needle."

She didn't know what was in the needle and by this time she didn't really care: sodium pentothal, Clorox bleach, battery acid, or heroin? It didn't matter. Just shoot me up and put me under. Stop the pain.

"Please, please make the pain go away," Linda pleaded with each of the four ruthless stooges.

"I don't know," she said to Elinor.

"Excuse me, Linda. What did I just say to you about lying?"

"Elinor, I really don't know which is which. I was very hung over that Monday morning when I made the switch. Remember, you called me asking me why I wasn't going to make the Sanderling marketing presentation? Well, when you did that, I had to pull away from the two paintings that were sitting on the dining room table to get to my cell phone, which was in the kitchen. When I finished talking to you and returned to the dining room, I couldn't remember which paint-by-number was the original and which was the one I had finished the night before.

"They were both equally awful. One was painted by a five-year-old, and the other by me, an intoxicated woman at 2:00 a.m. I just grabbed the one on the right and brought it over to Strunk's office before the closing. I don't know if the Larsons have the original, or if the Asps do."

"Oh my God."

The four henchmen were done with Linda. She just sat there, unconscious and slumped over in her chair like so many torture victims before her. Her face was bloodied, her body bruised and numb and her heart barely pounding. They would untie her shortly and drag her back to her cell. There would be more persecution coming. There would be depositions, hearings, teleconferences and registered mail. Lots of registered mail.

The attorneys would have a field day with this one. Like the feeling Cortes and his gang of conquistadors must have had when they first gazed across the golden cornfields of Teotihuacan in 1521, those dozens of legal experts knew that they had found the mother lode of all mother lodes. All that was left was to behead Montezuma and make off with the gold. Fun stuff for attorneys. Even Elinor Braun loosened her collar as she showed Linda Hinkle to the door. She wanted to be sure they wouldn't need to take a second swing when they proceeded to lop off her head.

"Well, I'll have to let you get to your meeting for now," said a despondent Elinor Braun.

"What should we do next?" asked Linda before heading through Elinor's French doors.

"Wait."

"How long?"

"Not long enough," answered Elinor.

She was right. Not long enough.

570-9514
Mildred Lee's Home Phone

It was 2:00 Thursday morning when Mildred Lee's alarm clock went off. "It's time to empty the new ice maker," she muttered to herself quietly. As Mildred slowly got up and hobbled to the kitchen she could hear it. She could hear it pounding on her rooftop. It was the rain.

Kandee was within 100 miles of Shoreside and the first outer bands of thunderstorms were hitting the island. The wind was picking up. The storm's fast upon us, thought Mildred as she stood quietly in the living room listening to the sound of rain on the roof. Fast upon us.

Mildred recalled the rainstorms she experienced with her late husband back in Chicago. There was no comparison between the two storms. The thunderstorms in Illinois were sprinkles compared with the rains that inundated south Florida during these tropical storms. If it was raining cats and dogs midsummer in Evanston, it was raining entire kennels on Mildred's rooftop as she stood there in her yellowed nightgown, her mouth agape, her eyes glassy and old.

The rain was falling hard. It quickly filled Mildred's gutters to overflowing and pooled along the edge of the house where her shrubs and ornamentals were planted. It ran down the driveway and settled in the swale between the driveway's apron and the street. That puddle grew logarithmically, exponentially with every passing minute. The puddle soon became a pond, the pond a lake and the lake wanted desperately to merge with the ocean. It rained so hard that the fires of hell would have been extinguished in a minute had the devil not been crafty enough to put an earthen roof on his inferno.

All the while Mildred just stood there. Her eyes looking up at the ceiling, her hands shaking ever so slightly, like the hands of the elderly always shake. She was saying a silent prayer to herself. Praying that everything would be all right. Thinking of her grandchildren in Chicago and wishing that this old house would sell before the "Big One" hit. Frightened.

After a spell, Mildred turned her attention away from the deluge that was now pounding on her roof, and continued toward the kitchen. It was time to empty the ice bin into one of her two coolers. She bent over and unscrewed the drain cap in one of the two white coolers. She had a little pie pan underneath it to catch the melted ice as it trickled out. After draining what little water came out, she put the cap on and shook the ice chest. She was making sure that all of the ice inside was settled before dumping in fresh ice.

Then she went to her refrigerator, bent over, opened the freezer and took out the ice bin. It was a quarter of the way full. "It's working good now," Mildred said to herself as she carried the bin over to the ice chest. She opened the cooler and dumped her ice into it like someone depositing her life savings in a safe-deposit box at the local bank. Her entire life savings; in coins.

The ice made quite a noise as it fell into the ice chest and one of her cats, Blackie, scooted from under the kitchen table when it happened. All three of her remaining cats were like that, spooky and darting around all the time. Neurotic, indoor cats.

Mildred put the ice bin under the wire arm of her ice maker and started meandering over to bed. She stopped in the same place in the living room to listen to the rain. It was still pouring outside. Now the winds had kicked up to the point where they were driving the rain into the corrugated aluminum hurricane shutters that covered all the living room windows. It sounded as though hundreds of people were standing outside Mildred's ranch throwing handfuls of gravel at the house. It was a very disturbing sound.

Mildred climbed into her single bed and took out her rosary. She knew that without it she would never be able to get back to sleep. She reset her alarm for 6:00 a.m., which was the next time she would empty her ice bin, and began saying her rosary. Mildred was still a devout Catholic. Everyone from Chicago is a devout Catholic, or a former devout Catholic.

Outside, the rains fell harder than the day before Noah's ark floated free. They saturated the earth and filled the canals, they fell in a darkness so thick that headlights passing in the night couldn't penetrate it. If they say that when it rains this hard, God is crying, then on this warm, windy tropical night, God must have just learned that his mother had passed away. God wasn't crying, he was bawling.

"Hail Mary, full of grace, the Lord is with thee, blessed art thou amongst women, and blessed is the fruit of thy womb, Jesus. Holy Mary, Mother of God, pray for us sinners now and in the hour of our death. Amen...Hail Mary, full of grace, the Lord is with..."

Mildred's muffled prayers were smothered by the sound of the wind-driven rain smashing against her thin hurricane shutters. They were so muffled by the wind and rain that only Mildred Lee, and her husband in heaven, Walter, could hear them. Walt prayed along with her for a while. He owed it to her, at least until she fell asleep.

Mildred repeated her Hail Marys as her arthritic hands slowly walked their way down the beads of her rosary. Every sixth prayer was the Lord's Prayer. "Our Father, who art in heaven, hallowed be Thy name, Thy kingdom come,

Thy will be done, on earth, as it is in heaven. Give us this day our daily bread and forgive us our trespasses, as we forgive those who trespass against us..."

The world outside Mildred's tiny, two-bedroom ranch was a scary place for a tired, 84-year-old woman who never wanted to leave Chicago. Her rosary helped. It helped immensely. In ten minutes, Mildred fell fast asleep.

The rain outside continued. Sometimes it would lighten to the point where it was little more than a drizzle in the relentless wind. At other times it would rain even harder, complete with the timpani of thunder and the flash of a million volts of lightning against a pitch black sky. It wouldn't stop.

It would rain all day Thursday and into Friday morning. The rains would fill all the ditches and swales on Shoreside Island to overflowing. Island swimming pools would run over and flood their surrounding decks. Lakes would spill out and double their former size, water would cover blocks of low-lying roads, roofs that never leaked would leak, and the world would be soaked with the tears of God.

Kandee would dump nearly two feet of rain on Shoreside before moving toward the northeast. The island would become a cold, wet dog shivering in the warmth of Friday morning's sunshine. It wasn't the first time this once-unnamed barrier island would become drenched to the bone, nor would it be the last. It was the price it paid for a winter without frost. It was the cost of being born in the tropics.

570-9898
The Main Switchboard; Thursday

"No, it's mostly rain. It's been raining here since early last night. There isn't all that much wind with this storm. Just rain."

It was 4:00 Thursday afternoon and Betsy was going through her well-worn monologue about the storm for the umpti-millionth time. Owner after owner had been calling asking her about tropical storm Kandee, and wondering how much damage their condos had sustained thus far.

The news media up north were to blame. They had hyped tropical storm Kandee completely out of proportion. They kept going on and on about how the storm was passing directly over the top of Shoreside Island and how all indications were that the intense winds and torrential rains were virtually certain to lay ruin to the island. They were bored.

Hurricanes and tropical storms in Florida made good copy for the television news media up north during late October. The weather around the rest of the nation consisted of little more than showing a national map indicating where the autumnal colors were peaking and reporting the local forecast, which called for more cold, wet rain.

The only weather happening in the continental United States was these few late-season tropical storms and, if they got lucky, an actual hurricane. The tornadoes of the spring were old news and it was too early in the year to report on any winter blizzards. Both snowstorms and twisters were good television copy, complete with either footage of downtown Fargo under 20-foot snowdrifts or helicopter shots of some Wichita suburb blown to bits by an errant tornado. Both cataclysms were out of season and presently unavailable.

So tropical storm Kandee became the default setting. Film crews were actually standing along the causeway in the drenching rain trying to make things look worse than they really were. Camera angles had to be modified in an attempt to make the three-foot chop on the bay look threatening. If the camera man shot the choppy surf while lying on his stomach, the whitecaps took on a far more sinister dimension than they actually had. Throw in some archival footage from Andrew and Camille while hinting that it was probably at least that bad on Shoreside and you have it: news. Not truth. News.

As owner after owner tuned in to CNN, The Weather Channel, or MSNBC, they were all led to believe that Shoreside Island was about to perish beneath the crashing surf, flooding rains and an unusually high storm surge. Of which only about ten percent was based on actual events. The other 90 percent was a result of local forecasters getting sick and tired of talking about the glorious fall colors in Vermont, or along the Blue Ridge Parkway. They all wanted action: roofs being blown off, frightened survivors climbing onto helicopter skids, house pets swimming to safety. Maple leaves and autumnal colors were boring.

No sooner would the owners turn off their television sets than they would run to the phone to call someone on Shoreside to see if their unit had collapsed into the Gulf. If they weren't in a rental pool, the only other 800 number they had handy was that of the real estate agent who sold them their condo or their island home. That's why Betsy's voice was down to the wire and her monologue as well rehearsed as a bad high school play.

"No, it's mostly rain. It's been raining since early last night. There isn't all that much wind with this storm. Just rain."

The owners all asked a variation on the same question. "How bad is it?" or "Is the storm as bad as it looks here in Dayton?"

Their next question would inevitably deal with their property. Questions like, "Is it going to cause any damage to Osprey Landings?" or "Is there any chance my roof will be ripped off in the storm?"

Betsy would calmly, methodically allay their fears. She would take a minute to talk the callers out of the hysteria the local weathermen had whipped them into. Whipped them into because they were tired of covering leaves. Because they were bored to tears with tranquil footage of some rolling countryside painted in rich, colorful sprays of yellows and orange. Television: It's a junkie for anything other than pastoral, thought Betsy. No wonder this country is so stressed out.

Between the owners' relentless questions and two dozen calls from various reservationists throughout the island wondering if the Sanderling grand opening party was going to be canceled, Betsy was beat. She couldn't wait for the bell to ring at 5:00 sharp and to turn over the telephone system to the answering service. She could fax them her standard response: No, it's mostly rain. It's been raining since early last night. There isn't all that much wind with this storm. Just rain. They could then carry the torch well into this rainy night.

Outside Shoreside Realty's office, the rain kept falling. If any of the owners who had been calling all day had bad roofs, they were in trouble. The storm had already dropped more than a foot on the island, and the local weather forecasters, who were not as prone to panic, were predicting another six to nine inches before Kandee moved toward the northeast. Kandee was a first-class soaker. Mr. and Mrs. Jensen, whose roof did have a problem, had to run to Kmart for more garbage cans. Their lawsuit meter was ticking big time over Kandee.

Betsy was a little worried about getting home. Her Pinto sat fairly high and she was pretty confident she could make it through the standing water. It had never stalled on her before. Still, it was going to be touch and go if the rain didn't let up.

Tonight, she had to make it home in time to fix her homemade lasagna for Mark, who was coming over around 7:00 for dinner. Despite Kandee, this was a dinner Betsy didn't want to have to cancel.

A few nights ago Mark had started hinting about an engagement ring and Betsy was hoping that tonight, with a belly full of her delicious lasagna and a head full of Cabernet, Mark might propose to her.

Her answer was yes. Yes times a thousand. Yes bigger than the Milky Way. Yes without reservation or second guessing or anything other than yes. It was a "yes," Betsy had said secretly to herself more times than she had explained how non-threatening Kandee was to stressed-out property owners all day. It was what she had wanted to say to Mark since the day she first laid eyes on him, dressed in his UPS brown and looking fine.

"No" was never even considered. "No" was unthinkable, almost as unthinkable as the thought of Mark not asking Betsy to marry him. "No" was no.

So as the clock ticked away and the phone lines kept lighting up time and time again, Betsy went into automatic. There were really two Betsys working the switchboard at Shoreside Realty that day, one was answering the phones, calmly relating that it was mostly rain. Or that the forecast was for sunny and clear by Saturday and that the "Sanderling grand opening party was not canceled." And the other person was dreaming about a romantic dinner for two in her little $450-a-month apartment on the mainland.

Two people, both of them good people. Betsy, the voice of Shoreside Realty. An angel really, an angel without wings.

813-980-2626
Infinity Trucking, Tampa

"How the hell do I know where the truck is?"

"It's your truck, don't you have a CB radio or any way to get in touch with the driver?"

"CB radios went out with the Johnson administration. Where the hell have you been hiding, for Chrissake?"

Adam felt like hanging up. It was his third call to Infinity Trucking that afternoon and he felt as if he was talking to a bunch of morons. Technically, he was. They just called themselves Teamsters because it was easier to spell. Most of them spelled "morrons" with two rr's. Teamsters. Besides, they reasoned, Teamsters sounded tougher.

"Well, call me if you hear anything. That truck was supposed to be here just after noon and it's now..." Adam glanced at his Rolex, "three thirty-eight. I need those pumps to be in place by daybreak if we hope to get any of this water pumped out of here. It's already rained 12 inches here on Shoreside. Have you seen much rain from tropical storm Kandee in Tampa?"

"I don't know. I haven't been outside."

"Have you heard anything on the radio?"

"No. I don't have a radio in the shop."

Adam took a deep sigh and continued, "Well, if you hear anything from your truck driver, please give me a call, okay?"

"Sure."

"Bye now."

The card-carrying Teamster on the other end of the line, whose name was Jake Lombardo, didn't bother saying goodbye. He just hung up. He was proud of himself for stonewalling that little prick on the other end of the line. He hadn't even bothered to write the 800 number down that Adam had given him on his second call to Infinity Trucking. Why bother? thought Jake to himself as he went back to reading the sports section of the *Tampa Tribune*. Little pricks like this Bartlett fellow always call again. Assholes, the whole lot of them. Rich sons-a-bitches from fancy barrier islands like Shoreside.

They don't know what it is to work for a goddamned living. They've never even driven a forklift. No, they drive Volvos and those expensive German cars.

Fuck-um. Fuck-um all.

Jake looked out at the pouring rain through the window in his office and turned up the radio. Over five inches of rain had fallen on the eastern outskirts of Tampa and more was expected before midnight. Jake hadn't felt like sharing any of that information with Adam. It would have made their useless telephone conversation just that much longer. Jake was more interested in the stats from the Tampa Bay Buccaneer game last Monday night and two commentaries about the upcoming game on Sunday with the Raiders. They're gonna kick some ass on Sunday, felt a very confident Bucs fan.

Deep down, Jake was getting concerned about his buddy, Terry Nelson, who was driving the three big pumps to Shoreside on a flatbed. He should have been there by now, or at least have called in. At first Jake felt sure that Terry had probably just ducked in for a quick bump at that topless truck stop north of Sarasota. The one with the big billboard saying, "GIRLS, GIRLS, GIRLS" on it and a huge blowup of three tramps pulled right out of a *Hustler* magazine. Hell, every truck driver with an hour or two to spare heading south stops by that joint for a quick bump.

But that would have put Terry in at 2:00, 2:30 at the latest, figured Jake. It was now past 3:00 and there wasn't any word from Terry and he sure as hell hadn't made contact with that Bartlett asshole yet. With all this rain, maybe something had happened. Infinity Trucking hadn't had a work-related accident in, Jake looked at his chart to double check, in 18 days. That was a new company record.

Over the course of the last hour, Jake had tried to reach Terry on his cell phone several times. He must have it turned off, reasoned a frustrated supervisor.

No, something had happened. Terry had stopped into the topless truck stop for a bump, which was to be expected. Well, his favorite stripper, Ashley Moore, was working that Thursday. The place was damned near empty because of all the rain and the weather and Ashley was bored to tears because of it. She decided to give Terry Nelson her undivided attention.

Dollar after dollar seemed to disappear into Ashley's skin-tight G-string while her silicone-filled double-Ds hung precariously close to Terry's hairy nostrils. One quick whiskey seven slipped into two less-quick whiskey sevens into three lazy whiskey sevens while Ashley worked over that metal dance pole on the stage like it was...well, you can imagine.

Terri had stumbled out of that joint about 2:30. He was legally drunk, but being a professional truck driver meant that he was familiar with operating a big 18-wheeler in this condition. He climbed into his Freightliner cab and headed to the on-ramp to I-75. God, Ashley has great tits, he thought to himself as he flipped his headlights on and started working through the 20 gears it took him to get up to speed. Fantastic tits. Damn near as big as footballs.

He was still thinking about Ashley's tits, which were really a product of Dow Chemical and not of Mother Nature, when he lost control of his big rig about 18 miles from the on-ramp. The rain that Kandee had been lambasting Florida with had saturated I-75 to the point where large inch-deep pools had formed along low points in the freeway. With his big rig hitting 70 miles an hour as he came off an overpass, his two front tires hit a large puddle and lifted right off the surface of the road. They had become a pair of 10-ply water skis.

The truck hydroplaned. Feeling the sudden loss of control, and too shit-faced to think of what else to do, Terry slammed on the brakes. He finally stopped thinking about Ashley's fine set of boobs, as thoughts of imminent disaster overruled his raging libido. His survival came before her jiggling tits, but not by any real measurable amount.

The instant he slammed on the brakes, the cab part of the truck hit a nice dry patch of concrete while the flatbed he was hauling kept skidding along the surface of a rain-slicked highway. It wasn't too long before the three large pumps he was hauling were passing him. He had jackknifed the truck and it was only going to get uglier.

By now, Terry Nelson was stone sober. Adrenalin had totally wiped out his whiskey buzz and the thoughts of Ashley's enormous breasts were a distant memory. He was in deep shit, sliding down a three-lane highway going 50-plus miles an hour and heading for the wooded median.

At this point in time, Terry did what all good Teamsters are trained to do in situations like this: he quickly apologized to God for being such a horseshit drunken husband and father all his life and prayed like a motherfucker. No, he quickly retracted the motherfucker part of the prayer and changed it to, prayed like a choir boy. An alcoholic choir boy.

He was in trouble and his truck, as well as his life, were in God's hands. The outcome would be decided in the next four or five seconds. He did manage to look around and note that this was probably going to be a one-truck accident. There wasn't another vehicle anywhere in sight. Just in case, and out of a sense of common humanity he didn't even know he had, he leaned on the horn like there was no tomorrow. At least he didn't have to take anyone else with him.

When the cab started hitting the soggy shoulder of the freeway, it miraculously didn't roll. The ground was so wet that it just gave way beneath the big truck like he had hit a median full of green, wheel-bearing grease. The same thing didn't hold true for the flatbed. With the extra weight of the three pumps making the load top heavy, as soon as it skidded onto the median it started tipping over faster than Terry had shoved dollar bills in Ashley's sequined G-string. Luckily, because it was in front of the cab at that point, it lifted the cab just high enough to free itself.

The entire flatbed, and the three huge pumps that were strapped down on top of it, tipped over sideways and kept skidding across the center median of the freeway.

It was still doing 35 when it hit a stand of slash pine that had been planted by Boy Scout Troop No. 44 out of Bradenton 15 years ago as a part of the I-75 beautification project. The small trees gave way quickly to the tons of tires, axles and hydraulic pumps that mowed them over.

But they didn't take a tumble without making those three pumps pay dearly for their indiscretions. Those three pumps would never so much as push a trickle of salt water or sewage overflow through their valves again. They were trashed. Ruined. Truck accident debris.

Without the weight of the flatbed propelling it forward, the Freightliner cab had little trouble stopping. When the big rig finally settled down, it stood just 20 feet from the lovely slash pines. Well, once lovely but now totally flattened slash pines, that is. Terry Nelson, his heart still skidding down the freeway, realized that it was over.

Terry turned off the engine and climbed out of the cab, which was facing north, northeast at this point, although Terry couldn't have told you how many revolutions his truck had made to end up pointing this direction. He walked away from his big white Freightliner about 30 feet and sat in a puddle that was over a foot deep. He was in shock. He was alive and that was all that mattered.

He thought about his wife in St. Petersburg, about his two teenage boys and wherever in hell they were this afternoon and, just for good measure, he gave one last thought about Ashley's outstanding set of jugs. Once a Teamster, always a Teamster.

Three cars went by before one of them stopped to help. Terry was still sitting in the warm rainwater as this stranger approached him.

"Are you okay?"

"Huh?"

"Are you hurt?"

"No, no. I don't think I'm hurt," said Terry in a daze.

"What happened?"

"I lost control."

"Yeah, it sort of looks like it. I'll go call the Highway Patrol. Come on, get in my car, you're soaking wet."

The good Samaritan called the Florida Highway Patrol and they arrived at the scene ten minutes later. It was a disaster. The pumps, now lying sideways, were leaking out all of their vital petroleum fluids. The oils and diesel fuel were adding a multicolored stained glass effect to the puddles forming in the middle of the median. The rain kept falling.

Statements were taken, flares set and an environmental damage control unit was notified. Terry was taken away in an ambulance to a hospital in Sarasota for observation. The officers never bothered to check his blood-alcohol levels. He didn't look drunk by the time they arrived. He looked scared.

One of the highway patrolmen at the scene got on the dispatch and had them call Infinity Trucking. Jake took the call just before 4:00 in the afternoon. When the gal who called said she was with the Florida Highway Patrol and that she was reporting an accident with one of their rigs that had just occurred on I-75, Jake's blood went colder than a glacial stream. He knew that it had to be Terry. God, he was going to miss that son-of-a-bitch.

She quickly added that the driver appeared to be okay but that they had taken him into Sarasota General for further observation. With the news that Terry was going to be fine, Jake felt the weight of the world fall off his big, right-tackle-sized shoulders. Thank God.

The rig was insured, as was the load it was carrying. Hell, Infinity Trucking lost a half-dozen loads a year in accidents not unlike this one. Jackknifing, rolling, chains inexplicably breaking, axles coming off, you name it. Loads were one thing. Losing a fellow Teamster, that's a whole different story.

Jake stood, walked over and poured himself another cup of coffee, and then went back to reading the sports section. It was a dangerous way to make a living, driving those big 18-wheelers, but somebody had to do it.

Adam's call came at 5:00 p.m. sharp, just before Jake had turned on the answering machine to head home for the day.

"Infinity Trucking," answered Jake.

"Please hold for Mr. Bartlett," said Chris to the Teamster.

As Jake reluctantly went on hold, he wondered why jerks like Bartlett can't make their own fucking calls. No, they've got some overpaid secretary to do it for them. They probably don't even wipe their own asses, he imagined just as Bartlett came on the line.

"Any news, Mr. Lombardo?"

"Yup."

"Well, where's the truck?"

"We lost her."

Christ, thought Bartlett. Not this bullshit again. Getting any information from this guy was like pulling teeth out of a hippo. Useless.

"What do you mean, you lost her?"

"She tipped. Luckily, Terry Nelson, one of the best goddamned truck drivers on Earth, wasn't hurt too bad."

"Was there an accident? Is that what you're trying to tell me?"

"Yup."

"What about my three pumps?"

"Goners."

"Can't we get them put on another truck and get them shipped here by daybreak?"

"Nope."

"Why not?"

"They're all busted up. The flatbed tipped sideways when the truck jackknifed and they went head first into a stand of pines. They'll never pump a lick of water again. They had to call in one of those goddamned environmental crews to contain all the fuel oil and shit. You'll just have to get along without your pumps, Mr. Bartlett. You know how it is, shit happens."

"Oh, for Christ's sake."

Jake heard Bartlett swear for the first time and suddenly had a little more respect for the man on the other end of the line. He almost felt sorry for him but then caught himself.

"Well, sorry about your pumps Mr. Bartlett. We'll adjust your bill some for the fact that they were never actually delivered to you. There will still be some loading fees and some processing fees coming. I'll have our secretary, Maggie, fax you the bill tomorrow morning after this storm gets the hell out of here. That's what caused the accident, ya know, all the rain on the highway. It's a dangerous way to make a living, Mr. Bartlett. Our driver was lucky he wasn't killed."

"Yeah, lucky."

"Bub-bye."

"Goodbye." Adam hung up and slumped in his leather chair. He looked out his window and saw the sheets of rain still falling. Falling, falling, falling. He was screwed and he knew it. He didn't know that a huge set of silicone filled implants were at the root of his undoing, but what did it matter? The pumps weren't going to be on the Sanderling site come daybreak and the swales were going to fill to overflowing with nearly 20 inches of rain.

Tomorrow and Saturday morning wouldn't be enough time to allow the tropical Florida sun to evaporate but an inch or two of the rain and the ground was already soaked to its limit. The pumps would have changed all that. Millions of gallons would have poured non-stop across the beach and into the ocean, had they made it. The retention areas surrounding the six buildings would have been bone dry by the time the barbecue dinner was planned. The project would have looked its best.

Adam had asked Chris to start looking into smaller, local pumps after his third call to Jake Lombardo and Infinity Trucking. They were all rented by folks in town trying to pump out recently dug foundations or unfinished swimming pools that needed to be bone dry before the contractors could apply the Marcite. Besides, those pumps were tiny by comparison to the ones that were now lying sideways in a ditch outside Sarasota. Thirty of them couldn't have done the job that those three defunct diesel pumps could have done.

Well, reflected Adam to himself, it was mostly just for looks anyway. He wanted the project to look its best. The long, winding driveway to the buildings would be high and dry and the parking area had plenty of fill. He just didn't like the idea of all that standing water. It looked a little too much like the swamp it was for Bartlett's taste. He wanted it to shine for those 32 families that were coming to spend the night on Saturday.

It will just have to do, he decided. It's a shame, but it will have to do. The forecast is still a go; sunny and clear with highs in the low 90s. They'll still have the beach, the pool and the tennis courts.

There was one more thing that they would have that Adam Bartlett had failed to take into consideration, being that Bartlett had always been a straight-C student when it came to high school biology. With seven acres of warm, fresh water, two days of sunlight, and plenty of time to hatch, they would also have a few mosquitoes to contend with come Saturday afternoon during their gala grand opening. A few million.

570-9219
Sam Goodlet's Home Phone

"Uh-ha. No. You're kidding? You're not kidding? When?" asked Sam.

Sam was on the phone to Dale Anderson of Anderson Realty. It was one of those unbelievable telephone conversations where you don't know whether to laugh hysterically or break down and bawl halfway through the call. Both options raced through Goodlet's mind as he listened to Dale bring him up to speed on the current condition of Mr. and Mrs. Grinstead, Dale's sellers.

"You have to try to get them to back off a bit. Things are getting serious, Sam. Real serious," said Dale.

"I'll talk to them for you, Dale, but my clients are impossible. The Hazeltons are simply relentless and I doubt that they'll back off any at this point. Bart feels that he's just got too much time and money invested in the purchase. You know how those good old boys can be sometimes, stubborn as mules."

"Well, Sam, do what you can. I've got a phone call in to Kurt Grinstead's brother in Michigan, but he hasn't gotten back to me yet. Maybe he can convince Kurt to come out of the house. Otherwise, the Shoreside police will have to get involved.

Dale Anderson continued, "I've just never run into anything like this before. Twenty-three years in the business and this transaction takes the cake. Mrs. Grinstead still in the hospital up north. Mr. Grinstead now locking himself in his house, tearing all the Sheetrock off the interior walls and throwing it through the dining room window trying to prove that his house is bug free. You can hear him all over the neighborhood, Sam. You can hear him shouting at the top of his lungs every time a busted-up piece of drywall flies out that window yelling, 'IT'S BUG FREE, IT'S BUG FREE, IT'S BUG FREE AT LAST!!!'

"I don't know what the hell to make of it."

Sam didn't respond. He didn't know what to say. The situation between the Hazeltons, himself, the Grinsteads and their agent, Dale Anderson, had deteriorated to a point of no return. Even the lawyers who had become involved were dumbfounded as to the next move. It was a case study on the effects of real estate gone south and how it directly affected a person's mental health. It was surreal.

"Well, I'll call Bart and Dolores and see what I can do."

"Thanks, Sam. Goodbye."

"Goodbye."

It was late Thursday afternoon and it was still raining. The rain bands kept sweeping across south Florida drenching everything in their path. Sam had originally planned to drive across the causeway this morning and go work at his office, but Kandee convinced him to stay at home. It wasn't the wind that made him change his mind. The strongest recorded gust thus far had hit only 47 miles an hour. The sustained winds were clocking in around 35 miles per hour. Hardly threatening.

It was the rain that kept Sam's Oldsmobile safely parked in his two-car garage. The rain that wouldn't stop. The rain that had flooded his yard and driveway, spilling across the empty fields behind his lanai and out across the vast, flat surface of Florida. Rain, rain and more rain.

Sam knew that some of the lower-lying areas would flood to the point where his Olds might stall trying to get through. That's a mess he didn't need to add to his list of messes. He wisely decided to stay at home and use his home phone as his base instead of his office phone. Betsy had made it in, and between her pages and his list of calls to make, Sam could keep himself plenty busy.

Sam had some other deals going - the Kessler house was closing in two weeks and there was that nice couple from Maine who were thinking about making an offer on one of the Promenade Units. Most of his energies were focused on the Grinstead disaster. It was a major disaster and it needed Sam's undivided attention.

Since last March, things had gone from bad to worse, to worse, to even worse. There was no closing in sight and if things continued sliding downhill, it was doubtful that there would ever come a day when Mr. and Mrs. Grinstead would sign a deed to Mr. and Mrs. Hazelton. Chances were that Mr. Grinstead would be committed if he kept on his present course.

Last March, after Kurt and Celia Grinstead had finally agreed to replace all of the pilings in the home, Baker, Baker and Strong recommended a firm out of St. Petersburg to handle the complicated replacement contract. The firm was called Davis Brothers Construction. They specialized in piling replacements like this, and they were willing to do it for the exact $38,000 figure Mr. Strong had estimated it would take. Little did anyone know that one of the Davis Brothers, Jimmy Davis, was married to Mr. Strong's sister, Martha. It was, shall we say, a convenient coincidence.

Because of prior commitments, the Davis Brothers Construction company couldn't get started on the Grinstead house until mid-May. That meant that Sam Goodlet, aka Shoreside Realty, and Dale Anderson of Dale Anderson Realty had to get another extension signed. By this time the Hazeltons had gone home to Alabama, and Mrs. Grinstead was finally out of the hospital from her toxic reaction to all the pesticides she and Kurt had used trying to get the carpenter ant and sugar ant problem under control. Celia Grinstead was still on medication for her nerves. Moderately heavy narcotics.

By and large it appeared that everything was finally going well. The closing was re-scheduled for late June to allow plenty of time for the piling work to be completed and re-inspected before the closing date. The siding was going to be reinstalled after the pilings were completed and Sam Goodlet was back on track.

Then, on that fateful afternoon of May 29, Sam got the call that derailed the Grinstead closing yet again. Apparently, Sam was told by Dale, the younger Davis brother, Mark Davis, had failed to properly shore up one end of the four huge timber piles that were temporarily holding up the Grinstead house while the new pilings were being installed. Because of it, a large house jack had unexpectedly shot out from under the weight of the house, nearly killing one of the construction workers as it clipped his shoulder, and the entire Grinstead house tumbled two feet down to the east.

Dale Anderson, who just happened to be at the site when the incident occurred, said you could hear the Grinstead house cracking and splintering apart like someone driving over a stack of two-by-fours with a Sherman tank. Everything - every corner, every door, every window, every cabinet in the house - was instantly set akimbo. There wasn't a door in the house that would open or close, pipes started bursting, outlets started shorting out and the burglar alarm went into some kind of burglar alarm seizure that it had never fully recovered from.

In effect, the Grinstead house had fallen and could not get up. It was an unimaginable situation. Fortunately, no one, except the house, was hurt in the incident. The construction worker's shoulder was badly bruised and he recovered within a few days, but the house, well, the house needed to be in traction. When the news reached Mr. and Mrs. Grinstead, who were staying in their summer cabin in North Carolina until the closing, Mrs. Grinstead had a traumatic seizure not unlike the one their burglar alarm had just endured. She was admitted into a psychiatric ward in Asheville, North Carolina, the very next day. She, too, had fallen and could not get up.

The purchasers, Mr. and Mrs. Hazelton, were aghast when Sam called them that afternoon in Bessemer, Alabama. They immediately called their lawyer. Bart quickly realized that the only house that they had ever found without a "fatal flaw" was now chock full of them. The vinyl siding was entirely off the house and spewed around the yard, the drywall from underneath the house was piled in one small corner melting and leeching everywhere in the pouring rain, and now, there wasn't a cupboard or door that would either open or close. The house had become the mother lode of fatal flaws. A cornucopia of domicile defects.

Like one of those television infomercials, little did Sam realize that, over the next few weeks, he would continue to call the Hazeltons in that classic infomercial style saying, "and that's not all, folks, if you order today, there's more!" Once the Davis Brothers managed to get the house jacked back up and on the level, mysterious aftershocks continued to lay ruin to the Grinstead home. The roof started leaking, probably from where all the trusses and framing joints had become twisted and bent. Nobody was aware of the dozens of pinhole leaks until it rained six days after the house had taken the big tumble. Ten gallons of roofing tar later, the leaks were under control.

A week after that, Sam called Bart to tell him that the electricians had found that the electric wiring within the house was no longer reliable. Circuit breakers would pop inexplicably and brand-new light bulbs would randomly explode. The entire house had that smell to it, that funny rubberish electrical smell. The one that always makes you want to dial 911 and scramble for the front door. Three different electrical contractors over the next two months couldn't find the source of the smell, although they did finally manage to stop all the light bulbs from exploding.

Then there were the drywall problems. Huge chunks of drywall had cracked and bent when the house tilted to the east. Over the next couple of months, some of the larger pieces fell without warning off the ceilings and walls throughout the home. Several electricians who were working on the wiring suffered minor injuries. In late August, after everyone felt that things had finally settled down and the new pilings were in place, the entire guest bedroom ceiling collapsed in the middle of the night.

When the contractor came in to wrap up some additional repairs the next day, he found the guest bedroom looking like an Associated Press photo of a Turkish earthquake. He didn't dare pick the big piece of drywall up that covered the double bed, fearing the worst. When he finally did muster the nerve to lift that 4-by-12 sheet of plasterboard, he was glad to find that no one had been sleeping in the bed. They would have been killed.

When he looked at the ceiling, lo and behold, yet another flaw made its presence known, this time in the form of clear evidence of a recent dry-wood termite infestation. The nest was quite extensive and the termites were all scurrying about, trying to relocate after the unexpected loss of their entire floor the night before. There was no denying it, the Grinstead house would have to be tented. That was a problem, because the timing couldn't have been worse.

By this time, Mr. Grinstead was on his way down from their summer place outside Asheville. His wife, Celia, was still in the hospital. Technically it wasn't a hospital, but a long-term mental health facility near Greenville. They had moved her from the Asheville psychiatric ward to a long-term facility after realizing the magnitude of Celia's problem. The shock had proved to be too much for her. Celia soon descended into a strange, somnambulistic state which had the psychiatrists at both facilities completely perplexed. She was under 24-hour surveillance and was undergoing a protracted series of psychological tests.

Mrs. Celia Grinstead had taken on that glazed-over look common to pre-catatonic patients. She didn't look good at all.

The contractor had found the new termite infestation the day before Mr. Grinstead arrived at his home, which Kurt thought was now fixed and ready for the upcoming closing. When they told him about the need to tent the home, his eyes, like Celia's, developed a blank stare and he started having weird, jerky movements. They were like those nervous ticks some people have in their upper lip, only in Kurt's particular case, they were occurring all over his body. His hands and fingers would jerk unexpectedly, his shoulders, hips, you name it. He didn't look good either.

They went ahead and ordered the tenting. It went pretty well. All of the siding had been put on before they treated the home and all of the drywall was underneath the house where the new pilings were now firmly in place. The closing, much to Sam Goodlet's delight, was reset for the fifth time to occur on October 1, just 24 days from the date of the tenting.

The Hazeltons had driven down from Alabama to attend the closing and Mr. Grinstead had obtained full power of attorney for his wife, Celia, who at this point could have done little more than drool all over the closing papers had they been put in front of her. Drool profusely.

Of course, Mr. Bartholomew W. Hazelton couldn't leave well enough alone. He had Sam Goodlet and Nuts and Bolts Inspection Service do a final, final, final, final walk-through inspection the day before the closing. It went well. All of the cracks had been repaired, all of the doors and windows opened and shut and even that odd, remote electrical smell was gone. Well, there was still a faint trace of it in the house, but not enough to merit putting off the closing.

On the way out the front door, just as Sam was patting the inspector on the back and Mr. Hazelton was reaching for his checkbook to pay him, a small sugar ant was noticed by Dolores crawling alongside the front door. She followed the ant up the wall and noticed it going into a tiny pinhole near the ceiling. It was soon followed by a second, then a third ant in a steady procession.

Dolores pointed it out to the inspector just as Bart handed him his $175 reinspection check. The inspector had never seen anything like this before. The house hadn't been tented but a week ago and there now seemed to be clear evidence of a sugar ant infestation. He recommended a new pest inspection.

The news of a fourth pest inspection was the last straw. Kurt Grinstead snapped like that camel's back we've been hearing about all these years. Snapped with a loud crunch you could hear for blocks. He put down his home phone without even bothering to set it back on the receiver. Then Kurt went downstairs to grab a hammer and a five-pound box of ten-penny nails and calmly came up inside the house.

With Dale Anderson still listening through the telephone receiver that was never properly hung up, he could clearly hear Kurt muttering to himself saying,

"It's bug free, it's bug free, it's bug free at last!" while the sound of hammering echoed over the phone line.

Within the hour, every door and window leading outside, except the one in the dining room, had been nailed shut. Not with one or two nails either. The front door alone had 127 nails in it. Many of them pounded through the very middle of the front door.

Now, three weeks later, in a soaking tropical storm, Kurt Grinstead was throwing large pieces of drywall out the dining room window yelling, "IT'S BUG FREE, IT'S BUG FREE, IT'S BUG FREE AT LAST!!!" Apparently, Kurt was using the back side of his claw hammer and his bare hands to remove all the drywall in search of that last elusive sugar ant nest. The closing had to be postponed once again. This time due to madness.

Mr. Hazelton was extremely upset. His attorneys were fast approaching the same mental state as Mrs. Grinstead. They were having trouble controlling their saliva and no one wanted to return Bartholomew's phone calls at the firm. Fear had overtaken them.

Sam was finished. Mildred Lee was off her rocker stockpiling ice, Mr. and Mrs. Hazelton were talking about having Mr. Grinstead committed and the neighborhood association was considering some kind of legal action.

In the middle of the night, Kurt was climbing out of the dining room window and removing all the vinyl siding for the second time, tossing it helter skelter around his yard. Between that and the leaching drywall, property values on Surfside Street had sunk to an all-time low. It wasn't good.

Mr. Grinstead had grown emaciated and pale from two weeks of being locked up in his own house. He wasn't eating right. Unbeknownst to everyone but Mr. Grinstead, he had actually started eating drywall dust mixed with some old cans of sweetened condensed milk. As a food source, drywall is very low on the nutritional scale. It's right up there with dirt and beach sand for complete lack of sustenance. It was also making Kurt extremely constipated.

Something was going to have to give.

570-7372
Betsy's Home Phone

"Hello," Betsy Owens answered her portable phone. She was expecting this call.

"Hello, Betsy, it's Mark, I just called to let you know that I'll be a little late."

"Thanks for calling, Mark, I appreciate it. I'll take the lasagna out of the oven in a few minutes. Besides, it's better if you let it sit for a while before eating it anyway."

"Is there anything you need before I come over - milk, ice cream or anything?" asked the courteous young man.

"No, we're just fine with everything. How soon will you be here?"

"Within half an hour. With all this rain, everyone's schedule ended up running late. It was just one of those things. You know, those UPS things."

"No problem Mark, the phones at the office were going crazy all day, too. These tropical storms really make people crazy, don't they?"

"You bet they do. I'll see you in a little while then. I've got a big surprise for you."

"What is it?"

"You'll just have to wait. If I tell you over the phone it wouldn't be a surprise, would it? Bye for now."

"Bye."

Betsy put down the phone and lingered. She was momentarily transfixed by the idea of Mark's big surprise. Could it be? She silently practiced saying the word "yes" several times before heading into the kitchen to take her lasagna from the oven. Should it be a quiet, surrendering "yes?" Docile and sweet like her inner nature? Or should it be a decisive and self-assured "yes," like the way she could handily put the president of the United States on hold if the switchboard was going mad. Until that moment came, Betsy could only guess how she might respond. The only thing she knew for certain was the answer, should Mark pop the question. It was "yes."

The lasagna came out perfectly. As she set the small casserole dish on her dining room table, the smell of homemade Italian cooking saturated the air. It smelled divine. She threw a small kitchen towel over the aluminum foil covering to help keep it warm while Mark made his way over. She opened the bottle of Cabernet to let it breathe before serving. Now all there was to do was to pick up the apartment a trifle and wait.

Mark arrived 20 minutes later. For Betsy it seemed like two hours had passed, she was so anxious and thrilled at what might be forthcoming. He brought her a lovely bouquet of flowers. Nothing fancy. Just one of those grocery store bouquets consisting of black-eyed Susans and inexpensive cut flowers. It didn't matter to Betsy that the arrangement in Mark's hand cost less than $8. It was the thought that counted.

"It smells scrumptious, Betsy! And I'm starving."

"Take a seat, you hardworking boy," said Betsy.

Starving was good. Betsy knew that Mark's job wasn't easy. He drove the truck, delivered and picked up packages all day and kept all the paperwork straight on his electronic notepad while doing it. Some of the larger UPS packages weighed in excess of 100 pounds and they could really wear a man out by day's end. Add to that all the rain from tropical storm Kandee and the stress of driving in the deluge and you end up with one tired and hungry boy for dinner.

They both sat and served themselves while making those adorable little looks across the table at each other. Lovers' glances, shy and delicious over a homemade dinner. As they sipped the wine and enjoyed the pasta, time quickly vanished into a delirium of laughter and joy. This was it. This was everything and all things Betsy had ever wanted from life. His name was Mark, Mark Thurston.

After dinner they sat on the couch and listened to Celine Dion's latest album. Betsy loved Celine. She has such a beautiful voice, thought Betsy about the Canadian singer. Once comfortable, they started hugging and snuggling together. Mark didn't bother to reach for the TV remote. That was Betsy's first indication that something big was about to happen. Mark didn't mind Celine, but he preferred listening to her while watching a hockey game on mute. They were both from Canada. It made sense in a UPS kind of way.

Tonight he hadn't even asked Betsy for the remote. Tonight he seemed a little pensive and withdrawn. Nervous.

A half hour passed. They had kissed several times and made small talk. Goofy, lovers' conversations that are not really important. Just the sound of each other's voices and a few cherished laughs in between. Endearing moments in our lives, fleeting and filled with the sheer sweetness of puppy love.

Just after one exceptionally tender kiss, Mark pulled away slightly and looked into Betsy's dark brown eyes. He looked beyond them, as though he were peering right into her angelic soul. Then he broke the silence.

"Betsy, I have something to ask you. Something that I have never asked anyone in the world ever before."

With that sentence, Betsy's heart raced. It jumped out of her pounding chest and ran half way to the moon in exhilaration. Her heart almost exploded inside of her, sending her flying into the very throes of love.

"Yes, Mark, what is it?" She asked but she knew.

"Will you...."

He hesitated. It was only an instant, but for Betsy it was longer than the longest of eternities. It was a pause that lasts a century.

"Will you marry me?" asked Mark. With that, he reached into his right-side pants pocket and pulled out a small, jeweler's box wrapped in a single strand of gold string. He handed it to his girlfriend, his strong hand shaking visibly.

Betsy smiled and took the box into her hand. She could see how nervous and exposed he was. How vulnerable. She knew what was in the box. It was her engagement ring.

Now Mark waited. He waited 100 years. He waited the way a million men before him have waited. Holding his breath in anticipation while the woman he had fallen in love with decides. Says either the one word they have prayed to hear, or God forbid, says something in response that means "no." That she will have to think about it, or that it's just too soon, or that marriage isn't right for her, or simply says, "no."

It was only another instant in time, but for Mark it was forever. He looked at her again, knowing that he would be devastated if she said anything other than that which he so desperately wanted to hear. That she would accept his proposal. That Betsy would say the word, the only word his heart could handle. The word "yes."

As Betsy's heart raced beyond the moon and toward the deepest reaches of the stars, she nervously looked at the man she was so gloriously in love with and in as tender a voice that has ever broken the silence of a proposal, Betsy said, "Yes."

It was the easiest thing she had ever done in her life. "Yes."

The rest of the evening was a symphony of joy; the opening of the jeweler's box, Mark's slipping his engagement ring on Betsy's finger. The kisses, the blushing, the delicate happiness of this special night. It was a symphony played on the strings of young lovers' hearts, played loudly and with a wondrous enthusiasm. It ended with the climax of 100 timpani, followed quickly thereafter by the silence of two exhausted lovers, falling asleep in each other's arms. Like lovers do.

574-9897
The Cliftons' New Phone Number

"Oh, Jennifer, it's simply gorgeous," said Mrs. Clifton, while standing in her brand-new kitchen on a clear, windy Friday afternoon.

Jennifer was on cloud nine. Floating in the ether of the angelic ending to her very first sale. Standing there, beside Dr. and Mrs. Clifton in their brand-new home, watching Marie Clifton run her hands over the silky smooth Corian countertops, seeing her open the pantry to inspect the handcrafted wooden shelving and listen to her "ohh" and "ahh" as she walked through each and every room of their new home.

"It's so bright and airy," added Marie Clifton. "It's even prettier than the photos you sent us last week. You've done such a fabulous job, Jennifer. We can't possibly thank you enough."

This was all Jennifer Willow had ever wanted out of real estate. She wasn't in the business to become a superstar or because she wanted to make $1,000 a day. She was in it to help people. People just like Dr. and Mrs. Clifton, who were doing the final walk-through on their new home on Palmetto Court just before heading off to First Federal Savings and Loan to close on the house, to convert their construction loan into a 30-year fixed-rate mortgage.

Everything was coming up roses for Jennifer. As forecast, tropical storm Kandee had moved right along, pushing north, northeast toward Jacksonville and drenching central Florida along the way. The back side spin of the storm had dragged down some unusually dry, slightly cooler air and by noon, just after having lunch with her clients at The Oyster Bar, the weather was chamber of commerce perfect. It was so unlike the cloudy, overcast day when the three of them had first seen the lot a year ago.

After lunch, the Cliftons had checked into the Radisson to freshen up after a long day of traveling, and the meeting with Jennifer at the house in Osprey Greens at 4:00 p.m. sharp. Once at the house, they would do the final walk-through and inspection, and then meet the builder to settle with him at the bank at 5:00 p.m. Needless to say, the inspection was going very well. Jennifer had taken great pains to ensure that every detail - every piece of molding, every tile, every light fixture and ceiling fan was installed and working flawlessly.

"James, just look at this shower. Have you ever seen such beautiful tile work?" asked Marie of her husband. They had left the pickled-ash cabinetry of the kitchen for the large master suite upstairs. Thus far, there wasn't a thing they could observe that needed to be punched out or fixed after closing.

"It is nice, isn't it," said James while flushing the toilet to make certain that nothing was leaking. "They've done a damn good job building this home, and that's a fact."

"They came highly recommended," added Jennifer, still adrift in her white, puffy clouds.

From downstairs, unexpectedly, Jennifer heard a man calling for her.

"Jennifer, Jennifer Willow, are you here?"

It was Ralph Hardwick, the developer of Osprey Greens. He and his wife, Lila, had just returned three weeks ago from their world cruise. The cruise was fantastic: Hawaii, Asia, the Suez Canal, Israel, Europe and eventually, back to New York. The trip of a lifetime, Lila and Ralph kept telling each other over their eight-month sojourn. The trip of a lifetime.

Jennifer excused herself and made her way downstairs to greet Mr. Hardwick. When she finally got to the bottom of the stairs, she noted that he looked very distressed. She had met Ralph only a few times over the years, once when he and Lila came to buy some accessories at the Decorating Hut, and then again at the Cliftons' closing 11 months ago. Both of those times he seemed so relaxed, so friendly. She sensed something was amiss.

"Hi, Ralph, is something wrong?" asked Jennifer.

"Jennifer, we have to talk. Can we step outside for a minute?" said Mr. Hardwick in a very solemn tone.

"What's the matter?"

As this brief exchange took place, Dr. and Mrs. Clifton started working their way down the attractive spiral-designed stairway that ended in the foyer where Jennifer and Ralph were standing. They, too, noted the nervous look on Mr. Hardwick's face and wondered what could possibly be wrong.

"I really think that this is a private matter and I would prefer if just the two of us could step outside and discuss it, Jennifer."

No, that didn't sit well with Jennifer. Cloak-and-dagger real estate was not her style. Everything was above board, fair and square, tell it like it is for Jennifer. She immediately dismissed Ralph's suggestion for a private meeting.

"Ralph, anything you have to say to me you can say in front of my clients. I simply won't have it any other way."

By this time all four of them were standing in the foyer. The sunlight was pouring in through the high arched windows above the front door, the smell of new carpet and freshly sanded handrails lingered in the air, and the excitement of owning a brand-new home came crashing to earth as Ralph Hardwick looked straight into Jennifer Willow's stunning green eyes and said, "Jennifer, you've built the house on the wrong lot."

There was, shall we say, a pregnant pause. Pregnant with mutants. Pregnant with aliens that had multiple appendages and glow-in-the-dark eyes. The nurses in the birthing suite wanted out. Jennifer Willow's firstborn real estate sale was an abomination.

"What did you say, Ralph?"

Jennifer, for some bizarre reason, wanted Ralph to repeat it. Dr. and Mrs. Clifton didn't want to hear it again. They didn't want to hear it the first time. They were supposed to be at First Federal Savings and Loan in 15 minutes to hand them a cashier's check in the amount of $72,345.98. They had just flown from upstate New York, had a nice lunch that was now coming back up on them, and they didn't want to hear it again, but Jennifer did. So Ralph Hardwick repeated it.

"Jennifer, you've built the house on the wrong lot."

There, now they were all fully apprized of the situation. Mrs. Clifton looked at Mr. Hardwick, realizing that he wasn't kidding and said, "I think that I'm going to be sick," and dashed into the guest bathroom, closing the door behind her. Dr. Clifton, wanting to set the record straight, jumped head first into the muck of it.

"Of course you're mistaken."

"No, I'm not. I built this subdivision, phase by phase, block by block and lot by lot, and I know, as sure as I'm standing here, that this house is sitting on lot "D," Phase IV, Osprey Greens North. I know because my brother-in-law, Andy Stoughton, and his wife, Deb, are sitting in my Lexus right now holding a deed to this property."

Ralph wasn't mistaken. That cloudy, overcast afternoon a year ago was the problem. That and Jennifer's trouble with those cute little north arrows they put on all those plats and maps and stuff that Jennifer never did have a very good handle on. Well, that cute little curly north arrow would sure have come in handy about now. Jennifer had accidently flipped the plat around. North was south. South was north.

Lot "A," which is the lot Dr. and Mrs. Clifton owned, was 200 feet away. Same size, same view, wrong location. It was one of those classic, "I can't believe it really happened," real estate stories. Two weeks after closing on the lot, Jennifer had met the builders to begin construction. Normally the new survey stakes would have tipped someone off, but all four of the lots had just been surveyed and the stakes all looked the same.

Jennifer had gone straight to lot "D," which she thought was lot "A," and said to the contractor, "Well, here it is." He said fine and got started the following week. Barbara Silberman, who would have caught the problem early had she been on Palmetto Court, never knew a thing. After selling the lot to the Cliftons and Ralph selling the other lot to the Stoughtons, there hadn't been a drop of activity on either of the two remaining parcels, lots "B" and "C."

Barb had done the classic, stick a sign in the ground and forget about it, on both of the properties. She hadn't been within a mile of Palmetto Court in the last year.

Ralph was on a world cruise and the real owners of lot "D" were out in Ralph's Lexus, ready to sue everyone on the planet.

Andy and Deb Stoughton had finally sold their double-wide, held a huge rummage sale and moved to Shoreside Island, ready to live the dream. When the three of them drove off to take a look at their lot this afternoon, to see whether or not it was still holding any water from Kandee, they were surprised to find a brand-new, four-bedroom house sitting smack in the middle of their lot. Surprised here being a very poor choice of superlatives. Shocked is a better choice. Aghast works too.

Jennifer, who was just standing there, her mouth agape and her lovely blond hair visibly turning gray right before Dr. James Clifton's eyes, was crushed. She knew that she had made a little clerical error. One that weighed in at roughly 38,000 tons, if you included the slab.

Jennifer's little cloud nine party was, needless to say, over. The fluffy little cosmos she was strolling around in five minutes ago was now an open-pit uranium mine. Jennifer had taken the quick elevator down. The one where you get in just as the cable breaks. As lovely as the view was from there in her "people person" heaven, it was every bit as bleak and dusty in this newfound uranium mine she was now working. The foreman was a sadist and no one had ever made it out of the mine alive. By week's end, Jennifer Willow's lungs would glow in the dark from all the radioactive dust she was about to inhale.

"Oh my God," was the next thing Jennifer said. She meant it.

"What can we do about it?" asked a derailed Dr. Clifton.

"I don't know, Dr. Clifton. I've never been in a situation like this before."

"Can we move the house to our lot?"

"I don't know. The concrete block foundation you've constructed won't move well at all. But even if you could, my brother-in-law and his wife are probably on my cell phone right now with their attorney. They've just spent months working with an architect friend of theirs designing the home of their dreams. When we drove here to check on whether or not Kandee had left any water on their lot, they all but died when they found this house on it.

"I can't tell you what they plan to do. They're really pissed off."

They were pissed off. It was the dream of dreams. Selling everything, even their bowling balls, and finally moving to Shoreside. Their winning lotto ticket, a brand-new home on one of the most renowned barrier islands in all of Florida. They had finally arrived. Arrived to find that somebody had put a house right in the middle of their lot. "An ugly house," added Deb in disgust.

"Really ugly," said Andy Stoughton while calling his attorney in Panama City. "Really ugly, and urine-yellow to boot!"

570-1995
Unit 2-A, Sanderling Condominiums

Saturday morning arrived just as it had been forecast: sunny, humid and clear. Tropical storm Kandee was gone. She had cut a rain-drenched swath diagonally across central Florida and exited near Cape Canaveral. Now she was heading back toward North America, expecting to make landfall early Sunday morning just east of Wilmington, North Carolina.

Kandee had picked up some momentum after hitting the warmer waters of the Gulf Stream. She was now a Category I hurricane. The natives of the coastal regions of North Carolina, from Beaufort to Cape Hatteras, were busy boarding up and buying supplies. They had been through this drill a dozen times before in the last ten years. They did it methodically and without much fanfare at this point. It was just another storm bearing down on them. There would be more to follow.

Adam awoke early and walked to the balcony of the condominium he had spent Friday night in. It was one of the three units Eugene Boyle had elected to purchase. It had the best view in the entire complex: top floor, north side. The ten-unit building, building "A," stuck out just enough from building "B" to give it an unobstructed view of the water and the sunsets to the west.

The night before, with Adam and Vanessa sitting on that spacious screened balcony, looking at a flawless October sunset while enjoying take-out Chinese, Adam felt that he was at the very pinnacle of his career. The world was his oyster. An oyster filled with pearls.

What could be possibly better? Last night, Vanessa was wearing a sexy nightgown Adam had purchased for her from a Victoria's Secret catalog. It was a birthday present from Adam, long and tight against her gazelle-like body. Exquisite. As she sat there, making small talk and enjoying her sweet-and-sour chicken, all Adam could think of was how he would be inside of her within the hour.

How they would both be lying together under that brand-new skylight in the master bedroom. Making love under a sky full of radiant stars. Passionate, romantic love, complete with wet, unending kisses and sweaty, entangled bodies. Resplendent, sensual and intense. Full of candlelight and the sweet, elusive scent of sex. Falling asleep in each other's arms just as Scorpio climbed the southern sky.

It was morning now, with the sun pouring in through the windows beside the breakfast nook on the eastern side of the condo. Adam was still a trifle hung over from the bottle of Dom Perignon he and Vanessa had finished around midnight. He didn't mind the hangover, remembering how he had earned it; savoring every sip of the expensive champagne between their extended sessions of lovemaking.

Adam walked to the balcony of the condo. He sat and gazed at the pure blue waters of the Gulf of Mexico, watching the slanted light of the sun shine across his kingdom. He saw the sunlight dance off the tops of the breaking surf as he inhaled the sea air and enjoyed this moment in time.

In a way, it was all his. Adam would eventually list every one of these 64 units at Sanderling. After the fabulous grand opening planned for this afternoon, he would put 32 of the units into the Multiple Listing Service next Monday morning. With the busy winter selling season fast approaching, they would sell quickly. Word would be out on the fabulous views, the huge pool and the private, secluded setting. The reservationists that were invited this afternoon would make certain of that.

Thirty-two new Gulf-front condos listed at an average selling price of $500,000. Over $16,000,000 in listings. He and Loggins had set the sales commission at six percent: split at three percent to the selling agent and three percent to the listing agent. At Adam's commission plateau with Shoreside Realty, that meant a cool $430,000, not to mention how many of the units he would end up listing and reselling over the years to follow.

When he factored in a half-dozen double-dips, Adam had calculated that the sale of Loggin's 32 unsold condos would gross him over $500,000. The second 32 units, the ones Adam had already sold to his group of investors at a flat two percent commission, would probably go back on the active market as the investors cashed out of them the following year.

Those were an even better slice of the pie. Those units Adam could list at full seven percent commission with a 3.5 percent co-broke. Prices would be higher by then, with the initial offering sold out and the demand increasing. He could easily look at $600,000 to $700,000 per unit for the sale of the investor condos next year. All totaled, Sanderling Condominiums could put $1.4 million into Adam Bartlett's personal coffers. Plenty of gas to keep him running down the freeway of real estate he was speeding along. Plenty of fuel.

He had a right to feel like a king on that exquisite Saturday morning. A lithesome redhead asleep in the master bedroom, a million dollars in inventory beneath and behind him, and a view of the world fit for an emperor.

He drew a deep, intoxicating breath of salt air and headed back inside to make a fresh pot of coffee. There were still plenty of details to tend to before the big kickoff barbecue scheduled to begin at 4:00 that afternoon, and Adam didn't want to leave anything to chance.

The trucking accident Thursday afternoon was bad enough. As he gazed out the back windows of the unit he was disappointed with what he saw; there was standing water everywhere. The site had never looked worse. Wherever there wasn't sufficient fill, there were dark, deep ponds. The place looked like a swamp for Chrissake, thought Adam as he made coffee. It looked like Lake Sanderling.

Had that flatbed from Infinity Trucking not jackknifed into a forest, the site would have been pumped out by now. Drained dry and looking sharp. The thought that all that standing water could spell mosquitoes later in the day never occurred to Bartlett. He wanted the water pumped out to make the project look good. Like having your car detailed before putting that "For sale" sign on it, or recarpeting your house just before listing it; removing the standing water, as far as Adam was concerned, was just for show.

The standing water would remind everybody that Sanderling was built on a former stretch of swamp, and Adam didn't care for that image. It had too many negative connotations. He wished like hell that those idiots hadn't put his three big diesel pumps in the ditch, but it was too late for that. He would have to make do with it. Take a different spin and make it work.

He had already decided that he would focus on how well the drainage plan worked. How high and dry the winding roadway was and how there wasn't a trace of water in any of the parking areas under the units. That would make all those acres of standing water look like they belonged there. That would put a positive spin on a careless trucking accident.

There were few salesmen on earth who could do what Bartlett did without so much as missing a step. That was his talent. Turning a negative into a positive as effortlessly as a master illusionist makes a tank disappear. It was a master salesman's sleight of hand, a trick of words and perspective. It was what made him untouchable.

Adam waited as the Krups coffee maker finished. As he listened for the final gurgles of water to work through the machine, he looked to the east across the 13-acre site that was the Sanderling project. The dark lakes looked pretty in a way, reflecting the morning sunlight. The buildings, six of them five stories high and one, the one way in the back, with only four units in it, looked elegant and majestic rising from the wetlands below them. There weren't any birds or wildlife to be seen that morning. They had long since abandoned their old habitat.

Just as well, reasoned Bartlett. All the racket those damn birds make.
Over time, a few of them would find their way back. Over time.

Adam poured two cups of coffee and headed into the bedroom where Vanessa was still sleeping.

"Vanessa, time to rise and shine," said Adam.

"What time is it, Adam?" she replied in a sleepy, muffled voice.

"It's 8:15, darling. Time to get up."

"It's too early, Adam. Let me go back to sleep. Please."

Adam had other plans. He wanted to make love one last time that morning before going around to all the units, checking to be sure that they had the welcome packs and sundries in each of them. He needed to call Ribs & Wings catering to confirm their arrival and he had some real estate deals to tend to in between. He needed to get started.

He gently shook Vanessa in an effort to wake her. Eventually, she sat up and joined him in drinking a cup of fresh-brewed coffee. After using the bathroom and freshening up, they made love once again. It was that sleepy, dreamlike love that everyone longs for. Slow and peaceable. Warm and secure.

This was it, this was the mountaintop that Adam had conquered, and the view from the top was breathtaking.

870-2162
Bartlett's Cell Phone

Its Latin name is *Aedes taeniorhynchus*. The people who work at the Shoreside Conservancy call it by its common name, the salt marsh mosquito. Over the millennia, it has adapted itself to the climate of south Florida. As an adaptation to the seasonal water supply, bone-dry winters and monsoonal summers, the tiny insect has learned to lay its eggs on dry land. Over the natural course of events that land will become flooded, either by freshwater rain or by exceptionally high tides, and once the soil is saturated, the eggs will hatch.

During the last Shoreside summer, September and early October had been particularly dry months. Several large tropical storms and one Category 2 hurricane had run up along the east coast of Florida, doing little more than wreaking havoc on the Bahamas and sucking all the cloud cover and moisture off the west coast. The few thunderstorms that did occur filled only the lowest points in the vast swale system that had been engineered in, around, and throughout the Sanderling Condominium complex.

Only the last few contractors remaining on the project took note of the mosquitoes on the site, and their numbers seemed to be in keeping with the mosquito population on the rest of Shoreside. With nothing out of the ordinary to convey, why would they even bother mentioning a few bugs to Loggins or his right-hand man, Ralph Galano? Besides, by this time, 95 percent of the tasks remaining to be completed prior to the final CO was interior work. Because of this, the mosquitoes and no-see-ums, which could be quite nasty at times, went unnoticed and unheralded.

Tropical storm Kandee changed all that. In the end, Kandee had dumped 17.5 inches of rain on Shoreside Island, give or take an inch in any given locale. The water in the swales quickly crept beyond its usual high-water mark and spilled across acres of former marsh. Hence, the creation of Lake Sanderling. Unbeknownst to the developers, the investors, or Adam Bartlett was the fact that locked deep within that dry soil lay billions upon billions of microscopic eggs. All of this insect biology eagerly awaiting the life-giving alchemy of common H_2O, a few days of warm, subtropical sunlight and upon hatching, as much blood as possible.

In a way, it was like a case study in spontaneous generation. Aristotle would have stood proud that fateful Saturday afternoon. Take old, hard-packed mud, add millions of gallons of ordinary rainwater and, as if by magic, there appears a mosquito population that rivals the arctic tundra in mid-July. Of course it wasn't spontaneous generation. It was what happens when one tries to fool Mother Nature by building a condominium complex on a 13-acre parcel of former swamp.

The pile drivers, roaring dump trucks and cursing construction workers had shagged off all the herons, otters and purple gallinules the first few weeks into the project. Their noisy Caterpillars and backhoes had quickly raked clear all the beautiful strands of buttonwood and sea grape along with the profusion of Brazilian pepper. None of this had any impact on the billions of tiny salt marsh mosquito eggs that were safely tucked inside those piles of dirt that the machines spent weeks shuffling about.

No, all those big machines ended up doing was to spread the dirt out and mix it up a bit. The weight of a 20-ton bulldozer meant nothing to an egg 100 times smaller than a grain of sand.

Now that the rain had finally arrived, soaking deeply into the soil, all those eggs were ready to give birth to mosquito larvae. The larvae, in turn, quickly transformed themselves into adults in the two warm days that followed Kandee's deluge. The males flew off in search of plant food and, as mosquitoes are prone to do, the females flew off in search of blood.

The unprecedented hatch on the island wasn't going to be limited to the Sanderling site either. Over the next week, until the county mosquito control people got a handle on it, there was going to be a problem with salt marsh and freshwater mosquitoes throughout the region. Baytex, Malathion and a host of other insecticides would soon be doing battle with the billions of tiny, winged bloodsuckers. Large, specially equipped DC-3s would be smothering vast tracts of land with deadly toxins in an effort to ward off the spread of St. Louis encephalitis or, as some County Health Department people feared, malaria. Eventually, the chemicals and their human champions would win, but their victory would come too late for Adam Bartlett. Far, far too late.

Adam's cell phone rang at precisely 2:30 p.m. The owner of Ribs & Wings was calling. At the time of his call, Adam was checking the last unit in the complex to be certain it had all the linens, toilet paper and the welcome package. His cell phone signal wasn't coming in very clearly, so Adam stepped onto the rear balcony to try to clear the static on the line. Cell phones can be so temperamental at times, he thought to himself as he closed the door behind him.

"Bartlett here," he said again, this time with a semblance of clarity.

"Yeah, Adam, dis is George down here at Ribs & Wings. We're packing up da truck now to come on down, but my guy here can't remember, did you order da baked beans or da coleslaw?"

Adam hadn't ordered anything. Chris had taken care of all of those details.

Adam was wondering how in hell this idiot had gotten hold of his cell phone number.

"I don't know, my assistant Chris did all the ordering."

"Well, which side dish do you prefer, da baked beans or da coleslaw?"

"Bring them both."

"There'll be an extra charge for dat, Mr. Bartlett."

"Fine, just add it to the bill."

Just as Adam said bill, he took his left hand and swatted a single, tiny little salt marsh mosquito that had landed beside his left ear. He never gave it a second thought. Just an errant bug on a calming, glorious afternoon.

"Okay then, sir, my guys should be out there with the barbecue truck in a half an hour. We're planning to serve all you guys around 5:00 or so, ain't dat right?"

"Right."

"Goob-bye den."

"Bye."

He had to be from Chicago, thought Adam. Chris knew where to find the best barbecue in town and the owner just had to be from Chicago. South Chicago at dat.

As Adam pulled his cell phone away from his ear, he noted that there were two small mosquitoes on the back of his right wrist. One of them had already taken a long, full drink of his blood. The other one was just getting started. Adam took his left hand and swatted both of them. One left a small black splotch, the other one left a red-and-black splotch, the way a mosquito looks like after they're smudged, all legs, wings and a tiny drop of blood. Your blood.

The three consecutive bites got Adam to thinking.

Bug spray. Damn, I forgot about bug spray. It's been getting calmer and calmer all day and I didn't even think about bug spray. Adam got on his cell phone immediately.

"Chris, this is Adam."

"What's up, Adam, I'm on my way out the door."

"Well, the wind has really died here at the site and there seem to be some mosquitoes coming around. It's probably from all that rain. Please pick up a half-dozen cans of Off and come on over. That should take care of it."

"Can I get anything else?" asked Chris before hanging up.

"No, the caterer just called and he seems to be all set. The beer truck and the bar people are already here setting up. I think we're all set except for some mosquito spray and the crowd. Just pick up the bug dope at Eckerd Drugs and come on down. It's looking great."

"I'm on my way, Adam."

"Great, see you soon."

"Bye."

"Bub-bye."

With that Adam put his cell phone back and headed inside Unit D-10 to finish his inspection of the units. Everything looked to be in order. In fact, everything was in order. Not exactly man's idea of order. Everything was in a perfect, natural order.

Little did Adam realize that the six cans of Off that Chris was purchasing at Eckerd's Drug Store would do little to ward off the coming salt marsh mosquito hatch. By 5:15, those half-dozen cans of insect spray would be empty. By 6:00 that night, 600 cans of Off might have helped, although they would have done little to ward off the millions of tiny no-see-ums that would join in the onslaught.

It was Mother Nature's order that Adam was up against and he was no match against the marvels of a billion years of insect biology. He, and the launching of his Sanderling Condominium marketing plan, were soon to be face to face with one of the most prolific hatches of salt marsh mosquitoes ever seen on Shoreside. As Adam headed out of the last condo and walked toward the beer truck, he swatted himself three more times before getting there. Twice on the shoulder and once on the forehead. It was only an inkling of what was soon to come.

The beer truck and the barbecue station were parked alongside the tennis courts. They had rented a big open tent to keep the rain off, had Kandee lingered longer than expected. Now the tent served as a cool, shaded area out of the tireless Florida sunshine. The setup looked good, thought Adam as he walked over toward it.

"How's it going?" he shouted as he neared the two Miller employees who were going to be pouring the beer.

"Fine," said the shorter of the two.

"Fine," said the taller one. "Except there're quite a few mosquitoes around here. Do you happen to have any bug spray around?"

"My assistant, Chris, is bringing some bug spray down shortly. It's just that it's getting so damn calm. You know how it is, they always seem to show up in the late afternoon when it gets calm like this."

"Yeah, we know," replied the shorter of the two.

Things were happening. The crew from Ribs & Wings arrived and fired up the big grill they had towed behind their custom catering van. The tables were being set and the guests were pouring in at a steady pace. Everything was right on schedule.

There were 32 investor units, 50 percent of the project, that were available for the kickoff of the Sanderling condo project. Adam and Vanessa had taken the best apartment in the complex. As a favor to Betsy, Adam had let her and Mark stay in a unit way in the back of the complex for their early wedding present. They were going to be married in January, but Adam thought that it would be a nice opportunity to get them something beforehand. Adam liked Betsy and even though she wasn't a reservationist, she deserved the getaway.

Everyone at Shoreside Realty liked Betsy.

That left a total of 30 condos for the top reservationists, their husbands, wives, or significant others. Most had individual units for the night, but quite a number had elected to double up, with one couple staying in the master bedroom and another couple in the guest bedroom. All totaled, there were 126 people expected to attend.

Single gals, young couples, older couples with children and empty-nest supervisors and managers all drove the long winding road looking for the exact location of their particular condo. Adam had hired two of Loggins' good-looking construction workers to hand out site plans and direct everybody to their free unit as they pulled into the driveway off the main road. That was like Bartlett, to leave no stone unturned.

The invitations said that things would get started at 4:00, with an open bar and a beer truck to start the party off on the right foot. Couple after couple made their way from their units after hurriedly getting settled in and started showing up by the beer truck. Showing up thirsty and ready to party. Their kids were jumping into the pool not 50 yards from the big tent. The complex was looking splendid in the falling afternoon sunlight.

"Great party, Adam," said one exceptionally attractive young reservationist from Johnson Realty.

"What a fabulous idea," said her nearly-as-attractive friend.

Adam took note of the two. Vanessa was still in first position, but there's never any harm in checking out some good backups. Had Vanessa not been expected momentarily, Adam would have tried to get a phone number or two. He was nothing if not consistent.

Things were going fabulously. Chris had arrived with the bug spray and, for the moment at least, the six cans of Off were keeping the mosquitoes at bay. The reservationists and their managers were all going on and on about their extraordinary views, the quality of the furnishings and appointments in the units, and what a delight it was to see a project that really showed off the beauty of Shoreside Island.

Adam was floating on a salesman's high made even more pleasant by the Blue Sapphire gin and tonic he was drinking. By this time, Vanessa had come to join him. She was wearing a tight red blouse and a black mini-dress that allowed 95 percent of her beautiful, pale white legs to show. Vanessa looked like sex in sandals. Scrumptious. Hanging on Adam's right arm like the sensual red-haired accessory to the undisputed czar of Shoreside Island real estate. With his tall G&T, the aroma of ribs wafting through the still air, and his gorgeous redhead at his side, Adam's tableau was complete and undisputable. Adam Bartlett had arrived.

Ironically, so had the salt marsh mosquitoes. They came in waves. The first wave hit around 5:00. Not a big deal. Chris went around passing out her six cans of Off and the initial hatch was easily repelled. With the guests now pleasantly liquored up, no one really made much to do about the first foray of bugs.

The second big hatch of mosquitoes came in around 6:00, just as everyone was wrapping up dinner. This one was ten times as nasty as the first assault.

Within a few minutes, all six cans of OFF had been completely drained of their contents. Some of the more scantily clad reservationists went to their condos to get on long-sleeved blouses and pants. Everyone, now quite in the bag from all the free liquor, and stuffed on spicy chicken wings and barbecued pork, found themselves spending 40 percent of their time swatting insects. It soon got worse.

By 6:15 things were going badly. Adam had sent Chris back to Eckerd Drug Store for more bug spray, only to have her return saying that they closed at 6:00 p.m. on Saturdays. She had stopped at a couple of corner stores but everyone was out. The bug problem was pandemic across the island and the run on bug spray had depleted the island's supply.

By 6:30, the skies around the Sanderling project were dark with salt marsh mosquitoes. Dark and hungry.

Everyone was talking about it.

"Wow, there sure are a lot of mosquitoes around this place," said someone while swatting six of them that had landed on her arm.

"Whew, you can say that again," agreed her friend.

"Well, did you know that this place was built on a swamp?"

"Yeah, and I heard that they had a heck of a time getting permits."

"Just look at all this standing water, no wonder this place is loaded with mosquitoes."

Adam quickly sensed it. For the first time in his life he couldn't think of a way to put a positive spin on a bad situation. The bugs were becoming terrible. Fierce and ravenous.

The gala celebration of the Sanderling Condominium project was turning into a scene from a Stephen King novel. It was the flying insect version of the film *Arachnophobia*. The crowd was losing it.

There were so many mosquitoes in the air that the sound of them alone started driving people mad. There were now billions upon billions of bugs surrounding the complex. They were making this incessant hummm, like the sound of a thousand fluorescent light bulbs or the noise of a distant airplane. A twin-engine Cessna having mechanical trouble, coming in low and heading straight for your house.

As the mosquito blitz continued, the celebration bash deteriorated. People started going bug crazy. They would start swatting, then itching, then dancing around in tight little circles. The more aggressive mosquitoes would get inside their ears and the noise would trigger even more aberrant behavior. One boyfriend became so unnerved by the incessant bugs that he jumped into the pool to escape them. He jumped in with all of his clothes on and his cell phone still in his pants pocket.

Several reservationists, in an effort to keep them off their legs and arms, discovered that smearing thick barbecue sauce all over themselves tended to keep the mosquitoes from biting. Soon, mothers started using the same desperate technique to keep the insects off their children while they ran and got the car.

The situation spiraled out of hand. Now dozens of people were running around screaming, their bodies smeared head to toe with dark red, extra hot barbecue sauce. From a distance, it resembled blood.

It looked like some crazed sniper had climbed into the penthouse of the "A" building with a massive stash of automatic weapons and a brain tumor the size of Texas. It looked bad. Really, really bad.

Adam felt helpless. Vanessa had long since run up to their penthouse, the little salt marsh killers having made quick work of her exquisite thighs. She was now soaking in the Jacuzzi bathtub, trying to get her swollen bites to go down.

At first, Adam had tried to make excuses. "Oh, you know, there are more bugs than usual because of all the rain." "They'll clear out of here once the sun sets. They always do." "It's not all that bad, just a few mosquitoes and some no-see-ums."

All of Adam's excuses ran out about the time a mother drove up with her two boys and said that they were leaving. Looking through the car window at her two children, scratching themselves silly in the back seat, and seeing them both covered in hundreds of mosquito bites, Adam couldn't argue with this lady. The kids looked frightening. They looked like they had the worst case of measles in recorded medical history. They looked like smallpox victims.

Not a half hour earlier, in an effort to survive the onslaught of bugs, both children had dived into the pool with straws. Holding themselves just below the surface by pushing off the pool stairs, the two boys were breathing through the straws to avoid coming to the surface. When the salt marsh mosquitoes figured out that they could still manage to crawl down these intake devices, the mother grabbed the kids and came over to say goodbye. Even their tongues had been bitten.

Soon the entire complex was filled with the sound of trunks slamming, wheels screeching and cars pouring back toward home. The mosquitoes, aided by their microscopic allies, the vicious no-see-ums, were winning. They were dive bombing the site by the millions and the hapless reservationists were fleeing for their lives.

By 7:15, the two Miller guys got into their truck and hauled ass out of the Sanderling project. They hadn't even taken the time to put away their beer lines. As the truck sped off, one of those lines snagged the tennis fence, and now a trail of dripping Miller Lite ran directly from the Sanderling project to the causeway and on into town.

Rumors had spread about the possibility of an outbreak of St. Louis encephalitis at the site and the rumor mill hadn't stopped there. There was talk of malaria, yellow fever and some kind of pox being carried by these bloodthirsty swarms. No one knew the exact kind of pox, nor did they care. They had heard that it was 100 percent fatal. People were in a complete panic.

Adam just stood there. Bug after bug drank from his uncovered ears. He didn't bother to swat them off after a while. What was the use? He saw three years of work collapsing before him in a cloud of tiny, swarming vampires. Let them drink away, he thought as the sunlight faded and the condos emptied. Drink they did.

By 8:00 p.m. it was all over. The caterers had gone, leaving half of their dishes and silverware behind in their rush to escape. There was no one left except for Betsy and Mark in the "F" building, and Adam and Vanessa. At 8:30 Vanessa told Adam that she had a terrible headache. She was gone by 9:00.

As the sun set to the west, Adam sat on the same screen porch he had sat on that morning. It was no longer a kingdom he overlooked, it was a ruin. Behind him was an empty project. They had all returned to the safety of their homes and apartments, far away from this bug-infested hell hole called Sanderling. By noon tomorrow the word would be out and there would be no stopping it.

Boyle, who never did end up showing, would hear about it through the grapevine by 4:00 in the afternoon, right after the Tampa Bay Bucs' victory over the Raiders. Loggins would get the call from Boyle a half hour after that. News would spread faster than the phantom encephalitis, which comes from freshwater and not salt marsh mosquitoes. For Bartlett, encephalitis would have been quicker.

The story would spill across the island like the news of the plague. Sanderling is a bug-infested swamp. Do not, under any circumstances, and I repeat, do not rent any of the units at Sanderling, even to your worst customers. That message would soon infiltrate the sales community as well. If you can't rent them, and the site is crawling with every kind of biting insect known to man, don't show them. The Sanderling kickoff party was a complete catastrophe.

As Adam finished his bottle of gin, Mark and Betsy, in an effort to get away from the mosquitoes and the no-see-ums that had made their way into the unit itself, played around under the covers of their brand-new king-sized bed. They eventually got around to making love. Unbeknownst to either of them at the time, Betsy was going to become pregnant because of this salt marsh mosquito hatch. They were just having fun at the time, but Betsy had forgotten to take her little pill earlier that morning.

Funny how things like that happen.

570-2331

Unit 2-G, Sanderling Condominium

"SEE IF THEY HAVE A FLASHLIGHT IN THE KITCHEN, BETSY."

Mark was shouting from the master bedroom. He was already under the blankets of the huge king-sized bed, safely out of reach of the mosquitoes and no-see-ums that were assaulting the complex.

"I CAN'T FIND ONE!" shouted Betsy from across the condominium. "WHERE WOULD IT BE?"

"LOOK IN THE CUPBOARDS UNDER THE SINK, THEY SOMETIMES PUT THEM THERE."

Betsy kept looking. She was in her flannel nightgown and the insects that had made it in with them when they ran through the front door were slowly finding their way under her loose-fitting gown. It was one of those sack-like nightgowns, like the kind that were popular at the turn of the 19th century. Victorian in style, prim and proper.

Mark should have been the one scouring the kitchen for the flashlight but he was allergic to no-see-um bites. One bite from those minuscule flying teeth would put a welt on him the size of a nickel. Because the two of them had left all the windows open before going to the barbecue, the condo was loaded with hundreds of no-see-ums. To tiny insects the size of a pinhead, screens offered no defense.

"I FOUND IT," Betsy shouted to Mark from the kitchen.

"GOOD, THEN COME ON BACK HERE AND BRING YOUR NOTEBOOK."

Betsy grabbed her pencil and her notebook and went into the master bedroom. She turned out the light and climbed into the king-sized bed. Once there, she slipped under the covers to join Mark. It was fun. Like a teenage sleep over with a friend.

By this time, unbeknownst to both of them, only three people were left at Sanderling. Vanessa had left Adam about a half hour earlier. All of the other reservationists and rental managers, their children and their significant others had cleared out. Most of them were already home, soaking their bug bites in the tub or calling everyone they knew to tell them about the mosquito infestation at the condominium complex they had just escaped from.

The gala Sanderling marketing kickoff party had come down to three people. Adam Bartlett sitting at the dining room table drinking straight gin, and Betsy and Mark under the covers in their king-sized bed, planning their wedding with a notebook and a brand-new flashlight.

"This is great, Mark. I'm glad we stayed."

"Me too."

They kissed again. Just a little peck of a kiss. They had work to do and there would be plenty of time for making love later.

"Well, let's start with the invitation list. I don't want a real big wedding. Let's try to keep it around 100 or so, don't you think?" asked Betsy.

"Sounds fine to me," agreed Mark.

They started making their plans. The wedding would be in mid-January, when the condo rates dropped to the shoulder season rates. That would help with the cost of putting up all the relatives. Betsy's would come from Indiana. Mark's family was from the Pittsburgh area. It was thoughtful of them to even consider such a thing.

Soon the notebook was full of names, dinner selections, locations where they might consider having the wedding, different bands that they liked for the reception, and a host of other notations. Even The Brown Truckers were considered for the dance, more as a courtesy to Mark than anything else.

As they chatted and planned their future, darkness fell on the Sanderling Condominium project. Adam was getting hammered, trying to escape the inevitable. The bottle of Blue Sapphire gin was down to two or three shots. He would finish off the rest before midnight, grab a blanket and sleep on the couch in the living room. Sleep poorly.

The mosquitoes outside would settle down as well. By midnight the waxing moon would reflect off the standing water in the surrounding swales. From the beach, the empty condominiums would look peaceful and luxurious, like pillars of stone rising from a huge lake. The noises of darkness would surround the complex. Sounds of crickets and raccoons fighting over discarded chicken wings. Noises of the wild.

By 12:30 the batteries in the flashlight would wear down to the point where neither Betsy nor Mark could see clearly enough to continue with their wedding plans. They would have to postpone the rest of their brainstorming session until daylight. That was fine with both of them, they were tired.

Mark crawled from beneath the covers and set the exhausted flashlight, the notebook and the pencil on the nightstand. Then he quickly crawled under the covers with his bride-to-be. They spooned quietly for a few minutes, Mark gently kissing the back of Betsy's neck. Betsy squirming and laughing because of it.

"Mark," she said, "you know how ticklish I am!"

Mark paid no attention to her sweet reprimand. He knew that she was enjoying it. This was romance: a waxing moon outside, two lovers entangled beneath warm blankets in an empty condominium complex, and the sound of the breaking surf in the distance. Their wedding plans on the night stand beside them and their warm breath mixing in the cool night air. Lord Tennyson's love poems could not describe this idyllic scene. Shakespeare, the bard himself, would have been at a loss for words.

As the moonlight shone through the skylight directly above the bed, the two of them made love before falling fast asleep. They made the kind of love that lovers dream of making. Tender and sweet, giving and warm. It wasn't sex. It was a dream of sharing souls. A moment in this hurried highway of life wherein all that is splendid is unveiled before us. Ethereal and sweet, like the sound of a waterfall, or the smell of spring in the air.

Their passions spent, they both fell fast asleep, safe beneath their warm blankets. Safe and ever so warm. Betsy, without knowing, was now with child.

570-1995
Unit 2-A, Sanderling Condominiums

Adam Bartlett awoke at noon. Hung over and depressed, he got up and microwaved some of yesterday's leftover coffee and walked to the balcony. The view from the fifth-story lanai was identical to that of yesterday's, only exactly one day later. The wind was now light and the air carried a touch of autumn in it. Just a touch of that cold, crisp air that had made all of the leaves change color far to the north of Florida.

He sat in one of the Brown Jordan chaise lounges and slowly sipped his cup of coffee. It was dark and bitter. Vanessa was no longer waiting for him in the master bedroom, wrapped in a bright red nightgown from Victoria's Secret. How things can change in 24 hours.

Yesterday, Adam was the sovereign of Shoreside Island, the undisputed real estate lord of millions of dollars in Gulf-front inventory. His future bright, his plans illustrious, and his dominion boundless. Now he was devastated. Reduced from prince to pauper because some whiskey'd-up Teamster had jackknifed his rig while thinking about Ashley Moore's massive double-D knockers. Without knowing it, that drunken Teamster had jackknifed Adam's life right along with those three diesel pumps. Adam's future became part of the accident. In two minutes of reckless driving, Bartlett's destiny was trashed. Ruined. More truck accident debris.

Adam just sat there, staring. A few no-see-ums had worked their tiny bodies through the useless screening and were biting him behind his ears. Adam didn't bother to brush them away. His ears were already smothered in bites, as were his wrists and the back of his neck below the hairline. The no-see-ums weren't even painful at this point. They were just a foreshadowing of larger, far more damaging bites to come. They were nothing when compared to the capacious chunks Tom Loggins and Charles Harris would soon be taking out of him. Not to mention the 23 other angry investors.

They wouldn't stop at the ear or the back of his neck either. They would all be going for the throat, or worse. Only Adam's aorta would satisfy them at this point. He would have to answer to each and every one of them over time. He would have to explain why he didn't know anything about the reproductive biology of salt marsh mosquitoes. That had he known about the swarms of insects that drove off all the tormented reservationists, he would have postponed the kickoff to the following week. He should have known. But he didn't.

Adam was just a man. He didn't know about salt marsh mosquitoes; nor did he know anything about reset geodetic survey markers, or a million Brazilian pepper seeds Ralph had planted to help Loggins secure the permits. No one knew about those midnight excursions. No one but Loggins, Harris and Ralph Galano. The investors might have forgiven Adam, or at least cut him some slack, had they known of the underhanded tactics TLD, Inc. had used to develop the McKinzie parcel. But the code of silence the three men had taken would not fail. Bartlett was to become the fall guy.

He was to bear the full responsibility for the disaster. It was Bartlett's idea and Sanderling was his undoing. With news of last night's fiasco now traversing the telephone lines of Shoreside Island faster than the speed of e-mail, the seven Sanderling buildings were effectively sinking back down into the muck upon which they had been built. The mosquito-infested muck.

Adam knew it. As he sat there on the porch, his cell phone turned off, both of his pagers chirping away and the condominium phone off the hook, Adam knew what was coming. By Monday morning a meeting would be scheduled. The topic would be self evident. How can we stop the spin? How can we save Sanderling from the salt marsh mosquito debacle? Who the hell's responsible? Why didn't we see this one coming?

The coffee Adam was drinking was hot, old and bitter. It had been left on the burner too long yesterday and it had cooked down into that awful, acrid state that old coffee descends to. Adam didn't give a damn.

For a minute he remembered something from his childhood. It was something obscure, something he hadn't thought of in 30 years. As a toddler, he and his father used to stay at the kitchen table after dinner. His dad, Dennis, would take out an old deck of cards and pull up beside Adam, still sitting in his wooden high chair. As Adam sat there watching, his father would build a house of cards on the tray of his high chair. All the while, as the house became higher and higher, Adam wouldn't move, or make a sound.

When it was all finished, his dad would wink at him. With that wink, Adam would take in a deep breath and say to his father, "Collapse, begin to fall." Once said, little Adam would quickly blow down that magnificent house of cards.

That's what he felt like doing to the Sanderling Condominium project as it stood empty in the mid day sun: Collapse, begin to fall.

Part IV
God Bats Last

570-9514
Mildred Lee's Home Phone

Mildred pushed the small red button on her remote and turned off her 12-inch television. The news was grim. She crept over to her stove to put on some tea and reflect on what she had just watched. As she reached for her teapot she noted that the fine white hair on her arms was standing straight up. Goose bumps.

I've got goose bumps just from watching it. This isn't a good sign.

Mildred Lee had been watching cable channel 39, The Weather Channel, all morning. It was late July and the world was full of storms. There were hurricanes and tropical storms rolling off Central America, moving over the steamy waters of the eastern Pacific. They were battering the hell out of the southern tip of Baja before setting their sights on Hawaii and the islands beyond. The Atlantic was crawling with them. As Dr. William Gray himself had forecast, it was going to be a very active season.

Already, wave after wave had been sliding off the equatorial coast of Africa. Three early Caribbean storms jump-started the season, but only one was named, tropical storm Amy. She hit just north of Corpus Christi, Texas. Mildred's chart had made note of some minor coastal flooding and one fatality. Some unlucky soul tried to ford a flooded arroyo in his new Land Cruiser. They found him three days later downstream, as dead as the bricks in the Alamo. They never found the Land Cruiser.

After Amy came Bret. Bret had potential, thought Mildred. He was the first Cape Verde storm of the season. Cape Verde storms are the monsters that begin their journeys as tropical waves coming off the tropical coast of Africa near Senegal and Guinea. These are the big storms. The storms that start their powerful pirouettes above the warm waters of the east African Atlantic and perfect their wrathful ballet as they cross the great, temperate ocean. They are dancing wildly out of control by the time they give their command performances along the coastline of North America.

Andrew was a Cape Verde storm, as were Betsy, Camille and Hugo. Bret had tried to join the ranks of these sordid hall of fame storms, but after achieving an impressive Category 3 status, he veered north without making landfall. Bret became a threat only to ships at sea, eventually falling apart over the cool, uninspiring waters of the north Atlantic.

After Bret came Celeste. But Celeste never even made it to Category 1 status. She had taken form just north of the island of Hispaniola, but never managed to reach maximum sustained winds of 74 miles per hour. Celeste's circulation hit a disappointing 65 miles per hour and waned. She brushed by the outer island of the Bahamas two weeks ago and caused some minor damage along with a few injuries. To Mildred, Celeste was just another in a decade of disappointments that had come and gone before her.

Next, spinning east to west, came Hurricane Dudley. Mildred felt the name fit the storm perfectly. Dudley was a dud. He never amounted to much, coming in just north of Barbados from the coast of Africa as a Category 2 storm and ending up breaking up over the Yucatan peninsula four days ago. Five deaths, less than a million dollars worth of damage and it was over for Dudley.

None of these first four storms amounted to much. They were just passing storms in a long history of forgotten cyclones. Named storms that never really gave the world a reason to remember them. Minor players with a good chance that their forgettable names would someday be used again, hopefully with some results. They would soon become obscure, recalled only in the dusty lists of last year's tropical storms. Insignificant.

The storm that made Mildred shudder and put all those goose bumps on her arms was as of yet unnamed. It was just a dark mass of squalls and thunderstorms presently leaving the western coast of Africa. There was something about it that frightened Mildred. Maybe it was the sheer size of it. Maybe it was the knowledge that the ocean it was now traveling over was warm and willing.

Perhaps it was her intuition. An old woman's sixth sense of impending danger. Whatever it was, Mildred couldn't get the image of this massive area of wind and rain from her mind. There was something about it, something that told her that this could be it, this could be the storm that Shoreside was long overdue for. The "Big One."

Mildred dropped her tea bag into the steaming water and waited. She would have to recheck all of her supplies again this afternoon: the ice in her coolers, the canned goods, the flashlight batteries, everything on her extensive checklist. There was always so much to do. She would have to get ready. This one could be it.

She walked over and picked up her hurricane tracking chart. Let's see now, after Dudley comes...she scrolled down the list for the thousandth time since June 1...comes Emily. What a pretty name, she thought. What a pretty name.

589-2923
Sam Goodlet's Cell Phone

"Hello, Sam Goodlet here." Sam wasn't expecting a call.

"Sam, it's Mildred. How are you doing?"

"I'm doing fine, Mildred. What's up?"

"Have you heard about Emily?"

"Who's Emily?"

Sam hadn't heard about Emily, nor had most of the people living in Southwest Florida. She was still only a tropical depression. The National Hurricane center hadn't even named Emily yet, her winds still below the 38 miles per hour minimum threshold required to become a named storm.

The unnamed Emily was more than 2,000 miles away, only now beginning her terrible spin. Harmless and distant, churning up a vast and empty ocean. There were no supercomputer models capable of projecting whether a depression would become a storm, and the storm eventually a hurricane. There was no way of predicting the eventual path of a storm that far away. It might veer northward toward Bermuda, or hook south into Mexico, or take 1,000 other unpredictable directions. At this point, no one could predict Emily's path, or predict that she would make hurricane status.

That fact made no difference to Mrs. Mildred Lee. Her hurricane tracking chart had a wobbly dotted line projecting all the way from 52.48.620 west, 015.58.430 north square into the center of Shoreside Island. Of course the dotted line was done in erasable grease pen just in case. Every storm that came up in the south Atlantic had Mildred's bull's-eye projection into Shoreside Island. One or two storms a year came relatively close, but most of the time Mildred had to use a slightly dampened sponge to remove her personal tracking forecasts. In a way, it was always a disappointment to her.

Sam was getting tired of it. Sam felt that Mildred was just having another incident of her chronic paranoia about tropical cyclones. Another case of the heebie-jeebies. Psychologists call it obsessive compulsive disorder.

"She's that huge storm in the Atlantic heading right toward us. She was upgraded last night to a tropical depression. She's going to be a killer, Sam. Emily's the "Big One!" said Mildred emphatically.

"Come on now, Mildred. Haven't we been through all of this before?

The chances of a major storm hitting this coast are less than four percent. The last one that came through this way was Donna back in '60. Why are you so afraid of every little storm that comes along? The chances of this new depression, what did you say her name was...Emily? hitting Shoreside are slim to none, Mildred. You shouldn't spend so much of your time worrying about it."

"I'm not worried, Sam. I'm prepared. My two ice chests are filled, my canned goods, flashlights, my rope, drinking water, radios, everything is set except for two little things."

Sam knew what was coming. He knew that there had to be a reason for the call. He was waiting for the other shoe to fall.

"Which two little things are those, Mildred?"

"Well, you know those two hurricane shutters in the kitchen you had me take down to help show the house? They're lying outside. Could you come over tomorrow and help me put them back up? Tommy, my errand boy, who usually helps me with things like this, is up in Orlando this week with his family. I would really appreciate it, Sam."

Sam couldn't say no. It was like saying no to his long-lost Great Aunt Claire. The one who always gave him cookies and candy. In Sam Goodlet's heart, Mildred had become that great aunt. Saying no was out of the question.

"Sure, Mildred, I can do it. I've got an appointment in the morning but I'm free early afternoon. How does 1:30 sound to you?"

Sam knew that anytime sounded good to Mildred. She never left the house and at that she seldom strayed far from her little color television set in the kitchen. The TV with its remote stuck on cable channel 39, The Weather Channel.

"One-thirty would be fine, Sam. Can I make you some soup for lunch? I've got 36 cans of Campbell's chicken noodle soup in my pantry. Wouldn't that be just wonderful for a little afternoon snack?"

"Sounds delightful, Mildred. I'll be there and I'll be hungry."

"Bub-bye, Sam."

"Goodbye, Mildred."

Sam flipped the cover down on his cell phone and set the phone on the empty seat beside him. He hated chicken noodle soup, but he didn't want to offend Mildred. That was typical of him, Sam would do anything to accommodate a client. He'd give them the shirt off his back if they asked for it. His T-shirt to boot. He might have a million different scenarios played out in his imaginary world, but in the end, Sam cared. It was his nature.

That's why he was in his car this morning, heading downtown to a hearing. He was just doing another good deed, this time on behalf of the Grinsteads, who technically weren't even his clients.

The hearing was called to decide what to do with what was left of the Grinstead residence. Mr. Grinstead's brother, Elmer, had flown down to attend the hearing, and there were several psychiatrists scheduled to appear before the judge as well. Something had to be done.

Neither Mr. nor Mrs. Grinstead was able to attend. Mrs. Grinstead was still in a long-term mental health facility outside Greenville, and Mr. Grinstead was likewise indisposed. He was in a padded cell not three miles from the courthouse. He was still wearing a straight jacket and saying, "IT'S BUG FREE, IT'S BUG FREE, IT'S BUG FREE AT LAST!!!" with a voice that sounded as raspy as a rusted wood file. He was under constant suicide watch and had a 24-hour surveillance camera placed in the corner of his tiny, windowless room. Even the heavy narcotics weren't helping.

As bad as Mr. Grinstead's condition was, the house was worse. Before Elmer had convinced this same judge to order the SWAT team to burst through the front door and subdue his brother, Kurt Grinstead, he had managed to remove better than 90 percent of the drywall from the interior of the house, and every section of the vinyl siding. He did so piece by piece, using nothing but his fingernails and a claw hammer to accomplish his tortured goal. By the time those half-dozen men wrestled Kurt to the ground, the rubber grip on the claw hammer was worn as smooth as polished granite and Kurt's calloused hands needed a serious manicure.

All that remained of the interior drywall were some scattered sections of ceiling near the top of the vaulted living room. Kurt, in his determination to find that sugar ant nest, had cleverly stacked all his furniture in the center of the room into a weird, extremely unusual suburban pyramid, allowing him to reach the very top of the vaulted ceiling 20 feet above him.

The SWAT team, after wrestling the claw hammer from Kurt and getting him safely into his new straight jacket, was mortified by the interior condition of the house; the white powdery dust, the pieces of drywall and torn remnants of pink insulation scattered around everywhere. But it was his living room pyramid that proved to be the *coup de gras*.

For the base of the pyramid, Kurt, formerly an engineer, had wisely selected all of the kitchen appliances, including the washer and dryer. He had determined these were heavy and solid enough to handle the next layer. That next layer consisted of the living room sofa, matching loveseat and two occasional chairs. Kurt had cleverly put all of the home's interior doors between the layers to keep the pyramid level. On top of the furniture rested the kitchen table with a single, bright blue kitchen chair at the very pinnacle.

It was really quite an impressive piece of engineering, thought the head of the SWAT team. Especially for a raving lunatic.

Since Kurt had technically harmed no one but his house, and had been eating a mixture of drywall and sweetened condensed milk for much of his sustenance during his bizarre three-week stretch of self-imprisonment, it was clear to the police that he would be far better off in a mental health facility than in jail.

He didn't argue with the decision. In fact he didn't say anything except to go on and on, in a babbling fashion, about the termites, ants and crawling roaches that were still somewhere in the walls of what was left of his home.

These were, of course, delusional insects, the real bugs having fled the home in panic long ago.

Since his committal, months had passed. With the electroshock therapy, the anti-depressant drugs and a score of other therapies, everyone felt confident that Kurt would eventually snap out of it. Everyone was optimistic that both Kurt and his wife would get over these little problems they were having with the closing of their house on Surfside Street and get on with the rest of their lives.

Everyone was wrong. Celia still had a terminal case of the drools, and after months in the wacky ward, Kurt Grinstead was still not exactly himself. From weeks upon weeks of going unshaven and unwashed, he looked a little bit like a cross between Charles Manson and the Unabomer, Ted Kaczynski. Not good. Not good at all.

Something had to be done. The drywall, which Kurt had thrown out through the one non-nailed-up dining room window and onto the front lawn, had disintegrated in the seasonal summer thunderstorms, turning into a chalky mush. The neighborhood homeowners association had managed to get a court injunction to have the pile removed but not before the white gypsum rock had permeated the surrounding soil. Everything in the yard had died. The lawn was dead, the shrubs were dead, as were all the trees. The huge, sprawling live oak that once had graced the west side of the yard looked like something out of *The Legend of Sleepy Hollow*: leafless, twisted and spooky.

The homeowners association had managed to get the company they had hired to remove the drywall to also neatly stack the vinyl siding underneath the brand-new pilings, but that didn't help things out much. The house looked macabre. Like a house that had been used in a top-secret bomb test. A cobalt bomb. No, make that a lithium bomb. Some kind of weapon that removes siding and drywall, kills all the vegetation and insects and leaves the homeowner mad as a hatter. Lithium bomb works. It has a nice ring to it.

The hearing had been called to decide if the sale should be canceled completely and the control of the home and the Grinsteads' estate handed over to his brother, Elmer Grinstead, or if the price should be adjusted and the property conveyed by court order to Mr. and Mrs. Bartholomew Hazelton.

Oddly enough, Bartholomew and Dolores still wanted the home, although Sam had no idea why. A person would have to be out of his mind to take possession of a house in this condition. Of course they had adjusted their offer considerably from the original contract price. Whereas the original contracted price for the property was for $450,000, they were now offering to take what was left of the home for $150,000. That figure was just slightly under actual land value.

Sam, in a surprise move, had actually decided to side with Kurt Grinstead's brother on this one. He felt that it wouldn't be fair to hand the house over to the Hazeltons for a song. It was their incessant search for sugar ants and cockroaches that had driven both the owners straight to the madhouse. Because the situation had so changed over the last year and half, Sam no longer felt that he had a fiduciary obligation to his clients.

To put all of this in simple layman's terms, he thought Mr. and Mrs. Bartholomew Hazelton were despicable. He had fired himself.

So he was there to argue that the house be handed back to the seller's brother and that the contract between the Grinsteads and the Hazeltons be voided due to insanity.

The listing agent, Dale Anderson of Anderson Realty, was also going to be there, as were several members of the neighborhood homeowners association. No one expected a decision this morning, but the judge wanted to hear everyone's story before proceeding. He had already read through the briefs and found the entire event beyond belief. He wanted to meet the Hazeltons, their agents and everyone involved in the debacle.

Sam laughed to himself as he pulled into the courthouse parking lot to find a place for his Oldsmobile. In a few days it might not even matter, he thought. Not if Mildred Lee is right about this new storm. What was it named again? Oh, yeah, Emily.

That's kind of a pretty name for a hurricane, isn't it? Emily. Maybe she'll solve the problem.

570-9898
The Main Switchboard; Tuesday Morning

Betsy could feel the baby kicking again. It was almost ticklish, but it felt just a bit too strange to be ticklish. Sometimes she felt as if there were an alien down there, growing inside of her. But most of the time she felt totally wondrous, knowing that she would soon be bringing a new child into this world.

Line six lit up and Betsy sprang into automatic. "Shoreside Realty, how may we help you?"

The phone call was for Adam again. It sounded like another attorney. Betsy didn't bother inquiring into any of the details. She didn't need to at this point. As glorious as things were for her and Mark - their soon-to-be born son, their new house in town and Mark's recent promotion - life was being exceptionally cruel to Bartlett. He didn't deserve it, thought Betsy. She was always so willing to forgive.

Betsy had put on quite a bit of weight over the course of her pregnancy. She had gone from being a "full-figured" woman to now being a "full-figured" pregnant woman. She was big. As big as any woman would want to be.

Her belly looked as though it held a globe in it. She had put on a little better than 50 pounds and gaining all that weight had been hard on her. She had developed varicose veins, leg cramps and her lower back hurt constantly. But it didn't stop her from coming to work. She loved answering the phones and hoped to stay on her job right up until her water broke.

Mark was all set. They had picked up a pager for him a month ago. Every afternoon around 3:00 Betsy would pull his pager up on the system and type in, *LOOKS LIKE WE WON'T BE GOING TO THE HOSPITAL TODAY!!* He would invariably panic when the pager went off. Drop his packages and double-check the message. Then he would read the message, laugh to himself and continue about his business. He fell for her little joke unfailingly. God, she was a gem.

He was as excited about becoming a father as she was about being a mother. She was planning to take a six-month leave of absence right after the baby was born. Everyone at Shoreside Realty, from Elinor Braun on down, was aghast at the thought of it. Her replacement was good but she had the personality of a snail when compared with Betsy. They were going to miss her immensely.

Betsy was due at any time. Her doctors felt that she shouldn't be coming into work, that all the extra weight and the commuting back and forth were too hard on her. She told them that she'd be just fine. She replied that she'd be bored to tears staying home and that it wasn't all that busy this time of year anyway.

Doris was being a sweetheart. She was coming in early to cover Betsy for lunch and helping her get comfortable on the little sofa over in the tiny lounge they had for employees and agents to grab their box lunches. Sometimes she would even go and pick up something special for her little mother-to-be.

No one was more excited about having a baby than was Betsy. It was her dream of dreams to have children someday. She didn't care that she was three months' pregnant when they got married. Only she and Mark knew that she was with child.

They both figured that it must have happened that night back in October at the Sanderling grand opening. It must have happened right after their flashlight went dead and there were too many bugs around to dare to come out from under the covers. Fooling around. That's how it always happens. Somebody forgets to take her birth control pill and they start fooling around. It was meant to happen.

The phones kept ringing and Betsy kept answering them, forwarding them and paging everyone on the planet, or so it sometimes seemed. Between her uncountable tasks she kept thinking of names. Nicole if it's a girl and Jonathan if it's a boy. Mark has a few of his own picked out, she thought. We'll just have to wait and see.

Just then, line four lit up. Betsy answered the call in her professional, courteous fashion.

Line four was for Linda Hinkle. It was Mr. Strunk. He was Dr. and Mrs. Asp's attorney, and Betsy knew that they were the in the middle of something to do with a painting. She was still working on the exact nature of the mix-up. It sounded like a good one.

Betsy put the call through and started daydreaming about the baby. They had just painted and fixed up the nursery last week. It looked adorable. She couldn't wait.

570-9898 Ext. 9
Linda Hinkle's Desk

"Yes, I understand," said Linda to the attorney on the other end of the line.

"No, I just don't remember. I know that I didn't sign it anywhere, not even on the back," continued Linda.

"Seven dollars and ninety-five cents. I paid $7.95 each and I bought three of them. Yes, that's right, from Billy's Craft Store in town."

"No, I threw the receipt away."

Mr. Strunk, the attorney on the other end of the line was drilling Linda Hinkle for the hundredth time. They were still trying to find out which painting was the original and which was the fake. No one could tell.

"Look, Mr. Strunk, we've been over this a million times. There are no markings, price tags or anything on my watercolor that would help let on to the fact that it's a fake. I made sure of that before bringing it over to the condominium and making the switch.

"Surely, one of your experts has to be able to tell. Isn't that what they're trained to do, expose forgeries? Isn't that their job?"

It was their job. The first one, Dr. Antonio Frazzetta, whom the Larsons had flown in from Milan, Italy, was reputed to be the world's leading expert in art forgeries. He had been schooled in Madrid, studied at the Louvre in Paris and had spent years researching all of the great masters, from Leonardo da Vinci to the post modernists.

Dr. Frazzetta, who had arrived a month after the discovery of the two paintings, had come down to Mr. Strunk's office to inspect the two watercolors and declare which was painted by little Rose Larson and which by that deceitful real estate lady. The same real estate lady who was footing the bill for his $3,000 first-class flight, his hotel room and his $4,000 three-day fee. Specialists like Dr. Frazzetta do not come cheap.

After spending two days with the watercolors in one of Mr. Strunk's conference rooms; after taking microscopic samples of the paint, analyzing, researching, checking and double-checking, Dr. Frazzetta walked out of the room with both of the watercolors, went straight into Mr. Strunk's office and said in his thick Italian accent, "I cannot tella whicha is a which."

Strunk was stunned. His contacts had assured him that Dr. Frazzetta was the best there was. He had uncovered and exposed countless forgeries throughout Europe over the course of his illustrious career. No one had ever come more highly recommended. He was the best.

And he was the best. For oil paintings done by extremely skilled painters. Thick, technical frauds that took years to paint. Forgeries done by artists damn near as skillful as Van Dyck or Rembrandt were themselves. Here, amidst the master painters and the master forgers, Dr. Frazzetta was the undisputed authority. He could quickly ferret out which was which. He could tell by how the oils were layered, swirled or textured. He could tell at a glance.

But here, on Shoreside, in this lawyer's small conference room, staring blankly at two stupid paint-by-number watercolors, Dr. Frazzetta was useless. He was out of his element. The only thing he could think of was to take the both of them and dump them in the garbage. Americans, he kept thinking to himself while scraping tiny flecks of lime-green paint from each of them for further testing, only Americans could call these paintings. These are, well, these are worthless pieces of trash.

Of course Dr. Frazzetta didn't tell any of this to Mr. Strunk. He just kept saying that he couldn't tell which was which. To him, they were identical. The were both garbage.

Of course, Dr. Frazzetta still got paid. He ended up flying a young lady in who, judging by her age and engaging chest size, was probably not his wife. The two of them ended up staying an extra week on Shoreside. Loretta Snyder actually showed them some property. They never bought, but Dr. Frazzetta and his young thing looked as if they were having a very romantic vacation.

Two months after that, Linda got more news. There was nothing left to do but to bring in another specialist. This time the Larsons decided that they needed someone more familiar with watercolors. They were getting to be quite the experts with regard to paintings.

The next specialist Linda had to pay to fly down was due in tomorrow. He was from the Boston Museum of Art. His name was Mr. Robert Hinds. He had graduated from the Chicago Art Institute, studied at the Guggenheim and was presently working on a textbook titled, *American Watercolors in the 20th Century.*

He had personally known Norman Rockwell and was considered by many in the art world to be the consummate expert of American watercolors. It cost Linda $1,000 to fly him down and another $3,500 in fees. He was arriving Friday from Boston.

Ironically, he was also bringing down a young lady who looked far too young to be his wife. She was his assistant. She looked like she would make a great assistant, in her jet black tights and skin-tight turtleneck. Oh, the wonders of the art world.

By Friday afternoon, this would all be over. The original paint-by-number would be handed back to the Larsons and the fake would be thrown away. Dr. and Mrs. Asp didn't ever want to see that painting again. In lieu of the painting, they were suing Linda Hinkle and Shoreside Realty for $25,000.

That suit had yet to get under way, because without clear knowledge that they had been handed the fake and the Larsons the original, there really weren't any grounds for the lawsuit.

It was such a mess. Linda took it in stride, however. She was having another banner year with Frank R. Estate and she wasn't going to let $40,000 to $50,000 in losses catch her off guard. She was going to persevere. She was going to hold her chin up right through Mr. Strunk's unending string of questions.

"Of course I'm willing to cover his per diem expenses, Mr. Strunk. I told you that I just want to get this whole thing over with. I'm sorry I did what I did and I think that everyone knows that I'll make good on this one."

"Friday at 4:00 at your office? Let me double check."

Linda opened her DayTimer and looked at Friday. She had a hair appointment at 3:00 p.m. to prop her coif back up but she could reschedule that for Monday.

"Yes, I can be there. Are you certain that this specialist will be able to find out which is which? That Italian, Frazzetta, didn't seem to be of much help."

Strunk explained that Hinds specialized solely in watercolors and that he had come with impeccable credentials. If anyone could tell, it was Robert Hinds.

"Fine then, Mr. Strunk, I'll plan to be at your office Friday afternoon at 4:00 sharp."

"Oh, one last thing - what if this new storm turns north? They're saying that the outer bands could start hitting Shoreside as early as Friday evening. If that happens, shouldn't we look at meeting Monday instead, after Emily has blown over?"

"Fine, I'll look for your call then. Goodbye."

Linda hung up the phone and went back to work. She had four contracts pending, a listing presentation to prepare and an appointment to make in 35 minutes. Her life was good, if you choose to call it that.

570-9898 Ext. 17
Adam Bartlett's Office

"Where are you, Adam?" Adam had called in.

"I'm still at home. Have I had any calls?"

"Eugene Boyle called again. He says that if he doesn't hear from you this week he's going to have to do something drastic," said Chris to her boss.

"Tell him to go screw himself."

"That won't work, Adam. You're going to have to deal with Mr. Boyle sooner or later. I'll tell him that you'll call him back later today."

"Tell him whatever you want, Chris. Tell him to take a flying fuck for all I care."

Chris didn't take the bait. She wanted to, but she knew that it wouldn't do either of them any good. This wasn't good.

"When are you coming in?" asked Chris.

"When I get there."

"Well, you've got a basketful of messages to deal with when you do. Try to lighten up, Adam. This mood you're in isn't helping the situation any."

"Thanks for the advice, Chris. I'll see you later."

"Goodbye, Adam."

"Bye."

Chris set down the phone and wanted to cry. She wanted to pack up her personal items, leave her letter of resignation on Adam's cluttered desk and walk straight out the front door of Shoreside Realty, never to look back. Chris wanted to vanish, just like Adam had vanished into his ocean of self pity.

God, these last nine months had been hell, Chris thought as she sorted through Adam's unreturned phone calls, trying to put the biggest fires on the top just in case he decided to come in later to deal with them. A living hell.

It all had begun that fateful afternoon last October. The Sanderling grand opening, the marketing plan that died amidst a swarm of salt marsh mosquitoes. An entire project brought to its knees by no-see-ums and the buzzing of a million biting insects. Since that notorious afternoon nine months ago nothing had been the same.

That following Monday, after the incident, Loggins, Harris and Bartlett met in the conference room for more than three hours trying to figure out a way to stop the hemorrhaging. Stop the negative buzz about the Sanderling Condominium project. They worked every angle, from deep discounting the first few sales to explaining that it was a once-in-a-million outbreak. But their efforts were like tiny fingers in a gigantic, collapsing dike. The 32 top reservationists on Shoreside Island were spreading the news about the Sanderling disaster faster than the best spin doctors in the world could operate to try and save the helpless project. There would be no stopping it.

Within weeks the story was everywhere. Sanderling was built on a swamp. A bug-infested swamp. There wasn't a travel agent or a reservationist on Shoreside Island that would dare book their clients into a unit at Sanderling Condominiums. The apartments sat empty all winter. Empty as echoes.

Adam had arranged a second grand opening in early December to try to turn things around. The swales had long since become bone dry and the bug problem wasn't any worse than elsewhere on the island, but it was a complete bust. No one accepted the invitations and no one showed. The reservationists were still keeping an eye on their kids for any signs of encephalitis or malaria. They wouldn't be caught dead in a unit down there.

News spread like news on a small island does. It spread like some kind of malignancy. Stories and events became twisted and exaggerated, building momentum with every sordid retelling. By midseason, rumors were circulating that two people had actually died because of their insect bites that dreadful afternoon. One was a child. They weren't sure what it was that took the two of them. Some said it was a rare form of yellow fever. Others heard that it was malaria. It was terrible.

Of course, no one had actually died. The only mortality was a condominium project that had fallen victim to a plague of ferocious insects that fateful afternoon. By February, it was evident to Bartlett that the island's salespeople were in the loop. No one was showing the apartments to their prospects. Thirty-two sets of keys lay hanging in the key closet collecting dust and tiny spider webs. Bartlett had managed to show the properties a half-dozen times but someone always got to his clients before he could get them on paper. Maybe it was the receptionist at the motel where they were staying. Perhaps it was the waitress that served them lunch the day after their showing.

Not that it mattered. Before a contract could be drawn up and signed, the customers bolted. They brought up hearing something about the site having an insect problem and before long the sale was as dead as the asphalt driveway that led to and from Sanderling. Hopeless. Abandoned.

Adam fell. He fell like Icarus. He fell from grace like so many a fallen soul before him. Deeper and deeper into an abyss without bottom. Chris bore sad witness to the fall, trying as she might to grab hold of Adam somehow on his graceless tumble down. Trying as she might to save what was left.

But it was to no avail. After a while, all she could do was to try to cover for him. Explaining that he was with clients when he was really at home drinking. Telling lawyer after lawyer that he would call them back as soon as he came in while knowing full well that he wouldn't come in. That he would remain at home in his apartment all day with the phone off the hook and his two pagers resting silently on his dresser, their batteries removed, sitting next to a pile of change. Quiet, despairing and incommunicado. His cell phone, once his lifeline to the world, permanently turned off.

Once again on this Monday morning, Adam was at home. Idly sitting on the living room sofa, flipping through the cable television channels looking for a way out. Looking for a station that specialized in fallen heroes whose BMW *750iL* had been repossessed three months ago. A program that could miraculously pull him away from his Scotch and soda. Some glorious savior-like talk show host that could make him pick himself back up and put the batteries back into his pagers. Make him push the power on button on his $900 Nokia cell phone. Convince him to rejoin the world.

But that channel didn't exist, nor was there such a talk show host. Adam just sat there, half drunk and depressed beyond recognition, filling up space.

He kept flipping through the stations, working his way back to Channel 2 every few hours. Back to go. Watching bits and pieces of everything over the course of his day. Indifferent. Disconnected.

Chris Taylor, his top assistant, was getting sick of it. She had considered quitting a dozen times in the last three months. All of the others were gone. Two of the girls had been let go on April 1 after a disappointing season, and the last staff member had left on her own in June. Supporting his staff, and trying to keep his real estate machine running through season had financially ruined Adam. Chris knew that it was over.

The Adam Bartlett selling machine was at a standstill, brought to its knees by indigenous insects. Chris had gone to three-quarter salary two months ago. She didn't know how much longer she could take it. Other job offers were coming in, and it would only be a matter of time before one of them became too good to refuse.

Chris didn't blame Adam. Under the circumstances, most people would have done the same. Crumbled.

At first they were civil about it. Loggins, Harris and their group of investors felt that somehow or other, Bartlett would pull it off. He would turn it around. Work through it. Charm his way back to the throne. But it was too massive for Bartlett to handle. It was like trying to stop a runaway train loaded with nuclear waste coming down the back side of the Rockies. It was too heavy and too lethal.

By mid-March all bets were off. The investors, defecting one by one, had hired legal pit bulls to cover their asses. Bartlett was buried under an avalanche of phone calls. The two Sander brothers had hired Pullman, Dooley and Sachs. Dr. Bethel had hired a firm from Tampa. Mr. Turlington found a local lawyer,

Mr. Sackler. Mr. and Mrs. Harding were using their family lawyer up north. The rest of them all followed suit.

Questions were raised about the condominium prospectus. Legal questions. Were the condominium documents properly distributed to the investors? There seemed to be clear evidence of misrepresentation. Were the investors informed of their risk of loss? Was there any concealment? Dishonest dealings? Breach of trust?

It was all bullshit. The investors were pissed because their units weren't selling and they wanted answers. They wanted their money out of the deal and if that meant ripping Adam Bartlett a new asshole in the process, so be it. The handshakes had turned to fists. The friendly congregation of deep pockets had turned into a pack of wild dogs. Angry dogs with plenty of cash to follow through with their threats of lawsuits.

Tom Loggins and Charles Harris were already gone. Loggins had coolly bankrupted TLD, Inc. and walked away. The 32 pre-sales along with the sale of all of the furnishing packages had covered all of his out-of-pocket expenses save for $187,000. First National Bank was welcome to the remaining 32 unsold condos. The bank foreclosed on the units without a fight. Charles Harris kept the dog pack at bay while Loggins formed a new corporation and went looking for some acreage to develop over on the mainland. To them, Sanderling was an inconvenience. A bust. Nothing gained. Most importantly, nothing lost. The big boys were walking away unscathed. That is how big boys become big boys.

The Water's Edge project four years ago had netted them $1.7 million after taxes. Harris had 40 percent, Loggins 60 percent. Losing a couple hundred grand on Sanderling was simply the cost of doing business. Would that it were that simple for Adam.

To Adam, Sanderling was a 64-unit nightmare. Lacking anyone else to blame, they all blamed Bartlett. Bartlett and his asinine marketing plan. Bartlett should have his real estate license revoked. Bartlett should have his fucking head examined.

His head was being examined. It was being examined by bottle after bottle of J&B Scotch. It was being soaked in a sea of despair. Bills were past due, listings were expiring, phone calls were left unreturned for weeks on end.

It was the fall of a lifetime. No hidden last-minute parachute, no solution in sight.

Adam took a deep, long drink of ice-cold Scotch and paused the television on The Weather Channel for no particular reason. The weatherman was giving the latest updates on Dudley and some new storm off Acapulco, Mexico. Adam didn't give a shit.

Just before he flipped the channel the weatherman added, almost as an afterthought, that a new tropical depression had formed just west and south of the Cape Verde Islands in the eastern Atlantic. The storm, which was expected to strengthen over the next few days, was going to be called Emily. It was an unusually pretty name for a hurricane, thought Adam. Emily. He liked the sound of it. Everyone did.

212-872-9897
Mrs. Herzog

"Is Emily really going to hit Shoreside?" queried a nervous property owner.

"That's what they're saying Mrs. Herzog. They're talking about a direct hit sometime around 2:00 Saturday morning. In the middle of the night."

"Oh, that's just terrible. It's all over the news up here in New York. They say that it could be worse than Andrew. What do you honestly think, Mr. Randazzle?"

Honestly? Jason Randazzle didn't give a damn about how much damage Emily was about to inflict on any of the properties located on Shoreside Island. He had quickly added natural catastrophes to his list of reasons why people should sell their properties. Death, divorce and now his newest addition: disasters. Anything that motivated party "A" to sell to party "B" was good news for Jason Randazzle's endless dial-a-thon. Thus far, since being named on Tuesday, Emily had made for a super week of leads.

On Monday, with the storm still 2,000 miles away, Emily was useless to him. She was just another tropical storm in the mid-Atlantic, doing her lovely pirouettes upon the indigo blue stage of the open ocean.

As the week unfolded, and Emily set her sights on south Florida, all of that changed. By Thursday morning, with all the computer models and weather analysts putting Emily's forecast track right over the top of Shoreside, the phone calls were heating up. Jason was carefully bending his listing presentations toward the dangers of ownership on a barrier island.

"With all the long-range computer models indicating that we are heading into a 20-year period of increased hurricane activity, perhaps you should consider putting your place on the market?" asked the manipulative genius with the ruddy skin.

"Provided your condominium survives the storm intact, I think we could put it on the market in the mid-$300,000 range," Jason would add as he wrapped up any number of conversations.

Because of the approaching storm and the immediate information Jason had access to, most of his cold calls were getting through. Most of the island owners he called were keenly interested in any recent news about the storm; the direction, the projected storm surge, the intensity, all of this was important to them as owners of property in the path of misfortune. That's why he switched his introduction on Wednesday morning to, "Hello, Mrs. So and So, I'm Jason Randazzle calling from Shoreside Island, Florida, to give you a personal update on Hurricane Emily."

Of course he wasn't calling to give them a personal update at all. He was calling to scare them into listing their property immediately after the storm because, as he put it, "Isn't it financial suicide to own property on a hurricane-prone island like Shoreside?" or, "Sooner or later a hurricane the magnitude of Emily is bound to hit a barrier island like Shoreside. With that catastrophe in mind, Mr. Smith, do you want to run the ongoing risk of losing everything, or do you want to do the prudent thing and sell your property before it's totally destroyed?"

This was sick behavior. Jason was playing on people's fears at the worst possible moment. Pre-sympathy conversations before the actual death. Planning the funeral before the patient had any indication that his stroke was in the works. Trying to get someone to sell before the hurricane was anywhere close to Shoreside was a callous and sadistic approach to getting a listing. And, true to character, Jason Randazzle was proud of himself for being so resourceful.

Besides, he thought, it was turning out to be a gold mine. He was highlighting lead after lead in either light blue, which meant that he was to call them back sometime soon after the storm, or green, which meant that, in all likelihood, as soon as Emily cleared the causeway, they were going to sell their island property and get the hell out. They were going to listen to Jason Randazzle's sound advice and quickly dispose of their home, lot, or condo, which, as Jason reminded them, was probably the most vulnerable part of their financial portfolio. Fear, to a master salesman like Randazzle, was beautiful.

Because it was Wednesday morning, and Jason had gone through 100 presentations just like this one all day yesterday, he didn't have to think about his answer to Mrs. Herzog's last question, "What do you think, Mr. Randazzle?" His response was as canned as tuna in oil.

"I think it's time you consider selling, Mrs. Herzog. With all the long-range computer models indicating that we are heading into a 20-year period of increased hurricane activity, owning a condominium on a vulnerable barrier island on Shoreside is a little like playing financial Russian roulette, don't you agree? Provided your condominium survives the storm intact, I think we could put it on the market in the mid-$300,000 range."

Mrs. Herzog, glued to the same Weather Channel as Mildred Lee was all year round, couldn't have agreed more. Owning property on Shoreside was crazy. Financial lunacy. She and Walter Herzog had always been extremely conservative in their investments and having a third of a million dollars sitting right in harm's way was foolish. Extremely foolish.

"You've been so helpful, Mr. Randazzle, how can we ever thank you? We'll be sure to phone you as soon as the storm passes to talk about a free market analysis of the property. I hope our place makes it through okay. It looks like it's going to be a terrible storm.

"Could you be so kind as to drive by and take a look at the complex as soon as you can make it back to the island? We'd both be so appreciative."

"Gladly, Mrs. Herzog. Anything I can do to help," said Jason Randazzle with absolutely no conviction.

"Goodbye then, and I hope you make it though the storm without any real trouble."

"Thanks, goodbye."

With that, Jason took out his green highlighter and circled Mr. and Mrs. Herzog, Unit 234, Jacaranda Condominium. He took his pen and added, "Call on Monday morning!" next to their name and telephone number. He was having a fabulous week thanks to this godsend called Emily. He hadn't used his green and blue highlighters this much since the stock market tumble back in the early '90s. Financial ruin was another one of Jason's favorites. Although most of the owners on Shoreside had a way of overcoming that market correction unscathed. Still, that 500-point drop a decade ago made for a good week of cold calling. Bear markets were good news to Jason.

The irony of it all was that the minute these properties became listed, the tables took a 180-degree turn. The floor became the ceiling, the risk became a sound investment and the spin reversed directions quicker than a Category 5 hurricane. Once there was money to be made in selling the recently listed property, the chances of a hurricane ever hitting the island again were one in a million.

If someone called a month from now and inquired about Unit 234 at the Jacaranda, they wouldn't hear any of the well-scripted presentation Jason had just delivered. They'd hear about how well it had weathered the storm. Jason would go on and on about how well built the property was and how unlikely it would be that another storm like Emily would ever come along again. "Not in our lifetime, that's for certain."

It was complete crap. Jason knew damn well that hurricanes could hit back to back, like the two big storms of 1926 and 1928 that battered the little towns around Lake Okeechobee. Hundreds died in the storm of 1926 that flooded Moore Haven and thousands perished two years later when the dike surrounding the big lake gave way and inundated Belle Glade. Those storms were only two years apart.

"With the storm of the century behind us," Jason was already planning his post-Emily performance, "it's probably the safest investment you can make."

Dialing for dollars. Daylight is dark and darkness daylight depending on whether you were buying or selling. Get out while you can or get in while you can still afford it. Buying, selling, trading and plotting, that was Mr. Randazzle's specialty. No one had it down with such ruthless perfection.

Give him a dial tone, three Magic Markers and his priceless notebook of names and numbers and he was a rabid dog unleashed. Twenty-three greens in two days of calling. Forty-eight light blues and a handful of stalwart yellows. Hurricanes are wonderful, thought Jason Randazzle as he picked up his telephone to dial, who is it? Mr. and Mrs. Freeman in Newport, Connecticut. They owned Unit 235, Jacaranda Condominiums. Good, thought Jason, that's a three-bedroom unit, according to the tax rolls. Three bedrooms are in high demand. I'd love to list this one.

495-0097
Adam's Home Phone

The telephone kept ringing. It was Wednesday morning and Adam still hadn't made it into work yet. Late Wednesday morning.

He wondered who in hell was calling him. Bothering him. The state-of-the-art answering machine he once had was no longer working properly. It malfunctioned after he slammed it on the floor two months ago after listening to a particularly vicious message from one of Boyle's particularly vicious attorneys. Adam was glad that it could no longer take any more goddamned messages. It was dead.

So his phone, were it not intentionally left off the hook, would just keep ringing. Eventually, even the most determined callers would give up.

Just for the hell of it, Adam would sometimes keep count. The all-time record was set last week: 27 rings nonstop. Probably some asshole attorney or investor trying to read me the riot act, thought Adam as he let ring after ring fall on deaf ears. He was impressed. To get to 27 rings you really have to want to talk to someone. Most gave up after ten.

The current ringing stopped. Twelve. Twelve rings was above average. Maybe it was Chris? No. Chris was tired of calling. It was someone else. Someone wanting a piece of me, someone serving papers or just calling to scream at me about the fucking Sanderling disaster.

Adam got up from the sofa and went to the bathroom to take a piss. He had been drinking beer all morning. Cheap beer. He put the television on mute. He had been watching one of those asinine talk shows on cable. Some guy had been sleeping with a middle-aged mother, her 20-year-old daughter and the 63-year-old grandmother. Screwing three generations at once.

Where the hell do they find these people? pondered Adam as he stumbled to his bathroom.

After urinating, Adam stopped at the sink to wash up. He looked in the mirror and for the first time in weeks he actually noticed himself. He hardly recognized the face staring blankly back at him. It was Adam Bartlett, but not the Adam Bartlett he knew.

The face in the mirror was unshaven, tired and tortured. The last time Adam had dragged a razor across his face was Sunday morning, and the three-day stubble on his face had grown coarse and dark. It had that homeless look to it. The kind of stubble-covered face you find on street corners, asking for change or looking through garbage cans in search of aluminum.

His eyes were still a vibrant blue, but now they were circled by sunken rings of sheer exhaustion. Sleep had long since betrayed him. Adam hadn't slept well in months. Scotch had become his ally in his battle with his chronic lack of sleep. Scotch helped him into bed and helped him out of bed. His head spinning and his body collapsing beneath him, Scotch was his ticket to another troubled night's rest.

But the rings beneath his eyes, deep and nearly purple, showed just how hard this fall from grace had been on him. The dirty T-shirt didn't help, all yellowed under the arms from forgetting to put on any deodorant. No, the plain white T-shirt completed the image staring back at him. A pathetic image.

Adam stood there, in front of that bathroom vanity mirror, for what seemed to be an eternity. He couldn't remember ever seeing himself look this bad, this strange and discarded. Never.

He decided to shave. He bent over the sink and washed his face with some soap and warm water. Then he got out his razor and shaving cream. He needed an entire handful of shaving cream to cover the deep stubble. As he lifted the razor to his face he saw his hand shaking. There was an element of disbelief to the entire scene.

It was as if, for just an instant, Adam Bartlett was someone else looking at himself from a distance. Someone standing at the foot of his king-sized bed looking down the short hallway into the bathroom. Watching this troubled young man lifting a razor blade to his three-day shadow. The man standing at the foot of the bed saw Adam's hand trembling as the blade touched his skin just below his sideburns. His hand was shaking now, shaking more than a hand holding a razor blade should.

The man watched himself put the razor blade down. Adam knew that if he tried to shave himself right now, he would cut himself. Cut himself repeatedly. He just couldn't get his trembling fingers to behave. He bent down and washed the lather off of his face. It had been a long, long way down.

Just then the phone rang again. Without giving it a thought, Adam walked away from that painful mirror and went to pick up the telephone. He didn't know why he was doing it. He just did it.

"Hello."

"Adam, is that you?"

"Who is this?" It was a woman's voice on the other end, but it wasn't Chris. It wasn't Vanessa either. She had left him long before his BMW had been repossessed by the leasing company. She had left him at the first sign of trouble. The voice on the other end of the line sounded familiar but he couldn't place it.

"Adam, it's me, Peggy."

"Oh."

"Are you okay, Adam? You don't sound good at all. Have you been drinking?"

"Just a couple of beers, Peg. You know that I can handle my liquor."

Peg knew that Adam could handle his liquor, but she also knew that no one could handle the hell that the faltering Sanderling Condominium project had recently put him through. She felt sorry for him. All through the years she had wished and waited for Adam to take a fall, but now that he had, there was a part of Peg that wished it had never happened. But it was too late for any of that.

"I'm calling about this weekend, Adam. Do you remember that this is your weekend with Danny?"

Adam had forgotten. He had not taken his son Danny in four months. At first it was because he couldn't find the time. He was still trying to deal with all the fallout from the busted project; the complaints, the price reductions, the lack of bookings, the whole bloodbath of it all. After that it became a money issue. He didn't want to see his boy under his present financial circumstances.

If he couldn't come to Peggy's door with a new CD-ROM, some tickets to an amusement park in Orlando, or a brightly wrapped board game, then he didn't come to Peggy's door at all. He didn't want his son to think that his father was a failure.

"Shit, Peg. I've forgotten. Maybe next month."

"No, Adam, and that's why I'm calling. You wouldn't be able to take him this weekend even if you pulled yourself out of your bottle of Scotch long enough to do it. You can't see him next month either."

"What the hell are you talking about, Peg. Of course I can see Danny."

"Not until you catch up on your past-due child support payments. I went to court Monday to have the judge rescind your visitation rights until you make good on your support payments. You're months behind, Adam, and we're having one hell of a time making ends meet. If it wasn't for Ken giving us a helping hand, Danny and I would be out on the street."

Adam didn't say anything. There was a long stretch of silence that said, "no contest."   "Adam, are you still there?"

"Yeah, Peg, I'm still here."

But he wasn't still here. Adam was gone. He had tumbled down a flight of stairs so long that there seemed to be no end to it. It just kept collapsing beneath him, as though he were falling down an up-escalator. Everything in Adam's life was tumbling down that long stairway with him: his business, his girlfriends, his dreams, his only son, his life. The pain was crushing him.

"Well, what are you going to do about it?"

"Go to hell, Peg, and take Danny with you."

With that Adam hung up the phone.

Worse. It was no longer a stairway he was falling off. It was the edge of the world.

480-9091
The Decorating Hut

"Oh, I'm so glad for you," said Elinor.

"Thanks, I never would have guessed it. Not after everything I put them through."

"Jennifer, it just goes to show you that there are still some wonderful people in the world."

"Well, the Cliftons certainly meet that criterion."

"Yes they do. Have you heard when my new patio furniture might come in, Jennifer?" asked Mrs. Elinor Braun, Jennifer's former sales manager.

"I think it's due in tomorrow afternoon. It's being trucked here from Orlando. Do you want us to deliver it to your house Friday morning?"

"No, not with that storm coming. Could you just keep it in the shop for a few days until Emily blows by?"

"What storm?"

"You haven't heard? There's quite a hurricane brewing just south of Cuba. They're saying that there's a pretty good chance that it could swing north toward Florida in the next 48 hours. If it does, having patio furniture delivered wouldn't be the wisest decision to make."

"Not a problem, Elinor, we'll just keep it in the back room until the storm passes. Just give me a call next week and we'll have our delivery boys drop it by."

"Thanks, Jennifer. Do you like it back at the Decorating Hut?"

"I love it, Elinor. Real estate and I just didn't get along. You know, all those forms and stuff. Here, you just sell someone a sleeper sofa, swipe a credit card and its over. No more forms, plats and no more north arrows to endure."

"I'm happy for you."

"Thanks, Elinor. And thanks for ordering your new patio set with us. We'll stay in touch."

"Bye, Jennifer."

"Goodbye."

Elinor Braun was glad to see that things were working out for Jennifer Willow. She was surprised to hear that the Cliftons had decided to use Jennifer to decorate their house. Especially after all the litigation.

After the fiasco that afternoon when everyone discovered that Dr. and Mrs. Clifton had built their home on the wrong lot, no one could have guessed that they would even talk to Jennifer again, let alone work with her on decorating their second new home in less than a year.

Their first house ended up belonging to Ralph Hardwick's brother-in-law and his wife, Andy and Debbie Stoughton. That was only after a long drawn-out court battle. The Cliftons had wanted to simply switch lots and generously compensate the Stoughtons for the inconvenience. Given your typical Shoreside resident, this might have worked.

But Andy and Deb Stoughton didn't fit that profile. They weren't college-educated, upper-middle-class professionals by any stretch of the imagination. They were beer drinking rednecks from Panama City who happened to get lucky twice. Once, when they bought a lotto ticket at their favorite bowling alley, and a second time when a rookie real estate agent forgot to double-check which direction the north arrow was pointing while she was showing her very first customers a vacant lot.

The Cliftons had built a house on the Stoughtons' lot and that was that. The house belonged to the person who owned the dirt beneath it, appliances and all. Of course it wasn't going to be quite that simple.

Not once the local lawyer population got wind of it. For them, it was the equivalent of an elephant kill. There was a ton of meat to be picked off this mess. No, make that seven or eight tons. The bank that financed the construction loan for the Cliftons had four of its attorneys looking into it. The Cliftons had two. The Stoughtons had one, and he was a perfect asshole. Shoreside Realty had five. The title company that had closed the transaction had six, including two paralegals. The survey company had two. The City of Shoreside had the city attorney and his staff looking into it and, last but not least, the developer, Ralph Hardwick, had his attorney on it for good measure. It was a big elephant. A big, dead elephant.

Three months later there wasn't a scrap of skin or meat on that carcass of a mess. There were so many suits and countersuits flying around that the judge involved was ready to have the house torn down just to get the damn thing over with. No one was winning.

Finally, after five months and nearly $100,000 in legal fees, the judge decided that the house should go to the Stoughtons. The Cliftons were disappointed, but the surveying company and the title company quickly covered any losses that Dr. and Mrs. Clifton had sustained and the only thing they had lost in the end was time and aggravation. That and roughly $19,000 in legal fees.

Jennifer Willow, per the terms of her independent contractor agreement with Shoreside Realty, had to pay her percentage of the company's legal fees. That amounted to $3,000 more than all the cumulative commissions she had earned thus far in her illustrious two-year real estate career. Upon hearing this news, her husband went ballistic.

A week after the final court settlement, Jennifer Willow walked into Elinor Braun's office and handed her a letter of resignation. Elinor had never formally asked for it, but it was tacitly understood by everyone at Shoreside Realty that it wasn't long in coming. There was talk, and plenty of it, about Jennifer's real estate license being revoked for culpable negligence. North arrows are pretty hard to miss, even for green-eyed blonds.

The day after hearing about Jennifer's resignation, the owner of the Decorating Hut was on the phone with Jennifer trying to convince her to come back to work for her. Business was down 11 percent since Jennifer had left the Decorating Hut. The young, good-looking agents were no longer bringing their clients over just to sneak a peek at the island's most gorgeous woman. Walk-in traffic had plummeted the day after Jennifer's long blond hair no longer graced the showroom floor.

It didn't take all that much convincing to get Jennifer back. By the end of a ten-minute conversation the owner of the Decorating Hut had already given Jennifer her next week's work schedule. The only form she needed to fill out was a standard W-4 payroll exemption form. At that, all she had to do was sign it.

Oddly enough, through all the trials and tribulations of the lengthy litigation over who the house belonged to, Elinor and Jennifer became friends. Elinor had always liked Jennifer and now that she had quit the business, she liked her even more. She was a people person, and people persons have a way of eventually getting devoured in the real estate profession. Eaten alive by the hyenas lurking in the shadow lands with law degrees in hand. Elinor could hear them crunching Jennifer's beautiful bones as the lawsuits and countersuits all piled up in the county courthouse.

Long ago, Elinor figured that something like this was bound to happen to Jennifer, but she couldn't do anything to prevent it. It was something that every neophyte has to discover on her own. The horror of it all. The horror.

Now it was over. The Cliftons had commenced work on their new home, on the lot they actually did own and their new house was already dried in. It would be completed mid-February and they were excited about it. They had modified the floor plan considerably from the house they had built on the Stoughtons' lot. The bedrooms in that first house were too small and they didn't like the flow of the kitchen. In a way, it was kind of nice to have a test house built.

They had also chosen a different exterior look, going with a stucco finish as opposed to the vinyl. The two houses were only 240 feet apart and they thought it would look odd to have them looking virtually identical.

The Stoughtons, who had insisted throughout the proceedings that they hated the house, the yellow color and everything else about it, settled in comfortably right after the judge handed down his decision. They talked about eventually re-siding the house in white, but for now the urine-yellow looked fine. Apparently, ownership changed their perspective.

So, as the old saying goes, all's well that ends well. The Cliftons had decided to use Jennifer to decorate their new place and they had now spent nearly $56,000 at the Decorating Hut. They were such nice people.

Jennifer and her husband were happy. The local male real estate agents were happy, and the Stoughtons were happy. The lawyers who were involved were very happy and the State of Florida was happy. The state had dropped the investigation into the negligence claim filed by the Stoughtons the day Jennifer voluntarily surrendered her real estate license.

Jennifer Willow's two-plus years in real estate had been a real adventure. She had lost roughly $1,500 a year when all was said and done. She wasn't the first Floridian to fall victim to the rocky shoreline lying near the beckoning sirens of a short-lived real estate career, nor would she be the last. Big commissions, easy money and a flexible work schedule have a way of luring in people like Jennifer Willow. Luring them in, then sinking them.

Especially when they have trouble with north arrows.

570-9898 Ext. 17
Adam Bartlett's Desk

Adam was at his desk. Thursday morning had arrived and he had decided the night before to make an appearance at the office. One of his few remaining listings was scheduled to close next week and he had to come in to put a few last-minute details in order. There were some inspection items that needed to be addressed and the time and place for the actual closing hadn't been set up with the title company yet.

It was Loretta Snyder's sale of one of Bartlett's listings. Adam himself hadn't made a sale in three months. Because of that, he knew full well that he had to keep this closing together. It had become a matter of paying the rent.

Chris was in shock. Although Adam had finally managed to get his trembling hands to hang on to his razor long enough to shave, her boss looked dreadful. His shirt was wrinkled and his sport coat looked tired. It was as if he had slept in his clothes. His hair needed a trim and his eyes were sunken and bloodshot. Even his once flawless leather penny loafers were scuffed and lacking polish.

Adam had arrived at the office just after 10:00. Chris handed him a stack of 43 messages and three certified letters she had signed for earlier in the week. To a real estate agent, certified mail is never good news. It means someone wants a bite out of you and wants to verify the fact that you've been bitten. Chris had been signing far too many return receipt requested slips these last few months. The investors, his fair weather friends, were eating Adam Bartlett alive.

There was more. Unread office memos, Realtor magazines, conference announcements and a score of faxes. Ugly faxes with large **CONFIDENTIAL** notices at the very top from legal firms with multiple lawyers' names on them. Faxes demanding responses. Immediate responses.

First National Bank had sent a single fax to Adam yesterday afternoon. They were pulling the listings. All 32 units were going to another, as yet undisclosed, real estate firm. It stated that prices were going to be slashed. Bartlett hadn't sold a single unit since the repossession and the bank felt it was time to give another island firm an opportunity. They were demanding to be immediately released from their listing agreement with Shoreside Realty, even though there were three months remaining on the contract.

Adam didn't care. They could take their listing agreement and put it where the sun never shone. He couldn't deal with the Sanderling Condominiums any longer. He couldn't handle the cost of running the ads, keeping 32 listings posted in the MLS and a host of added expenses, all for a project that had not sold a unit in nine months.

The investor units Adam once had listed were already lost. One by one, Boyle, the Sander brothers, Dr. Bethel, Mr. and Mrs. Harding and the rest had already pulled their properties from Shoreside Realty. Some had re-listed them with other firms, and still others didn't even bother putting them on the active market. The results were the same.

Elinor Braun had attached a memo to the bank's faxed request to withdraw its properties. She was unhappy with losing the listings. Very, very unhappy. She knew that when the prices got low enough, there were always bottom feeders out there. There were always buyers like Sophie Doren just waiting in the wings for properties in distress. At $275,000 per unit, even the bugs wouldn't keep people like Sophie away. Sanderling would start to sell soon and she was disappointed in Adam for losing the listings.

Chris was equally disappointed. She knew that Elinor was right. The bank had kept the prices high hoping that the rumors would eventually become yesterday's news and the condos would start moving. But rumors die hard on a small island and there had been only half a dozen showings at Sanderling over the past three months. Adam accounted for three of those showings himself. The insect issue wasn't going away. Sanderling meant swamp.

Without the 32 Sanderling condos in his inventory, the former crown prince of Shoreside Realty was down to three listings, with one due to close next week. That left Adam with a vacant lot listed for $119,900 and a tired condominium at Osprey Towers for $345,000. A very tired condominium, complete with lime-green carpeting and a yellow, floral print living room set. Exhausted would have been a better description of 543 Osprey Towers. Exhausted and starving to death.

With all of that in mind, Chris kept wondering when she would tell him. She had to tell him personally, and not let Adam find it out through the office grapevine.

I'll tell him just before lunch, she decided.

What she was going to say to Adam was inevitable. Yesterday afternoon Mr. Al Smith from Island Accounting had called with another job offer. Word was out that Chris was available, and everyone on Shoreside knew that she was good. She was better than good, she was fabulous.

Al had heard from Sam Goodlet about her looking for work. Goodlet had been using Island Accounting to do his taxes for years. Sam had mentioned the fact that Chris had recently taken a major pay reduction because of Adam's situation and thought that Al might be interested in a new assistant. Al certainly needed the help. His accounting business was brisk.

When Chris met with him after work on Wednesday, she honestly didn't know if Adam would ever make it back into his office. She was tired of it all and didn't really see any point in hanging on. The fax from First National Bank, arriving at 4:30 that afternoon, was the final straw. Losing 32 listings at once hurt, and Chris knew that Adam would have to let her go sooner or later.

Al Smith, sensing an opportunity, offered Chris more than she was making before the fall, and with Adam apparently unable to pull himself out of it, she couldn't turn him down. She had been with Bartlett for five years, but it was time to move on.

How am I going to tell him? Chris kept asking herself. She just couldn't picture Adam picking up his own phone calls. He hadn't done so in years. At the height of his career, Adam had five assistants, including Chris. Now, just before lunch, she planned to go into his office and tell him that she too was leaving. He wouldn't take it well.

All morning long, Adam kept taking calls and doing the best he could. There was no way for him to catch up. There were just too damn many urgent messages to reply to in one day. It would take him a week just to clear through all the attorneys. There were depositions coming up, subpoenas and some letters from the Florida Real Estate Commission. Certified letters with more dismal news inside.

By the time noon rolled around, Adam had only managed to scratch the surface. He felt like having a drink. A long, refreshing drink of some J&B Scotch, on the rocks, in a tall glass beside a pool somewhere. Somewhere far away, like Aruba. These were his thoughts when Chris interrupted Adam via the intercom.

"Adam, I have to speak with you. Do you have a minute?"

"Sure, Chris, come on in." Adam's imagination put his tall Scotch down on the small glass table beside his chaise lounge and watched as Chris came in and sat down at his desk.

"Adam, I don't know how to tell you this."

With that, Adam picked his Scotch back up and put the glass to his lips. He tipped his weary head back and as some metaphysical tropical sun beat down on him, he emptied the glass. It tasted sublime. He knew what was coming.

"What is it, Chris?"

"I'm giving notice, Adam. I've been offered a position with Island Accounting Services and I'm going to take the offer. I'm sorry."

Adam sat there looking at Chris for the longest time. His eyes were watering but he never lost his composure. Adam finally spoke. "Don't be sorry, Chris. We had a great ride together, you and I. We were there, Chris, we were at the top.

"But it's over now. That fax yesterday from First National Bank was the final insult. You bust your ass for years on a project and just when the sellers decide to sharpen their pencils and liquidate the property, they pull the listings. It's one hell of a business, Florida real estate. One hell of a business. Don't be sorry at all," said Adam.

"I'll be leaving two weeks from tomorrow, Adam. I can still help with the closing next week and put everything else in order before I go. I don't know how to tell you this, Adam, but it's been wonderful working for you these last five years and I'm going to miss you."

Chris was baring her soul to Adam. She was going to miss him. Over the years he had been good to her. When things were rolling, one Christmas he had given her a $5,000 cash bonus under the table. It was a lot of cash, and Chris was always appreciative of it.

As much as Chris was going to miss Adam, he was going to miss her 1,000 times more. Chris had picked up, babysat and delivered his boy, Danny, dozens of times for him, scheduled his dates; and she had managed scores of Adam's listings. She was in charge of paying the other four assistants, booking his appointments and making sure that Mildred Lee never got through. Chris was Adam's voice for many of his longtime clients. He was going to be lost without her.

"Chris, I'm going to miss you too. But let's face it, I would have to let you go sooner or later. When 4564 Long Key Drive closes next week, we'll be down to two listings. I don't exactly need a personal assistant to handle two listings now do I?

"You're a damn hard worker Chris, and if Island Accounting needs a letter of recommendation from me, have Al give me a call and I'll be glad to write one for you.

"And one more thing, Chris. Thanks for coming in here and telling me personally. I appreciate it."

Chris was crying. She quickly got up and headed out of the office. She didn't want Adam to see her this way. It broke her heart to be leaving him, especially now. Now that he was so down on his luck. She felt as though she were abandoning ship just when he needed her the most.

Mentally, Adam went back to his island in the Caribbean. He took the liter of J&B that the waiter had left next to his glass on the small table beside the pool, and unscrewed the top. He refilled his glass with the auburn-colored liquid. Once filled to the top, he lifted the glass and shook it gently in his hand, listening carefully to the crackling sound of the ice melting from the warm Scotch being poured over it.

He waited just a minute before lifting the second drink to his thirsty lips. He waited for the Scotch to cool down a bit, as hot as it was on this particular afternoon. Then he drank deep and long from the tall, endless glass of his dreams. The Scotch burned as it poured into him.

He glanced back over at the bottle and noted that it was half empty. He knew that he would have to flag down the waiter the next time he came around the pool.

"Just put it on my tab," Adam would say.

"Just put it on my tab and give yourself a $20 tip."

Adam was like that, generous with his own demise.

495-0097
Adam's Apartment

Adam left his office at 6:30. Chris was already gone. She had left five minutes after the phone system had been switched over to the answering service. She stuck her head in the door and meekly said, "Bye, Adam," before leaving. She was uncomfortable with the knowledge that she was resigning.

Before heading home, Adam put everything in order, at least as much order as he could manage under the circumstances, grabbed some paperwork to look over later back at his apartment. After that, he walked out the back door to the parking lot. Vince Cricket was still in his office on the phone with a client, so Adam knew that he didn't need to shut off the photocopier or lock the back door as he left. Vince could take care of all that bullshit later.

It was understandable that Adam never gave a thought to the irony of these two men being the last to leave this particular Thursday evening in late July. Two fallen superstars working late trying to save what they could of their once-illustrious careers. Vince never gave it a thought either. They were both too preoccupied with their private hells to consider what someone else's hell might feel like. It was always about them. Always.

As he climbed into his Porsche, Adam remembered that he was getting low on Scotch. He had been dreaming about an ice-cold glass of J&B all afternoon and the thought of not having enough liquor at home to fill that tall glass to the very top was unsettling to him.

I had better swing by Shoreside Liquor and pick up a liter before heading home, he reflected. Once in his Boxster and under way, he drove straight to the package store.

Financially, things were getting very tight for Bartlett, but not bad enough to keep him from buying the best. He grabbed a bottle of J&B and paid for it with cash. By the time he made it home he could almost taste the icy drink going down.

Once inside his apartment he walked over and took his phone off the hook. Adam felt that he had done more than his fair share of real estate today and he wanted to be alone. Alone with his Scotch, his television remote and his thoughts. Dark thoughts.

Dinner was never considered. For the past few months most of his nourishment had come from liquor. Beer, wine, Scotch and gin had supplied him with whatever nutrients they had to offer. Occasionally he would order take-out Chinese or call for a pizza delivery, but for the most part it was alcohol for breakfast, lunch and dinner. Tonight it was J&B over ice for dinner. Mouth-watering. Delicious.

Adam held the eight-ounce glass under the ice dispenser on his refrigerator until it was filled to nearly overflowing with ice cubes. Then he went over and took the liter bottle of Scotch out of its brown paper bag and unscrewed the top. He did so in a ritualistic fashion that spoke tragically of how many times he had performed this same sad dance. The dance of a drunk.

The ice crackled and popped as the warm Scotch tumbled over it. When the glass was filled to the very brim, with some of the ice cubes floating above the edge of the rim, Adam picked up the drink and walked over to his favorite corner on the couch in the living room. The couch that now held an imprint of his body that said more than anything about where his time was being spent, where his priorities had descended to.

He set the drink next to the couch and picked up the remote. With the silent click of a button the television sprang to life. Adam's life. Before he could decipher what was on the channel that came up, Adam had already pressed the channel key and the mute button. His long, meaningless journey to nowhere had begun.

Adam put his feet on the ottoman and reached for his glass of Scotch. It had cooled sufficiently, he thought. The perfect temperature. He quietly lifted the glass to his lips with the reverence of a priest at some kind of faithless communion, unholy and fulfilling at once. The eternal sacraments of despair.

Time passed.

Not time as we calculate it, but a time distorted by the curve of an emptying bottle. Time twisted and numb, measured not by minutes but by melting ice and bloodshot eyes. Intoxicated time, painless and fleeting.

By 10:00 p.m. his liter of J&B held two more tall ones at best. The rest had been poured into the empty vessel that was once a man. In the strange blue light of a muted television, Adam had refilled his glass with ice, with Scotch, with ice, with Scotch too many times to keep track of. There was no reason to keep track. Not in the brave new world where Adam Bartlett existed.

Thoughts of sleep eventually entered the cloudy picture of Adam's mind. Sleep, what a useless function that had become. Disrupted, disjointed and senseless. But the same could be said about Adam's waking hours. So deep, and so cold, this land below the frozen ice of a man's despair.

After a time Adam decided to go to bed. He got up from the television and went to the bathroom. The mirror over the toilet caught a glimpse of him and he foolishly looked back. It was the same unrecognizable person he had seen there Wednesday morning, the same victim of science.

He realized just how much he hated that man in the mirror. Hated him with all of his heart and soul. Hated how he looked, how he drank, how he sat there on that goddamned couch watching that goddamned television that never offered him one minute's worth of advice as to how in hell he could get out of this awful place he was trapped in. This living shit storm.

The person in the mirror, whoever it was, looked frightening. He realized that his eyes were bloodshot beyond redemption. Murine, Adam remembered, I've got some Murine in the medicine chest, thought the drunk looking at the drunk in the mirror. That will solve everything. Murine.

When Adam opened up the medicine chest he quickly spotted the bottle of Murine. Standing there beside it, as if placed there by the devil's own hand, sat a second container. A bottle of sleeping pills left ages ago by Vanessa. Prescription sleeping pills for another restless soul. Trazadone. Take one and sleep finds you. Take more than that and death finds you.

Adam didn't bother picking up the small dispenser of Murine. He took the amber drugstore bottle into his hand and read the warning label carefully. It stated emphatically that these pills are never to be taken in conjunction with drinking alcohol. Serious injury, or death might occur.

Death might occur. Adam was fascinated in the sound of that phrase. Death might occur.

He opened the bottle and poured all of the pills into his shaking, empty hand. As empty as his will to live. There were nine pills left. Nine was enough. He went back to reading the label. The recommended dose was one. He had eight more than he needed for a good night's rest.

He knew. He knew how he could get rid of that son-of-a-bitch in the mirror. How he could escape that fool with the bloodshot eyes who had just had his assistant quit, told his ex-wife and kid to go to hell and lost 32 listings that morning. That man who had no reason to go on. No reason at all. He knew how he could escape from this roomful of reflections. How he could finally go to sleep.

His trembling hand slowly poured the nine pills back into the childproof container they had come in from Walgreens. He closed the medicine cabinet without returning the bottle of sleeping pills. These, he kept tightly clenched in his hand. These pills, Adam's intoxicated thoughts had decided. These, I need these pills.

Adam went back into the kitchen and poured one last drink of J&B. One final tall one. He took the drink and the sleeping pills back to the couch with him. Back to see what pictures were flashing on the muted television. He stopped to put on his favorite CD. He put on "Surfacing" by Sara McLachlan. Her thin, melancholic voice soon filled the noiseless living room.

After setting his drink down he fell back into his favorite position; feet on the tattered ottoman, pillow behind his back, television remote in his left hand, ice-cold drink in his right hand and a look on his face like a man on death row. He was a man on death row.

It had come down to this. This place where they kiss the musty, rotting floor of the basement of the world. Suicides. Where they surrender and vanish. Vanish into a kingdom of such frightening solitude that only the dead can explain why. The dead who can't explain. That is where Adam was at that instant, in the foyer of hell.

He set his drink down, with beads of cold water sweating off it, and opened the bottle of sleeping pills. He poured them all into his empty right hand. As empty as self pity always is. His left hand kept flipping through the channels, faster and faster and faster, as though it were searching for a stay of execution. For a call from the governor granting a pardon to this drunk on a couch. Granting an 11th-hour reprieve.

Time stopped breathing. "In the arms of an angel..." reverberated across eternity.

For reasons beyond understanding, Adam hesitated. His channel surfing had stopped at The Weather Channel and the news was grim. He took the television off mute without knowing why. He turned the volume up. It battled with Sara's lonely song.

A large aerial shot of Florida, taken from some satellite in outer space, was displayed before him. The time lapse kept playing back the last 24 hours of weather. A man off screen kept talking about the size and magnitude of the approaching hurricane. Adam could see it clearly. Hurricane Emily was heading toward south Florida and she was in the throes of her devastating dance, spinning savagely out of control.

Her powerful counterclockwise rotation was easy to see from this vantage point high above the globe. The Weather Channel kept repeating the time-lapse footage as the man said that, by morning, hurricane warnings would be issued for all of south Florida and that, unless the storm changed directions, computer models were indicating that it would hit somewhere along the west coast of Florida in the next 24 to 36 hours. Emily now packed sustained winds of 147 miles per hour with gusts exceeding 180. She had grown up to become a great hurricane, a 100-year storm.

It came to Adam in a stroke of genius. He smiled as he put the nine pills carefully back into their container. If it has come down to this, then so be it. If I am going to die, then I am going to die in style.

The plan unfolded before him in perfect order. He would find some excuse to get down to Sanderling before they evacuated the Island. He would think of something to tell Chris. Then he would stay. Stay and face the storm, like some twisted post-modern sea captain, he would go down with his ship.

He would park himself on his top-floor-west apartment, the same unit he had stayed in that last glorious night with Vanessa, and he would wait for her, for

Emily. He would sit on that porch, overlooking a Gulf gone mad with wind and waves and wait for the embrace of a force-five hurricane. No one would know it for what it was.

When they found him dead, his ex-wife and son would receive double the amount of his current life insurance policy: not a half-million were he to swallow these nine pills and commit suicide, but a full million. Adam had elected to add the coverage to his policy three years ago: accidental death, double indemnity. It was all Adam could do for his ex-wife and child at this point and it was the only thing he was able to do for himself. Emily would take him and that godforsaken development right along with him.

It was the perfect plan. A suicide at Sanderling.

Adam put down his glass of Scotch and went to bed. He slept better than he had in months. Now that he knew he was going to die, he had everything to live for.

570-9514
Mildred Lee's Home Phone

"I knew it, I knew it would be just a matter of time." Mildred kept mumbling to herself while shuffling around her little two-bedroom canal home. "Just a matter of time."

She was getting ready. This was it. This was the storm she had planned for ever since the day she stepped off that nonstop flight from O'Hare International. The "Big One," the storm of the century. A channel-cutting storm.

"Emily's on her way and there's no stopping her now. I tried to warn them, all of them, but they wouldn't listen. History always repeats itself when it comes to hurricanes and the State of Florida. Always.

"It might be ten years, it might be 50 years but sooner or later God bowls another big storm off the coast of Africa and sooner or later it hits Florida harder than any king pins have ever been hit. This is it. This is the 'Big One.'"

Mildred had been mumbling off and on like this since Thursday afternoon, when the computer models started confirming what Mildred had known since Monday: that Emily was going to hit Shoreside Island. As the barometric pressure dropped, Mildred's mumbling increased proportionately. At this point, with the eye of the storm less than 24 hours away, she was muttering to herself nonstop.

"I've got to go over my checklist again. Now where is it? Where did I set it down? Oh, God forbid that I've gone ahead and lost that checklist. Not now, not at this crucial time."

She found her checklist. It was on top of her little color television, which was still locked on channel 39, The Weather Channel. By noon she could switch it to one of the local channels, since they were commencing continual coverage of Hurricane Emily beginning at 12:00 sharp.

In a way, everyone on Shoreside and in town was both excited and afraid. The animal within them sensed the steady drop in air pressure and reacted accordingly. Complete strangers talked to each other at Home Depot while buying sheets of plywood and supplies. People helped others without even being asked, lifting heavy sheets of 5/8-inch plywood onto those big orange carts and showing them where to find the flashlight batteries.

It was our tribal instinct kicking in. There was a sense of imminent disaster that was gathering the local human tribe together. It broke down the distance people normally tend to keep from each other. Conversations began at checkout lines in the grocery store, people talked to other tables at restaurants and no one thought twice about it. It was a built-in survival mechanism that overrode our fear of strangers. I became we.

Of course Mildred Lee couldn't share in this community-wide outbreak of comradery. Her *esprit de corps* was limited to her three remaining cats, Blackie, Buttons and Mittens. They wanted no part of the approaching storm or of Mildred Lee, their eccentric owner. Their usual spookiness had taken on a new sense of urgency in the last 12 hours. They were dashing and darting about Mildred's darkened ranch with a vengeance.

Blackie, the big tomcat, kept climbing straight up the curtains in the living room. He would reach the top, run across the valance and scurry down the other side. Halfway down he would leap across to the top of the sofa. He did so repeatedly, mimicking the behavior of a caged panther. The barometric pressure was definitely affecting Mildred's cats. They were going completely mad.

Mildred hardly took notice. She was standing in front of her tiny pantry with her checklist in hand, continuing her marathon mumbling session.

"Water. Yes, 17 gallons."

"Canned goods. Tons."

"Batteries. Two hundred."

"Manual can openers. Four."

"First aid kits. Nine."

"Mosquito repellent. One case of 24 cans."

"Bleach. Twelve gallons."

"Trash bags. Two hundred."

"Duct tape. A case."

"Tarps. Nine."

"Candles...? Where are my candles?"

Mildred looked at the shelf where her cardboard placard said "CANDLES" and noted that there were no candles stacked neatly behind it. She couldn't be without candles. Not with a storm the size of Emily 18 hours away.

"Where are they?" Mildred continued murmuring to herself. "Where the heck could they be?"

She shuffled over to check the guest bedroom closet. Sometimes she put them in with all the extra pillows, wool blankets and emergency flares that were stored in that small walk-in closet.

The candles were the last item on her list. Sam Goodlet had come over as promised and put her two hurricane shutters on last Tuesday and everything else appeared to be in order. Because she had planned for, stocked for and in a strange kind of way, waited for this hurricane the last ten years, there was no way in hell that she was going to evacuate Shoreside for the storm.

"No way am I leaving the security of my home." Mildred said to herself as she slowly bobbed over to the guest bedroom, her gray hair spiked in a Phyllis Diller hairstyle. "No way."

A mandatory evacuation order was already in place on Shoreside. Of course they couldn't force a person to leave her home, they could only insist. Not that the local police would know that Mildred was even in her little bungalow. She didn't own a car. With no car in her garage, and the house all shuttered up tighter than a Nazi bunker, the local constabulary would, in all likelihood, drive right by on their final check of the residents. Little would they know that Mildred was hunkered down deep inside that dark house. Hunkered down and ready.

"Oh, here they are!" said a relieved Mildred. "Right where they all should be."

Mildred bent down and double-checked. Her candles were under one of her 14 wool blankets, which in turn were safely sealed in double plastic lawn bags. Wool blankets ain't much good if they're all darn wet, Mildred was fond of repeating to herself as she stuffed them one by one into the big, black plastic bags.

She had found her misplaced candles. All 600 of them.

Mildred Lee was ready.

773-2123
The Shoreside Conservancy

"Scott, there is nothing we can do at this point."

"I know. But it's such a shame, a storm of this size and magnitude; it will really take a toll on the island's wildlife."

Scott was on the phone with Mr. Burnham, the new chairman of the Conservancy. They were trying to decide what, if anything, they might be able to do before Emily bore down on Shoreside. Bore down hard.

"What I recommend is that you board up the office, take the three computers and stick them in your trunk and get the hell off the island as soon as possible. The weathermen up here are saying that this might be the worst storm to hit south Florida since Andrew back in August of '92. The last thing I want is to learn that you tried to ride out the storm on the island, Scott.

"Whatever wildlife is left on Shoreside after the wind and the storm surge pass through is going to need you alive. So put up our storm shutters, grab the computers and our backup disks and get the heck out of there. Do you understand?"

Scott understood. He understood the devastation. He had been reading up on past Florida hurricanes for the last few days, trying to get some kind of idea what to expect should Emily actually hit Shoreside. The prognosis was bleak.

Hurricanes kill. They not only kill people. They kill mangroves, herons, bobcats, opossums, otters, manatees and everything in between. They blow apart rookeries, destroy entire forests and drown whole populations on barrier islands like Shoreside. They have since time eternal.

They were innocent killers, a strange by-product of the warm equatorial seas. The trees and wildlife would eventually recover, slowly recover. It would take decades for all of the scars to heal. As much as Scott understood and appreciated the cycle of tropical hurricanes in south Florida, it broke his heart to think about how many creatures would die over the course of the next two days.

Still, he knew that there was nothing he could do. He couldn't very well go around and put each and every gopher tortoise crawling around Shoreside in the trunk of his Honda Civic. He couldn't find and rescue every palm rat hiding in the strangler figs and palmettos throughout the 7,000 acres of the island. They were in harm's way with no knowledge of what was coming at them or any means of getting off the island. It meant certain annihilation.

"I understand, Mr. Burnham. Do you want me to try to save the monitors, or just take the CPUs?"

"If there's room, take them both. But the main thing is to save those hard drives. Save all of our mailing lists, our research data and our accounting. The Conservancy would be a mess if we lost all that information.

"Tell me, Scott, where are you planning to go?"

"I thought that I'd take I-75 north. Maybe as far north as Lake City if I have to. The projected path of the storm brings it diagonally across the state. Normally, everyone would head inland to Orlando, but the forecast track puts it just south of Kissimmee. Orlando won't work for this one. Maybe I'll head southeast, back over to the Greater Miami area. They're saying that Emily will miss Miami entirely."

"Where's the storm now?"

"My last alert radio announcement put Emily about 375 miles south, southwest of Shoreside. The barometric pressure is still dropping. It's at 27.80 inches and falling. Her sustained winds are now clocking in around 145 miles per hour and they are warning everyone that further strengthening of the storm is likely. She's a Category 4 storm, Barry, and she might damn well be a Category 5 before she finally makes landfall.

"If she is, the plywood I've nailed over our windows won't do much to slow her down. The island will crumble beneath a 15- to 20-foot storm surge and winds will be hitting 160 miles an hour. She's a killer storm, Barry. She's a great hurricane."

"Just get the hell off the island, Scott. I've gotta run. Call me when you get settled into a motel later."

"I promise I will."

"Goodbye, Scott, and God bless you."

"Thanks, Barry. Goodbye."

Scott thought that it was odd that Barry was asking God to bless him. That was always a difficult subject for Lindsay, the subject of God. He wondered about it, thought about it often, but never really came to much resolve.

God is so confusing, thought Scott to himself on many a sleepless night. God is hard to figure. Even when Scott felt that nature and God were the same, he still couldn't quite figure it. God was always so paradoxical, so at odds with himself.

Like hurricanes. Here, on Shoreside Island, life had spent the last 50 years growing thick and plentiful. The mangroves, the black mangroves, red mangroves and the buttonwood were tall and strong, the racoons stuffed with wild guavas and whatever they could dig out of the local Dumpsters. The birds were everywhere: 46 osprey nests, both the white and glossy ibis and the countless wrens, warblers and southern cardinals. Life, despite the development of the island, was still abundant on Shoreside. But not for long.

Scott recalled reading about one huge storm that blew through the Everglades in the '40s and took out 385,000 herons and egrets in a single day. That is a hell of a lot of birds.

Hurricane Andrew had kicked the crap out of the mangrove forests of the southern Everglades. Scott knew firsthand the damage that monster 'cane had caused just north of Flamingo. Andrew destroyed thousands of acres of mangrove forest. Scott knew because he had canoed through it with his wife in '94. He saw it up close and first hand. It was a mess.

The shoreline of Whitewater Bay was a hopeless tangle of trees, leafless and turning bone white in the relentless Florida sun. A forest that looked like a twisted boneyard.

But it wasn't only hurricanes that wrought such massive devastation. It was whenever Mother Nature turned ugly. Tornadoes, hailstorms, tsunamis, earthquakes, lightning, forest fires and volcanoes. All of them were every bit as ruthless to nature as they were to man. In fact, many were worse.

Man could be warned. We have communication. We could use everything from cell phones to ham radios. We have satellites that could track the storms, seismic equipment positioned everywhere on the planet, helping us to anticipate that next rumble. We know when the tidal wave is to hit. The wildlife knows nothing.

They could smell a fire, and if the species was mobile enough, it might be able to outrun it. Some animals can sense a hurricane or an earthquake, but not in time to get out of its way. Some catastrophes, like volcanoes and tornadoes, treat both people and animals with the same disregard. They were both instant. Both completely devastating.

After Mt. St. Helens blew apart, Scott gave up on God. He had hiked the base of Mt. St. Helens, as well as the base of Mr. Rainier, just after high school. The forests below those peaks were glorious. Elk, mule deer, bobcats, lynx and mountain lions abounded. There were beautiful stands of timber and stunning alpine meadows. It was as pristine a natural environment as Scott had ever known.

On May 18, 1980, all that ended. In the time it took that person to snap six color photos, they all died. Scott might spend a year trying to save 400 acres from the developer's bulldozers and Mt. St. Helens could whisk away a million acres in a minute. Flattened. Trees knocked down like matchsticks 100 miles east.

Ash, ash and more ash. In some towns located downwind, it soon became two, three inches deep. Yakima, Washington, had to deal with 600,000 tons of ash alone. A mud slide buried an entire lake. Scientists had estimated that 5,000 black-tailed deer, 1,500 elk and 200 black bear perished instantly. Not to mention thousands upon thousands of owls, crows, ducks and woodpeckers.

Devastation of a scale unimaginable to us. Unimaginable unless the human race went mad. Totally mad. Mad to the point of using nuclear weapons for kicks. Not that the thought of our doing such a thing hadn't crossed Scott's mind now and again. We'd done worse.

But aside from doing something that foolish, there was only war that rivaled the instant ruin of a volcanic eruption. And war was nothing when compared with the eruption of Krakatau in 1883. That explosion was so great that the pressure echo of it could be felt around the world seven times. The sound of the blast itself was heard clearly 3,000 miles away.

The entire island, part of the Sumatran Island chain, vanished. Blown away. Every plant, insect, bird of paradise, every rare rhino, Sumatran tiger on that island was instantly annihilated. Vaporized. The tidal wave that followed the blast was 130 feet high. Thirty-six thousand people living near Krakatau died. Many, many more animals perished as well.

What kind of God does this? That's what ran through Scott's mind as he unplugged all the Conservency's CPUs and placed them one by one into the trunk of his little Honda, the one with the new solenoid.

He kept thinking about the injustice of it all. The travesty. It wasn't an easy question to ask: Why do disasters happen? Why does God kill? The question kept Scott's restless mind busy while he hammered up the last few 3/4-inch plywood sheets. It had kept his restless mind busy for years.

There would be no resolution to it this afternoon. It was an enigma. A small piece of the grand puzzle of infinity. Scott would never understand it.

Nor will you. Nor will I.

570-9898
The Main Switchboard

It was time. Adam awoke from a long night's sleep and felt rested and at peace with himself for the first time in months. But Adam's peace was a strange, contorted peace, like the unholy satisfaction a man might have after selling his soul to the devil. Deep within, Adam Bartlett knew that the bargain had been struck. His last deal finalized. Now it was only a matter of time.

Adam showered. He took a long, hot shower with the steam billowing from the top of the shower enclosure and filling the room with a hot mist. He kept turning up the hot water. The steady stream of water became hotter and hotter. He finally got it as hot as he could possibly stand. Only then, when it was almost scalding, did the shower feel as if it was helping, cleansing him in an unclean way.

He shaved, got dressed, and packed up his briefcase. Everything was fine. He was going to go into the office for a little bit to catch up on some paperwork, make up some half- assed excuse to run down to Sanderling, remain there into the night, and kill himself by using a Category 5 hurricane like another suicide might use a .38-caliber handgun. Everything was fine.

Before leaving his apartment, Adam phoned Chris to tell her not to bother to come in today, with the storm approaching and all. Chris readily agreed. She didn't really want to come in again anyway. In her heart of hearts she wished that Emily would sweep Shoreside Island clean, taking Shoreside Realty and the Sanderling Condominium project right along with it.

After hanging up with Chris, Adam went down and climbed into his Boxster. He tried to find a radio station that was offering something besides the nonstop coverage of the approaching catastrophe but he couldn't. At this point, the local news media were in a hurricane feeding frenzy. This was the "Big One." CNN, CBS, NBC, ABC - all of the majors were arriving in town. It was all Hurricane Emily; the storm of the century. They were having a field day.

He turned off the radio and put on a CD. As an old Doors album blared out the disenfranchised voice of Jim Morrison, Adam drove down highways crowded with cars heading the other way. Steady lines of automobiles filled with passengers and drivers streaming away from the barrier islands toward the safety of the mainland. Streaming toward higher ground. Only a handful of cars were traveling in the same direction as Adam's Porsche. Traveling toward the approaching danger.

Jim Morrison's anxious voice fit Adam's mood perfectly. The restless lyrics, the impassioned edge to his hypnotic voice. The songs melded into one another as the Porsche headed toward the causeway and the island beyond; "L.A. Woman," "People Are Strange," "The End." The Doors belong to hurricanes, reflected the troubled driver. Both are natural disasters.

When Adam pulled up to the office he noted that there were only two cars in the parking lot. The makeshift wooden hurricane shutters were up and only the back door to the office building remained uncovered and usable. One of the two cars belonged to Betsy, which Adam found unusual. The other was Jason's dark blue Mercedes four-door. An expensive-looking luxury automobile. Hard to miss.

Adam grabbed his briefcase and went inside. The top was down on his Boxster and although it looked like rain, Adam didn't bother to put it up. What does it matter, he thought as he went in through the back door and headed down the hallway toward the wing that held his office. What does it matter?

"Adam, what are you doing here?" asked Betsy as she unexpectedly crossed paths with him in the hallway.

"I've just got to pick up some papers and files before the storm," replied a nervous Bartlett, caught off guard by actually running into someone at the office this morning. Someone so filled with life.

"You know about the mandatory evacuation, don't you?"

"Sure I do."

"Well, they want everyone off the island by 3:00 this afternoon, Adam. I've already told Jason and now I'm telling you. This hurricane is a big storm and they're saying that it's going to get really ugly just after sunset."

"Yeah, that's what they're saying."

"Well, don't stay too long, Adam. I just came out to pick up my things. I've decided to take some vacation time until the baby comes. I'm due in 10 days and I've got two weeks' vacation coming. After the baby, I'll be staying at home for three or four months, so I guess I might not be seeing you for a while, Adam."

"Guess not."

"Bye, Adam."

"Bye, Betsy. Good luck with the baby."

With that Betsy picked up the large paper shopping bag she had set down while talking with Bartlett and headed toward the back door. The paper bag contained all those little things that had decorated her tiny office space near the switchboard. Photographs of Mark, of Betsy's sister and her mother and father. Keepsakes with little value beyond sentiment. Priceless only to those who know the faces in the photos. Those who know whose birthday party it was. Whose graduation. Irreplaceable, really.

But even in those few, fleeting minutes in the hallway, Betsy felt it. Perhaps it was a mother's instinct, sharpened by the upcoming arrival of her firstborn. Perhaps it was because she cared for Adam, still feeling badly for the way things had gone for him these last six months. She felt that nobody should have to be put through the gauntlet Adam was running.

It wasn't the way he looked on this particular morning. No, thought Betsy as she walked over to her car, Adam had looked good for a change. His hair was combed, his sports coat pressed and his face clean shaven. If anything, he looked too good.

It was something else that Betsy had sensed. A quiet, invisible resignation. Nothing Adam said, did, or how he looked gave any indication of the trouble Betsy had sensed. It was an intuition. Something was wrong.

As she started her old Pinto and headed toward the causeway and the safe harbor of the mainland beyond, Betsy had already decided to check on Adam later in the day. Just to be sure he had gotten off the island okay. Just to follow through on the knot that was slowly being tied in her stomach. Following up, checking on Adam later, would help untie that knot.

Adam, of course, didn't take note of Betsy's observations. He was aloof and unaffected by the concerns of the living. Everything he did was done on automatic, like an airplane full of lonely passengers put on autopilot. An airplane steering directly into the side of an empty mountain range. Everything on this meaningless Friday morning had an inevitability to it, a crushing certainty.

He went into his office and sat behind his desk. He wanted to call his ex-wife Peggy and speak with his boy, Danny, one more time, but he held himself from doing so. He knew that it might tempt him to take hold of the controls, to switch off the autopilot. It was too goddamned late for that. Way too goddamned late.

The sound of his boy's voice over the telephone might snap him back into the realm of the living. Adam wouldn't let himself go there. He was smarter and stronger than that. His telephone sat untouched.

He sifted through some messages and opened his briefcase. The only real business Adam had to tend to was to perish in the approaching storm, but the eye of that storm was still 20 hours away. Adam wished that Emily was already ripping Shoreside apart. The time between then and now was painful. God, he wished that the storm would hurry.

As he sat there he wanted desperately to say something, anything. To leave a note. To explain to Danny why he was doing this. He took up a pen and a blank piece of paper and he began.

Dear Danny,

I know by the time you receive this letter I will have died. I'm sorry for that. I want to let you know now how much I love you and will always love you. I

*didn't do this because of you, or because of your mother, and you need to know
that.*

*Peggy is a wonderful mother and she always has been. She will take care of
you like she always has. I should never have left her, but it is too late for all of
that now.*

*I'm going away because I cannot deal with it any more. Everything I once
had is gone and there is no reason for me to go on. I can no longer deal with the
nightmare Sanderling has made of my life; the incessant telephone calls, the
lawyers and the constant harassment have become too much for me to take. I
have lost everything, my savings, my assistants, my business and I can't go on. I
feel that...*

With that Adam stopped, ripped the page from his notebook, and tore it into
a hundred tiny pieces. There would be no note. A suicide note would cost his ex-
wife and child a half-million dollars. Accidental death, Adam reminded himself,
double indemnity.

He wanted to write that note but he couldn't. They would never know why
he was found down at Sanderling after the storm. They would all be so
perplexed by it, how Bartlett could have been so stupid. That was how it would
have to be. Just a floating corpse in a failed project. A fool. A statistic.

In the distance Adam could hear Jason Randazzle talking on the phone.
Between gusts of wind and occasional sprinkles of light rain tapping on the
hurricane shutters, Adam could hear the smooth unbroken monologue of a
salesman in action. The actual words Jason were saying didn't matter, and
Adam knew it.

It was a cadence, the perfect rhythm of a well-trained professional. Adam
didn't need to hear the dialogue. The dialogue was immaterial.

As it was, Jason Randazzle was selling fear this morning. He was still on his
hot streak fueled by an approaching calamity. He was feeding on the falling
barometric pressure, getting owner after owner alarmed at the thought of
ownership here, on this vulnerable, helpless island. An island forever placed in
harm's way.

The owners, seeing the news coverage, hearing the predictions, were easy
prey for Jason Randazzle's well-scripted solicitations. They were quick to agree
with Jason's well-timed logic, all of them ready to sell as soon as the storm made
its way inland.

Had they been told by their salesperson of the danger of ownership on an
island like Shoreside they probably never would have purchased here in the first
place. They thanked Jason for his honesty, for setting them straight before the
storm. For offering his help and professional expertise in marketing their condo;
their three-bedroom, two-bath piling home; their vacant lot after the storm. The
world needed more sincere people like Jason Randazzle. How lucky it was for

him to have called.

Not that any of them would have phoned Jason the following week to hear him explain that now was the time to buy. Now that the storm had hit the island, depressing values and assuring the prospective purchaser that the odds of another storm hitting in the next 100 years were a million to one.

The quintessential salesman. Real estate, used cars, vacuum cleaners, encyclopedias, water softeners, stocks, bonds, oil wells - the product didn't matter. Buy low, sell high, buy high, sell low, all of it was irrelevant. They were the masters of churning. Adam knew what Jason was saying because he was cast from the same deceitful mold.

A skill honed by years of selling. Listening to their customers' dreams spill out before them and using that knowledge to consummate the sale. Saying what the buyers or sellers want to hear. It was the best floorplan on Shoreside, it had the best view, it offered the most amenities. Or, if they wanted out, that the association in this complex is too demanding, ocean views are boring, they don't maintain the greens like they used to. Float. Say everything and nothing at once.

Stay out of the traps. Stay noncommittal. Black is white, and white looks good on you. Up is down. Never take a position that might entrap you. Keep the monologue coming all the way to the paperwork. Silver tongues selling encyclopedias to the illiterate. *Crème de la crème*, the top producers.

All that mattered to people like Randazzle was a small percentage of the motion itself. Trading up, trading down, buying, selling, exchanging, it all cooked down to the 2.57 percent he cleared from the gross selling price. A quarter of a million dollars a year dialing for dollars. The thief with a fountain pen. The master of the dial tone.

Give either of them a $3.47 notebook full of names and numbers, a long-distance telephone company that didn't cost an arm and a leg and Randazzle or Bartlett were good to go. Geniuses at the art of selling, immune to rejection and as ruthless as a starving leopard at midnight.

Yes, Adam knew what Jason was saying without actually hearing it. He knew instinctively that Jason was on a roll. Building a list of leads a mile long with hurricane Emily as his silent partner. Going for the jugular when the animal on the other end of the line was weak and vulnerable, just like a good salesman should.

"God," Adam said quietly to himself, "I wish this fucking storm would hurry!"

570-9514
Mildred Lee's Home Phone

"Hello," answered an excited Mildred Lee.

"Mildred, it's Sam. Sam Goodlet," said her concerned listing agent. "Why are you still home, Mildred? Hasn't anyone offered to take you off the island?"

"They're on their way to get me now, Sam. Don't you fret over me any. I'll be out of here in a half an hour. Those nice people over at Friends of the Island, you know, that volunteer organization, are sending a van over to take me and the cats off Shoreside before Emily gets any closer.

"Isn't it exciting, Sam. I mean to be here when the "Big One" finally hits. Like I've said all along, it's just a matter of time. It looks like sometime around 3:00 or 4:00 Saturday morning is going to be when the eye passes over us. That nasty old Emily is going to lay ruin to Shoreside, Sam. I can just feel it in my bones."

"Well, you be sure to call me immediately if they don't show up soon to take you off the island. There's still some time left, but these rain squalls are starting to pack some punch and I want to make sure you're still around to sign that deed when we sell your place this coming season," said Sam in an optimistic tone.

"Oh, don't you worry none, Sam. I'll be out of here within the hour."

"You'd better be, Mildred. They're saying that the storm surge might go as high as eight feet. According to that certificate of elevation you handed me a year ago, your floor sits at nine feet above sea level. That's cutting it pretty darn close, Mildred. Whatever you do, I sure as heck want you off Shoreside when Emily makes landfall tomorrow morning.

"If they're wrong about the size of that surge, you'll find yourself under water. Those hurricane shutters of yours aren't going to do much good in a flood. They'll fold in like tinfoil if the storm surge reaches the height of your windows. The safest thing to do is to cage up Blackie, Buttons and Mittens, and head toward the mainland and higher ground."

"That's my plan, Sam, and I'm waiting for the doorbell to ring any minute now."

"Well that's good to hear. You be sure to call me if they don't show up, okay."

"I promise, Sam. You're always so concerned. Too bad you're married, you're such a sweetheart."

"Goodbye now, Mildred."

"Bye, Sam."

Sam hung up the phone and went back to watching the television. Hurricane Emily had commandeered all the local television stations. The coverage on all four channels was nonstop hurricane updates, warnings, watches and spin. Hurricane spin. Predictions of what kind of damage area property owners might anticipate during the long, dreadful night ahead.

Footage of the latest satellite shots, showing the tightly wound eye of Emily, was interspersed with footage of past hurricane damage. Andrew footage. Georges footage. Old, grainy, black-and-white Donna footage. Frightening scenes of roofs being torn off and mobile home parks reduced to a curious montage of twisted aluminum, pink insulation and splintered two-by-fours. As the camera panned the surrounding devastation, nothing remained standing across acres and acres of residential subdivisions. Nothing remained intact.

The message being repeatedly blasted from every local station was exactly the same - GET OUT! Evacuate, clear out, leave immediately, withdraw, pack your valuables and your pets and run. Run to high ground just like the Calusa Indians must have done 500 years ago. Find shelter inland, or gain high ground before the big wind and the big waves bury you.

The technology had improved a million times over but the message to the natives had not changed in 100,000 years. Flee before the storm. Move away from the coast, from the low-lying barrier islands and the mangrove-lined islands behind them. Head inland and seek shelter. This was the same message that was spread through the primitive villages of the native Americans when they first noticed the long, sweeping waves that foreshadowed the storm.

It was the only warning nature provided back then, before the advent of radios, television and geostationary orbiters. Long, booming swells that traveled ahead of the hurricane's steady march. Unusual in their power and intensity, the Calusa, the Seminole and all the native Americans who lived along the coast must have known what they meant. Must have taken them as their warning to seek high ground and safe haven.

God help them if they did not.

Sam Goodlet sat down in his La-Z-Boy recliner and went back to watching the coverage. They would break off for updates from the head of the National Hurricane Center in Miami, or commentary from various hurricane experts throughout the country. The message to the viewers was always the same: Run. Run for your life.

Mildred hobbled over to her tiny television to turn the volume up. She laughed to herself as she did. She had them both fooled. She had told the people at Friends of the Island that Sam Goodlet was coming to evacuate her. Now she had told Sam that Friends of the Island were coming to take her off Shoreside. Little did either of them know that she wasn't planning to leave.

She had been waiting for Hurricane Emily for a decade and she wasn't about to miss out at this point in her life. She had planned, tracked, plotted and calculated, and she was ready. Canned goods, flashlights, hurricane shutters and coolers filled to overflowing with ice all reminded her of how much effort had gone into getting ready, getting prepared for a night just like the one slowly descending on Shoreside. A night in hell.

No, it was final, Mildred Lee was staying. She had spent years preparing for a hurricane just like Emily and she wasn't about to miss out on the opportunity of a lifetime. The storm surge was projected to be no more than eight feet because the hurricane was coming ashore during a particularly low tide. That left Mildred a one-foot margin of error.

Hell, thought a determined Mildred Lee, if I have to, I'll just get up on my bed for a bit until the storm surge subsides. I'll be fine. I didn't go through all this effort for nothing, getting all those supplies, having Sam come over and put up my last two shutters. If I was planning to evacuate, why go through the bother of getting ready for a hurricane? It doesn't make any damn sense if you ask me, pondered an 84-year-old lady in her lonely canal-front house on the north end of Shoreside Island before an approaching monster.

A foot. That was all Mildred had to gamble on. Each cubic yard of seawater weighs nearly a ton. It can crush solid brick walls as if they were made of cardboard once the ocean surrounds a house like Mildred's. Hurricane shutters are useless in a flood.

Tiny, vulnerable and ready, Mildred Lee watched her 12-inch television show her the eye of Emily hooking toward the west coast of Florida. Coming to finally visit Mildred Lee, like her long-lost sister from Chicago or a distant niece that she had not seen in years. Coming to spend the night. Maybe Emily would like a cup of tea, or some nice chocolate chip cookies Mildred had baked just for this special occasion.

Emily was going to visit Mildred. It sounds innocent enough. Quaint. Perfectly civil. She would drop by for an evening and head north, northeast by first light. Mildred had spent her entire lifetime awaiting her good friend. She wasn't about to evacuate and spoil their little social. Their time together.

As Mildred watched her little TV she felt oddly calm. She wasn't anxious or afraid in the least. The newscaster's voice faded away into some distant noises, like children playing in a vacant lot a quarter mile away. As Mildred listened, their words began to sound like a song, a song whose name she couldn't quite remember. A song she liked.

Their warnings went unheralded, much like the unheralded warnings of Dr. Isaac Cline as he drove his buggy along the beaches of Galveston on the afternoon of September 8, 1900. The day more than 6,000 people died.

Mildred was safe. Her friend was finally coming. Everything will be as it is meant to be. Emily. It's such a pretty name for a hurricane, thought this sweet little old lady from suburban Chicago. Such a pretty name.

570-1995
Unit 2-A, Sanderling Condominiums

Adam's dark green Boxster rolled down the long, empty driveway that led into the Sanderling Condominium property. Adam had put the same Doors CD back on his stereo. Because the wind had picked up dramatically, he had turned his car radio up to the point where the sound of the music was overwhelming. Ray Manzarek's organ solo in "Light My Fire" became reality. The music transcended loud. It became the moment itself.

In advance of Emily, the rains had also arrived, soaking the light cream leather of the $50,000 sports car in some bizarre ritual known only to the long-dead Morrison and the visionary poet who had given the name to the band, William Blake. Adam didn't care about the car or the leather. Where Adam had descended, only the rhythm of the music mattered.

"When the doors of perception are cleansed, man will see things as they truly are: infinite," wrote Blake 200 years ago. Truth has a way of echoing down through the centuries. A way of reminding us. At times like these, it becomes a haunting, prophetic echo, like the song that now filled Adam's head.

Adam pulled under the "A" building and parked the car directly behind the ten small personal storage units located under the condo. If the Shoreside police even bother to check to see if anyone is staying at Sanderling, thought Adam, they won't see my car unless they pull all the way in. It was a calculated precaution. He was hiding.

"Come on baby light my fire. Try to set the night on fire. Try to set the night on fire. TRY TO SET THE NIGHT ON FIRE!!!" As Morrison screamed that last foreboding line, the left-front speaker on his Porsche blew. Adam's $2,000 custom Bose system couldn't handle that scream any more than Jim Morrison could before his death decades ago. It was too raw. Too primal.

Adam didn't take notice of the blown speaker. He had been steadily turning up the volume on his stereo all the way to Sanderling, just like he had turned up the hot water in his shower earlier. Likewise, the music was scalding him, boiling him in some self-destructive rage. Morrison's voice and Bartlett's soul had fused, becoming a helpless beast without reason, an animal left standing in the pouring rain.

The last organ solo ended and Adam turned off the car. A second speaker blew just before the engine died, but Adam took no note of that either. Internally, he had already entered the tomb into which he was soon to die. Everything else meant nothing. Nada. Only Morrison's screams remained, reverberating through the emptiness of his desolate soul like the memoirs of a fellow suicide.

"TRY TO SET THE NIGHT ON FIRE!"

Adam grabbed his briefcase, his bottle of J&B, and headed up to the top-floor unit. Once out of his car, he noticed the weather. It was worse. The storm was drawing closer and closer to mainland Florida and the weather was deteriorating as it did.

As he walked up the exterior stairway, Adam grew nearer and nearer to the ominous sky stretched above him. The storm bands were clearly visible. The slow curve of the dark clouds disappeared into the distance like the curve of an empty highway in a desert. There were still broken patches of blue sky peering from between the bands, but they were few and far between. As Emily drew closer to Shoreside, these patches would disappear. By nightfall, the cloud cover would be thick and impenetrable.

Adam took his master key and opened Unit 2-A, the top-floor-north apartment. It was the same apartment he and Vanessa had made love in nine months ago. It looked unchanged.

No one had stayed in it and only two agents had shown it since that fateful afternoon. Ironically, remembered Adam, this particular unit was owned by Boyle. Boyle, the man who would have liked all the details of Adam and Vanessa's romantic interlude that wonderful night before the grand opening. How they did it in the hot tub, after washing each other's hair and covering each other with her expensive conditioner. How their lovemaking had felt that heavenly night. Rapturous and sensual.

But Adam never told Boyle about that night, or the morning after, when they made love slowly and passionately. Boyle had never asked. He didn't want to know how Adam had been fucked any longer. Not since he realized that he was getting fucked. He no longer found it entertaining. All Boyle wanted was out.

At the moment, Eugene Boyle was up north. He was 1,300 miles from hurricane Emily. He hadn't talked to Adam since he had unleashed his lawyers upon him seven months ago. Unleashed them good. Adam smiled to himself at the thought of it all. He would never have to talk to that asshole again.

Adam stuck his liter of Scotch in the empty refrigerator and walked to the front porch with his briefcase in hand. The condominium didn't have any hurricane shutters. They were over budget, and TLD, Inc.'s policy was to never add any extras that would put a project over budget. If the purchasers wanted them, Loggins could put them in at his builder's discount: $4,000 per unit. Electrically operated. Capable of withstanding winds up to 140 miles per hour. Adam smiled again. They said that Emily was gusting to 180 miles per hour.

They would have been blown away regardless.

He opened the sliding glass doors to the screened patio and looked across the Gulf of Mexico. The sea beyond was furious. Waves were smashing onto the beach with an imperative Adam had never witnessed before. They were fast and choppy, looking as though each and every wave grew that much higher than the one that preceded it. White sea foam and saltwater spray were being shot ahead of the waves by the gusting winds. The view was inspiring.

This is the ideal location, thought Adam. The perfect vantage point to watch a great hurricane descend on Florida. Watch it come ashore like 100,000 storms have come ashore before it. Decades of storms, centuries of storms, eternities of storms. Watch it batter the hell out of the sabal palms and mangroves. Watch it kill.

Adam sat and opened his briefcase. The only file in it was this one, the Sanderling Condominium project, and it was more than two-inches thick. Adam took out the file and left on the large brown rubber band that held it all together. This file was going down along with him. It was part of his plan.

Adam got up and went into the kitchen through the sliding glass doors he had left slightly agape. He opened one of the cupboards and got an eight-ounce drinking glass. Filling it to the very brim with ice from the ice maker, Adam was glad to note that the electricity was still on. He knew that there was plenty of ice inside the tray once the power failed. Plenty enough to get him to where he was going. J&B tastes better over ice, he decided. Much better.

He opened the fridge and grabbed his liter of J&B. He cracked it in the fashion that he had cracked so many a bottle before it over these last few months. He cracked it with a sense of purpose. The smell wafted up to him as the seal opened. The smell of success.

He poured the Scotch over the ice until it nearly ran over the polished edge of the glass. Rattling it gently as he lifted the drink up to his lips, he knew that the race was on. The race to nowhere. Only now it came with a view.

He walked back to the lanai and took the rubber band off the file. He wanted to read through it all one more time, from the purchase of the 13 acres to the bill for the pumps that never arrived.

In his desperate fashion, Adam was prepared for the storm. His survival kit consisted of a briefcase, a cell phone that was turned off, a bottle of J&B Scotch and a legal file that was two-inches thick. Two inches of personal hell.

It was going to be a beautiful afternoon, thought Adam as he took a long, second drink of Scotch. Absolutely beautiful.

570-9514
Mildred Lee's Home Phone

Sam watched the television in horror. Emily was 95 miles off Shoreside, spinning wildly out of control. At her present speed of 15 miles per hour and her current track, her vacuum-like eye would cross directly over the island around 3:00 in the morning in this, the darkest of nights.

Her barometric pressure was 27.56 inches and falling. Emily was a monster, a cataclysm of wind, rain and seawater. The worst part of the storm surge would happen to the right of the eye, just south of Shoreside. Even with the storm coming ashore during low tide, the newscasters predicted a storm surge approaching 16 feet. The entire coastline was being evacuated from Marco Island to the edge of Tampa.

The only saving grace was that Emily was a tight, compact storm. Her eye was no more than 12 miles across and her spiral bands stretched little more than 100 miles from her center. She was like her brother before her. He came ashore in 1992 just north of Homestead on the other coast. He was the single most expensive natural disaster to ever hit North America. Her brother, Andrew, was also a Cape Verde storm, tightly wound and ever so bitter.

As Sam watched and waited he kept thinking back to that catastrophe. He remembered the blocks and blocks of flattened buildings. Thirty-billion dollars in damage. Twenty-five thousand homes destroyed, another 100,000 damaged. Fifteen-thousand boats lost, and countless cars, trucks and airplanes laid ruin beneath a fury of wind and water.

The aerial shots of Homestead Air Force Base after the storm showing multimillion-dollar jets destroyed. The entire complex looking as though it had been shelled by Fidel Castro's army. Hangars with their roofs blown off, dozens of Piper Cubs strewn around the runway like discarded toys.

And the rumors after Andrew. The rumors of 5,000 dead migrant workers, stacked in makeshift morgues like cordwood. Human cordwood. Nameless migrant workers who were buried nameless. Cover-ups and secret mass graves because the United States government didn't want to admit that they had perished. A shameful government that didn't want these illegal aliens included in the death count.

The official death count for Emily's brother, Andrew, was reported at 52.

That included those who perished when the storm reformed and slammed into Louisiana. After the storm, the hearsay was that if you didn't have a green card, you didn't exist. If you didn't exist, you couldn't have died. The official death count should have been 5,052. The gymnasium filled with corpses would have verified it. But in the chaos that followed Andrew, verifications were impossible. No one will ever know for certain, thought Sam Goodlet as he stared at the television. No one.

As Sam thought about all of this he heard the local newscaster announce that the causeway to Shoreside would be closed to everyone in 30 minutes. Everyone but officials and emergency vehicles. If there was anyone left on the island who had not evacuated, then they needed to do so immediately or risk being cut off by the approaching storm surge.

Sam knew that Mildred was safe. She had been taken off the island by Friends of the Island and was now probably in a shelter. Some high school cafeteria far removed from the vulnerable coastline. Safe.

But in his heart, Sam feared that hurricane Emily wouldn't allow anyone to be completely out of harm's way. She was too powerful, too violent. Like her older brother, she probably held hundreds of deadly tornadoes in her eye wall. Micro-storms dancing within the perimeter of the larger vortex. The best estimate was that Hurricane Andrew spawned 280 individual micro-tornadoes, some of them reaching 20 miles inland. Safety was a myth in a storm like Emily. A comforting delusion.

Just then the phone rang. The ring startled Sam back into the present tense. He had been so absorbed with the television and the grim forecast before him. He got up, walked over and picked up the ringing telephone. He wasn't expecting a call and he knew the news, whatever it was, wasn't good.

"Sam?"

"Mildred, is that you?"

"Yes, Sam, it's me. My electricity has just gone out but my phone still works fine, doesn't it?"

Sam Goodlet was instantly slammed back into reality. He knew.

"Where are you, Mildred?"

"I'm fine, Sam. I've got all my supplies, my hurricane shutters are all up, thanks to you, and I'm going to be just fine."

"Where are you, Mildred?" repeated a frightened man.

"I'm at home, Sam."

"Mildred, you told me earlier that Friends of the Island were going to take you off the island. What happened?" said Sam sternly. Angrily.

"I told them you were going to take me off the island, and I told you that they were going to take me off the island. But I had never planned to leave my home, Sam. I'll be fine here. I was just calling you to check to see if the phone still works. It works fine, doesn't it?"

Sam stood silent. Frozen. Unable to respond to Mildred's question. Unable to think of what to do next. Every option was laden with danger at this stage. Every alternative had more than its share of risk.

"Mildred, what the hell were you thinking!"

Sam was angry. He was angry because he knew that Mildred had gone too far this time. This wasn't a Kandee, or a Category 1 hurricane. Emily was the real thing, a major hurricane slamming almost perpendicular into Shoreside. Mildred's house would more than likely be under water in the next four hours. Her pantry full of canned goods and flashlights submerged beneath 15 feet of ocean.

"Don't be mad at me, Sam. I've been getting ready for a storm like this for years. You really didn't think I would go running off Shoreside at the first sign of trouble when a big storm finally came along, did you?

"I'm ready for Emily, Sam. I've got all my canned goods, my blankets and my candles right here with me. You've got no reason to worry."

He didn't even think about what he said next. The words just sprang from his mouth automatically. They were words that he didn't want to be saying but had to say. Like an uncontrollable scream a person lets go at the county fair when the bottom drops out of the spinning cyclotron. Words without thought.

"Stay where you are, Mildred. I'm coming to get you."

"No you're not, Sam. I'll be just fine."

"Stay where you are and that's final."

Mildred had never heard Sam sound so stern, so demanding. She felt like a little child who had just been caught stealing candy at the local grocery store. She felt hurt, reprimanded for something she felt was harmless enough. Penny candy. That's all she had taken. Just penny candy.

"Okay, Sam. You can come and get me if you insist. But I'm telling you, I would be perfectly safe here in my house. I'm ready for the "Big One," Sam. I'm as ready as I'll ever be."

Sam knew what he had to do. Time was running out, as time tends to do in a disaster. First, he had to tell Mildred to find her cats and have them ready to go as soon as he arrived. That would be critical.

"Mildred, listen carefully. Round up Mittens, Buttons and Blackie and put them in that traveling case that Tommy uses to take them in to the vet. We have very little time and there won't be a second to spare. I'll leave as soon as I get off the phone. It will take me every bit of 30 minutes to get to Shoreside and the traffic should be nonexistent this late in the game.

"When I get close, I'll call you on my cell phone. Pack no more than two suitcases with anything you want to save and be ready to head out the door with me as soon as I arrive. The storm surge they are predicting will be starting to build right after 10:00 p.m. so we'll have no room for error. I'm on my way, Mildred. Please be ready."

"I'll be ready for you, Sam," said a reluctant survivor.

"Goodbye, see you in half an hour."

"Goodbye, Sam."

Sam was fortunate that he didn't have to say anything about his plans to Mrs. Goodlet. His wife had gone to spend the evening with her mother at her condominium. Her mother, since her husband's death four years ago, lived alone in a small apartment not three miles from their house. It was too small for the both of them to stay the night, so Sam offered to hold down the fort at home. He left a note on the kitchen table. His last four words were, "Love you always, Sam."

Sam went to the garage and started his Oldsmobile 88. He would have to hurry. God, thought Sam, why do things like this have to happen?

276-4345
Jason Randazzle's Home Phone

At 8:00 Friday night, Jason Randazzle, like everyone else in town, was hunkered down at home with his face glued to the TV. The news, for all the barrier island property owners and those living anywhere near the coast, was bleak. Because of it, Jason was elated.

All the local programming had been suspended. NBC, CBS, ABC, FOX and even the local PBS station had switched to coverage of Hurricane Emily. Only cable held onto its meaningless monopoly of reruns of *Seinfeld, Star Trek,* and bad Fred Astaire movies. The rest was 100 percent storm.

All the stations promised to continue nonstop coverage of Hurricane Emily until the power was knocked out. Which would happen at precisely 1:35 Saturday morning, when Emily's eye made landfall.

Until then, it was all hurricane spin. Clockwise spin, opposite that of the storm's rotation. It was down to announcing and re-announcing what to anticipate; what to have on hand, what shelters were open, how high the storm surge might go, what sort of damage to expect and where the storm might head once it made landfall.

There were satellite images every 15 minutes showing the exact location of Emily's 12-mile-wide eye and live links to any number of scientists at the National Hurricane Center in Miami. Even Dr. Gray from Colorado had an occasional cameo. Everyone was in complete agreement on one point: Emily was going to be bad. More than once during the course of the coverage, she had been referred to as Hurricane Andrew's twin sister. That was because she was the same kind of storm - fast-running, tightly wound and immensely powerful. More like a tornado on steroids than your typically large, sprawling storms. Storms like Hugo in 1989 or Gilbert back in 1988.

Aside from the storm surge that was certain to inundate Shoreside and one smaller barrier island to the north, localized flooding from the accompanying thunderstorms wasn't anticipated. Unlike tropical storm Kandee, hurricane Emily wasn't a rainmaker. Although the rainfall amounts might vary by several inches across the projected path of the storm, the consensus was that no one area would receive more than six inches. Kandee dumped 18 inches on some locales nine months ago. Bartlett and three million salt marsh mosquitoes knew that better than anyone.

No, Emily wasn't a rainmaker. She was a wind machine. A nervous, high-strung bitch of a hurricane who now packed sustained winds of 152 miles per hour with gusts over 187 miles per hour. At 8:05 p.m. she had a barometric pressure of 924 millibars, or 27.24 inches. Although that pressure had been holding steady, there was considerable speculation out of Miami that she might strengthen somewhat before hitting Florida. She had three miles per hour to go before becoming a Category 5 hurricane.

At this point it hardly mattered. She was a first-class bitch with a world-class attitude. A bad attitude. Shoreside Island was her first stop on the mainland, and it wasn't going to be pretty.

All the forecasters, scientists and disaster personnel were resigned to the fact that Shoreside was going to be totally devastated at the hands of this wicked woman. Image upon image of Homestead and south Dade after Andrew's nasty visit were pulled out of archives and flashed across the television. Piles of rubble that once were homes, twisted street signs and people standing bewildered in their uprooted yards kept dancing across Jason's huge screen. Portraits of catastrophe.

At 8:15 that Friday evening Jason Randazzle's phone rang. He put down his beer, placed the television on mute and walked over to get the phone.

Jason lived alone. He had a girlfriend once, but that was three years ago. She ended up leaving him for a carpet installer who she met when she had some new Stainmaster carpet installed in her apartment. Jason handled her rejection like he did most everyone. Water off a duck's back. She was fat anyway, he kept reminding himself. Fat.

At this point in his uncharismatic career, it hardly mattered. He liked living alone. Calling his mother now and then and watching continuous sports coverage on ESPN on his Mitsubishi giant-screen TV. That and making absurd amounts of money.

"Hello, Jason Randazzle here."

"Mr. Randazzle, this is Cynthia Parker calling you back. Remember, you called me earlier today."

Jason didn't remember. He had called nearly 100 people earlier today. Their names and numbers ran together like watered-down tomato soup. All dull orange and washed out. "No," was the answer he should have given, but that would have been out of character.

"Sure I do, Cynthia. How can I help you?"

"Well, like you said earlier this morning, after the storm my condo might not be worth what it is now, but I was wondering how much of a price reduction I might expect when all the damage is repaired?"

"Well, that depends...."

Jason was hedging. To begin with, he had no idea who Cynthia Parker was, where she was calling from, or what condo she owned. Without his notebook filled to overflowing with names, numbers and notations, it was all soup. A bland, diluted soup, featureless and being served ice cold.

"Depends on what?" inquired a nervous Shoreside property owner whose face was likewise buried in CNN up in St. Louis, Missouri.

"Depends on quite a number of things. How much damage, what the view looks like after the storm, any number of factors."

Cynthia was becoming suspicious. Her condo complex was a mile from the beach. Her view consisted of the parking lot. Maybe he didn't remember her. In the meanwhile, Randazzle was trying desperately to think of something. He needed his notebook. Without it, all he could do was throw bullshit at Mrs. Parker. Sometimes bullshit sticks. Sometimes it doesn't.

Jason continued, "I'll tell you what, Cynthia. You don't mind if I call you Cynthia, do you?"

"No, not at all."

"Well, Cynthia. I really need to go to my car and get my notes on your condominium before I can answer that question. Do you mind if I call you back in a few minutes?"

"That would be just fine."

"Let me get a pencil and paper and jot down your number."

"My number is 714-876-0991. I'll be home all night. I'm here watching the news on Hurricane Emily up in St. Louis. It looks pretty bad for Shoreside, doesn't it."

"I'm afraid it does. I'll call you back in no more than ten minutes."

"Thank you so much, Mr. Randazzle."

"You can call me Jason, Cynthia."

"Thank you, Jason. Goodbye."

"Goodbye."

Jason set the phone on its receiver and pretended to wipe his forehead with his right hand. He had dodged a bullet. The name Cynthia Parker meant nothing to him. He had logged so many names, numbers and properties in the last few days that they had all become a blur. The good news was that virtually everyone wanted to sell and he had it all carefully recorded in his notebook.

It was a week in paradise for a telephone salesman like Jason. With a massive storm bearing down on Shoreside, everyone wanted out. Sell, sell, sell. For Jason Randazzle, it was like a Black Friday on Wall Street. They were all ready to unload, dump and liquidate. It was panic selling at its finest and that fact never bothered Jason. He loved playing on people's emotions when it came to helping them make decisions. For Randazzle, it was never about people - their dreams, their plans or their problems. It was about 2.57 percent.

Jason headed to the garage to grab his notebook. Of the 87 calls he had managed to squeeze in before the mandatory evacuation order, 46 owners were interested in listing their properties in the next few weeks. Jason knew that some of them, depending on the damage and the depreciation in the aftermath of the hurricane, would reconsider. Fallout like that was fairly typical.

Still, odds were that Jason would pick up at least a dozen listings in the next 30 days. Possibly 20 listings. Either number would be a record for the month of July. Life, from the pockmarked and twisted perspective of Jason R. Randazzle, was great.

When Jason got to his dark blue Mercedes he could hear the wind-driven rain pounding against the garage door. It was getting pretty ugly out there already, he noted to himself, and the storm was still seven hours off.

He opened the passenger door and started rifling through the files he had grabbed before leaving the office. He didn't want to lose any of his currently active files so he wisely decided to take most of them home with him. They would be safer at home than at the office, with the projected storm surge and the havoc it would wreak. Jason lived well inland and the chances of the surge making it this far up the interior were nil. Thinking ahead, that was Jason.

He started looking through the files. Jason's invaluable notebook was somewhere in that eight-inch stack of legal-sized files. Somewhere.

After going through the stack of files the first time without finding it, Jason became concerned. Not panicked, but concerned. He thought that he couldn't find it because of the lighting. It was dark in the garage and the dim interior light of his Mercedes didn't help. He flipped his headlights on to give himself some extra light.

After sifting through the stack twice, he came up empty-handed. This wasn't good. He picked up all of his files, pressed the armful of paperwork against his chest and headed into the living room. Then Jason plopped the whole stack down beside his glass of beer. Budweiser Light, his favorite. In the rush to get inside and find his notebook, he had left the passenger door open and the headlights on high.

Now, under the blue-green glow of his big-screen television and the two lamps on either side of his couch, he carefully sifted through the stack of files. It's in here somewhere, he knew. Somewhere.

But it wasn't in the pile. It had to be. But it wasn't. He went back to the Mercedes with a big six-volt flashlight, figuring that it had slipped between the seats of the car. It had to be under the seat, or in the back seat, or between the seats. But it wasn't.

He checked the trunk. It wasn't in the trunk. He checked the glove box and the two compartments that held maps and things behind the driver's seat and the passenger's seat. It wasn't there either.

He checked the side-door compartments, where he kept his maps and sunglasses. He knew damn well that it couldn't even fit in those small plastic compartments but he checked them anyway. He retraced his steps into the house from the garage to his couch and came up empty-handed. All the while his interior light, his trunk light and his headlights were shining on brightly. It took him half an hour to find out it was gone.

His bright red $3.47 spiral, college-style notebook wasn't anywhere to be found. His bright red spiral notebook that held 18,000 names, numbers, office numbers, property addresses and 46 red hot listing leads had gone missing. He finally broke down and admitted the obvious to himself.

I accidently left it at the office. Shit. Shit, shit shit!

Jason Randazzle, without giving it a second thought, knew that he had to do what he had to do. He had to go back to Shoreside Island and retrieve it. It was like leaving his best friend out there to die. Without his notebook, and his collection of telephone numbers and names, he was completely helpless. His notebook was his lifeline to the land of plenty.

He knew that it would probably be lying right on his desk. What an idiot I am, he thought. I shouldn't have left in such a hurry. See, haste makes waste. Now I've got to figure out how to bullshit my way past those police barricades and get to the office. It won't take me over an hour and half total, unless the winds pick up.

Then it dawned on him. He had to call Mrs. Parker back before leaving. It was an ideal situation for him to look like a hero in front of a customer. He would call her and explain he had left his notebook at the office and he was willing to go the extra mile for her and retrieve it.

That is exactly what he did. He called her back.

"Hello," answered Mrs. Parker some 1,200 miles away.

"Hello, Cynthia, this is Jason Randazzle. Remember, you phoned me about an hour ago regarding your property on Shoreside?"

"Why, yes, of course."

"Well, as things sometimes happen, I went to my car and found I've accidently forgotten my notebook back at the office. Because I know how important this information is to you, I'm going to run there right now and retrieve it."

"Don't you think that a bit unwise, Mr. Randazzle? They're saying up here on CNN that all the barrier islands up and down the coast have already been evacuated."

"Well, sometimes we have to go the extra mile for our clients, Cynthia. That's the kind of agent I am."

Cynthia was having a problem with Jason's magnanimity. She thought he was pretty much behaving like a complete imbecile, offering to run out to Shoreside just for her in the midst of an approaching Category 5 hurricane.

"I don't think that it's all that important, Jason. Why don't you wait until Sunday when the storm has passed?"

"A man's gotta do what a man's gotta do."

"Well, you certainly sound determined. If that's the case, then good luck to you, Mr. Randazzle."

"Thanks, Cynthia. I'll phone you when I get back. You're an hour earlier than we are, so I hope it won't be too late."

"No, please do call me. I'll be worried about you if you don't."

"Talk to you in just a bit. Goodbye."

"Goodbye."

Jason felt strangely proud of himself. It was the feeling a person has when he's standing underneath that elm tree with his aluminum ladder in hand about to rescue a kitten from the third limb up. Or the swimmer, just before diving in, who brings the two-year-old safely from the bottom of the swimming pool. Jason was now on some kind of heroic mission. He had to save his notebook from the deadly grip of Hurricane Emily. Of course Mrs. Parker was right, Jason was acting like a complete idiot.

With that, he grabbed his raincoat and the oversized golf umbrella he had won at last year's Shoreside Realty golf jamboree, and got into his dark blue, four-door Benz. He was on his way to recover his personal El Dorado. His bright red spiral, college-sized notebook had now become his damsel in distress.

It had been more than an hour since the search for his notebook began. When he went to start the Benz, after leaving almost every light in his car on the entire time, it was very slow to start. The battery had run down.

It finally started though, and Jason figured it would recharge itself during the run to Shoreside. He hit the automatic garage door opener and pulled out. He was on his way, flying down the deserted streets and empty highways on his valiant journey back to Shoreside Island. He was going to save that notebook if his very life depended on it.

589-2923
Sam Goodlet's Cell Phone

"Hello."

"Mildred, this is Sam calling you back. Can you hear me okay? My cell phone is breaking up. It must be from the storm."

"I can hear you okay, Sam," replied Mildred.

"I'm on the causeway. It took some convincing on my part to sway the Shoreside police to let me through the evacuation barricade. It's to a point where unless you can prove to them that it's a dire emergency, they won't let you drive on the island.

"When we come back out in a few minutes, if they even bother to ask you, just say that you're my aunt. If I hadn't told them that we're related, I don't think they would have let me back on."

"The police are saying that we've got an hour, maybe less, before the water rises too high and the roads become impassable. Are you all set to evacuate, Mildred?"

"Almost," answered a weary old woman.

"What's the matter?" Sam could hear the troubled tinge in Mildred's voice.

"It's Blackie. I can't find Blackie anywhere. All three of my cats have been climbing the walls since this hurricane started getting close to us and now Blackie's disappeared. It's so dark in the house with the electricity out and, well, you know how black he is."

"You've got to find him, Mildred. I'll be there in five minutes to pick you up. The water's rising quickly. Here at the causeway it's already washing over in a few low spots. Keep looking, Mildred, and I'll give you a hand when I get over there."

"Thanks, Sam."

Mildred hung up her telephone and went back to searching for her third cat. Buttons and Mittens were already in their respective carrying cases. They were both unhappy. Extremely unhappy. They were clawing at the inside walls of the cases as cats are prone to do when confined, and making weird cat noises. Low, guttural moans followed by loud, crazy screeches. Awful noises. Disturbing.

Mildred went back to looking. She had a large flashlight in her hand and she kept shuffling from room to room scouring every nook and cranny of her bungalow.

The single beam covered such a small area at any one time that Mildred realized just how easily Blackie could elude her.

With the electricity on, and all the 15-watt lightbulbs lit brightly, it was easy enough to spot a large black cat darting from under the sofa to under the sideboard to under whatever Blackie could squeeze under. But with nothing more than candlelight and the narrow beacon of a single halogen flashlight, Blackie could avoid capture forever. It was an unfair match up from the start - this shuffling octogenarian and a nimble, neurotic cat.

Blackie, amidst the screams of the other two cats and the plummeting barometric pressure, was convinced that Mildred Lee was going to kill him. He could hear the moans and cries of Buttons and Mittens from his hiding place behind the refrigerator and had no intention of ever coming out. Here, he was safe. Blackie somehow knew that Mildred couldn't move this large object away and reach down to snatch him. Snatch him and shove him in that tiny box that Tommy put him in when he went to the vet. To the doctor's where he went to get jabbed and pricked, needled and abused. Went to get tortured just like the other two cats were soon to be tortured.

The truth being that Blackie was no longer an ordinary house cat. He was a paranoid schizophrenic house cat, delusional and hellbent on staying out of the clutches of his sadistic owner. Catching Blackie in his present mind-set was impossible.

Mildred figured as much as she wobbled from room to room looking for her third cat. She knew that Blackie was always the hardest cat to catch, even for Tommy, who was young and quick. She tried to calm Blackie down by talking to him while she searched,

"Blackie, this is Mildred. Remember, I'm your friend. You had better come out and evacuate with me and Mr. Goodlet or you will probably drown. Sam thinks that the whole house is going to fill with seawater and you know how you hate to take baths, don't you Blackie. This will be worse than a bath, Blackie, because this will be salt water and lots of it. Come out, Blackie, or you will more than likely be left here to be totally submerged and die."

It wasn't a very effective approach, but it was done in the classic Mildred Lee style. Mildred was getting ever more anxious for Sam to arrive. He could find Blackie. He was such a nice man.

Just then Mildred heard a loud knock on the door. It surprised her. She had expected to hear the doorbell ring but then remembered that the electricity was out. The doorbell wouldn't ring even if Sam had pushed it, which he had tried to do without thinking when he first arrived.

"Coming. I'm coming," hollered Mildred at the top of her lungs, making Blackie crouch down even further behind the fridge.

Mildred slowly worked her way from the guest bedroom, where she was scouring the walk-in closet for the third time, to the front door. After undoing all the deadbolts and locks, she opened it to see Sam Goodlet standing before her in a driving rain.

"Come on in, Sam."

"Just a minute, Mildred. Hand me your flashlight for a second."

Mildred handed Sam her big flashlight and stood there as he ran off. She didn't bother to look to see where he was going, but figured that it must be important.

Sam took the flashlight and ran around to the back of the house. He wanted to see how far the water had come up the seawall behind the house. He needed to know approximately how much time they might have before the roads flooded. The last thing in the world that Sam wanted to have happen was for him and Mildred to be stuck on Shoreside when Emily came ashore. Even the thought of it sent shivers down his back.

As he reached the canal side of the house he focused the narrow beam on Mildred's concrete boat dock. It was gone. The beam landed on what should have been a large concrete patio dock but it was already submersed beneath tons of rising seawater. This wasn't good.

Then he shone the beam up along the edge of the seawall. Normally, the seawall sat two to three feet above an average high tide. This was anything but normal. The cap of the seawall was level with the seawater. In some lower spots, where the white, wind-driven foam of the salt water had built up, you couldn't even catch a glimpse of the seawall. It was sinking beneath an ocean gone mad. Quickly disappearing beneath a mountain of water.

Sam knew at once that there wasn't much time. He ran back to the front door to find it still wide open, with the aged Mildred staring blankly into the windy darkness. Mildred had actually hoped Blackie might bolt for the door. If he did, she was ready to snatch him. Sam walked in and closed the door behind him.

"Where did you go, Sam?"

"I went to the canal, Mildred. I needed to see how far the water has come up. We've got to hurry, Mildred. It's just a matter of time. Have you found Blackie yet?"

"No, Sam. I think that he might be behind the refrigerator. You know, where sweet little Buffy died."

"Oh, God."

Sam grabbed the last cat-carrying case and hurried to the kitchen. He could spare five, maybe ten minutes at most trying to capture Blackie. After that, the water would be in the swale of the apron that ran between Mildred's garage and the street. That concrete apron wasn't much higher than the top of the seawall cap and it would be the first to go under water. Five, ten minutes at best.

When Sam put the case down on the kitchen table he finally took a minute to look around. That's when he saw all the candles. Hundreds upon hundreds of candles. Mildred had spent all afternoon amidst the increasing winds and squalls placing half of her 600 candles around the house. As soon as the electricity had failed an hour and a half ago, she had meticulously lit them all.

Chills ran up Sam's spine as he looked around the room. There were 50, maybe 60 candles in the kitchen alone. Each of them had been carefully placed in a little dish, or a cup or a saucer. Some of them were in their own glass containers, and some of them were in elegant candle holders.

There were tall, thin candles like the kind people display during the Christmas holidays and short, scented candles that you buy at malls to put in bathrooms when you have guests over. Scores of designs, shapes and sizes graced Mildred's island home.

Cast in the light of these flickering candles, every room in the house took on a strange, ethereal aura. Like a scene from the *Exorcist*, or a documentary on voodoo, Mildred's home had suddenly taken on an eerie, undescribable sense of fear. Sam was now caught up in it, whatever it was. He turned off the flashlight, whose clear white beam didn't belong in this overwhelming candlelight, and stood in silent awe.

For an instant, it reminded him of his boyhood up north. He had once been an altar boy, standing in front of rows of votive candles that were placed on either side of the altar. Offering candles, each in a dark red glass, each and every candle burning for the sins of the men and women who lit them. The fallen souls who knelt before these glowing holdovers from the Dark Ages and whispered Hail Marys and the Lord's Prayer until their lips were dry and their voices worn thin as Eucharist wafers.

For Sam Goodlet, the mad alchemy of the moment was overwhelming; the two cats crying out from their cages near the front door, the wind howling and the driving rain smashing against the aluminum shutters, the smell of dozens of scented candles mixing with the relentless odor of cat urine, and the mysterious ochre glow of hundreds of flames left him frozen and speechless. He knew at that instant that death was near. His death.

Like a mountain climber 100 feet beneath the summit, caught in a blinding snowstorm, arms no longer able to pull himself up, legs buckling from unbearable cramps, Sam knew that he would never reach the top. He knew instinctively that he and Mildred would not make it off Shoreside Island.

Or like the airplane passenger. Feeling the unexpected, sudden jolt of the plane and knowing instantly that he or she would die. That rush of terror. Knowing that something has broken and that the plane will soon be falling from the sky. Tumbling. Breaking apart as it falls.

That horrible place in time when the victim sees the fiery blast of the gun his ex-wife is holding, or the stainless steel flash of that knife the thief raises for that final, fatal stab. A foreboding intuition that Sam never wanted to feel. The knowledge of impending doom.

Just then Mildred, who had been hobbling behind Sam all the way from the front door, made it into the kitchen.

"What's the matter, Sam. You look like you've just seen a ghost."

Her voice, still rich in her Chicago accent, snapped Sam back into the present. He was glad it had.

"Oh, nothing really, Mildred. Just a funny feeling. Where's Blackie's cage?"

"Right next to the flashlight you just set down on the kitchen table, Sam. Big as day."

"Thanks."

With that, Sam went over and started taking the six candles off the top of the refrigerator. He didn't want one of them falling over when he pulled the appliance away from the wall.

"Mildred, be prepared to grab Blackie if he tries to jump from behind the fridge when I start pulling it out. The commotion is bound to startle him."

"I'm ready for him, Sam."

Sam grabbed both sides of the small white refrigerator and started wrestling it away from the back wall. It came out easily, in part because it was one of those models that come with rollers on them. And in part because of all the replacement ice makers this fridge had received over the years. The rollers on this appliance were well used and moved freely. Sam pulled the fridge well away from the wall in less than a minute.

He then took the flashlight, leaned over the abutting counter and peered behind the fridge. Staring back at Sam, with his glowing red eyes, was a spooky, horrified Blackie. Mildred was right, he was hiding in Buffy's warm grave.

Sam pulled the fridge out even farther into the center of the kitchen, allowing enough room for him to crawl into the space where Blackie was crouched in terror. That took another minute.

Then Sam got on all fours, put the flashlight on the kitchen floor and went after Blackie. What followed should have been expected.

When Sam's hands finally took firm hold of the paranoid cat, Blackie exploded. It was like clutching a cherry bomb of claws and fangs. Blackie completely lost control. He bit Sam several times, clawed both of his wrists and tried to slash his face. But Sam wouldn't release Blackie, knowing how important saving this cat was to Mildred.

As he crawled back out, Blackie managed to land one quick blow to Sam's face. Blood followed the outline of the scratch marks immediately. When Sam rose to his feet, Mildred looked on in horror.

"Blackie, you're a bad cat," Mildred scolded. "A very bad cat."

Sam dropped Blackie in the carrying case and slammed the cover shut. Inside, Blackie went insane. He jumped and slammed against the top and walls of the cage, screaming like a wildcat. Mildred had never seen him behave like this. Not ever.

"Are you okay, Sam?"

"Just a few scratches, that's all, Mildred. A few little scratches."

"I've never seen Blackie behave like this. It must be that hurricane, Sam. That hurricane is making everybody act just crazy, isn't it?"

Sam sat in one of the kitchen chairs. He felt dizzy and disoriented. Nothing was going right. The candles, the screaming, frenzied cat, the rising water and incessant noise of the wind were all working on him, keeping him from finding his bearings in this world gone mad. He looked down at his wrists.

They were bad. Blackie had landed a half-dozen vicious bites and ten times that in scratches. Blood was streaming from both of his wrists as though he had just tried to commit suicide.

"Mildred, do you have anything that we can bandage up these hands and wrists of mine. They're bleeding pretty badly."

"Sure I do, Sam. I've got a half a dozen medical kits in the pantry."

Mildred went over and took out one of her larger kits. She placed it on the kitchen table beside Sam.

He opened it and took out the large Ace bandage that was generally used for sprained ankles or pulled muscles. There wasn't time to search for anything else. He undid the packaging and wrapped it around his left wrist, using the little metal pin to hold it from unraveling when he was through with it.

"Mildred, I'll need a second kit for the other wrist."

Mildred shuffled back to her pantry and removed a second first aid kit. She set that one next to the last one.

"Could you please give me a hand with this one?"

Sam was right-handed, and wrapping his right wrist and palm was going to take another set of hands. Mildred's arthritic hands fumbled with the bandage for what felt like forever. It wasn't working.

"Oh, the hell with it, Mildred. We've got to get out of here now."

He quickly undid the bandage from his right hand and stood. Sam picked up the carrying case holding Blackie and headed for the front door.

"Sam, you can't leave the fridge like that, it looks awful."

"Don't worry about the fridge, Mildred. No one is going to be showing your house any time soon, Mildred. I promise you that."

"But, Sam."

"Mildred, we've got to get out of here. There's a goddamned hurricane six hours away and we haven't got time to straighten out this little fucking house. Okay?"

Sam was getting angry. He had a right to be getting angry. His wrists were torn to shreds, his right cheek was bleeding and the noise of the incessant wind was driving him off the edge. Add to that an 84-year-old woman who suddenly cares about how her kitchen shows and it was more than any real estate agent is expected to handle. Even a good one like Sam Goodlet.

"Don't yell at me, Sam. You've got no right to yell at me like I was some kind of a child."

"I'm sorry, Mildred, but we have to get moving."

"Fine, I'll start blowing all the candles out and you put the cats and my two suitcases in the car."

The candles. Sam had overlooked the candles. They couldn't leave the house with any of these hundreds upon hundreds of candles burning. If the storm surge didn't reach the house, any one of these miniature fires could end up burning the house down. Mildred was right, all of the candles needed to be put out before they could abandon the house.

"Fine, but hurry."

Sam opened the front door and took Buttons and Mittens out first. They were still moaning and making bizarre cat noises but at least they weren't jumping around like Blackie was. He opened the back seat of his Olds and put both cats' cases in back. Leaving the back door open, he went around and opened the trunk to have it ready for the suitcases.

When he did that, the trunk light shone into the intense darkness surrounding him. Fifteen feet behind him, Sam could now clearly see that the salt water had risen dramatically since he pulled in. The driveway apron was buried under water. From this vantage point, it looked to be a least a foot deep. Maybe deeper.

"Oh, Christ." Sam mumbled to himself as he looked back toward the growing pool of ocean between Mildred's driveway and the road beyond. "This is bad. This is very, very bad."

There wasn't time to bemoan his situation longer than an instant. Time was everything. Seconds now mattered.

Sam rushed up the driveway, in through the front door and grabbed both the suitcases. He would toss them in the trunk and come back for Blackie and Mildred on his final run.

After closing the trunk he ran back to the house for the last time. The seawater was rising at an alarming rate. The water wasn't five feet behind the back of his car when he slammed the trunk shut and headed into Mildred's house, casting a scouring glance at his real estate sign as he did. It had a banner across the bottom saying, "CANAL FRONT!" It was worse than that now, thought Sam to himself, it had canals on all four sides at this point. It was an island.

When he got back inside the ranch, he called for Mildred.

"Mildred, we've got to go."

"I'm still putting out candles, Sam. There's so darn many of them ya know. Maybe you could give me a hand."

In the three minutes Sam had taken to load the two cats and the luggage, Mildred hadn't even managed to put out all the candles in her master bedroom. It was understandable enough. It had taken her all afternoon to set them out and an hour and a half to get them all lit. There was no way on earth that she could extinguish them all in three minutes.

Sam joined her. He ran into the kitchen and started putting out candle after candle after candle. Some he blew out, some he pinched out, some with the fingers on his right hand and some with the fingers on his left hand. It was taking forever. Forever is what neither Sam nor Mildred had.

Minutes went by. Candle after candle was extinguished. Both of Sam's thumbs and index fingers were blistering from the repeated pinching of the countless candle wicks placed between them. It was terribly painful.

Sam had grabbed a second flashlight just before he finished dousing the last half-dozen candles. Mildred was still putting out the last three candles in her bedroom when Sam yelled to her.

"Hurry, Mildred. We have got to leave."

"I'm going just as fast as I can, Sam." And she was. She would slowly, methodically place her cupped little palm behind each and every flame. Then, with her feeble breath, she would try to blow out the candles. Most of the time, her tired aim would miss the fire entirely, with her tiny puff passing above, below or on either side of the solitary fire. She was old, and the candle flames were young and spirited. Sam could put out ten candles to her one.

She finally extinguished the last candle and came bobbing out of her master bedroom. "I'm ready, Sam. Let's get going."

Sam grabbed Blackie, who had now quieted down some, and opened the front door. The wind was picking up. Whereas before it was steady and powerful, now it was howling. A long, steady scream of a wind, filled with pelting raindrops.

Mildred was just behind Sam as he put his foot out the front door without looking down. When it hit the seawater Sam knew. He knew instantly.

He looked down and saw that the storm surge had already reached the edge of the foundation. Knowing that, he figured that the swale in the driveway apron was now probably two, maybe three feet deep. He doubted that his low-riding Oldsmobile would clear it.

"Get in the car, Mildred," Sam shouted to her over the driving wind and rain.
"What?"
"JUST GET IN THE DAMN CAR!"

Sam and Mildred made their way down the driveway and as they did, the water became deeper and deeper. When they opened the two front doors, salt water poured into the floor of the Olds. Sam stuck Blackie between them and sat down to start the Olds. It started right up.

Sam knew that his only chance of making it onto the main road was to first pull up all the way to the garage and then slam the car into reverse, hopefully with enough momentum to blast through the expansive lake that had now formed behind them. Once on the higher grade of the roadway, they just might be able to drive to the causeway and get help from there. Sam remembered seeing a Humvee at the roadblock 20 minutes ago that could easily drive in these conditions. It drove so much higher than his Oldsmobile.

That thought reminded him of the problem. Twenty minutes ago. He had counted on this taking no more than five, ten minutes at most. It had taken double that. It had taken too long.

With those apocalyptic thoughts in his head, he pulled the Olds up right to the point where it nearly touched Mildred's garage door. Then, in the pouring rain, with his windshield wipers making that relentless ticking noise that wipers do in rains like this, he put the car into reverse and floored it.

When the Olds hit the waist-deep puddle, the water lifted up and floated the car. The air in the trunk and the passenger compartment proved too buoyant for the depth of the enormous pond Sam had just backed into. Once his tires failed to keep contact with the concrete, they simply spun wildly out of control. The momentum took the car six or seven feet into the swale and ended.

With the tires off the pavement, the big eight-cylinder engine raced wildly. It raced while the car floated helplessly in the salt water. They weren't going to make it to the road. Sam had somehow known that when he first stood in that strange, candlelit silence a half an hour ago.

Death was surrounding them, like the darkness and the wind-driven rain. It was no longer a question of why? It was only a question of when.

911
Earlier; The Police Barricades

"I'm sorry sir, but we're not letting anyone back onto the island at this time." The highway patrolman leaned into the open passenger-side window of Jason's wet Mercedes. The highway patrolman had his law enforcement act going full tilt. Bright yellow raincoat, glasses and a voice like Charlton Heston. It was his finest hour, the entire "To Protect and Serve," thing in spades. Hurricanes tend to bring out the cop in cops.

Jason had prepared for this. "I understand, and I appreciate your concern for my welfare, officer, but I have to get back onto Shoreside."

"Why's that?" asked the cop who sounded not unlike Moses.

"My sister might still be out there. She's a paraplegic. She was supposed to be taken off the island by that nonprofit group, you know, Friends of the Island, but I just phoned them and they thought that I had evacuated her. You have to understand, since the accident, she's the only family I have left."

Jason was lying. He didn't even have a sister. All he had was a mother. A very weird mother whose husband had walked out on her 36 years ago when Jason was just a boy. He knew that the police wouldn't let him across the causeway just to retrieve his personal money machine, his bright red spiral, multisectioned, $3.47 college-style notebook, so he had concocted this deplorable lie on his way to the barricades.

He had rehearsed the script so often over the last 15 minutes that he believed it himself. By the time he ran into this *Ben Hur* imitation, Jason felt that he loved his crippled sister. He continued...

"The accident was terrible, you know. Her husband, my two nieces and my mother were all taken from me that same afternoon.

"You probably remember it. That minivan accident that happened up on Highway 41. Remember, about two years ago?"

The patrolman did vaguely remember that accident. It had been a bad one, making all the local television news that night and headlining the following morning's newspaper. Jason had thought that the highway patrolman might recall it. In fact, he had counted on it. Everyone had died except the driver, and she was left paralyzed for life.

Of course, none of them was even remotely related to Jason R. Randazzle.

He had only remembered the tragedy on his way down and thought that it was his best ticket through the police barricade. Saving his paraplegic sister from the hands of Hurricane Emily. Great stuff. Who wouldn't let you past the barricades for heroics like this?

"Yeah, come to think of it, I do remember hearing about that one. Nasty mess. Even the semi's driver was hurt. That was your sister driving, huh? Tough break. Are you sure she didn't get off the island any other way?"

"No, I'm not sure, and that's the problem. I've been trying to reach her all afternoon and evening but her line has been busy. I've even had the Sprint operator interrupt the line to try to get through but it's impossible. There's something wrong with the telephone system in her condominium building. It's probably due to the storm.

"My sister lives alone in a small apartment complex just west of Shoreside Drive. I've got to find out if she's there. I'll never be able to live with myself if I don't. It won't take me but 20 minutes to find out if she's trapped there in her home. If she is, then I'm saving her life and I'll be back here in..." Jason looked down at his Rolex, "25 minutes max. If not, in less than that.

"You just have to let me through," pleaded this smooth-talking salesman.

"Well, under the circumstances."

The cop buckled. Jason was way too damn good for a highway patrolman's feeble defenses. Charlton Heston himself would have let Jason through. Jason could have probably sold either of them a condo in town had he a little more time. But he didn't.

"Well, you get in and get right back out. They say the storm surge from this hurricane is going to start hitting us hard in the next hour or two. After that, this causeway will more than likely be under a couple feet of water. There's no saving either of you then."

"Thanks, officer."

"Good luck to you, sir."

With that, the officer waved Jason Randazzle through, opening one of the barricades just wide enough for his dark blue Mercedes to slip onto the causeway and the barrier island beyond. Jason had done it, he had lied his way back to the office to retrieve his notebook. The rest was a piece of cake.

As Jason approached Shoreside he noted how dark it was. The power on Shoreside had been out for hours, taken out by falling limbs and flying palm fronds. Somewhere along the north end of the island, hundreds of hand-lit candles burned inside Mildred Lee's two-bedroom ranch, but aside from that and a few emergency lighting systems that hadn't yet burned out their backup battery systems, the island was as dark as it was back in the Stone Age. Darker.

Only the blue, red and orange flashing lights of the emergency vehicles maintaining the barricade behind him shone into the all-encompassing darkness. As he sped toward Shoreside, those lights soon faded behind him.

Now, in the driving wind and light rain, only his headlights and the dim glare of his instrument panel offered him any comfort.

Jason had never seen a darkness as thick as the darkness that was swallowing Shoreside Island that night. By this time, the storm bands had been shoved tightly together, blocking even the faintest trace of starlight from hitting the battered palm trees and Australian pines far, far below. Everything was black, as black as the face of terror.

The office of Shoreside Realty was two miles down Shoreside drive on the left hand side of the street. When Jason pulled in, his headlights flashed across the building, allowing him to see that all of the hurricane shutters were up. Even the back door, which was accessible earlier, had now been securely covered.

"Oh, Christ," swore Jason as he swung the car around to shine its headlights on the back door. "I forgot about these goddamned shutters."

He parked his Mercedes in such a way as to allow the headlights to shine on the back door of the office. He figured that it was the easiest storm shutter to remove. He turned off the car and took his keys to open the trunk to get that small tool kit that comes with every new automobile. The standard-issue tool kit, with all the cheap, useless tools in it. Screwdrivers that never fit anything, pliers that slip. Placebo tools.

Luckily, the Mercedes headlights were designed to stay on even after the ignition keys were removed. It was German engineering at its finest, thought a fortunate Jason Randazzle. He flipped them on the high beams before getting out of the car and opening the trunk.

He was going to need a pair of pliers to loosen all the wing nuts that held up the sheet of half-inch plywood covering the back door. He knew Al Jensen, the maintenance man who did all the repairs for Shoreside's rental division, would have done his job by tightening those wing nuts to a fault. Jason's wrists were weak, accustomed to little more than taking down names and numbers, and because of that, Jason knew he would need a pair of pliers to undo them.

Even with the pliers, removing all nine of the wing nuts from the studs was a daunting task. The quarter-inch bolts that came out from around the frame of the door were well rusted, and Jason soon discovered that he needed the pliers for almost every turn of the wing nuts. It was taking forever.

"Why couldn't management spring for electric hurricane shutters?" muttered a frustrated salesman. "Too damn cheap, that's why," he answered his own question. It was the correct answer.

After a ten-minute struggle, Jason pulled the heavy piece of unpainted exterior plywood away from the door and set it to the side. He unlocked the deadbolt and the door handle and went inside. He had counted on the backup lighting system to get him to his office should the power already be knocked out on Shoreside. But the old batteries in that system hadn't been replaced since Elinor Braun had installed it four years ago. Corrosion had taken its toll. The backup system was defunct. The batteries dead.

Jason ran to the trunk of his Mercedes and got his emergency flashlight. It hadn't come with the car, but he had purchased it nearly a year ago when tropical storm Kandee hit the islands. When he pushed the top button to turn it on, it too failed to respond. He hadn't checked the batteries in the flashlight since last year. Inside, they looked like a junior high school science fair project demonstrating common household forms of toxic waste. The two inexpensive Eveready D-cells were all greenish brown and fused together. They were both as lifeless as the soil around the Love Canal. Useless.

He put down the dead flashlight and went to the passenger side of the car. Maybe I've got a lighter, or some old matches in the glove box, thought the clever salesman. He rifled through his glove box for the second time that night and came up empty-handed. Jason didn't smoke. It was a long shot to think that he might find a lighter or any matches in there, but it was worth a try.

Things weren't going as planned and Jason knew it. Leaving his headlights on high, he dashed inside and decided to try to find his office in the dark. He figured it couldn't be that difficult. After all, he had walked in through the back door a million times before, and he knew where his notebook was probably lying once he got back to his ten-by-ten cubicle.

It would have been easier with a flashlight, or a lighter at the very least, but he had come up empty-handed on both counts. He would have to relax, take a deep breath and go in blind. Just as blind as cold calling.

To understand the overwhelming task Jason Randazzle now faced, a person has to understand the layout of Shoreside Realty's office complex. Originally, back in the late 1960s, the office was a small 1,200-square foot building just east of Shoreside Drive, the main drag that runs up and down the island. In 1974, due to the increase in sales agents, a long hallway was built between the first expansion building and the original office.

The new addition was only 750 square feet and held four small offices and a small lobby area for the increased sales force. In 1981 a second small building was added, with a second hallway coming from both the other offices.

Over the following years, two more offices were built and the company acquired a small fabric shop that sat across the old driveway to the north. All six of these buildings now connected in a curious maze of hallways, foyers and a reception area near the front door. Finding your way around Shoreside Realty's convoluted floor plan was challenge enough in broad daylight. Now, in the pitch blackness of an approaching hurricane, it became a bit like entering those tunnels that run helter skelter through the belly of the great pyramid at Giza, or the catacombs under the streets of Rome: dark, mystical and smelling of death.

That's what lay ahead of him. Jason Randazzle had to work his way down three hallways, past the little snack area and the second foyer to get to his office. Because the hallways were narrow, there were no pictures hung on them or any other tactile landmarks that could help him find his way; it would all come down to remembering how many footsteps he took on his way into work every morning. It would all come down to rote.

Jason started into the formidable maze cautiously. He knew that he had to move slowly to avoid running into a wall on any of the four 90-degree turns he had to make to reach his office. Using his hands in the same way that a blind person might, he slowly, cautiously, worked his way deeper and deeper into the nefarious labyrinth.

He kept count of his footsteps and turns along the way, knowing that keeping track would come in useful on his journey out. Because he was being careful not to trip, or injure himself in any way, it was taking longer than expected. Quite a bit longer.

Finally, he felt his fingers reach the end of the third hallway. He was in the old fabric shop, and his office with the third door on the right. Halfway down that final aisle he heard a tremendous noise coming from the roof of the building. It startled him to the point where he pulled away from the tactile security of the wall and looked toward the roof, where the noise was coming from. It sounded as if the roof itself was about to rip off.

Unbeknownst to Jason, a sudden gust of wind had just sheered off Shoreside Realty's sign, sending it tumbling across the rooftop of the complex. It was a large, plywood sign with the company's logo and name painted on it. It made one hell of a racket as it headed toward the main drag. The roof itself was fine. It wouldn't blow off until 2:35 a.m., when the second half of the eye wall charged the island.

Thank God, Jason reflected. I thought I was a goner. In a way, he was. When he had let go of his wall, he had really let go of his landmark. Jason also had failed to take note of the fact that he spun around when he first reacted to the startling noise. When he went back to finding his wall, it was now the other side of the hallway he was hanging onto.

There were eight offices in the old clothing store, with four offices across the aisle from each other, offset just enough so that none of them looked directly across the aisle into any other. Jason was now heading down toward the end of the building on the wall opposite his office.

Jason counted down the one last doorway in the overwhelming blackness, and slowly opened the door to his office. But it wasn't his office. It was across the hallway and up just a tad. Not that he had any way of knowing this in the pitch-colored world that surrounded him.

The office he did go into actually belonged to the newest member of Shoreside Realty's residential sales team, Mr. Elliot Pindle. He had been brought in to replace Jennifer Willow.

Not that Jennifer Willow had ever used this particular office before. No, when Jennifer left, one of the two Daves decided to take her office, Bob took

Dave's office and Bob left his office open for Elliot. It was a curious by-product of real estate companies, this nearly constant office shuffling. It was standard operating procedure. Musical chairs.

Elliot, before he decided to give real estate a try, had been a clerk at the local 7-11. Everyone who came in kept telling him that, with his good nature and charming smile, he should be in real estate. He had never considered that everyone who came into the local 7-11 on Shoreside Island couldn't afford to own anything on Shoreside Island. For the most part, his customers were construction workers, housekeepers and service workers. They could barely afford to make the rent.

Still, encouraged by all their comments, Elliot had plowed ahead with their plans for his future. After taking all of his real estate courses and passing the state exam with a 93, he came to work for Elinor and the other real estate professionals at Shoreside Realty. Keeping Jennifer Willow's story in mind, he tended to shy away from selling vacant land. Probably a wise decision.

Elliot, in an effort to succeed, had decided to copy those things he noted that other successful agents did to make themselves successful. He attended seminars like the two Daves attended, he sat open houses like Marlene Flannigan did, and he kept a dark blue spiral notebook just like Jason Randazzle did. Dark blue being the operative difference here.

Since all of the offices were basically identical, Jason had little trouble finding his desk once he got inside. Make that Elliot's desk. Then, by fumbling around the top of his beige Formica desktop, he had little trouble finding his bright red, college-style, multisectioned spiral-bound notebook. Wrong. It was Elliot Pindle's dark blue, college-style $3.97 (inflation) spiral-bound notebook. This is where the complete absence of any trace of light can play tricks on you. Color tricks.

Jason was ecstatic. He had done it. He had found his notebook and now all that was left was to walk out a door, take a left and make his way to the back door and onward toward home. Because he was not on the side of the hallway he thought he was, his left turned out to be a right. He made his way back toward the hallway, only to find it a dead end.

Coming to the dead end should have tipped Jason off, but it didn't. He clutched his notebook that much harder in his left hand and doubled back. Five minutes later he stood in the back doorway of Shoreside Realty, under the warm glow of a pair of slowly dimming headlights and looked down at his rescued prize. That's when it hit him.

He quickly noted the complete absence of red on the cover. Opening it up, he found little more than a handful of names and telephone numbers and an extensive collection of what is commonly referred to as doodles.

Lacking any money with which to buy property on Shoreside Island, not a single person who had told him that he should get into real estate back when he was working at the island's only convenience store had ever called him since Elliot received his license. It was a common occurrence in the real estate industry. Everybody tells you that you would be good at it until you actually start practicing real estate. Then they all pretend not to know you. Elliot wasn't the first to fall for that old ploy. Nor would he be the last.

Without any real client base to work from, Elliot had an excessive amount of time on his hands. When he got tired of playing computer solitaire, which he played roughly four hours per day, he would spend the rest of his day doodling in his notebook. Over the four months he had been with Shoreside Realty, Elliot had gotten pretty good at it. At doodling.

Jason Randazzle, now growing quite despondent, even thought that some of Elliot's doodle art was pretty impressive. There was this really sharp two-page spread of the Shoreside lighthouse that sat on the southern end of the island. It was done in blue ink with an assortment of fluorescent Magic Markers adding just a dash of color. Elliot had talent, Jason had decided around page 20. Real talent.

Now here is where a bad decision was made. Jason Randazzle, having failed to retrieve his notebook from the coal mine-like depths of Shoreside Realty's office complex, should have walked out that back door, started up his dark blue Mercedes, the same dark blue as Elliot's notebook by the way, and driven straight home. His dimming headlights would have been the cue from which such a prudent decision could have been made.

But that wasn't his style. He handled the situation just like another rejection. He had grabbed the wrong notebook and his only option was to go back into the building, find the right office and grab the right notebook. Nothing could stop Jason once he set his mind to a task. Well, almost nothing.

So that's what he elected to do. He put Elliot's doodle book down on the photocopier next to the back door and started his long journey back into the abyss. This time, the sign didn't startle him and within 15 minutes he was standing in the doorway with his 47 fresh leads and a notebook filled to near overflowing with 18,000 names, addresses and numbers. Filled to overflowing with money to be made. Easy money.

Back at the doorway, the very first thing he noticed was that it was now difficult to tell the color of his bright red, college-style, spiral notebook. That was because the once brilliant white lights that emanated from his Benz had slowly faded to a faint, distant yellow. Anyone who has ever walked back to his car in the parking lot of a movie theater knows what that color looks like. At least anyone who has ever left his lights on.

He ran to his Benz without so much as closing the door behind him and turned off his headlights. Sticking his car key in the ignition, he turned it to the right and prayed.

His prayers went unanswered. Totally unanswered. The engine turned over a half-dozen times in that slow, lethargic fashion that car engines do when you know they're not going to start. His Mercedes made that loud, grinding noise that all those pistons, camshafts, crankshafts and mechanical things make when they fail to engage. Like the sound you might expect from a dying elephant.

After trying one more time to start his Benz, the grinding noise dwindled to a simple, solitary click. Click. Click. He kept trying but the answer always came up the same. Click.

Jason was now in serious trouble. Two miles of tropical storm-force winds, rapidly rising salt water and a darkness as deep as a buried coffin separated him from the beginning of the causeway. The police barricades, provided they were still there when Jason made it, were two miles beyond.

He sat there for a minute and weighed his options. In essence, there were only two options left. One was to stay on Shoreside and hole up somewhere on the island and ride out the storm. Somewhere higher than 15 feet. Some condo or piling home away from the coast, which was sure to take a beating when Emily made landfall early Saturday morning. That option was riddled with pitfalls.

What if I find a place only to find it locked up tight? What if all the hurricane shutters are up and I can't get in? The office won't work; it will be totally under water if the storm surge hits 15 feet. No, option one won't work.

The second plan was to get going. Plan B was to brave the wind, water and weather and try to get back to the police barricades he had lied his way through a half an hour ago. Try to make it across the causeway before the rising ocean swallowed it.

That's my only hope. Running as fast as I can down Shoreside Drive and then crossing the causeway on foot. Four miles, give or take a block. If I run, I can make it in less than an hour. It's my only chance.

Wait. There's one more possibility. I can dial 911 on my cell phone and maybe they can send someone out in that military Humvee to come and rescue me. That's the best plan yet. That's my ticket back to the mainland.

Jason pulled out his cell phone and flipped it open. For a brief instant, the little battery signal looked like it was sitting at 60 percent. Plenty of power. As he punched in 911 and pressed send, he watched in horror as the battery signal fell rapidly. Fell to zero. He hadn't given a thought to plugging it in his lighter on the way out, so it had been left on since this morning.

Jason Randazzle was having a bad battery day. The emergency lights, his corroded flashlight, his car battery and now his cell phone. It had something to do with his karma, the negative force field he enjoyed living in, but Jason was too self-enthralled to take note of it. He would have to hoof it to safety.

305-554-9091
Room 427, a Miami Motel

Barbara Silberman sat on the edge of her double bed and watched the television screen in horror. She knew.

This time her fears were not unfounded. She and her husband, Stanley, had fled the island on Thursday morning, leaving the vast majority of her belongings in their new spec home on Sabal Sands Lane. They had just listed the house last week. The ad copy kept echoing through Barb's mind as she watched Emily's eye zero in on Shoreside: "Just steps from the beach."

A week ago, that ad copy made her phone ring three times in one afternoon alone. Now her near beach location, with a 15-foot storm surge certain to inundate Shoreside, smacked of trouble. Being near the beach was a real selling point up until Emily took the shine off the old real estate maxim, "location, location and location."

With a Category 5 hurricane bearing down on a vulnerable barrier island, values had inverted. The absolute worst place to own property on the island was Gulf-front, with the storm almost certain to damage or decimate every home or condominium complex lining that seven-mile stretch of sand. The next worst was being near the beach, and the best location was as far inland as possible. Hopefully, some of the interior homes would survive the storm, sheltered by the trees and buildings that stood between them and the open ocean. Hopefully.

Barb and Stanley knew that their 200 yards from the beach wouldn't be enough. Because of it, their clever ad copy, *"Just steps from the beach,"* took on an entirely new meaning. Barb listened to the newscaster announce that the National Hurricane Center had just officially upgraded Emily to a Category 5 hurricane as she mentally rewrote last week's copy to *"Just steps from disaster."* It was good copy, but it was doubtful anyone would call on that ad.

That's what Barb was worried about more than the loss of her new house on Sabal Sands Lane. She was worried about what was going to happen afterward. Five years ago she had sold a single-family home in Osprey Greens to a retired agent and her husband from Cutler Ridge, Florida. They had owned and operated a small real estate company there when Andrew made landfall in August of 1992.

Now, as Barb and Stanley sat there, listening to the newscaster revise their projected storm surge from 15 to 17 feet because of Emily's increased wind velocity, Barb remembered the stories.

After Andrew decimated south Dade, real estate sales virtually stopped. For the first year after the storm, it was all about insurance claims. Eleven different insurance companies collapsed under the strain of thousands upon thousands of claims. Shortly after the storm, another 40 companies pulled out of Florida entirely. The losses were staggering. More than $30 billion was needed to rebuild, re-roof and reconstruct entire neighborhoods.

Buying into this quagmire of claims and counter-claims was unthinkable. Selling became a question of selling what? A pile of sticks in a yard stripped of vegetation down a street without a street sign in a subdivision reduced to 100,000,000 tons of rubble?

Condominiums didn't fare much better. Insurance coverages were often insufficient to cover the higher replacement costs, leaving condominium owners at risk for the additional funds needed to rebuild their units. Lawsuit followed lawsuit as questions arose from the rubble as to who was to pay for what? Who would cover the cost of the new pool? What was considered common ownership and covered by the association, and what was covered by the individual owners? Lawyers were having a field day. Realtors were starving to death.

Barb's customers said it took years before things settled back to anything approaching normal. The first few years after the storm were lean times for the men and women who had made their living buying and selling property from Cutler Ridge to Homestead. Very hard times.

"It'll be worse on Shoreside," said Barb.

"What do you mean?" asked her husband, Stanley.

"The build-back; it will be worse on Shoreside than it was for Andrew."

"What makes you think that?"

"The codes, the questions of nonconformity, the changes and reductions in density, the new state regulations, the revised coastal construction control line. All of it will be worse than it was in 1992."

Stanley didn't respond. He watched the latest satellite image of Emily for the hundredth time that night and tacitly agreed with Barb. She was right, the rebuilding of Shoreside Island after a catastrophe like the one that was about to occur would be worse than the disaster that struck Dade County in 1992. The issues involved had become more complex, the ramifications of a storm this size were mind-boggling.

Older condominium complexes that had residential densities of 16 units an acre would, at rebuild, be forced to comply with the new regulations of eight units per acre. Ground-level, pre-1979 complexes would have to be rebuilt on pilings. The legal quagmire surrounding these issues could take years to resolve. Would the first-floor unit owners become the first-floor owners again once the building was rebuilt on pilings? Would the state grant a blanket rebuilding waiver on the new density reductions and, if not, who would compensate the unit owners for their losses? The insurance would cover the construction cost of the loss but that might be $80,000 on a condominium whose value could hit $500,000. If the owners weren't allowed to rebuild, who would pay the $350,000 mortgage?

Stanley, who kept thinking through 1,000 different impossible scenarios finally said something.

"It will be worse, Barb. Way worse."

Then Barb said something that took them both by surprise.

"Let's get out, Stanley. Let's settle our claim, sell the lot for what we can and quit."

Stanley smiled. The thought of packing it in had crossed his mind more than once over the last few years.

"Where do you want to move to?"

"Taos, New Mexico," said Barb.

"Yeah, Taos works."

870-0710
Jason's Dead Cell Phone

The first mile of Jason's exodus from Shoreside went well. Although the wind was blowing wildly, gusting at times to better than 60 miles an hour, the flying debris consisted mostly of leaves, small sticks and garbage. The darkness was more trouble than the incessant wind. The darkness, like the air itself, was thick and all-pervasive.

Jason had left his dark blue Mercedes behind, knowing that just after midnight his $65,000 automobile would be submerged under a deluge of salt water. Totaled. Another expensive victim of this powerful force of nature. Not a problem, thought Jason as he hurried down Shoreside Drive. It's insured.

The only things Jason had with him were his wallet and his notebook. He had left his dead cell phone back in the car. No sense carrying a lifeless cell phone with me back to safety, he had reasoned. It too, Jason knew, would soon drown in the rising sea. It too, was insured.

No, the first mile went well. It was the second mile that didn't. When Jason reached the halfway point to the start of the causeway, right across from the island's only 7-11, he came to an impasse. Some time over the last hour, while he was feeling his way, like Helen Keller, through the maze of offices at Shoreside Realty, a large pine had toppled over, blocking most of the road. That, by itself, wasn't a problem. Jason could easily have walked around it.

But when it fell, it took a set of power lines down along with it. In the darkness, Jason could barely see them, but he could see well enough to note that they were there. They were lying everywhere, like thin black snakes coiled on a damp roadway. Since the power throughout the island was down, Jason was 99 percent certain that all those high-power electric lines were dead.

But what if they weren't? Jason looked down at his wet penny loafers and looked back at the tangle of power lines that were spewed about everywhere before him. If one of them were still alive, he could easily be fried alive trying to get through. The wet shoes, the damp highway and the ability of the high-voltage electricity to arc in these conditions would mean certain death. Death by electrocution. It was that remaining one percent that made Jason reconsider.

He would have to double back. He could head down the island half a block, take Turner Street one block down, then head up Whiteside Boulevard, back up and onto Shoreside via Palmer Street and then along Shoreside Drive to the causeway. Ten minutes longer by taking the alternate route. Longer, but safer.

It was when Jason took that unexpected detour that all hell started breaking loose. He had made it to Whiteside just fine, with the blowing refuse and limbs proving to be little more than a constant nuisance to him. But upon heading down the tree-lined Whiteside Boulevard toward the intersection with Turner Street, a large branch broke off high in the canopy of one of the tall Australian pines and clipped him on the way down.

In the windy darkness, Jason could neither hear nor see the branch coming. It just slammed into his right side without warning. The force of the large branch instantly knocked him onto the pavement. It had hit his right shoulder, just missing his neck. The branch was four inches across and seven feet long. Had it hit him in the head, it would have snapped his neck vertebrae instantly. It would have been over.

But it had missed his head and landed squarely on his right shoulder. Jason could feel the bones in his shoulder blade crushing as he fell, and by the time he hit the ground, his right hand couldn't respond in time to break the fall. His shirt sleeve tore off and his right arm was useless, with all the tendons and muscles up in the shoulder torn and dislocated.

It was as though someone had just taken a ten-pound sledgehammer, lifted it high over his head and come down on his right shoulder blade with it. The pain shot through him like fire. His cherished notebook, which he was clutching desperately with his right hand, holding it rolled up like a small newspaper, flew out of that hand the second the tumbling branch struck him. He nearly passed out from the overwhelming shock of the impact. It hurt beyond measure.

Now, he was lying there, in the middle of an empty boulevard, with the tree limb next to him and his notebook sponging up the rainwater from the pavement beside him. For the moment, it was too painful to get back up. Far too painful.

He let his pockmarked face feel the wet, equally rough asphalt. He was lying half on his stomach, with his left side touching the street and his right side up, not holding any of his body weight. The thought of putting any pressure on his right shoulder at this moment sent him into near panic. Jason knew that the damage was extensive. If he had fallen directly on it, he would have blacked out.

As he lay there on the abrasive asphalt, he watched his notebook disintegrate before him. First, it soaked up all the surrounding dampness, as paper does when it touches water. Then, with the heavy cover holding firmly to the ground, he watched the wind tear page after soaking page away, the wet paper easily ripping off the spiral binding. In a few minute's time, it was completely gone.

Gone were his 18,000 names and numbers. Gone were the 47 hot listing leads he was planning to start phoning come Monday. Page after page was now blowing down Whiteside Boulevard, and after that, up and down the back streets of Shoreside, carried away by the fury of Emily.

There was nothing Jason could do to save his notebook at this point. The only thing left was to try to save himself. Ten minutes later, with his body starting to go into shock, Jason Randazzle finally managed to get on his feet. He started limping down Whiteside in the same direction he had been traveling. He had only a half a block to go before taking a left on Turner Street. It seemed much farther.

By the time Jason turned toward Shoreside on Palmer Street, he saw it. The first rush of salt water had made it all the way up to the road grade. It was not what he wanted to see on this wretched, foreboding night. He knew as that first wave of seawater ran across Palmer Street that the swales and low spots along his planned evacuation route were now well under water.

With his feet sloshing through the salt water and his arm and shoulder in excruciating pain, his progress slowed. Before the sledgehammer took him down, Jason had been making good time. Now it was going slowly. Too slowly.

Every step was brutal. Time, it seemed, slowed down along with him. Everything entered that strange, inexplicable zone that occurs to people who are in terrible accidents. A zone where seconds last forever as cars collide, trains derail and injuries happen. Time in slow motion. Time before the end.

Jason finally made it to Shoreside Drive and turned right again toward the causeway. The wind was growing stronger. The flying debris, which, half an hour ago had been little more than a nuisance, was now a menace. The sticks had grown larger, even leaves striking his face at 80 miles an hour stung him like uncountable wasp bites. The twigs and leaves kept scratching and cutting his face and eyes. In the total darkness that surrounded him, ducking or avoiding any of this was impossible. The debris flew from the jet-black sky, sliced at his exposed arm and face and continued into the darkness beyond. It was as though he were being slowly murdered by shadows. Shadows made from razor blades, knives and rocketing hammers.

Jason noted that the hurtling debris now included pieces of tin roofs and plywood. The objects being rocketed through the air kept getting larger and heavier. Staying upright became a challenge, let alone making any headway.

Then the noise started. The noise that is the noise of hurricanes. Freight trains, jet engines, none of these describe the intensity of the noise. They just try to.

As the pressure continued to drop, his inner ears started to throb in pain. Everything was caving in around him, and Jason knew it. He was a tragic figure to behold, stumbling blindly down Shoreside Drive, his face bleeding, his left hand crossing his body holding his limp, damaged right arm and shoulder, his ears pounding and his heart telling him that it would soon be over. His heart telling him that he was not going to be able to reach the barricades. Not tonight. Not ever.

Two blocks farther down, Jason's progress ended. The storm surge had increased dramatically in the last ten minutes. It was now nearly up to his knees. On the far end of the island, Sam Goodlet was measuring how high it had come up the doorway without being aware that two other agents were also trapped on Shoreside. One of them, stumbling down the main drag, trying frantically to save himself. The other, overlooking an ocean gone insane, trying desperately to die.

In the knee-deep water, Jason had no way of seeing that another string of downed cables had fallen. This time, it was submerged telephone lines. They had snapped a half hour before under the strain of a falling Norfolk pine. As his footsteps were now down to tired shuffles, getting tangled in these hidden telephone lines seemed inevitable. The irony absolute.

He tried doubling back but it was no use. The more he turned and twisted to free himself, the more the vine-like telephone lines wrapped and tangled around his feet. Within minutes, they had ensnared him up to the point where he couldn't keep his balance any longer. He fell over.

Once fallen, the rest was inevitable. He tried to use his left hand to unwrap and free his two legs but that was impossible. Nothing could free him at this point. He was hopelessly wrapped up in the telephone lines with the rising tide rapidly gaining on him. The cuts on his face burned as the salt water rushed over it.

Ten minutes later, after struggling hopelessly to free himself, Jason was exhausted. He resigned, inhaling the dense, acrid taste of seawater. A minute later, his heart stopped. Jason Randazzle was a corpse. He had become the first Floridian to die at the hands of Hurricane Emily. They would find his body on Sunday, only guessing as to how painful and horrid his last few minutes must have been. They would unwrap his bloated body from the telephone lines and place it into one of those black plastic bags, zipping it tight before loading it into the emergency vehicle.

By 3:00 a.m. not a single page of Jason's prized notebook would remain intact. The phone calls he had promised to make on Monday would go unmade. Cynthia Parker would wait up until midnight in St. Louis awaiting a return call from Mr. Randazzle that would never come.

The fear Jason had sold all of the island owners over the last few days was real. Jason R. Randazzle had turned out to be its biggest purchaser.

A World Without Phones

Sam and Mildred were huddled around Mildred's battery-operated radio listening to the local announcers giving constant updates on Hurricane Emily. The water at their feet was ankle deep. Mildred's three cats were still in their cages.

To keep their incessant wailing and caterwauling from driving him mad, Sam had put the three cages in the guest bedroom. He put one of them on the highboy and two on top of the vanity, and covered them with some of Mildred's wool blankets to deaden the sound of their unrelenting shrieking. Then, in a final effort to silence these three crazy cats, Sam closed the door to the bedroom tightly behind him. He and Mildred had enough to deal with. Blackie, Buttons and Mittens only made a difficult situation worse.

Mildred's all-weather radio confirmed what their wet feet already knew. The storm surge was going to be much higher than originally predicted. At 11:00 that night, the National Hurricane Center in Miami had increased the estimated height of the storm surge from the original eight to ten feet to the present 12 to 15 feet. Possibly higher.

Sam had done the arithmetic 1,000 times in the last hour. The first-floor elevation of Mildred's ground-level ranch sat 9 feet above mean high tide. The house had your standard eight-foot ceilings. It was an older house and, as was often the case back then, the contractor hadn't bothered putting in an access ladder into the attic. It was just another cost-cutting decision that meant absolutely nothing to the builder 30 years ago. As fate would have it, that decision presently meant everything to the two people sitting around the kitchen table. Without an attic crawl space, they were trapped between the floor and the eight-foot ceilings.

"What are we going to do, Sam?"

"Pray, Mildred. We're going to pray."

Mildred knew that Sam was scared. Really scared. Nothing had gone well since they had backed his Oldsmobile into the salt water surrounding the house. After the engine finally stalled, Sam had one hell of a time getting his car door open, with the outside seawater pressing against it.

When he finally did manage to push the door open just a crack, the water started rushing in, nearly drowning Blackie and the other two cats in the back seat.

But that wasn't the worst of it. The worst of it was that Sam had failed to consider the locale of his cell phone as he struggled to open the car door.

It was in his right-hand pants pocket. Within 15 seconds of prying that car door open, it was totally submerged in salt water. Completely useless. Fried.

After wading to the other side of his Olds, rescuing Mildred and carrying her into the house, going back and getting all three cats, Sam realized what he had done. He realized that he had submerged his lifeline to a possible rescue. For an instant, the idea of not having a working cell phone didn't bother him. There was always the land line.

When he picked up Mildred's home phone a few minutes later, only to find it stone silent, he understood. He knew that both of them were now cut off. Totally cut off.

There wouldn't be any attempt to rescue them. By now, just past midnight with the storm only three hours from landfall, the emergency crews manning the barricades along the causeway were gone. The water there would be two feet deep. Even the military-style Humvee would have headed for higher ground.

Helicopters couldn't fly in these winds, now gusting to 90 miles an hour. Boats were worthless in these demented seas. Sam knew that no one was coming to save them. With rescue out of the equation, all that was left was prayer.

Prayer and the hope that the storm surge prediction would prove wrong. That the water would stop rising at 11 feet and not 17. At 17 feet, Mildred and Sam would run out of air. The two-bedroom, two-bath listed at $349,000 would become their watery grave. They would drown.

Going outside was unthinkable. The winds were hurling debris at speeds nearing 100 miles an hour. A small branch thrown at a person going that fast could kill him. A piece of roofing tin, torn off one of the many "Olde Florida" homes that adorned Shoreside Island, could slice a hand or an arm off a person like he was made of butter.

As if the winds weren't enough, there was the water now submerging the island. With that in mind, Sam got up and sloshed over to the front door to check the water level outside again. He could tell how high the surge had come up by noting where the water was presently squirting in along the tiny cracks on either side of the front door. The water outside was much higher than the ankle-deep water on the inside. The concrete block construction of the home was acting like a dam, keeping out the water from the massive storm surge.

Eventually, when the water level outside reached the aluminum hurricane shutters and the window openings they were covering, that would change. Seawater weighs nearly a ton per square yard. The thick concrete block appeared to be withstanding the pressure. The aluminum hurricane shutters would not.

Sam studied the seams along either side of the front door and noted that the water was spraying in just below the doorknob. The door, which opened out, was holding up better than Sam had expected. Eventually, it too would fail from the weight of the ocean against it. At its present rate of rising, the storm surge would hit the window sills within 15 minutes.

As he stood there with his flashlight studying the water squirting in along the door jam, he went through in his imagination what the next few hours might be like. When the deluge hit the windows, it would flood the house. The pressure on the outside of the concrete blocks would be equalized with the pressure on the inside. The water would flow freely into the house through all the open windows until it reached the drywall on the ceilings.

Somewhere along the line, it would simply be easier to inhale a breath of salt water than to continue to struggle to stay alive. Struggle with your face pressed against the sheet rock on the ceiling and your unsteady legs standing on the kitchen table.

Sam knew that Mildred would be the first to go. She wasn't strong enough, or tall enough to handle what would happen when the hurricane shutters, one by one, started buckling in, started failing, allowing the salt water to rush in and inundate their safe haven. Mildred simply wouldn't be able to keep standing as the tons of water came pouring in, causing all the wooden furniture to float around the rooms and the three howling cats to drown.

No, Mildred would die first, and there was little Sam could do to prevent it. The inflow of water would be overwhelming and chaos would ensue.

He could do little to help her as he tried to save himself. Tried to climb on top of the refrigerator, or stand on the kitchen table. All the while hoping and praying that the surge would stop at 15 feet, leaving him just enough air to breath as Emily marched inland, heading toward Orlando and then back to sea south of Titusville. Hope and pray. Hope and pray. Hope and pray. That's all that was left to the two of them. Hope and pray.

Time passed quickly.

Mildred Lee did die first, inhaling her first mouthful of seawater a little before 1:00 in the morning. Somehow Mildred Lee knew that it was meant to be. Thinking as she died that she had become one of the first casualties along Emily's march of death and destruction, she and Jason. The first of 847 people Hurricane Emily would kill during her brief journey to America.

Victims killed in stalled and flooded cars, or huddled in bathrooms that unexpectedly blew apart. Drowned and mortally injured, letting go of that stalwart live oak they were clinging to, surrendering to the silence they knew death would deliver. Eternal silence, far removed from the screaming noise of this cyclone.

Mildred could see her hurricane chart as she passed through the gates of the living into the land beyond. She saw Emily's tight eye hooking right into Shoreside, and could only guess where the track of the storm might go from there. She made note of how her ears hurt as the pressure continued to drop.

Just like a descending airplane. An airplane descending all the way to hell.

She thought of her three cats as she expired, her cats and her husband, and finally Mildred came to the realization that her death at the hands of Emily was inevitable. That her decades of paranoia about hurricanes could only have ended this way. That there was an element of karmic justice surrounding her final few moments on Earth.

Maybe Emily is my long-lost sister?

Now that she was surrendering to the force of the storm, Mildred Lee felt unexplainably at ease with herself. She felt unafraid. It was as though Emily had come to take her out for lunch and not to drown her and her three neurotic cats. Mildred harbored no bad will toward the storm at all in those last few minutes in her life. She felt at ease.

These storms, she thought, they are not evil. They are just a curious combination of wind, salt water and rain. The colossal cooling vents of the equatorial seas. As innocent as the showers they were ten days ago, falling on the thatched-hut roofs in Senegal and Sierra Leone. Falling on the dark-skinned people of Africa, 4,000 miles to the east. They are not monsters, or killers, or any of the names we unfairly lend them. They are the hand of God, thought Mildred as her lungs filled with the bittersweet taste of salt water. The work of the Almighty. As we all are. As we all are, she thought, as she died.

The storm surge from Hurricane Emily hit 18 feet, even higher in places.

Sam died a half-hour later, thinking of his wife and his family as he did. Hoping that they were all safe and secure on the mainland. Glad he had tried to save Mildred until the very end.

Thinking about what the Grinstead place must look like now. The exposed plywood siding ripped off by the relentless wind, the massive dead oak tree having fallen on top of the house an hour ago. Cutting the house in two with its fall, damaging the property beyond repair. Glad in a way. Glad that Bart and Dolores Hazelton wouldn't ever own it. Glad that Mr. and Mrs. Grinstead would survive the storm, safe and incapacitated in their institutions.

They'll get better, Sam thought as his face pressed up against the skip-troweled surface of the white ceiling. Pressed hard against it, looking for space to breathe. They'll both snap out of it eventually and they'll start over. They'll collect the insurance money, sell the lot and move somewhere up north, where winter comes every year and the insect world is held in check. Sam prayed for them as he realized there was no more reason to pray for himself.

He didn't regret trying to save Mildred, or wish for a moment that he had turned back at the barricades along the causeway earlier. He loved Mildred Lee the same way he had loved his Great Aunt Claire. He would have done exactly the same thing for Mildred tomorrow if it came to that. Service was just a part of his nature. Going the extra mile. Getting the job done.

Sam was like that: He was a good Realtor up until that final heartbeat.

Thinking of his customers, hoping that they were better off than he was at the moment. Inhaling that first mouthful of seawater and choking on it. Thinking that life had been good to him. Wishing that it hadn't been quite this short. And then vanishing.

578-5654
Attorney Strunk's Office

At exactly 12:27, the storm surge that inundated Shoreside Island reached to the top of attorney Bruce Strunk's four-drawer legal-sized filing cabinet. It was your typical beige office filing cabinet, filled with file after file of court settlements, closing statements and legalese. Nothing out of the ordinary. Just your usual legal excess of paperwork. More "Form Nazi" fodder.

The water had been rising steadily since first pouring onto the island around 9:00. It had found its way in through the doors and windows of Strunk's office, meeting little resistance along the way. Like most of the older commercial office space on Shoreside, it was a ground-level building. The island hadn't experienced a storm surge of this magnitude since the great Miami hurricane of 1926.

The memory of that cataclysm was too distant to be of any concern to the developers who had discovered Shoreside Island in the mid 1960s. Ground-level buildings were easy to throw up and no one was around to offer any testimony to the insanity of placing most of your commercial real estate in a potential bathtub. Besides, ground-level buildings were cheaper to build. Pour a slab, toss up some block and truck in some trusses, and you were ready to start signing leases. Cheap is good.

Strunk and his staff had little time to even consider taking all their innumerable files with them Friday morning when they closed up the office. They knew about the projected storm surge but there were far too many files, briefs and law books to evacuate even if they had been given a week's notice.

They took what they needed and left the rest for their insurance company to sort through later, should the seawater actually rise high enough to flood their office building. They took the backup tapes for all three of their computers, their escrow checkbook, some particularly active case files and their personal belongings. The rest would have to weather the storm.

Included among those items not worth jamming into the crowded trunk of Strunk's 1972 bronze Benz coupe were two inexpensive watercolors. Strunk had grabbed the file, now two inches thick and jammed with memos, expert depositions and court orders, but elected to leave the paintings behind. It made sense. The combined value of the two paint-by-number watercolors was less than a ten-spot. Besides, reasoned Strunk as he held the two paintings in his hand just before heading off island, both of them sucked.

He laughed to himself. The legal battle over which painting was the original and which was the forgery had now run to $43,000. It was still up in the air as to who was going to foot the bill. Possibly Shoreside Realty, possibly the buyers, probably Linda Hinkle but that matter was still open for debate. The primary issue was still unsettled.

The Italian specialist had failed to distinguish the original from the imposter, as had the watercolor expert from the Museum of Fine Arts in Boston. Both specialists had enjoyed a glorious week on Shoreside Island with their respective squeezes; walks along the beach at midnight, dinners at Viscaya, sex every morning, but both had failed at telling which painting was which.

That's why Strunk chuckled to himself as he closed his office door and left the two paint-by-numbers to fend for themselves in the face of Emily. They deserved it, the whole lot of them. They deserved a $43,000 legal fee over two painting that most adults would be embarrassed to put up in a playroom. They deserved being charged $400 an hour for behaving exactly like the five-year-old who had painted one of these two paintings more than a decade ago. It was the insanity of it all that made Strunk laugh. The implausibility of it.

Hell, he thought as he started his Benz and drove toward the safety of the mainland, that's not even the tip of the iceberg. He had seen so many real estate transactions fall apart over the most idiotic of reasons that nothing could surprise him at this point. There was the time the seller came back after closing and took half the furniture they had just sold to the buyers away in a U-haul. Took it back to Miami and resold it to a consignment shop. From there, the buyers had to trace and recover the furniture from Homestead to Boca Raton. That one took two years to clear up.

There were hundreds more. The fight over the Italian mirror that damn near killed a $400,000 sale. The seller who took down the mirrored wall, the buyer who wanted the two cars that were in the garage on the day of closing to convey along with the property. The list was endless. People behaving like children. Children with money. Too damn much money.

When the salt water finally hit the bottom painting, which was the original by the way, it didn't float away at first. The weight of the forgery on top of it kept it from floating off. What happened first was that the colors started melding and fusing together, as watercolors tend do when they get wet.

If either Dr. and Mrs. Asp or the Larsons would have been there to see it, they both might have been pleasantly surprised. As the inexpensive pressboard that the paintings had been done on became saturated, the tans, dark greens and blues gently lifted from the painting and slid into each other. Three minutes into this process, the bottom painting was stunning.

It had taken on that rare quality of delicate tones and colors indicative of the

French Impressionist movement in the late 19th century. Had the specialist from Boston seen the work at that exact moment, he would have wanted to meet Rose Larson. He would have wanted to see more of her work, thinking that she was a child prodigy.

"It has an astute spontaneity of color and texture reminiscent of Monet. Expressive, but not overly complex. The work of a young genius, no doubt," the specialist would have remarked. Remarked with that snobbish affectation that the fine art crowd requires of their art critics.

Four minutes into the soaking, Rose's painting had jumped almost 100 years into the future. By then, the colors had grown vague and opaque, similar to the style of Mark Rothko of the New York School of modern art. The faint pastels seemed to return to the abstract wholeness of the color field, symbolizing a transcendent unity that combined surrealism with abstract expressionism. A superb example of contemporary art.

A few minutes after that, both paintings, which were now floating and free, seemed more like part of a montage piece by Robert Rauschenberg. A wonderful work completed in 1955 and presently on display at the Metropolitan Museum of Modern Art. Beautiful in its passion, and an expression of visual possibilities. A piece that typified Rauschenberg's work, combining the use of commonplace objects and painting in a form of pop expressionism.

Ten minutes later, with both paintings rubbing against the low ceilings of the office, they disintegrated, becoming nothing more than wads of faintly colored cardboard in an office full of similar wads.

The argument over which was which would never be settled. Shoreside Realty and Linda Hinkle would end up splitting the bill, and both parties would finally agree to accept that lighthouse painting. The exact same painting they had been offered a dozen times before. Down deep, they both preferred that painting.

It was a lucky break for Jennifer Willow, who ended up selling them both the same print for full retail. Funny how things work out. Very funny.

870-2162
Bartlett's Cell Phone

The darkness had descended. From his vantage point on the top floor of the "A" building, Adam Bartlett had watched it arrive. It was as though the wind had carried the darkness in, blowing it across the island like a thick black smoke. By 8:00 that evening, it had suffocated the final remnants of daylight, smothering all traces of hope as it did.

Now, nearing midnight, the darkness was absolute. A solid black sky circled the condominium, engulfing it in a nothingness darker than Adam had ever known. In this near total absence of light, Adam's other senses intensified. He could feel the cold beads of sweat running down his glass when he reached to take a sip of his Scotch. He could hear the wind, howling like a billion lonely wolves in the void beyond.

By this time, the wind had become hysterical. The noise it made as it drove up from the south was total. It was the noise of hell. The sound of Lucifer's blasphemy: deafening and godless. Adam was terrified. The fear of dying had overtaken his desire to die. In this darkness all-encompassing, he could feel the very pulse of death.

Adam had left the front porch half an hour ago, drunk and afraid. He knew that it was too late to reconsider his decision but every minute, every second, he wished inside that it wasn't. Now that death was growing nearer, riding on that howling, screaming wind, it frightened him more that he had anticipated. He wished that he had taken those nine sleeping pills the night before, vanishing silently in some drunken slumber. That demise would have been easier. That would have spared him these hours of terror. Spared him this incessant noise.

He sat on the new sleeper sofa that backed up to the common wall between the two apartments. The sleeper sofa with the name tag and care instructions still dangling from one end. The epitome of model furniture: new to a fault. Even in the blackness, Adam could still faintly see the pages of his Sanderling file whirling about on the screened lanai. He had left the file out there when he came into the apartment an hour ago. The file was useless to him now. Useless to everyone.

His liter of Scotch, now stuffed inside the ice bin, held one last tall one in it, no more. The gathering noise outside reminded him that he might not get to that last drink. The noise that grew louder and louder with every passing minute. It demanded his undivided attention. It insisted upon it.

As Adam watched, a sudden gust ripped away all the screening on the front porch, taking 100 documents along with it. Surveys, memos, certified letters and legal hate mail took one last whirl around the porch and vanished into the bellowing ebony beyond. Adam smiled to himself as they flew off, knowing that he was soon to follow.

Far below him, the storm surge had long since submerged his dark green Boxster Porsche. With every gigantic, crashing wave, his $50,000 boy-toy was being smashed and re-smashed against the surrounding pilings. The storage units he had parked it behind had long since broken apart and washed away. The Porsche, now little more than a 3,000-pound battering ram, kept being thrown back and forth within the confines of the parking lot pilings. Like a caged beast, it kept ramming the concrete pilings with every surge of the pounding sea, chipping away at their integrity. Trying to escape. Escape to nowhere.

The rising ocean had been quick to find the Sanderling acreage. Loggins, Harris and Galano had easily fooled the State of Florida with their hacksaws and shovels. They had raised the survey elevations by three inches in six hours of labor on a night nearly as dark as this one. The state had been fooled, but they had not fooled Emily.

Their plan had worked because man is to man as fool is to fool. Neither the county nor the state had ever challenged TLD, Inc.'s benchmarks. The new surveys, with their surprisingly higher elevations, were welcome news to the government employees who had reviewed them. The word from up top was that Sanderling is a go. They were eager to issue the building permits and collect the annual real estate taxes. Growth is good. Development is mankind's destiny.

Deceiving those whose agenda invites deception was easy. Deceiving a hurricane is not.

As the huge storm surge that ran before the storm built up along the coast, the barrier islands became mainland Florida's first line of defense. It was what they always had been, a string of sand spits formed by the prevailing currents and wind, sand spits that rose little more than 10 feet above mean high tide. They had absorbed these terrible blows and tropical storms for untold millennia. They stood like flanks of windswept soldiers, ready to defend their peninsula to the death. Eager to die in her honor if so summoned.

As the water continued to rise, it poured through the two narrow channels on the north and south end of Shoreside Island. When they could no longer handle the sheer volume of water the approaching storm was pushing against the shoreline, that water naturally sought out the low points along the coastline. Like a breach in a dam, the low-lying areas would afford the least resistance.

Here is where the rushing salt water would first come inland, creating a tidal river as it moved quickly toward the interior. Emily did not care, nor take any note of the imaginary three inches that TLD, Inc. had created that night over two years ago. Those spot surveys existed only on paper, now lying in a file somewhere in the Army Corps of Engineers' office in Tallahassee. The land that really was Sanderling had not changed at all. Instinctively, Emily knew that.

Now this titanic storm surge, finding the lowest point mid-island, quickly flooded into the Sanderling Condominium project. With the mangroves long since uprooted and burned off, there was little native vegetation left to hold on to the sandy soil below. The numerous hibiscus plants, the coconut palms and the ornamentals planted by the developer had long since been swept away. With every incoming wave of salt water, the sand beneath the two Gulf-front buildings soon began to scour and wash away.

Emily, now a Category 5 storm, was trying to carve a new channel into the back bay behind Shoreside Island. There was too much water coming ashore for the old channels to handle the sheer volume pressing against the island. The Sanderling Condominium project, the old McKinzie parcel, was becoming Sanderling Pass.

As the water rushed inland, the sand behind the pilings vanished. Although the project was built to the new state standards, those standards did not anticipate what nature was capable of. Nothing man has ever built, or will ever build, is capable of that.

The State of Florida had always known that many a pass and inlet had been cut through the barrier islands of the west coast of Florida in the past from storms like Emily, but they had never experienced a storm violent enough to do so since the onslaught of development that had occurred in the last 50 years. They had never planned for a channel-carving storm. They could not have imagined a force of such magnitude. Energy so compact and powerful that one day in the life of Hurricane Emily could power the entire electrical needs of the United States for six months.

Emily was now a great hurricane. She had pushed a mountain of sea-water ahead of her and that seawater needed room. Emily was demanding a new pass, and she was demanding it now. Sixty feet below a terrified Adam Bartlett, Sanderling Pass was being dredged. Dredged by a crew of 100,000 workers who came in the form of this wind-driven ocean. They worked in a fury known only to God.

At 12:35 a.m., the six pilings that ran along the south side of building "A" began to buckle. The water beneath the condo was now 20 feet deep. Like a giant water cannon, the onrushing water had scoured away a million tons of sand and ancient seashells, leaving the long, cement legs of the building exposed and weakened. Standing like the thin legs of some concrete heron in the wind and rain.

The engineers who had so carefully designed the stress loads for those pilings had done so with the knowledge that they would always be surrounded by the compacted sand they were driven into. With that sand swept away by the energy of the storm, the long, thin cement pilings couldn't handle the weight of the five-story buildings above them. It was never a part of their calculations.

Adam, drunk and terrified, had been trying to decipher the mysterious voices inside the screaming wind when he felt the building shudder and lean as the first row of pilings buckled. It did so without the benefit of noise, since nothing, not even the crushing sound of those collapsing pilings, could now be heard over the sirens that had become the voice of the wind. The sirens of Emily's catastrophic song.

Now it was real. Adam could only guess at what was happening below the building. Earlier, when there was still a hint of light left in the world, Adam had noted the huge river of seawater that was being funneled through the swale that ran between the two most seaward buildings of the project. That deep swale that had been part of the original drainage plan; a long, narrow retention area that came right up to the edge of the beach.

Adam felt the sudden jolt, and reached for his Scotch as the building suddenly listed, catching itself on the next row of pilings before completely collapsing. Should the building fall over, Adam would die instantly. Like a sleeping peasant in a Turkish earthquake in the dark of some Middle Eastern midnight, the crash of concrete and rebar would kill everyone inside. Unlike those dusty calamities, building "A" would fall into a 20-foot deep torrent of seawater. Even if Adam could miraculously survive the fall, he would live only long enough to drown.

But the "A" building's fall was caught by the second row of pilings and the direction of the storm's winds. They were further in from the swale, and although battered and chipped from the trapped Porsche, they held. The condominium leaned in the darkness, like a misplaced tower of Pisa along a deserted stretch of coastline in south Florida.

Building "B" did not fare as well. The swale had been cut closer to that building and, as a result, the scouring was more intense. A half-hour later, as Adam stumbled over to the refrigerator to pour his final cocktail in his listing penthouse, building "B" tumbled into Sanderling Pass. Adam never heard or saw the crash. At this point, the winds were beyond plausible. They were blowing steady at 136 miles per hour. The noise was pounding, gnashing and rabid. A noise indescribable to anyone who has not heard it. The noise that is the roar of nature's beast unleashed.

Building "B" had collapsed because the scouring had weakened the north pilings and because of the direction of the wind. In essence, the force of the south wind had helped to push building "B" over once the first outside row of pilings had failed. The pressure of that gale acted like the hands of a giant, relentlessly shoving against the southern face of the structure. Finally pushing on it until it tumbled into the sea, then moving on. Because of the slight offset, it fell just behind building "A," missing the back steps by 20 feet.

Once the five-story building hit the water, it formed a temporary dam along the path of the newly carved channel. Within another half-hour, the onrushing water had cleared away most of that dam. Couches, appliances, fans and window treatments were all swept inland with the flow of the storm surge. Within the hour, nothing would remain but a pile of twisted rubble ten feet below the surface.

The same winds that had toppled building "B" were pushing so hard against the building Adam was sitting in that they were preventing it from falling. The relentless wind was bracing up building "A," stopping it from joining the other building now submerged beneath Sanderling Pass.

The other five buildings at Sanderling were holding their ground. They were scattered about the 13 acres but all of them were set farther back from the beach. The smallest building, the four-unit building in the back of the complex, was the least damaged of the seven. Because it was low and set near the rear property line of the parcel, it had not been as pounded and pummeled as were the other units.

At 2:00 a.m. Adam was drunk, wide awake and unable to move. He was in a trance, a paralyzing combination of too much liquor and 1,000 times more fear. He just sat there. Afraid. Waiting. Waiting for his world to end.

In this stupor of Scotch and shock, Adam's thoughts turned to Danny, his only son. As the edge of the eye approached Shoreside and the winds hit the maximum velocity of 158 miles per hour, Adam Bartlett sat motionless on a brand-new sleeper sofa in a penthouse apartment at a failed condominium project thinking of his boy. He remembered playing in the pool with Danny, back when he was three. Tossing him up in the air and catching him on a warm spring day. Memories of being a father. Comforting memories amidst the noise of 10,000 jet engines screaming around him. Good memories. Safe and reassuring.

At 2:15 every window in Unit 2-A blew out. The barometric pressure outside had dropped so low that the pressure inside the apartment needed to equalize. Adam had closed the sliding glass doors when he had come inside just before midnight and the thought of cracking a window or door had never occurred to him.

The windows and sliding glass doors on the abutting penthouse, facing into the wind, had blown out hours ago. They had been smashed by wind gusts and flying debris. The north unit, the one Adam had come to die in, was shielded from that debris. But it was not shielded from the falling barometric pressure.

In an instant, the condo was now open to the storm and the swirling back eddies of that wind. The sound of the hurricane, already intolerable, doubled. Adam's ears started pounding, unable to equalize to the falling air pressure. Like a scuba diver going to 1,000 feet in a minute's time, the pain inside both of

Adam's ears became excruciating. He wanted it to all go away. To vanish. To stop.

As he sat there on that unused sofa, the large framed print behind him was grabbed by a swirl of wind and lifted off of its hanger. Being too heavy to fly off, it dropped straight down on Adam. The 1/8-inch glass that covered the print of four people picking up shells along the shore of some Florida beach, smashed into Adam's head and shattered upon impact.

Pieces of broken glass were imbedded into the top of Adam's head and blood poured down the side of his face, staining his shirt in the dark red colors of the wounded. Everything had happened in less than a minute: the windows and sliding glass doors blowing away, the winds rushing in and the framed print smashing down on top of Adam. It had startled him back into the present. The pain had sobered him.

As the glass covering the framed print shattered, scores of tiny pieces of glass had also been thrown down forcefully along Adam's shoulders and arms. He had been holding the last few sips of Scotch in his right hand when the accident happened and the impact had caused him to drop his drink. Shards of broken glass had been driven into his extended arm. It was as if he had been sandblasted by broken glass. He had scores of tiny cuts across his head, arms and shoulders. Blood was everywhere.

Still he did not move.

At 2:34 the wind began to die. It fell off quickly and unexpectedly. Adam stood up and wiped the blood and sweat away from his eyes. The rain stopped. He walked onto the balcony, careful not to trip over the scattered furniture and pieces of window framing that were tossed about the apartment.

He knew what had happened. His ears still throbbed from the lack of air pressure. He walked to the very edge of the balcony and looked up. Above him, clear and beautiful on a July summer night, a sliver of a moon and a sky full of stars shone like beacons of hope. Adam was there. He was standing in the eye of the storm.

Tears were running down his cheeks. He was crying for himself, for his boy, for all the terrible ways of the world. The tears mixed with the blood and ran down his neck onto his stained and torn shirt. The hero was helpless.

Once again, his thoughts turned to Danny. He knew that the end was near. He remembered the last forecast he had heard about Hurricane Emily and what that now meant. Like Andrew, her brother, she was a quick and angry storm. Adam remembered that her eye was only 12 miles across and that she was moving toward the coast at 14 miles an hour.

As Adam stood there, looking at the infinity of the heavens above, he did the math. Fifty minutes, possibly less. He would be in the eye of the storm for a little less than an hour. Then the winds would return. But this time the winds wouldn't be coming from the south. They would come from the north. The back side of the hurricane would reverse itself. The winds would switch 180 degrees in less than an hour. Building "A," already listing to the south, would now have winds in excess of 150 miles per hour pushing against it. The giant would walk around to the other side of the building, place his huge windy hands upon it and shove it into the sea. In less than 50 minutes Adam Bartlett knew that Adam Bartlett would perish.

He reached inside his pants pocket and took out his cell phone. He needed to make one last call. He figured that his cell phone probably wouldn't work but he had to try. He needed to hear his son's voice one last time before his death. It would comfort him as 100,000 tons of concrete toppled into the sea. As he fell into his watery grave.

Adam took his cell phone and flipped it open, pushing the "on" button as he did. He watched its LCD light up and waited as it searched for a signal. What Adam could not have known is that three years ago the City of Shoreside had reinforced its microwave tower for just such a catastrophe. They had learned from Andrew and other storms that cellular telephones can be crucial during and after a hurricane and they had gone ahead and made the island tower virtually indestructible. Adam's cell phone, unexpectedly, had a signal. A strong signal.

He pushed a few more buttons and recalled Peg's home phone. If the power was out in town, he knew that he wouldn't be able to get through. It was out. All Adam heard was an unusual sounding busy signal. He would have to try Peg's cell phone.

With that, he pushed a couple more buttons and recalled her private cell phone number. He then pushed "send" and waited. He knew full well that it was 2:30 in the morning but he didn't care. In his intoxicated delirium, all Adam wanted to do was to talk to Danny one last time. He didn't even know what he was going to say.

It didn't matter. He could just ask if they were all right. He imagined the conversation as the call went out.

"Peg, this is Adam. Are you and Danny okay?"

"We're fine Adam. We evacuated to Miami late Friday afternoon. Where are you?"

"That's not important, can I speak with Danny just a minute or two?"

"Fine, Adam. We haven't been able to sleep all night, watching the coverage of the storm and all. It's a bad one, Adam. Emily is devastating the west coast. Things will never be the same after she gets through with Shoreside, will they?"

"No, never."

"Hang on, Adam, here's Danny."

A few seconds might pass.

"Hi, Dad. How are you?"

"I'm fine Danny, are you and mom all right?"

"Yeah, we're at Auntie Amy's house over in Miami. The power isn't even out over here. Mom and Auntie Amy have let me stay up all night to watch the storm. Cool, huh Dad?"

"Cool, Danny. Cool."

But that conversation would never happen. Peg and Danny had evacuated over to Miami and they were staying at Aunt Amy's house but the both of them were fast asleep on the sleeper sofa downstairs. Peggy's cell phone was lying in her purse, turned off and silent.

After a few rings a computerized woman's voice came on saying, "The cellular customer you have called is unavailable or has traveled outside the coverage area. Please call again later."

With that message, Adam flipped his cell phone shut and slid it back into his pocket, neglecting to press the "off" button as he did. He started weeping. He sat down on the ceramic tiles that covered the screened lanai and dangled his legs over the lip of the porch. He knew that he would never hear his son's voice again. He had felt like telling that personless voice on the line, that computer-generated woman, that for him, there was no later. For Adam Bartlett, death was 45 minutes away. He wept openly while listening to the incessant drum roll of thunder in the distance. His time had come.

570-8783
The Stoughtons' Home

Shortly after 2:00 a.m., an intense suction vortex whipped through the northern section of the Osprey Greens Golf Course. Winds inside the vortex topped 200 miles per hour. The two homes that were standing on Palmetto Court, one nearly completed, and the other recently re-sided in a white vinyl, were destroyed. In less than a minute, the Stoughtons' new home, the home that Jennifer Willow had inadvertently bestowed upon them, was gone.

The storm surge, which presently covered every square inch of the island, had long since taken the breakaway walls that made up the garage and workroom areas below the homes. Once removed, the sheer force of the wind ripped the framing of the two houses off their 32 wooden pilings. The sheet-metal hurricane straps that had been installed to prevent this from happening were designed to withstand winds up to 128 miles per hour.

Cast-iron hurricane straps couldn't have saved either home from Emily's fury. She paid no attention to Shoreside's well-meaning building codes and structural engineering requirements. The industries of man fail woefully against the industries of the natural world.

All that was left of the Stoughtons' home, and the Cliftons' home three lots over, were the pilings. Some of the pilings had splintered sections of the floor joists still attached. The Cliftons' home still had the front steps going up to it. The door into the home was gone, as was the home itself.

Emily had decimated 1,245 homes on Shoreside thus far, and the back side of her eye wall was slowly weaving its way toward Shoreside. Another 523 homes, nine older Gulf-front condominiums, a number of motels and 24 commercial buildings would collapse beneath the pounding surf or blow apart before the storm had passed. That and both the "B" and "A" buildings near the rapidly forming Sanderling Pass.

Thousands of island homes were damaged. Virtually every human endeavor, from the bridges along the causeway to the stop signs, were affected. The island was laid ruin.

The Jensens' home, the one that had the leak, now had a much larger one. The top of a nearby pine had rammed through the roof of the house as if it were shot out of a cannon. Ironically, it came through in the same area as the former leak.

Five months later, when the brand-new roof trusses and shingles were put on, the leak came back. The Jensens called Linda Hinkle to list the house the day it started leaking again. It sold a week later.

904-732-9878
Room 218, The Sabal Palm Motel

Scott Lindsey, safe and sound in a small motel room in Lake City, Florida, kept thinking about what it must be like on the island. As he watched the eye approach the island on cable television, he knew that it must be a living hell on Shoreside.

It was the real-life version of *Nature's Wrath Unleashed*. Palm trees had been completely stripped of their fronds, every Australian pine on the island was either sheared off to a bare trunk or toppled over. The salt water intrusion was soon to kill every lawn, every ornamental, every exotic and imported plant on the island. Only the natives would survive, thought Scott: the sabal palm, palmetto, the coconut palms, the mangroves and the gumbo limbo. The others would be poisoned by the salted soil. It would take years for the rainwater to leech the remaining salts out of the topsoil. In some areas, decades.

It dawned on Scott that only our wars rival the singular power of the natural world. At that, war was no match when compared to the destruction wrought when worlds collide. When that errant meteor slammed into what is now the Yucatan Peninsula some 65 million years ago. In the flash of an instant, an entire ecosystem perished. The great reign of the dinosaurs ended as a fireball the size of a billion hydrogen bombs ripped across the face of the Earth. A billion years of evolution erased in a heartbeat.

Earthquakes, firestorms, hurricanes and volcanoes can alter a landscape in a matter of hours. The great volcano of Tambora, south of Sumatra in the Indonesian Chain, which erupted in 1815, darkened the skies for two years. Crops failed, and people around the world starved because this solitary eruption ejected more than 20 cubic miles of volcanic dust and debris into the atmosphere. The year of 1816 was known as the year without a summer. Record cold temperatures were recorded in Switzerland and New England. Sunsets lingered for hours in the red, dusty haze the explosion had created.

Tsunamis have been recorded better than 15 stories high, waves sweeping entire islands clear of all living things. Pyroclastic flows, with toxic gases killing everything in their path. Like the eruption of Mount Pelee in 1902. That disaster killed 30,000 people on the island of Martinique as a cloud of deadly gases slid down the mountainside and smothered the inhabitants of St. Pierre.

Earthquakes have taken millions, and no doubt they will take millions more.

No, the best laid plans of man pale against forces far more powerful and far more divine. Thinking that we somehow have conquered these forces is nothing more than vanity. Arrogance and vanity.

Hurricanes paid no attention to which house was on lot "A" and which was on lot "D." These lines in the dirt were the designs of man. The lots, the blocks, the surveys meant nothing to her. The cities, the countries and the nations were all treated equally under nature's heavy hand. The division of the world into a million tiny pieces of real estate and nations was the work of man.

It meant nothing to Emily or to the natural world that hurricanes are a part of. The wild Florida panther doesn't know if it's in Dade or Hendry County when it makes its kill. The migrating birds of the world do not recognize the sovereignty of Venezuela any more than they do that of Canada. These are the creations of man, the territorial imperatives of this animal who so long ago ventured forth from the same equatorial regions of Africa where Emily was born.

These lines in the sand are his doing and undoing both, reasoned Scott. The natural world, the fishes of the great ocean, all suffer at the hands of these artificial zones and barriers created in the marble hallways of the great nations. The hallways of power and the armies created to defend that power. One nation protects the whales while the nation across the ocean eats them. One tries to save a migrating swan while the other slaughters it. These great lines of division stand as terrible reminders of our vanity as the animals and wildlife who do not understand them suffer.

In many ways, Emily and mankind were alike, reflected Scott. They both herald from the great rainforests of central Africa. The both belong here, equally a part of the natural order of life. But whereas Emily could not cease her deadly spin, we can. We can put down our axes, our chain saws and our bulldozers. Unlike these cataclysms that surround us, we have the gift of consciousness.

We can take a long, deep breath and slow down our terrible machine. This deadly human hurricane that has been spinning madly out of control for the last million years. Increasing our population until it strains the limits of Earth's ability to sustain us. Spinning faster and faster and faster in a universe that knows nothing of time. Spinning for naught. Thinking, ever so foolishly, that we are the world's master.

The world of man is not the world, nor will it ever be, reasoned a lonely conservationist in a quiet motel room in north-central Florida. Emily, as her calm and ominous eye slowly marched across Shoreside Island, reminded Scott as it reminded all of Florida who has the last say. Reminded everyone that, indeed, God bats last.

664-8786
Room 2124, Gulfcoast General Hospital

Betsy Owens went into labor at 6:00 that Friday night. Like a natural Pitocin, the falling barometric pressure caused by the approaching hurricane put Betsy into early labor. Betsy's doctor had anticipated something like this might happen, having seen the same phenomenon during last year's tropical storm and many a storm before that.

No one knows why it happens, but it does. As the low-pressure system approaches, late-term women go into labor and give birth. Perhaps it's a remnant of instinct, knowing that the baby is safer from the approaching storm once outside the womb. Perhaps no one will ever know why. All that is known is that it happens.

Mark drove Betsy to the hospital at 6:30 p.m. He drove poorly, as first-time fathers are prone to do. He ran three red lights and kept nervously glancing over at his new wife, watching her clutch the door handle as her labor pains set in. The storm had made him anxious enough. Now the birth of his first child was being thrown in for good measure. Mark Thurston was a complete mess.

Once at the hospital, Betsy was placed into a wheelchair and wheeled over to a birthing suite. She was lucky. It was the last available birthing suite. The next nine mothers who came in that night ended up in standard hospital rooms. Every woman in town who was anywhere near full term was going into labor. Hurricanes have a way with wombs.

The nurse on staff did a quick examination of Betsy and found that she was barely dilated. Three centimeters; Betsy was going to have a long night ahead of her. It was real though, and the nurse went to call her physician right after the examination.

First-time mother, thought the experienced head nurse, six hours at least, maybe more. A long night when you add a Category 5 hurricane into the equation. A very long night. Her doctor had better come in early just in case.

Betsy was doing fine. She and Mark had taken all the classes, the Lamaze breathing exercises, the whole ten week course. She was excited and scared. A *prima gravida*, a new mother all the way. As preoccupied as she was with this child now trying to come into this world, Betsy couldn't get her mind off Adam.

It was that look he had in the hallway, a look that was etched into Betsy's soul.

Between contractions, she kept going on about it with Mark.

"I don't know why I'm so worried about him, Mark, but I just am. It was that look on his face, a look that I've never seen on Adam before. I just know that he wasn't himself this morning. I just know it."

"Betsy, Adam's a big kid. He can take care of himself. You and I both know that there's no way that he could have been so stupid as to stay on that island. He'd have to be an idiot to even think such a thing," said Mark as Betsy's face contorted from another round of contractions.

A minute later, she continued. "Mark, I know that I'm asking a lot, but could you please call him. Just to make certain that he's at home. Please."

Mark couldn't say no to his bride. He picked up the telephone and smiled.

"It's 495-0097." Betsy rattled off Adam's home phone from memory. She could have rattled off the home phones of 80 percent of the agents who worked on Shoreside, for that matter. That's how good she was.

Mark made the call for her from the phone in the birthing suite. Adam's home phone rang and rang and rang. No answer. Bartlett wasn't there to take it off the hook and his answering machine had long since been thrown against the floor. Mark knew that Adam wasn't home. He couldn't have known that Adam was drinking a bottle of J&B in a penthouse unit at Sanderling, waiting for the end.

"No answer, Betsy. Maybe he's just not picking up?"

"Try his cell phone number, Mark. It's 870-2162," said Betsy just as her next contraction was coming on.

Mark dialed the number only to get this computerized woman's voice telling him that the person had left the coverage area and to try again later. Adam's cell phone was still turned off. He hadn't tried to call Danny yet.

Betsy was right. Adam was in trouble. Her intuition had taken note of it in the hallway and her intuition was good. He had been depressed lately, drinking heavily and rarely showing up at work. Now he had done something stupid. Very stupid. She had to try to save him.

"He's out there, Mark. I just know it. He's either in the office or he's gone down to Sanderling. I just know it."

"Oh, Betsy. Don't go getting yourself all worked up over Adam. You're having a baby, Betsy. Our baby. We just can't run down to Shoreside and rescue Bartlett. Besides, they've probably got the whole place evacuated by now.

"Even if Adam was out there, no one can get to him at this time, with the storm surge starting to come ashore and the wind picking up, no one can save him. Just try not to think about it, Betsy. Try and relax."

But Betsy couldn't stop thinking about it. She dropped the subject with her husband for 20 minutes before bringing it back up again. Surely there had to be something they could do.

"Maybe he's with Loggins."

"Betsy, are you starting in about Adam again? I thought that we weren't going to bring that subject up again."

"Oh, Mark. I'm just so worried about him. Please, pretty please call Mr. Loggins and ask if Adam's with him. Loggins lives miles from the coast. Maybe Adam decided to stay there tonight."

Mark was helpless. Sitting there, beside his lovely bride. Checking his watch to time the intervals between contractions, getting her water when she asked, or wiping the sweat off her brow after a particularly strong contraction; he would do anything she asked of him at this point. Anything.

"What's Loggins' number?"

Betsy recited it without so much as giving it a thought. She knew his office number, his cell phone number and his home phone. Betsy Owens was a walking Rolodex. The best telephone receptionist Shoreside Realty had ever known. The best any real estate company had ever known.

Loggins picked up on the third ring. In another two hours, all the land lines would go down, but for now the storm had yet to knock them out.

"Hello."

"Is Mr. Loggins there?"

"Speaking."

"Mr. Loggins, this is Mark Thurston calling. You know, Betsy's husband, the guy who works for UPS. We're at the hospital right now because Betsy's in labor but she's asked me to give you a call."

"What's this about?" Loggins was lost with this one.

"Betsy wants to know if Adam's at your place. Is he there?"

"Adam Bartlett?"

"Yes."

"I haven't spoken with Bartlett in months. Once the bank foreclosed on Sanderling, Harris and I didn't have any reason to stay in touch with him. He's not here, that's for certain. Why are you asking?" Loggins sensed that something was up.

"Well, we think he might be on the island. Betsy saw him at the office earlier this morning and she thought he looked depressed. We tried his home phone and there's no answer. We tried his cell phone and it's turned off, so we're just calling around to see if he's staying with friends."

"Oh shit!" Loggins knew. Through the grapevine, Loggins and Harris had been keeping tabs on Bartlett. They knew about the drinking and the depression their former golden boy had fallen into. The fact that Adam might do something as stupid as staying on Shoreside when Emily hit didn't come as much of a surprise. It made sense in a way. Terrible sense.

There was a pause in the conversation while Loggins reflected on the situation. Maybe there was something he could do. He continued.

"Mark, I'll call Ralph and have him try to find Bartlett. Ralph knows him and he lives only a couple of blocks from Adam's apartment. Maybe he can run over there and check to see if his car's in the garage. I'll get back to you in a bit. Give me your number at the hospital. Which one are you at, Gulfcoast or St. Mary's?"

"We're at Gulfcoast, in a birthing suite, Room 2124. Wait a minute while I get the number from the nurses' station."

Mark put down the phone, which was labeled with nothing more than the extension number, winked at Betsy, and ran over to get the main hospital number from one of the nurses. He was back in less than a minute.

"The number's 664-8786, Room 2124. Please call us as soon as you find anything out."

"I will. I promise."

"Bye now."

"Goodbye."

With that, both Mark and Tom Loggins put down their telephones. Betsy felt better. At least she was doing something. Trying to help Adam, wherever he was. Now she could get back to the business of giving birth. Now she could get back to becoming a new mother.

❖

Loggins picked the phone back up and followed through with his promise. He did so reluctantly. He didn't give a damn if Bartlett was on Shoreside. To hell with him, anyway.

It was Bartlett who had come up with that lame-brain idea to have this big grand opening fiasco to begin with. It was Bartlett who had single-handedly put the Sanderling Condominium project in the toilet. Loggins felt that it was poetic justice that Bartlett should go down with the project. They could tumble into the sea together when Emily slammed into Shoreside sometime after midnight. If Loggins could have had any say in it, he would have lashed that little asshole to one of the "A" building pilings.

But he made the call to Ralph anyway. He made it because he liked Betsy and he owed her the favor. Everybody liked Betsy. If she was worried about Bartlett, then Loggins would do what he could to allay her fears. It was the least he could do, especially with her being in labor and all. Loggins punched in his speed-dial code, and called Ralph Galano.

Ralph's phone rang twice before he picked it up. He wasn't expecting any calls, glued to the local news on TV like everyone else in south Florida. At least until the power failed.

"Hello."

"Ralph, this is Tom. Got a minute?"

"Sure, Tom. What's going on?"

Ralph had known Loggins for decades. Their relationship spanned a dozen major projects: condominiums, townhouses, Water's Edge development, Sanderling and the golf course project in town that they currently had on the drawing table. Loggins never called Galano to socialize, especially on this harrowing Friday evening. Something was up.

"It's Adam. I just got a call from Betsy Owens, you know, the telephone receptionist over at Shoreside. She's worried about Bartlett. She's at the Gulfcoast Hospital right now having a baby, but she ran into Adam at the office this morning and apparently their meeting didn't sit well with her.

"She thinks he's out there, on the island. She didn't come right out and say it, but I think Betsy thinks Bartlett's trying to kill himself or some damn fool thing."

"Wouldn't surprise me," replied Ralph.

"Nah, me either. He's been taking a hell of a lot of flack over Sanderling. I heard that the bank pulled the listings a couple of days ago. Between that and all the shit Boyle and the boys have been throwing at him, I wouldn't doubt that he has held a gun to his head more than once these last few months.

"Anyway, Betsy has asked me to find out if he's home. She's tried calling both his home phone and his cell phone but no one answers.

"Frankly, Ralph, I don't really give a shit what happens to Bartlett. But I like Betsy. Since she's having a kid and all, I just can't see letting her go on worrying all damn night about Bartlett. Especially tonight, as if there ain't enough shit going down with this hurricane and all."

"So what do you need from me, Tom?"

"If I remember right, you don't live too far from Adam's apartment complex, right?"

"Two blocks max."

"Well, Ralph, what I'd like you to do is to take a quick drive over there and see if he's there. Bust down the goddamn door if he doesn't answer. I'll pay for the damages. And check to see if his Boxster's in the garage. If he's not in and his Porsche is gone, then Betsy's probably got it right. The fool son of a bitch is on Shoreside, kissing a Category 5 hurricane in the face.

"If he's in the apartment, take your cell phone with you and give me a call. I promised I'd get back to Betsy with some news within the hour. Can you do that for me, Ralph?"

Of course he could. He had done 10,000 tasks for Loggins in the past and figured to do 10,000 more in the years to come. Ralph Galano was a "yes" man. He liked it that way. Following orders was easier than making the decisions about those orders. A model employee, that was Galano, eager to please and ready to serve.

"No problem, Tom. I'll get back to you in a half an hour tops."

"Thanks, Ralph. Be careful out there, this wind is really starting to kick up, so watch yourself. And if Bartlett ain't there, don't you dare try to go out to

Shoreside to save his ass. If he's there, he's on his own. You hear me?"

"I hear ya, Tom. I've got no intention of being a hero. Not tonight."

"Good. I'll wait to hear from you. Bye now.

"Bub-bye."

Ralph hung up the phone and got right to it. He went over to the small closet by his front door and took out his bright yellow rain gear. It wasn't raining all that much, but he didn't want to be caught unawares if the rain did start to pick up. He grabbed his Jeep keys off the kitchen table and headed out the front door, stopping to throw the dead bolt before walking to his car.

It was dark and windy. The gusts were hitting 60 miles an hour but the sustained wind wasn't anywhere near that yet. It was blowing steady at 35. Not a real problem for his Grand Cherokee to maneuver through. Besides, it wasn't far.

He arrived at Bartlett's townhouse in five minutes. Aside from some blowing debris and a few nasty gusts running between the houses, driving over was without incident. He was disappointed to see that the garage door to Adam's place lacked any outside windows. It would have spared him the trouble of having to break the damn door down to find out if Adam was home.

Ralph walked to the front door and rang the bell. No answer. He followed that by knocking several times. Knocking loudly. Once again, no answer.

Shit, I'll have to break in. The good news is that nobody's going to hear me. Not in all this wind. As dark as it is, no one's going to see me either. I might as well get on with it.

Ralph stepped back a few steps, dropped his left shoulder and slammed into the front door like a first-draft linebacker. The cheap deadbolt and hardware buckled and the door flew open. The ease with which the door blew open didn't surprise him a bit. He'd seen this project go up. It was your typical "throw 'em up in a month" Florida apartment construction. Built like shit.

Once inside, Ralph took a quick look around and knew straight away that Adam was on the island. The deplorable condition of Adam's apartment verified that fact at a glance. Ralph, having known Bartlett for years, might have thought he had busted the door down to the wrong unit, had he not been to Adam's place several times in the past for cocktails.

Now, as Ralph surveyed the empty bottles of Scotch strewn around the living room, the six pizza boxes, some with slices of old pizza still sitting in them, the unopened bills and piled-up newspapers his worst fears were realized. Ralph, like everyone else in the business, had heard about Adam's slide, but he had never expected Adam to slide this far. This was a slide into hell.

Even though Ralph was convinced that Adam had gone to Shoreside to embrace the approaching storm, he had to check the rest of his two-bedroom apartment to be certain. Then he had to check the garage, to make sure that the Boxster was gone.

Every room in the house told the same dismal story. The kitchen was a pigsty. Dirty dishes stacked in the sink, stinking of moldy sweet-and-sour chicken, pots half-filled with black beans and rice sitting on the range, with the food dried and stuck to the sides. The floor littered with J&B bottle caps, empty Dunkin Donut bags and dust from months of not being swept.

Ralph took a look in the fridge more out of curiosity than anything else. He knew what to expect. The fridge was empty save for one bottle of J&B that held no more than half a shot in it, a soured quart of milk, some condiments and two closed containers of Chinese takeout. He didn't bother looking inside the containers. He knew that they were a case study in mold culture. There wasn't any reason to look.

As he went through the rest of the apartment it was more of the same. The guest bedroom was the only place untouched by the derelict who lived there. The door was closed and everything inside the room was untouched by the despair that echoed through the rest of the apartment.

It was Danny's room. Danny's computer sat in the corner, posters of race cars, frogs and the venomous snakes of Australia covered the walls. A baseball bat, three hardballs and a glove rested untouched in one corner and an electric piano sat silently in the other. Dust had settled on everything, giving the room an eerie, haunted feeling, as though the boy had died.

But the boy hadn't died. His father had. His father had died inside, slowly poisoned by people who wanted to get their money out of the Sanderling Condominium project People who wanted results and wanted those results yesterday. Danny's father had been poisoned by law firms, bankers and a deluge of legal hate mail. Dead inside, as dead as someone still living can be.

Ralph silently pulled the door to Danny's room closed and went to look into the garage. As he passed through the living room heading toward the garage door across from the front door, he saw the bottle of sleeping pills sitting on the end table next to the remote. He picked up the bottle and carefully read the label: Trazadone.

Take one and you rest comfortably. Take the nine that Ralph found inside the prescription bottle and you rest forever. Hamlet's sweet sleep, the sleep of suicides.

Ralph remembered the quote from a high school play he had performed in, "Now cracks a noble heart. Good night, sweet prince, and flights of angels sing thee to thy rest." It all made sense. Sad, tragic sense.

When Ralph opened the garage door and flipped on the light he found what he expected to find. The Porsche was gone. The golden boy had taken his dark green chariot out to Sanderling to make peace with the gods. A restless, despairing peace, but a better place than this world was now offering him.

Ralph flipped off the light, closed the door behind him and went to find Adam's phone to call Loggins and make his report. He would tell Tom that

Betsy is right, Adam's probably on Shoreside. Adam's down at the Sanderling project with a bottle of Scotch and an unstoppable death wish. Judging by the disgusting condition of his apartment, Adam's been in a serious despair for months. There would be no saving him, at least by the hand of man.

When Ralph found the phone, he picked it up only to discover it was dead. The phone lines had already gone down. He would have to use his cell phone. Ralph punched in Loggins' number and pushed send. Loggins picked up a minute later.

"Loggins here."

"Tom, this is Ralph. The news ain't good. I'm at Bartlett's place now and his apartment looks like hell. It looks like a flophouse on skid row. I've counted nearly 20 empty Scotch bottles, a half-dozen bottles of wine and empty beer cans every goddamned place.

"You'd die if you saw this place, Tom. It's not the Bartlett we knew. It's somebody else living here; a wino or a drunk of some kind. Not Adam Bartlett."

"What do you think? Is he out there, like Betsy figures he is?"

"Yeah, he's there," answered a sullen Ralph Galano. He paused for a minute and continued. "I found a bottle of sleeping pills right beside the couch. He might have thought about suicide the last few days and changed his mind. Maybe he figured that it would be better just to perish in the storm. After what he's been through lately, life probably ain't worth living.

"The car's gone and there isn't any note that I can find. I know he's not seeing Vanessa anymore and I doubt we'll find him staying at his assistant's place. I heard Chris's going to work for Island Accounting next week. No, he's more than likely still on Shoreside. That's my guess anyway."

"Thanks, Ralph. Have you tried calling him?"

"No."

"Well, give that a try after hanging up with me. Betsy tried earlier but maybe he's turned his cell phone on. It's worth a shot. I'll try to figure out some way to reach the hospital to let Betsy know about what you found but that might be a real bitch now that the land lines are down. You get back to your place and keep trying to reach Bartlett.

"If you do get through to him, Ralph, do all of us a favor and try to get him off the island if it ain't too damn late. Do whatever it takes to convince him that it ain't worth dying for. It's just a piece of swampland we should have left for the fucking bugs and turtles. It's just a lot of wasted time and money at this point. It's a bust," said Loggins to his right-hand man.

"I'll keep trying to get him, Tom. I'll keep trying all night if I have to. If I do get through to him, I'll let you know."

"Stay safe, Ralph. Watch yourself driving back home, the weather's falling apart out there."

"Thanks, Tom. I'll get back to you later."

"Thanks, Ralph. Bye now."

"Goodbye."

Ralph flipped his small cell phone shut and headed to his Jeep. He stuffed a piece of cardboard in the doorjamb before leaving and pulled as tight as he could. That would help to keep the front door closed for a while at least. By midnight, with the hurricane coming, the roof would probably blow off this complex anyway, so the cardboard would work just fine until then. Besides, he thought as he fired up his four-wheeler, who the hell would want anything from that apartment now. It would be like breaking into the Dumpster behind a liquor store. One look around and the thief would head right back through the front door.

Ralph drove carefully the two blocks to his apartment. The wind had picked up a notch or two while he was in Adam's apartment. Now it was angry. It was a sneering, bitter wind that buffeted his Jeep on the short drive home. Emily was on her way.

Once back in his apartment, Ralph found that his electricity was out. With the winds gusting to 80 miles an hour, that fact didn't surprise him. He would have to get his transistor radio and listen to updates on that for the rest of the night. He was prepared for the storm. Not prepared like Mildred Lee was, with enough canned goods and supplies stockpiled to last through a year of hurricanes, but prepared for the most part. Ralph had the candles, the transistor radio, some spare food and water and most of the items found on checklists. Ralph would be fine.

He had tried calling Bartlett right after calling Loggins. There was no answer other than the standard computerized response that everyone receives when a cell phone is turned off. But Ralph had resolved to keep trying to call every half-hour until morning if need be. It was the only thing he could do to try to save Adam. Maybe Adam would turn his cell phone on sometime during the night. Maybe Ralph would get lucky.

Ralph lit a candle, turned on his radio to keep abreast of the storm's progress and noted the time. He would call every half-hour. Religiously.

The night deteriorated. The news reporter on the radio station he had tuned in to kept updating the strength of the approaching storm and increasing the predicted surge that rode before it. Emily was fast becoming the biggest bitch to hit Florida since Donna. She was going to rip into Shoreside as a Category 5 hurricane. The storm of the new century.

The storm surge, which only yesterday was projected to be around 12 feet, was now predicted to hit 18 feet. Every ground-level home on the island would be completely under water should that happen. The winds in the eye wall were projected to be approaching 160 miles per hour sustained when Emily slammed ashore. Gusts would exceed 200 miles an hour in the many suction vortexes embedded within the eye wall.

These were the same "evil winds" that flattened thousands of homes in Kendall and Homestead the night Andrew came ashore in August of 1992. The news was grim and the forecaster's voice, worn and tired from telling his listeners to stay indoors, get to shelters or evacuate, reinforced that grimness. Emily was the real thing. She was a channel-making storm. This woman from the Cape Verde Islands was now a colossus.

At 2:30 a.m., just as the winds were fiercest and the eye had passed over the back side of Shoreside some 25 miles seaward of Galano's house in town, Ralph tried calling Adam for the seventh time.

To Ralph's complete surprise, Adam Bartlett, his face bloodied and his legs dangling over the edge of the balcony of Unit 2-A, reached into his soaking pants pocket and answered his cell phone. Without so much as giving it a thought, Adam flipped his cell phone open and said, "Hello."

870-2162
Bartlett's Cell Phone

Bartlett unexpectedly answered. He was in shock. Had he not been, he would never have reached into his damp pants pocket, taken out his cell phone, and automatically flipped it open. It rang and he answered it. It was a conditioned response. Nothing more, nothing less.

"Bartlett, is that you?"

"Speaking."

"This is Ralph, Ralph Galano. Loggins' friend. Where the hell are you?"

"I'm at the project."

"What project? Not Sanderling, for God's sake."

"Yes, that's where I am. I'm at Sanderling. And it's unreal here tonight Ralph. Totally fucking unreal. It's the end of the world. It's unreal."

Adam's speech was broken and slurred. Ralph knew that he was hurt. Ralph had heard that kind of broken dialogue before. Just last year when that cable busted and dropped a load of cinder block on that Mexican kid. He sounded the same way Adam did while the construction crew worked to get his right leg out from under the pallet. Distant and estranged. Injured.

"Are you okay, Adam?"

"I'm okay. Just a few cuts. Some dried blood on my shirt. It's not bad now. It's calm here. The storm's passed. It's calm and I can see the stars shining."

Ralph knew that the storm hadn't passed. From listening to the exhausted reporter on his FM radio, Ralph knew that Adam was in the eye of the storm. The back side of Emily was fast approaching. And it would be every bit as vicious as the first wave of wind that tore through Shoreside.

"Listen to me, Adam. You're in the eye. It's not going to be calm for much longer and you have to work with me here. Do you understand?"

"I'm fine, Ralph. I've got to run."

"**NO!**" Ralph stated emphatically. "Don't you dare hang up on me, Adam. We need to talk. There's some shit you need to know about Sanderling and you need to know about it now!"

Adam pulled the phone away from his ear and started to flip the cover shut. For some reason, unexplainable even to himself, he didn't hang up. Maybe it was just curiosity. Adam thought he knew everything there was to know about this hell hole of a project. If Galano had more to add to this miserable tale, then he was willing to listen. He put the phone back up to his right ear and said, "What about Sanderling?"

"It ain't worth dying over, Adam. Tom and I never told you about the crap we pulled to get the permits for Sanderling in the first place. That project didn't fail because of you and your screwed-up grand opening. It failed because we built those goddamned condos in a swamp.

"Loggins and I dug up the government benchmarks and lowered them three inches the same night we put the property under option. How the hell do you think we got the Army Corp of Engineers off our backs? Without changing the elevations, there was no way in hell we would have gotten those permits for Sanderling.

"And the Brazilian pepper. Shit, Adam, it would have taken the blackbirds 100 years to put down that much pepper. Before we cleared the Water's Edge development, Tom and I took three gunny sacks full of those red pepper berries and stashed them in an air-conditioned storage locker. Before we put Sanderling under option, I personally planted those pepper seeds. Christ, it must have taken me ten hours to plant those 13 acres."

Adam was listening. He had always wondered how Loggins had managed to get the green light from Tallahassee. Now he knew.

"That's not all of it either, Adam. We helped fix the environmental study, we took care of plenty of the good old boys downtown and we kissed some royal ass for those building permits. It's not your fault the place was full of mosquitoes. It's a goddamned swamp, Adam. Why the hell are you killing yourself over a useless stretch of shoreline?"

Ralph was on a roll; he knew that he would have to break through to him soon, or the chances of Adam surviving the next onslaught of weather were nonexistent.

"What about your boy? He needs you, Adam. He needs a dad and you've always been one hell of a dad. Don't do it, Adam. For your kid's sake, don't do it."

Adam's legs dangled idly 60 feet above the ocean. It was becoming quiet now. As the terrible windstorm known as Emily marched farther and farther inland, a silence descended upon the broken world that surrounded him. A silence twisted and glorious, disturbed only by the drum roll of thunder in the distance.

After a lengthy pause, Adam replied, "It's all my fault, Ralph. Sanderling's my fucking fault."

"No, Adam. Sanderling's not your fault at all. Sanderling's all about money, Adam. All about making money. And money ain't worth a shit when compared with one hug from your little boy."

Adam started crying. Ralph was getting through. Like the priest trying to talk the suicide off the ledge, Ralph had found the key to keeping Adam from jumping those five stories to his death. The key was the love of his son. Nothing else in the world could have persuaded him from staying there, waiting for the other side of the storm to arrive and shove the building over. Push the "A" building into the waiting arms of the newly formed channel below.

Only Danny's love could save him. It was the only sacred thing left in a world filled with sin.

On the other end of the line, Ralph could hear Adam sobbing. As he listened to him cry, Ralph knew that he was getting through. It was all or nothing at this point, so he continued, "Adam, where are you now?"

"I'm in Unit 2-A, on the front porch. It's blown apart, Ralph. All the doors and windows are gone. The whole building's leaning and the water's up over the first floor apartment downstairs. It's been so scary, Ralph. I couldn't possibly explain..." Ralph cut him off.

"Don't try to. You've got to get out of there, Adam. If you're going to survive, you have to get out of that building. It sounds like the foundation's failing The pilings are probably buckling. When the other side of the eye wall hits, the "A" building will collapse. You've got to get as far back in the complex as possible. Can you walk?"

Adam was reawakening. He couldn't explain it, but his will to live was coming back to him. There wasn't any time to explain where this newfound sense of survival was coming from. It just came.

"Yes, but I'm cut up pretty bad. A big picture lifted off the wall and fell on me when all the windows blew out. There's a lot of blood and I'm cut pretty badly, but I can walk."

"Then go and look off the back porch. Is building "G" still standing. You know, the low one way in the back that has only four units. Is it still there?"

"I'll check."

Adam got up and walked through the debris scattered throughout the condominium to the back of the apartment where the front door once was. In the dim starlight he could see the entire project. That was when Adam noted that building "B" was gone. Not a trace of it remained, buried now beneath 20 feet of ocean. The rest of buildings were still visible, and all of them except for the one he was in appeared to be standing straight.

"It's still there, Ralph. But the "B" building is gone. Totally gone."

"It's collapsed. Look, Adam, from here on in you're on your own. You have to figure out how to get back to the "G" building. I don't know how in hell you're going to be able to make it, but you have to try. The wind will be coming from the opposite direction when the back side of the eye hits and, judging from the scouring that has already occurred, the taller buildings might start collapsing. Only the "G" building will offer you a chance. If the water's up to the first floor, you'll have to climb to the second floor when you get to it.

"You're not in a safe place, Adam. If you want to live, then you have to get going right now. It's up to you. You and the Almighty."

The question had already been answered, the one about wanting to live. The love of his son Danny had answered it for him. The question about the Almighty allowing Adam to survive was not.

"Thanks, Ralph. I've got to go."

"God bless you, Adam."

"I'll talk to you later, Ralph. Thanks for being straight with me."

"Goodbye."

Adam flipped his cell phone closed and stood on the small entrance area shared by the two penthouse units. It was quieter now. The scream of Emily's song had been replaced by the sound of endless thunder in the distance. A constant drum roll of lightning and timpani, but nothing when compared with the voice of a hurricane wind.

For a moment, Adam stood and surveyed the island landscape before him. Shoreside was devastated. The tall, graceful Australian pines were gone. All that remained were twisted and splintered stubs. In the distance, Adam could faintly make out some of the homes a half a mile away. They weren't homes anymore. They were roofless skeletons and piles of broken sticks. Nothing was left unscathed by her, nothing had escaped the first slap of Emily's awful hand.

Ralph was right. To save himself, Adam had to go deep inside. Pull all his energies together and survive. He had to survive.

He walked back to the screen-less porch and looked into the distance toward the open waters of the Gulf. From his vantage point, 60 feet above the ocean, he could see it. It was like a towering thunderstorm five, maybe six miles in the distance. The constant flashes of lightning illuminated the night sky and outlined the edge of the eye. Emily's back side was dancing toward Shoreside. Dancing madly with winds in excess of 150 miles per hour. Adam had a half-hour at best. Possibly less.

He would have to swim to the "G" building. That was his only chance. Swim to the "G" building and find some kind of shelter there. That was it.

Adam quickly thought through his hurried plan. If I could get over to the back building in the next half-hour, I could then get to the second story and hide in the south-side apartment. In the master bath, tight against the common wall between the two units. It's my only chance.

With that simple plan, Adam headed out the back door and started working his way down the emergency stairway. It was scattered with debris. Broken pieces of glass, door frames, torn and soaking cushions were in disarray before him as he carefully worked his way toward the first floor.

Halfway between the second and first floor, as he turned the last switchback in the stairwell, he saw the water. It was over the first floor by a foot or more. Adam stared in disbelief.

He knew that the state standards had made Loggins put the first-floor elevation at 17 feet above mean high tide. Seeing the salt water covering the first floor of the "A" building meant that the storm surge was higher than that. The storm surge was at least 18 feet high. No one in Tallahassee could have anticipated a storm like Emily when they decreed the new coastal construction control line guidelines. No one would have believed a hurricane like Emily was possible, save Adam.

He walked into the seawater and stood almost knee-deep in it. From here, he couldn't see the "G" building. Two other buildings blocked his view. But he knew it was there, roughly 600 feet away. What he saw next was unexplainable.

In the eye of Emily, the barometric pressure had dropped to 27.17 inches, nearly as low as Hugo. The winds had completely died but the ocean had been so shaken, so disturbed by the vortex surrounding it, that it was still unsettled and wild. In the absence of air pressure and wind, the waves became strange. The seas formed huge cones and queer, surrealistic shapes that drifted skyward. Adam had never seen a sea behave like this, leaping toward the starlit sky as though freed from the forces of gravity and the very laws of nature. Few people have seen these strange seas and survived to tell others about them.

Swimming through this bizarre ocean without the aid of a life jacket or some sort of flotation was going to be impossible. Some of the cones dancing before him were ten feet high. He would need something to hang onto or risk losing his way amidst this weird, freakish chop.

He looked into both of the first-floor units to see if there was anything he could use as a life vest or a piece of flotsam to hang onto as he attempted to swim to the "G" building. But there was nothing left in either of the units. The sea had carried everything off.

Adam went upstairs one flight. The unit to the south was likewise empty, having faced into the fierce winds of Emily for the last three hours. The unit to the north had fared better. It was there, amidst the scattered furniture and broken cupboards, that Adam found what he was searching for.

It was an old cooler. A cooler accidently left by one of the panicking reservationists last October as she, her husband, and their two children fled the onslaught of salt marsh mosquitoes that had wreaked havoc on Sanderling. The cleaners had emptied it of sodas and beer and stuck it in a small utility closet near the front door. The closet door ripped away when all the windows blew out, but the cooler had been wedged inside and miraculously remained.

Adam looked at it and knew that it would work. It was a 40-quart, extra-duty cooler. It had deep, foam-filled walls and a three-inch-thick cover. He knew what to do. Trying to swim the length of two football fields with the whole cooler wouldn't work. But the cover, he reasoned, the cover would work.

He grabbed the cooler and pulled it from the closet. Then he put his right foot inside the cooler, bent down and with one sweeping motion, ripped the white cover off. It was just what he needed.

With the cover in hand, Adam went down a flight of stairs, stopping just above the water to remove his shoes and jumped into the ocean. The water was warm. It was the very same warm water that was feeding Emily - 85 degrees. The salty fuel of hurricanes.

When he first hit the salt water, the scores of tiny cuts stung him. It was just like pouring salt on an open wound. But it didn't really bother him. In fact, Adam welcomed the pain because it made him feel more alive. Life is pain.

Using the top of the cooler like a small surfboard, Adam kept it slightly in front of him and kicked his feet methodically. Although the cones formed and unformed around him, in the absence of wind it wasn't that hard to make headway toward the back of the complex. Not with the makeshift surfboard held in front of him. The white foam that covered the sea kept blocking his view, but he could easily push it away with his right hand when it became too distracting.

Ten minutes later, swimming with all of his strength at 3:00 in the morning in the eye of a hurricane, Adam Bartlett was within 50 feet of the "G" building. Now the noise had started coming back and the wind was beginning to pick up.

As he swam that last few feet he laughed to himself. He laughed because he realized that the same swarm of mosquitoes that had driven him to suicide had chased a family out in such a hurry they had forgotten the very cooler that was now helping to save him. Fate, Adam reflected, is an impossible mistress.

In a few minutes' time, he made the stairwell below the first floor. The water was already receding, he noted. The wind, which only an hour ago had been pushing the ocean into the land, was now reversing and pushing the ocean outward. It was like a 20-foot tide coming and going in half the allotted time. The channel Emily was digging would never have time to cut clear through the island. The sea was fast receding.

Adam held onto the cooler lid and scrambled up the stairwell. He ran to the second story first, like Ralph had suggested, and looked inside. Half of the roof was gone. It wouldn't work. The top floor wouldn't work. When the winds kicked back in, Adam ran the risk of being sucked right out of the master bathroom. He would have to stay in the first-floor unit, already soaked from seawater but safer than the upstairs. A 6-inch concrete floor would prevent him from being lifted into the rushing wind. It was the only safe haven he had.

He went into the master bedroom and found it empty. Even the carpet had been stripped clean by the wind and seas. The walls to the master bath were almost gone, but a few pieces of studs and drywall remained above the Jacuzzi tub. The storm surge water, which only minutes before was knee-deep, was almost gone.

This is where I'll have to stay. Here, in this plastic tub on the leeward side of the building. It's all I have left.

Adam crouched in the tub, still filled with salt water and held onto the cooler top. He wisely thought it might come in handy as a shield when the hurricane's winds kicked up. Its three inches of foam might help protect him from whipping shards of glass and flying sticks. Flying at him at speeds greater than 100 miles an hour.

Now the noise was coming back. The peculiar cone-shaped waves had flattened out and realigned themselves with the driving north wind. The noise increased, approaching the island like the oncoming rush of 1,000 locomotives. The lightning flashes intensified, cracking and thundering above the howl of the wind. Adam knew, as he huddled in fear, that it was no longer up to him.

From his crouched position in the half-filled tub, he could just glimpse the top of the "A" building, the building he had just abandoned. As the wind kept howling, screaming, announcing boldly that she was the storm of the new millennium, Adam watched the "A" building shudder, buckle and fall.

There was no noise accompanying the fall, since nothing could now be heard above the continuous din of the wind. A cannon could have been blown off in the empty master bedroom beside him and Adam would not have heard that report over Emily's deafening screams.

As Adam watched the condo he had planned to kill himself in, watched it fall silently into the receding sea, he began to pray. It had come down to that which it comes down to for all of us when we surrender.

Naked and vulnerable, weak and humbled, without hope and without any chance of survival save a miracle, Adam turned to prayer. As he did so he knew that it had been years, no, decades since he had asked anything of God. In the secular universe where Adam was the crown prince, there was no need for God. Prayer was what others did. Prayer was for fools.

But his prayers on this wicked, stormy night were not the prayers of the faithful on a Sunday morning in a small-town church in America. Adam's prayers were 1,000 times more heartfelt and intense. Adam's prayers were as strong as the wind that roared around him. His prayers came from the exposed core of his soul. He was praying for his very life and he knew it.

Adam understood that at any moment an errant board might come ripping around the back eddies created by the swirling winds and drive itself straight through his pounding heart. Impaled and dying in a world gone mad. Death surrounded him, raging and howling in this devil's wind. In this insane dance of vortexes and cyclones.

He prayed 1,000 prayers that he might be allowed to live again, live long enough to see his son Danny once again. Not more than once, just once. Just to tell him how much he loved him.

"Oh, God," he mumbled silently to himself. "Please let me live. Please let me see my son again." Like the chant of a lonely monk, Adam's prayers went on and on forever. Like Daniel in the lions' den, Adam realized that this hurricane could devour him at any moment. His head, his entire body was in the mouth of the lion.

He prayed for forgiveness. He asked God to forgive him his sin of wanting to kill himself. Of vainly thinking that it mattered. Any of it: the condominium project, the money, the cars, the stuff of fools. He prayed until, like a vessel pouring itself empty, there was nothing left inside him but prayer. Like Siddhartha beside the river, or Jesus in the desert, Adam prayed until his lips were parched and his soul unveiled.

Hours passed.

The noise became all-consuming. The sound and the fury of the hurricane had entered into him, overwhelming the frailty of Adam's mortal consciousness. The wind was no longer external, but had swept inside him, blowing wildly within like the hurricane of human madness. Emily and Adam had become one, and in this impossible transformation, all sense of fear abandoned Adam.

The young man crouched in the fiberglass tub enclosure was empty. So many pieces of broken glass and perilous missiles had flown by, smashing themselves against the tattered drywall of what was left of the bathroom that it didn't matter any longer. Living through this hurricane was not his decision to make. It was God's.

Because he knew that without reservation, Adam let go of fear. He let go of fear the same way that a holy man lets go of self. He could no longer be afraid, just as he could no longer hear the noise. All he could hear were the whispers of his prayers. He, and the God who listened.

Emily slowly moved inland, marching across the peninsula on her way toward the Atlantic, killing hundreds upon hundreds as she did. People trapped in their cars, crushed in their broken homes, drowned and dying beneath this powerful force of nature.

But not killing Adam. Not killing the one man who had come to Emily to be killed. Sparing him. Allowing him to survive the storm. The hand of God at rest. The hand of forgiveness.

✸

It was well before 6:00 in the morning when Adam stepped out of the bathtub he had been huddled in for the past three hours. He was stiff and exhausted. He dropped his plastic shield and walked to the front porch. The winds were gusty but light, 30 miles an hour at best. Maybe less.

He went to the edge of the front porch of the condo and looked across the Sanderling Condominium site. Five of the seven buildings were still standing. Building "C" was leaning to the south. The rest of the structures, like the building he was in, were shells. The furniture, the appliances, the walls, the decorating, the carpet, the tiles, even the paint had been peeled away by the wind. The complex was in complete ruin, looking as if a nuclear blast had ripped across the hellish landscape laid out in desolation before him.

Adam looked down and saw that the water was gone, pushed back to sea by the reversed wind direction. All that was left was a deep, sandy gully that looked like an eroded hillside somewhere in the foothills of Wyoming. As his eyes followed the gully toward the ocean, he noted that water was still collected in the deeper sections. Near the beach, huge chunks of concrete and steel re-bar were damming the canyon. These were remnants of the two fallen buildings, both having collapsed toward the channel being dredged by the storm.

Trash and flotsam were everywhere; appliances, pieces of roofing, air-conditioning units, mattresses and rubble. The beautiful coconut palms, traveler palms and ornamentals that had once graced Sanderling were gone. A scattering of sea oats was still clinging to the sand near the beach but the rest of the site was completely stripped of green. It was a lifeless, littered wasteland before him. It was over.

Adam walked down the stairwell and jumped the last three feet onto the soft, water-soaked mud and sand below the end of the stairwell. The ocean had scoured away the top three feet of soil. Taken it inland with the storm surge, dumping it along streets and yards blocks away.

He walked cautiously toward the beach, breathing the air along the way as though each breath he took was his first. Nothing could have prepared him for the damage Emily had wrought. Nothing.

He walked along the deep canyon that ran past the back property line of the property. Nearer the shoreline it was still filled with salt water, looking like the mouth of a small river. Emily had wanted to cut the island in half, but she was too impatient. She had moved inland too soon, anxious to make her way to the Carolinas. Had Emily moved more slowly, this inlet might have made it across the six blocks that separated the Gulf from the bay at this point.

Next time, thought Adam as he reached the empty beach. Maybe the next storm will finish cutting this channel. Adam stopped 30 feet from the edge of the surf and sat down on the wet sand.

As Adam rested on the beach, the light of the rising sun began to extinguish the starlight shining above him. One by one, the delicate flicker of those distant suns surrendered to the closer star that now rose in the east.

Adam sat motionless, listening to the sound of the surf and the cries of seagulls reappearing high above him. A moment of repose after the storm. The sounds of a stretch of empty beach at dawn, nothing more than that. He drew his knees up, and wrapped his arms around them, looking like a tiny ball to the gulls and magnificent frigate birds that soared high above him. Helpless and vulnerable. Utterly alone.

He noticed an unusual swirl in the surf not 30 feet from the water's edge. It was like the boil in the water made by a porpoise, or the prop wash of a boat.

A moment later he knew what it was that had made the water churn so mysteriously.

At first he thought it was a piece of trash, floating along with the hundreds of boards, planks and damaged crab traps that littered the beach. But it wasn't trash at all. It was a giant sea turtle, a loggerhead.

Adam suddenly realized she was coming ashore to dig her sandy nest and lay her clutch of eggs. Just like she had a million years ago. Just like she had ten million years ago. Just like she had 100 million years ago. The hurricane had passed, and it was her time.

Adam didn't move, didn't so much as flinch as the 300-pound loggerhead dragged herself onto the beach. Because of his stillness, the sea creature took no notice of him. He was just another piece of flotsam on a beach littered with it. Adam posed no threat to her or her eggs. As she lifted her round, dark eyes and surveyed the shoreline near her, she completely ignored him. He was just a broken thing washed ashore. She kept on her cumbersome journey up the beach, needing to find a patch of sand beyond the high-tide line.

She crawled to within ten feet of Adam and stopped, putting her large head into the air in search of the scent of danger. The wind was still flowing from the north but Adam sat motionless to her south. Had she smelled him then, her instincts would have made her turn back to sea. But she was upwind of this broken man on the beach. She did not find anything that signaled danger in the wind.

Now the turtle buried her nose in the sand, as though smelling this stretch of beach to be certain she had found the place of her birth decades ago. Hers and the birth of countless sea turtles before her. Satisfied, she started digging into the sand with her powerful front flippers. Adam watched in silent amazement, realizing what a rare and wondrous thing he was witnessing.

After a few minutes, she crawled up the beach a body length farther and continued the excavation with her large back flippers. She curled each of them carefully, converting her two hind flippers into huge sand scoops.

Her nest must be perfect. It must not be too shallow, allowing it to be found by the raccoons or the sea birds, and it must not be too deep, keeping her young hatchlings from being able to climb out about 45 days from now. Twenty minutes passed as this ancient mother carved a home for her clutch of more than100 eggs.

After digging the sand, the immense turtle positioned herself over the hole she had laboriously made and began laying her eggs. Her eyes were covered in tears, as though she was crying for all the sins of the world as she labored and gave birth. Tears flowing down her mottled face as she pushed out her eggs, sometimes one at a time, sometimes two or three at a time.

Time stood still.

After pushing out her last few eggs, the huge sea turtle turned around and began kicking the sand up and over her clutch. She moved so slowly, so methodically as the sun kept pouring more and more light into the morning sky. Adam began weeping. He did not know why.

Was it for the turtle? Was it because he now realized that he would live? He didn't know why he sat there crying as the first shafts of sunlight broke across the horizon behind him. He wept openly and it no longer mattered to him that he did.

The loggerhead, having finished burying her nest, lifted her huge body on all four flippers and dropped on the nest, compressing the sand below as she did. She was compacting the soil, trying to conceal the fact that she had ever crawled up this lonely stretch of sand. Five, ten times she raised herself and then fell onto the sand, until exhaustion overwhelmed her.

Then she turned and headed back to sea. Adam could hear her labored breathing as she worked her way toward the surf. He could see how hard it was for her to be on land, away from the buoyant world of the ocean. It was as though the weight of the universe rested upon her barnacle-encrusted shell. Perhaps it did.

At the very edge of the surf, she stopped. This ancient creature, whose species had outlived the age of the dinosaur, whose tireless faith had witnessed a million extinctions during the last 150 million years, raised her head high and, with tears still streaming down her face, looked back at her nest. It was the look of a mother saying goodbye. A look eternal.

In that last glance, her eyes met Adam's. Her dark, mystical eyes looked directly into his soul and in an instant, the empty vessel that he had become was refilled with life. She knew instinctively that he would not harm her clutch, or willfully cause harm to any living thing from that moment forward.

With that, she turned away and with a few more ponderous steps disappeared into the vastness of the sea before her.

Adam, tears pouring down his face, stood and watched her swim into the Gulf of Mexico. Her final, beautiful glance had overwhelmed him. The sunlight now warmed his back as he watched her vanish into the abyss. It was the closing of the circle, her slow, glorious work of creation.

He turned around and looked once more at the Sanderling site, smiling as he did. He knew there wouldn't be any lights along this stretch of shoreline to confuse her tiny hatchlings when they crawled out of their nest nearly two months from now. The damage was too severe. Sanderling would be torn down. Demolished.

If all went well, hoped a reborn Adam, the mangroves and buttonwoods would be replanted and the land restored to a useless stretch of swamp along an empty stretch of beach. Useless to whom? thought Adam. Not to these ancient loggerheads. Not to the otters that were trapped and relocated to some inhospitable island in the back bay. Not to the herons, alligators and bullfrogs that once flourished here.

Useless to us. That was what she was trying to tell me, he realized. That it is much more than us. That she has glanced back upon races like us since time unfathomable and watched them come and go across the eons of her humble existence. Fools like us.

Adam, so glad to be alive, suddenly saw the world in a new and wondrous light. In the turtle's tearful, jet-black eyes he had a vision of the infinite. The endless world of time uncountable, of starlight yet unfound, of galaxies stretching beyond the imagination of this humble servant now standing on the beach. He perceived what few ever do.

That we are only part of the whole. That no one rises above the shell of the tortoise, or conquers, or ever rules. That in the infinite lies the moment, and that the moment is held in the hand of God. That God is all things, all beings and all life and all death at once. The doors of perception, in her one exquisite glance, were thrown open. Adam knew.

The man standing on the beach looked out to sea and started praying again. He no longer prayed for the storm to spare him, because the storm had taken Adam Bartlett. He prayed for God to spare us and forgive us. Spare us from our vanity, our transgressions and our sins. Forgive us for the damage we have wrought.

He turned and walked down the timeless beach as the sunlight warmed the battered west coast of Florida. Hoping that this time, more than ever before in his life, his prayers would be answered.

*This book is dedicated to the wildlife of the world,
with special recognition going to "Digger,"
an island gopher tortoise.*

Epilogue

Way Under Contract is a work of fiction. What has occurred in Florida over the past 50 years is not. In 1950, the population of Florida was 2,771,305. The projected population from the 2000 census is expected to exceed 15,428,000. On average, for every decade during the past 50 years, Florida's population has effectively doubled.

For the wildlife of the Sunshine State, this unprecedented growth has been devastating. Golf courses, suburbs, condominiums, apartment buildings, shopping centers, freeways, office buildings, the immeasurable uprootings of man, all serve to displace animals who once called those pastures, swamps and forests home. They retreat in silence. Some, like the Florida panther and the manatee, retreat to the very brink of extinction. Extinction being the longest silence.

Way Under Contract is not **a** Florida story. It is **the** Florida story. It is the story of section, township and range. The tale of men who see the world, not through the childlike eyes of wonder, but through the eyes of lot and block. The eyes of money. The men who clear the slash pines, burn the saw palmetto and lay the footings for the next exclusive subdivision, complete with lighted tennis courts, Olympic-sized swimming pools and exotic landscaping from every corner of the planet. All this while the native trees and shrubs lie smouldering in the distance, and the gopher tortoises, egrets and indigo snakes try to find a patch of land unscathed by the merciless roar of the bulldozer. Search to find someplace, anyplace to call home.

When you purchased this book, one dollar of the proceeds went to the Sanibel-Captiva Conservation Foundation. The foundations members are dedicated to the acquisition, restoration and preservation of wildlife habitat. They purchase the land, clear it of the invasive exotics such as Brazilian pepper, and let it be. In effect, they buy the land for the native flora and fauna which can hardly afford to own property in Florida any longer. Purchase it for the herons, river otters and butterflies who don't know what fee simple title is. For the animals who cannot read the fine print.

But it isn't just for the wildlife. It's for us. It's for a future that has William Blake's immortal *"Tiger! Tiger! burning bright"* still in it. It's to ensure for our children that there will always be panthers out there, prowling the primordial hammocks of the Everglades, and that they will be there forever.

It is for them and the generation after them, and for a thousand generations to come. Because if you really want to invest in tomorrow, purchase land, restore it and walk away. That investment is for you, your children and for the creatures, insects and plants who share this glorious Earth with us.

But one dollar is not enough. Nor is money all you can give. If you have time, volunteer. If you have talent, teach. If you have ability, lead. Find an organization nearest you that is dedicated to acquiring and preserving land and get involved. A nature conservancy, a land trust, a conservation foundation that strives to keep that ten-acre swamp from being drained, filled and used for yet another shopping mall. The ceaseless paving of paradise.

Do whatever you can, but please do something. Help to preserve the wondrous beauty of this irreplaceable planet. If you can, make a tax-deductible contribution to the Sanibel-Captiva Conservation Foundation, P.O. Box 839, Sanibel, Florida 33957. Or go to **www.indigopress.net** and find the link that takes you to a list of conservation groups throughout Florida. You will also find a link to organizations dedicated to saving Florida's endangered sea turtles.

Each of us, working alone, can do little to stop this alarming march of progress. But together we can save an acre here, a hundred acres there and, hopefully over time, a hundred thousand acres and more. The late Dr. Archie Carr, who dedicated his life to turning the tide on the extinction of our sea turtles, summed it up by saying, **"For most of the wild things on Earth the future must depend upon the conscience of mankind."**

We must speak for those whose voice is the song of the mockingbird and the wind rustling the fronds of the cabbage palm. Do it for that child within yourself and the generations of children yet to be. But most importantly, please do it.

Charles Sobczak
October 2000

Also by Charles Sobczak:

Six Mornings on Sanibel *(1999)*
ISBN 0-9676199-5-5 $13.95

Rhythm of the Tides *(2001)*
ISBN 0-9676199-1-2 $13.95

A Choice of Angels *(2003)*
Hard Cover: ISBN 0-9676199-7-1 $25.00
Trade Paperback: ISBN 0-9676199-9-8 $16.00

Questions regarding ordering information and/or comments are encouraged and welcome via:

Toll Free Number:	877-472-8900
Local Number	239-472-0491
Fax Number:	239-472-1426
Email:	indigopress@earthlink.net
Web Address:	www.indigopress.net
Mailing Address:	Indigo Press, LLC
	P.O. Box 977
	Sanibel Island, FL 33957

- VISA or MasterCard Accepted -
Orders may be placed via our website, telephone or US Mail.

Six Mornings on Sanibel
Among the best selling books on Sanibel Island for 3 years!

Six Mornings on Sanibel is a moving story for readers young and old. Two unlikely men meet one morning at the fishing pier on Sanibel Island, Florida. Over the course of the next six mornings, they share more than just snook runs and cold Cokes.

Richard Evans is an over weight, stressed out divorce attorney who measures his success by how much money he can manipulate from his clients. Under duress from his wife, Helen, he has taken his estranged family on vacation to Sanibel Island. Helen, who's life has grown to revolve around her soap operas, bridge games and excessive spending, has anything but time for her family. Subsequently, both their teenage boys are spoiled beyond measure with every toy and game produced. Spoiled with everything except love and time from their parents. Sadly, their big, beautiful Midwestern house resembles anything but a home.

Carl Johnson and his wife, Marie, moved to Sanibel decades ago to raise their family in the peaceful serene environment that island life has to offer; Carl as a fishing guide and Marie tending their family, garden and volunteer work. He has lived a long full life and is now old and retired. With his children living out of state and Marie having passed away to cancer the previous year, Carl is living the last years of his life with his fishing tackle and memories.

Over the next six mornings, while catching and releasing fish, Carl and Richard share tales of love, losses, heroism, vanity, suicide and life. They share bait, fishing gear and poignant conversations. With each passing morning, something happens to Richard. He begins to realize how superficies and shallow his life has become, and contemplates changing, no matter how difficult that change may be.

Rhythm of the Tides
A Collection of Essays, Short Stories & Poetry

From a blind peddler in the Grand Bazaar of Istanbul to a simple bicycle ride through Acadia National Park in northern Maine, these stories, like modern parables, explore the deeper meanings concealed in the most unlikely of settings. A few of the articles have won *The Florida Press Award* and many of them have appeared in local newspapers causing readers to spill their morning coffee laughing, or find themselves teary-eyed on a Sunday afternoon.

There is a story for everyone. The essays, poems and lyrics take a philosophical, theological, comical and existential look at family, friendship, romantic love, raising children, the loss of loved ones, religion, life, death, as well as the crazy antics of raccoons, or the fact that "The Bugs Have Won" in the battle against the human race.

There is the essay entitled *I Could Learn to Love Kansas*, where we are taught that "In the end, it is not the landscape that surrounds us that makes us who we are, but the landscape within. The landscape of the human heart." On the lighter side, there is a humorous look at ice fishing. "My uncle's ice house, as ice houses go, was an upscale model. The first thing you did upon entering this Hobbit-sized shelter was to start a fire in the wood stove. Starting a fire while sitting on six inches of ice has never struck me as sound thinking." From the poetry section, there is a simple comparison of love to mist, "Hanging in the evening air suspended upon itself./Needing only the moon to add proportion./ That, and two hearts to blend."

A Choice of Angels
A Love Story For Our Times

Scheduled for publication in April 2003, *A Choice of Angels* is a story of two cultures colliding. When Ayse Yalçin, a Muslim exchange student, meets Daniel Harris, the son of a Southern Baptist minister, an innocent study date quickly evolves into a budding romance. Daniel's father, Clayton, tells his son not to pursue the relationship, but his father's stern warnings go unheeded.

Set in contemporary Atlanta, Georgia, and Istanbul, Turkey, *A Choice of Angels* explores the depths of religious intolerance in the modern world. The story brings the reader into the strained dynamics of two families as they attempt to deal with an unexpected marriage between a Christian and a Muslim. Daniel's father disowns his son, and distances himself and his family to the point of putting a protection order on Daniel. What follows is a river of tears, heartache and, ultimately, redemption.

To better understand the culture, the author, Charles Sobczak, went to Istanbul in May of 2001. He also studied Islam with an Imam in America. The novel takes a hard look at the current rise of 'Born Again Christianity' in America as well as the historical conflicts that have existed between the two largest religions in the world. This is a book that is as sure to inspire as it is to spark heated debates.

Island Writings
A Collection of Florida Stories

Island Writings is a collection of three Florida fiction and non-fiction books by Sanibel Island writer, Charles Sobczak. The box is beautifully designed by Bob Radigan and inside, each book is personally signed by the author. Take a little piece of the islands home with you in this limited Sanibel and Captiva Special Edition! This set is available only via our webiste (www.indigopress.net) or our toll free telephone number (877-472-8900) for only $37.95. Island Writings makes the perfect gift or island keepsake!

Inlcuded in this set:

Six Mornings on Sanibel
This simple tale of two strangers meeting on the Sanibel fishing pier has become an island clssic. Over twenty-four consecutive months as an island's best-seller, this is a story of the wise old sage and the young fool.

Way Under Contract
Winner of the pretigious 2001 Patrick D. Smith Award for Florida Literature, this madcap novel unveils the underside of Florida real estate set against the backdrip of a savage category five hurricane.

Rhythm of the Tides
A Collection of stories, essays and poetry, this intriguing book is the ideal beach read. Several of the essays have won Florida Press Awards. You will laugh, cry and never want to stop reading.

About the Author

Charles Sobczak lives on Sanibel Island, Florida, where he has enjoyed living for nearly 20 years. He and his wife, Molly Heuer, have two boys, Logan (14) and Blake (12). Both children share their father's love of writing and their mother's musical talents.

Charles began his writing career over thirty years ago as a regular columnist for *The Statesman*, a weekly newspaper for the University of Minnesota at Duluth, where he was pursuing an English degree. After being exempted from Freshman English he spent the rest of his college years in advanced courses, studying writers from Shakespeare to Emily Dickenson.

After college, he was a member of a small coffeehouse group called *Easy Steam* for which he wrote lyrics, sang and played the flute. They toured professionally across the United States for four years and recorded one album, *How Does it Feel to Be Alive,* which had modest success. *Easy Steam* broke up in the late 1970's.

For the next fifteen years, Charles did little in the way of writing aside from keeping a journal and writing an occasional poem or short story. In 1994, at the request of an island editor, he started writing a fishing column for the *Island Reporter*. His familiarity with both offshore and inshore fishing around Sanibel gave him ample material for the next several years. The columns were well received, with two of them winning *Florida Press Awards*.

In 1997, with encouragement from Scott Martell, the editor of the *Island Reporter* at the time, he began writing a novel set at the fishing pier on Sanibel. *Six Mornings on Sanibel* was completed and published in November 1999, with an original print run of 3,000 copies. The first printing sold out in four months and went on to be the best-selling book on Sanibel for the next 24

About The Author Continued:

consecutive months. *Six Mornings on Sanibel* is now in its fourth printing with over 14,000 copies sold from Cape Cod. Massachusetts to San Francisco, California to Christchurch, England.

His second novel, *Way Under Contract, a Florida Story*, published in November 2000, won *The 2001 Patrick Smith Award* for Florida Literature. Given by the Florida Historical Society, the award is granted every year for the best work that depicts some aspect of life in the Sunshine State. With over 5,000 copies sold, *Way Under Contract* is currently in its second printing.

His third book, *Rhythm of the Tides*, is a collection of Charles' columns, including some of his pieces from *The Statesman* (1969), as well as short stories, essays and poetry.

A new novel, *A Choice of Angels*, is scheduled for release in April 2003. Set in Atlanta, Georgia and Istanbul, Turkey, the novel tells the story of the unexpected romance between Daniel Harris, the son of a Baptist Minister from Macon, and Ayse Yalçin, an Islamic exchange student from Istanbul. This novel explores the historical and modern divisions that exist between the two cultures.

Charles and his wife, Molly, visited Istanbul in May 2001, and he began writing the manuscript for the novel on August 13, 2001. Although in the works prior to the tragedy that occurred on September 11, 2002, *A Choice of Angels* is definitely a tale for our times.

Charles Sobczak is a lifetime member of the Sanibel-Captiva Conservation Foundation, a long-standing member of the Sanibel Fishing Club, President of Lee Reefs, and a member of the Sanibel and Captiva Board of Realtors. When he is not writing, Charles makes his living selling island real estate and is currently a top-selling Realtor with Coldwell Banker Previews International. Charles enjoys extended vacations with his wife and two sons, fishing and reading. His favorite works of literature were written by such varied authors as John Steinbeck, Kenneth Patchen, Kahlil Gibran and Joseph Heller.